This book should be returned/renewed by the
latest date shown above. Overdue items incur
charges which prevent self-service renewals.
...se contact the library.

...worth Libraries
Renewal Hotline
011... ...28
...rth.gov.uk

Wandsworth

March 2014

April 2014

May 2014

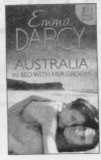

June 2014

July 2014

August 2014

Emma DARCY

AUSTRALIA
IN BED WITH THE BOSS

Published in Great Britain 2014
by Mills & Boon, an imprint of Harlequin (UK) Limited,
Eton House, 18-24 Paradise Road, Richmond, Surrey, TW9 1SR

AUSTRALIA: IN BED WITH THE BOSS
© 2014 Harlequin Books S.A.

The Marriage Decider © 1998 Emma Darcy
Their Wedding Day © 1996 Emma Darcy
His Boardroom Mistress © 2003 Emma Darcy

ISBN: 978 0 263 24608 7

010-0614

Emma Darcy's life journey has taken as many twists and turns as the characters in her stories, whose international popularity has resulted in over sixty million book sales. Born in Australia and currently living in a beachside property on the central coast of New South Wales, she travels extensively to research settings and increase her experience of places and people.

Initially a French/English teacher, she changed careers to computer programming before marriage and motherhood settled her into a community life. A voracious reader, the step to writing her own books seemed a natural progression and the challenge of creating exciting stories was soon highly addictive.

Over the past twenty-five years she has written ninety-five books for Mills & Boon, appearing regularly on the Waldenbooks bestseller lists in the USA and in the Nielsen BookScan Top 100 chart in the UK.

THE MARRIAGE DECIDER

Emma
DARCY

CHAPTER ONE

IS YOUR MAN ABOUT TO DUMP YOU?
SPOTTING THE EXIT SIGNS

THE headline teaser on the glossy cover of her favourite magazine caused a roll of nausea through Amy Taylor's stomach. It was the new December issue, out today, and the advice it contained was too late to be of any help. A pity the article hadn't been written months ago. She might have recognised what had been going on with Steve, at least been somewhat prepared for the bombshell that had hit her over the weekend.

Though that was doubtful. She wouldn't have applied the exit signs to her relationship with Steve. Although neither of them had pushed for marriage—free spirits should never shackle themselves, he had insisted—after *five* years together—a mini-marriage in anyone's book—continuity had become a state of mind. She'd been hopelessly blind to what was really happening.

Free spirits! Amy gnashed her teeth over that remembered phrase. There was nothing free-spirited about rushing headlong into marriage with someone else! The blonde he'd bedded behind Amy's back, was shackling Steve with an ease that was painfully insulting. With the result that Amy was certainly being left *free!* Though hardly free-spirited.

Here she was, comprehensively dumped, twenty-eight years old, single again, and suffering the worst case of

Monday blues she could ever remember having. It was sheer masochism to pick up the new issue of the magazine with *that* article in it—a clear case of punishing herself—but maybe she needed to have all the signs spelled out so she'd know better next time. *If* there ever was a next time.

At her age, the market for unattached men was slim, especially men worth having. Amy brooded over that depressing fact as she paid the news vendor for the magazine and walked down Alfred Street to her workplace, the last office building facing the harbour on Milsons Point, a highly privileged piece of real estate which she was in no mood to appreciate this morning.

Ahead of her, summer sunshine had turned Sydney Harbour into a glittering expanse of blue, patterned harmoniously by boats and ferries carving white wakes across it. To her left, Bradfield Park offered the peaceful green of newly mown lawns, invitingly shadowed by the great Coat-hanger bridge that dominated the skyline, feeding the city with an endless stream of commuter traffic. Amy was totally oblivious to all of it. For her, there was only the dark gloom of her thoughts.

Dumped for a blonde, a smart, pregnant blonde. Nobody got pregnant by accident these days. Not at thirty-two. Amy was sure it had been a calculated gamble, the hook to pull Steve in and tie him up for better or for worse. And it had worked. The wedding date was already set. One month from today. New Year's Eve. Happy New Year, Amy thought bitterly, seeing a long stretch of loneliness for herself.

Maybe at thirty-two, she'd feel desperate enough to snitch someone else's man. After all, if he was willing, as Steve must have been…but how could you ever really trust a man who cheated on the woman he was living with? Amy wrinkled her nose. She'd be better off on her own.

But she didn't feel better off. She felt sick, empty, lost in a world that had suddenly turned unfamiliar, hostile, her bearings torn away. Tears filled her eyes as she pushed open the door to her workplace and barged into the foyer, needing the safe mooring of her job to fight the flood of misery she could barely contain.

"Hi! Boss in?" she aimed at Kate Bradley, her vision too embarrassingly blurred to meet the receptionist's eyes directly. Besides, Kate was a gorgeous blonde, a typical choice for Jake Carter's front desk woman, and another reminder of pain for her right now.

"Not yet," came the cheerful reply. "Something must have held him up."

Jake was an early bird, invariably in his office ahead of Amy. She was intensely relieved to hear he was late this morning, giving her time to get herself together before those yellow wolf eyes of his noted anything amiss.

She certainly didn't need the humiliation of having to explain why her mascara was running, which it probably was from her furious blinking. Moisture had to be clinging to her lashes. She pressed the elevator button, willing the doors to open instantly.

"Have a good weekend?" Kate asked, addressing Amy's back, blithely unaware of any problem.

Amy half turned, not wishing to appear totally rude. "No. It was the pits," she blurted out, giving vent to some of her pent-up emotion.

"Oh! Guess things can only get better," Kate offered sympathetically.

"I wish," Amy muttered.

The elevator doors obligingly opened. The ride up to the floor she shared with Jake was mercifully brief and she headed straight for the washroom to effect repairs. Once safely enclosed in privacy she tore tissues from the box on the vanity bench and began wiping away the smeared make-up around her eyes.

She couldn't afford to look as though she was falling apart. As Jake Carter's personal assistant, she had to stay on top of everything, as well as maintain the class image of the company. *Wide Blue Yonder Pty Ltd.* sold its services to the mega-rich who had no tolerance for bungling. Perfection was expected and perfection had to be delivered. Jake had drummed that into her from day one.

Two years she'd been working with him and she knew him through and through. Nothing escaped his notice and she needed cast-iron armour to stop him from getting under her skin. He was a brilliant salesman, a masterly entrepreneur, a stickler for detail, and a dyed-in-the-wool womaniser.

He was certainly single, and frequently unattached, but the chance of forging anything but a brief physical affair with him was nil. She couldn't help fancying him now and then—no woman alive wouldn't—but Amy had too much self-esteem to ever allow herself to be used for fun. Casual intimacy did not appeal to her.

Jake was into *experiences* with women, not relationships, the more exciting and varied the better. To Amy's accumulated knowledge, he had a low threshold of interest in any woman. They came and went with such regularity, she lost track of their names.

Though they did have one thing in common. They were all stunning to look at and made no secret of their availability to answer any need Jake Carter might have for them. He didn't have to chase. He simply had to choose.

Jake the rake, Amy had privately christened him. As far as she could see, he never scratched more than the surface of those who rolled through his life. Amy had figured very early on that keeping an impervious surface to Jake Carter was a prime requirement for keeping her job. Let other women fall victim to his animal magnetism. She had Steve.

Except she didn't anymore.

Tears welled again.

She stared at the soggy mess of herself in the mirror, battling the sense of defeat that was swamping her. Maybe she should dye her hair blonde. The ridiculous thought almost made her laugh. Her emphatically arched eyebrows and the double rows of lashes were uncompromisingly black, her eyes such a dark blue they were almost violet. She'd look stupid as anything other than a brunette.

Besides, she liked her hair. It was thick and glossy and the feathery razor cut around her face gave the shoulder-length bob a soft frame for her rather angular features. She didn't mind them, either. The high slant of her cheekbones balanced her squarish jawline and although her mouth was on the wide side, it did not look disproportionate. It more or less complemented the slight flare of her nostrils and the full curve of her lips was decidedly feminine. Her nose was straight, her neck was long enough to wear any jewellery well and her figure was fine, curvy enough in the right places and slim enough to carry off the clothes she liked.

There was nothing wrong with her looks, Amy fiercely asserted to herself. Jake Carter wouldn't have hired her if he'd found her wanting in that department. His clients expected glamour. After all, they bought or chartered luxury yachts and jet planes. *Wide Blue Yonder* catered to their every whim, and charged them the earth for it. Jake insisted that his staff be as pleasing to the eye as everything else connected to his business. Image, he preached, was every bit as important as supplying what was demanded.

Though Amy had little doubt he was pleasing himself as much as anyone else. He made no secret of enjoying the visual pleasure of his female work force. He might call it *class,* but he was such a sexy beast, Amy was certain he revelled in exercising his right to choose a stimulating environment for himself.

She took several deep, calming breaths, opened her handbag, fished out her emergency make-up kit, and set to work, creating an unblemished façade to present to her boss. His lateness this morning was a stroke of luck. She couldn't bank on any more luck running her way. Somehow she had to shut Steve and his pregnant wife-to-be out of her mind and concentrate on performing every task Jake handed her with her usual efficiency. It was the only way to avoid drawing unwelcome attention.

Satisfied she looked as good as she could in the circumstances, Amy returned her make-up kit to her hand-bag. Having washed and dried her hands, she smoothed the skirt of her scarlet linen shift over her hips, wishing linen didn't crease quite so much. But it was *in* this season, despite its crushability, and the bright colour was a much-needed spirit-booster. At least, that was what she'd argued as she'd donned it this morning.

Pride had insisted the expensive dress should not be wasted. She'd bought it last week, planning to wear it to Steve's office Christmas party. Now she saw it as a too belligerent statement that she would not mourn for him, a pathetic statement, given the heartsickness she was trying to hide. Still, it was too late to change her mind about it now and it might distract Jake Carter from picking up on her inner distress.

The tension of having to face him eased when she discovered his office empty and there was no sign of his having arrived for work. Puzzled as she was by his uncharacteristic lateness, Amy was nevertheless relieved to have the extra time to establish an air of busy occupation.

She settled at her desk and slipped the magazine she'd bought into the bottom drawer, out of sight and hopefully out of mind until she could read it in private. Concentration on her job was top priority now. She turned on her computer, connected to the Internet and brought up the E-mail that had come in over the weekend.

She was printing it out for Jake's perusal when she heard the telltale whoosh of the elevator doors opening to the corridor which ran adjacent to their offices. Her nerves tightened. Her mind raced through defensive tactics.

Jake would probably drop into her office to explain

his lateness, then use the connecting door to enter his own. After a perfunctory greeting she could plunge straight into discussing the mail with him. It contained a number of queries to be answered. The sooner they got down to business, the better.

Jake had a habit of throwing personal inquiries at her on Monday mornings and she desperately wanted to avoid them today. This past weekend didn't bear thinking about let alone commenting upon. Not to Jake Carter.

If there was one thing more difficult to deflect than his sizzling sex appeal, it was his curiosity. Give him even a hint of an opening and he'd capitilise on it, probing for more information every which way. The man had a mind as sharp as a razor.

The door to her office rattled as it was thrust open. Amy's heart kicked in trepidation. She kept her gaze fastened on the printer as she steeled herself not to reveal even the tiniest crack of vulnerability to the dangerous impact of her boss's strong charisma.

In her mind's eye she ticked off what she had to meet with perfect equanimity; the tall, muscle-packed physique exuding male power, skin so uniformly tanned it seemed to gleam with the warm kiss of sunshine, a face full of charm, a slight smile accentuating the sensuality of a mouth that somehow combined strength and teasing whimsy, an inviting twinkle in eyes all the more fascinating for their drooping lids, causing them to look triangular in shape, accentuating the intensity of the intelligence burning through the intriguing amber irises. Last, but not least, was an enticing wealth of dark, wavy hair, threaded with silver, giving him an air of maturity that encouraged trust in his judgement, though Amy knew him to be only thirty-four.

She suspected he'd look no different in ten or even twenty years' time. He'd still be making every woman's heart flutter. It was a power she resented, given his fickleness, and she clung to that resentment as she looked up from the print-out to give the necessary acknowledgement of his presence.

Her gaze caught on the capsule he was carrying.

Shock wiped out her own concerns.

Jake the rake with a baby?

A baby?

Steve's pleas for understanding pounded through her mind...responsibility, commitment, the rights of the child, being a full-time father...

Jake the rake in that role?

Amy lost all her moorings. She was hopelessly adrift.

"You don't think fatherhood becomes me?"

The amused lilt of his sexy, purring voice jerked her gaze up. He chuckled at her confounded expression as he strolled forward and plonked the capsule on her desk.

"Cute little tyke, isn't he?"

Amy rolled back her chair and stood up, staring down at what looked like a very small baby who was blessedly fast asleep. Only its head and a tiny clenched hand were visible above the bunny rug tucked snugly around the mound of its body. How old it was Amy couldn't guess, but she didn't think it was newborn.

"This...is yours?" Her voice came out like a strangled squawk, disbelief choking more than her mind.

He grinned, enjoying having provoked her obvious

loss of composure. "More or less," he answered, his eyes agleam with wicked mischief.

She belatedly registered the teasing. Resentment flared out of her control, fuelled by the pain of having to accept Steve's full-on commitment to fatherhood with a woman other than herself.

"Congratulations!" She arched her eyebrows higher. "I take it the mother is happy with this more or less arrangement?"

"Uh-oh!" He wagged a finger at her, his sparkling amusement scraping her nerves raw. "Your bad opinion of me is showing, Amy. And it's absolutely undeserved."

Like hell it was! She hastily constructed a deadpan look to frustrate him. "I do apologise. Your personal affairs are, of course, none of my business."

"Joshua's mother trusts me implicitly," he declared loftily.

"How nice!"

"She knows I can be counted upon in an emergency."

"Yes. You always do rise to an occasion."

He laughed at the dry irony in her voice. "I see you've recovered. But I did have you lost for a word earlier on," he said triumphantly.

"Would you like me to be speechless more often?"

"What fun would the game be then?" Sheer devilment in his eyes.

Amy deliberately remained silent.

He heaved a sigh. "Determined to frustrate me." He shook his head at her. "Challenge is the spice of life to me, Amy."

She ignored the comment, giving him nothing to feed off.

"Okay," he conceded. "Joshua's mum is my sister, Ruth. Everything fell in on her this morning. My brother-in-law dislocated his shoulder, playing squash. She had to take him to hospital. I was elected as emergency baby-sitter so I got landed with my nephew for the duration. Ruth will come by here to pick him up when she can."

Light dawned. "You're the baby's uncle."

"And his godfather." The teasing grin came back. "You see before you a staunch family man."

From the safe distance of being once removed, Amy thought cynically.

"I'll just pop him down here." He lifted the capsule off her desk and placed it on the floor beside the filing cabinets. "Great little sleeper. Went off in the car and hasn't budged since."

He was leaving the baby with her!

Amy stared at the tiny bundle of humanity—the result of intimacy between a man and a woman—a bond of life that went on and on, no matter what the parents chose to do—a link that couldn't be broken—a baby.

Her whole body clenched against the anguish flooding through her. For this Steve had left her. For this Steve was marrying another woman. Their years together meant nothing...compared to this. He'd covered up his infidelity. Amy hadn't even suspected it. It was the baby who had ended their five-year-long relationship...the baby the man-trap blonde was having...part of Steve he couldn't let go.

And Amy couldn't blame him for that, however deeply it pained her.

A baby deserved to have its father.

But the betrayal of all they'd shared together hurt so much, so terribly much...

"This today's mail?"

She hadn't been aware of Jake backtracking to her desk. The question swung her head towards him. He'd picked up the sheets from the printer. "Yes," she answered numbly.

"I'll take it into my office." He made a beeline for the connecting door, waving at the capsule as he went. "There's a bottle of formula and a couple of disposable nappies in that bag at Joshua's feet. Shouldn't be a problem."

So arrogantly casual, dumping his responsibility for the baby onto her!

Resentment started to burn again.

He opened the door and paused, looking back, oh so sleekly elegant in his grey silk suit, unruffled, uncreased, supremely self-assured, the tantalising little smile quirking his mouth.

"By the way, you look utterly stunning in red, Amy. You should wear it more often."

He winked flirtatiously at her and was gone, the door closing smoothly behind him.

Amy saw red.

Her mind was a haze of red.

Her heart pumped red-hot blood through her veins.

Her brain sizzled. All of her sizzled.

Since Jake Carter enjoyed cracking her composure, he could damned well enjoy a monumental crack! She was *not* going to look after someone else's baby…a baby who had no connection to her whatsoever. It wasn't her job. And today of all days, she didn't need a vivid reminder of what she had lost and why. Let Jake Carter look after his own…the staunch family man! The Godfather!

She looked down at the baby, still peacefully asleep, oblivious to the turbulent emotions it stirred in Amy. She looked at the plastic bag at the foot of the capsule. It was printed with fun Disney characters. Today, Jake Carter could have *fun* with his nephew. The game with her was over and she didn't care if he fired her for it. In fact, if he dared to try any pressure on her over minding his nephew she'd get in first and dump him.

It would probably be a new experience for him, getting dumped by a woman. And he wouldn't be expecting it, either. There hadn't been any exit signs for him to spot.

A savage little smile curled her lips.

She was about to give Jake Carter a red letter day.

And serve him right, too!

CHAPTER TWO

AMY barged into her boss's office, wishing the capsule swinging in her hand was a cudgel to beat him with. It infuriated her further to find him leaning back in his executive chair, feet up on his executive desk, hands cupping the back of his head, gazing smugly at the panoramic harbour view through his executive windows.

No work was being done. The mail she had printed out for him had been tossed on the in-tray. He looked as if he was revelling in recalling the pleasures he had undoubtedly indulged in over the weekend. While she had been dealt one killing blow after another.

It wasn't fair!

Nothing was fair!

But by God! She'd make *this man* honour his commitment!

Her unheralded entrance drew a bland look of inquiry. "Some problem?"

Welcome to hell on wheels! she thought, marching straight up to his desk and heaving the capsule onto it. She did refrain from knocking his feet off. She didn't want to wake the baby. It wasn't the infant's fault that his uncle was a male chauvinist pig.

With her hands free, she planted them on her hips and took her stance. Apparently fascinated by the vision of his normally cool personal assistant on the warpath, Jake stayed locked where he was, which suited Amy just fine. She opened fire at point-blank range.

"This baby...is your responsibility."

Her voice shook, giving it a huskiness that robbed it of the authority needed. She hastily worked some moisture into her mouth and resumed speaking with more strength.

"Your sister elected *you* to be her son's baby-sitter."

She stretched her mouth into a smile designed to turn Medusa to stone. It must have worked because he still didn't move. Or speak.

"She trusts you implicitly," Amy said sweetly. "As she should since you're his godfather. And a staunch family man."

It gave her a fierce pleasure to throw that claim back in his face, an even fiercer pleasure to see him look so stunned and at a loss for a ready reply. Join the club, brother, she thought, and fired the last volley.

"Looking after your nephew is not my job. Hire someone who specialises in baby-sitting if you can't do it yourself. In the meantime, he belongs with you."

She swivelled on her heel and headed for the door, her spine stiff, her shoulders squared, her head tilted high. If Jake Carter so much as breathed at her she would wheel and attack him again.

There wasn't a sound.

Silence followed her to the door.

She didn't look back.

She made her exit on a wave of righteous fervour.

It wasn't until the door was shut and she was alone in her own office, that the silence she'd left behind her took on an ominous quality in her mind.

Silence…

Like the silence after Steve had walked out.

She'd lost her man.

Amy closed her eyes as the realisation of what she'd done rushed in on her.

She was about to lose her job.

Lose everything.

This black day had just turned blacker.

CHAPTER THREE

AMY lost track of time. She found herself sitting at her desk and didn't remember sinking into her chair. It was as though she'd pressed a self-destruct button and her whole world had slipped out of control, shattering around her.

Vengeance...that's what she'd wreaked on Jake Carter...paying him out for what Steve had done to her. And she'd had no right to do it. No right at all.

A personal assistant was supposed to personally assist. That was what she was paid for. Any other day she wouldn't have blinked an eyelid at being left with a baby to mind. She would have taken it in her stride without so much as a murmur of protest, cynically accepting that Jake, the rake, wouldn't want to be bothered by a baby. Besides which, in business hours, his time was more important than hers. He was the one who pulled in the profits.

She slumped forward, propped her elbows on the desk and dropped her head into her hands. Dear merciful God! Was there some way out of the hole she'd dug for herself?

She couldn't afford to walk away from this job, not now she was alone. Steve's departure meant the rent on the apartment would double for her unless she got someone else in to share the cost. These few weeks before Christmas was not a good time for changes.

Besides, who would pay her as much as Jake did? Her salary was more than generous for her qualifications. And she would miss the perks that came with meeting and doing business for rich and famous people.

Her gaze lifted and ruefully skirted the photographs hanging on the walls; celebrities on their luxury yachts, on board their private jets, travelling in style to exciting places, wining and dining in classy surroundings, perfect service on tap.

Of course Jake was in all the photographs, showing off his clientele and what he had provided for them. The man was a brilliant salesman. The photographs were public proof that he was the one to deliver what was desired.

And the plain truth was, however much he provoked her with his teasing and wicked ways, Amy did, for the most part, enjoy the challenge of matching wits with him. He kept her on her toes, goaded her into performing at her best, and the work was never boring. Neither was he.

She'd miss him.

Badly.

Especially with Steve gone.

She'd miss this plush office, too.

Where else would she get a workplace that could even come near to matching what she had here at *Wide Blue Yonder?*

Her gaze drifted around, picking up on all she could be about to lose. The carpet was the jewel-like turquoise colour of coral reef lagoons, the paintwork the mellow yellow shade of sandy beaches, outlined in glossy white. Fresh arrangements of tropical flowers were brought in every week, exotic blooms in orange and scarlet mixed with glowing greenery. Every modern technological aid for business was at her fingertips—no expense spared in providing her with the best of everything.

Then there was the million dollar view—an extension of the vista that could be seen from Jake's office—Darling Harbour and Balmain directly across the water, Goat Island, and stretching along this shoreline, Luna Park with its cluster of carnival rides and entertainment booths.

Mortified at her own lunacy for giving none of this a thought before barging in to confront Jake, Amy pushed out of her chair and moved over to the picture window overlooking the grinning clown face that marked the entrance to the old amusement park. Fun, it promised. Just like Jake. Except she'd hot-headedly wiped fun off today's agenda.

She should go back into his office and apologise.

But how to explain her behaviour?

Never had she struck such a blistering attitude with him. He was probably sitting in there, mulling over what it meant, and he wouldn't gloss over it. Not Jake Carter. No way would he leave it alone. If he wasn't thinking of firing her for insubordination, he was plotting how to use her outburst to his advantage.

She shivered.

Give Jake even a molehill of an advantage and he could build it into a mountain that put him on top of any game he wanted to play. She'd seen him do it over and over again. If he let her stay on...

The sound of the door between their offices being opened froze her train of thought. It raised prickles around the nape of her neck. Panic screamed along her nerves and cramped her heart. She'd left it too late to take some saving initiative. In helpless anguish she turned to face the man who held her immediate future in his hands.

He stood in the doorway, commanding her attention by the sheer force of his presence. The absence of any hint of a smile was stomach-wrenching. He observed her in silence for several tension-riven seconds, his eyes focused intensely on hers. Amy's mind screamed at her to say something, offer an olive branch, anything to smooth over what she'd done, but she couldn't tear her tongue off the roof of her mouth.

"I'm sorry."

Soft words...words she should have said. She stared at his mouth. Had they really come from him or had she imagined it? Yet how could she imagine an apology when she hadn't expected it?

His lips twisted into a rueful grimace. "I was out of line, dumping Joshua on you and taking it for granted you'd mind him for me."

Incredulity held her tongue-tied.

The grimace tilted up into an appealing smile. "Guess I thought all women melted over babies. I didn't see it as an imposition. More like a novelty."

She felt hopelessly screwed up. Her hand shot out in an agitated gesture. "I...over-reacted," she managed, her voice a bare croak.

He shrugged. "Hell, what do I know? You're so buttoned up about your private life. There must be some reason you're not married to the guy you've been living with all these years." His eyebrows slanted in an expression of caring concern. "Is there a problem about having a baby?"

The sympathetic tone did it.

Like the trumpets that brought down the walls of Jericho, it struck chords in Amy that triggered a collapse of her defences. Tears welled into her eyes and she couldn't find the will to stop them. She wanted to say it wasn't her fault but the lump in her throat was impassable.

She had a blurry glimpse of shock on Jake Carter's face, then he was moving, looming towards her, and the next thing she knew his arms had enveloped her and she was weeping on his shoulder and he was muttering a string of appalled comments.

"I didn't mean it... Honest, Amy!... I was just testing...never thought it was true..."

"'Snot," she sobbed, her hands clenched against his chest.

"Not true?" His bewilderment echoed in her ears.

She couldn't bear him thinking she was barren, making her even less of a woman than Steve had left her feeling. She scooped in a deep breath and the necessary words shuddered out. "He didn't want a baby with me."

"Didn't?" He picked up sharply on the past tense.

The betrayal was so fresh and painful, it spilled out. "Having one with her."

"He knocked up some other woman?"

Jake's shock on her behalf soothed her wounded pride. "A bwonde," she explained, her quivering mouth not quite getting around the word.

"Well, I hope you've sent him packing." A fierce admonition, giving Amy the crazy sense he would have done it for her, given the opportunity, probably cracking a bullwhip to effect a very prompt exit.

"Yes," she lied. It was too humiliating to confess she'd sat like a disembowelled dummy while Steve had gone about dismantling and removing his half of their life together.

"Good riddance," Jake heartily approved. "You wouldn't want to have a baby with him, Amy. Couldn't trust a man like that to stick around."

"'Sright." She nodded mournfully, too water-logged to make any cynical parallel to Jake's attitude to women.

"Still feeling raw about it," he murmured sympathetically.

"Yes."

"Guess you only found out this weekend."

"Tol' me Sat'day."

"And I had to slap you in the face with Joshua."

The self-recrimination stirred her to meet him halfway. "Not your fault." There, she'd finally got it out. "Sorry," she added for good measure.

"Don't worry about it, Amy. Bad timing, that's all."

He was being so kind and understanding, patting her on the back, making her feel secure with him, cared for and valued. His warmth seeped into her bones. Her hands relaxed, fingers spreading out across the comforting heat of his chest. She nestled closer to him and he stroked her hair.

Like a wilted sponge, she soaked in his tender compassion, needing it, wanting it. She'd felt so terribly alone these past two days, so bereft of anyone to care about her...

A baby cry pierced the pleasant fuzziness swimming

around in her mind. Joshua! Left alone in the other office! Amy lifted her heavy head, reluctant to push out of Jake's embrace but she couldn't really stay there. Kind understanding only went so far. This was a place of business. A line had to be drawn.

Jake might start thinking she liked being this close to him. In fact, weren't his arms tightening around her, subtly shifting their body contact, stirring a consciousness of how very male he was? To Amy's increasing confusion, she found she wasn't immune to the virility she'd always privately scorned. For several electrifying moments she was mesmerised by its effect on her.

Another baby cry escalated into a wail, demanding attention.

"Responsibility calls, I'm afraid," Jake said wryly, confusing Amy further as he gently loosened his hold on her.

Had she imagined the slight sexual pressure?

He retained one supporting hand at her waist as he lifted his other to tilt her face up. His eyes were a warm, caressing gold. "Got your feet back?" he softly teased.

It drew a wobbly smile. "Firm on the floor again."

"Good!" He nodded approval. The warm molten gold hardened to a glitter. "Better go and wash that guy off your face, as well as out of your mind."

In short, she was a mess and he wanted his personal assistant back in good form. Of course that was all he wanted. Jake Carter was too smart to muddy up his business with pleasures he could get so easily elsewhere.

Then his fingertips brushed her cheek. "Okay?"

Her skin tingled, most probably from the flush of embarrassment rising to her cheeks. "Yes," she asserted as strongly as she could.

He gave her a lopsided grin as he dropped his hand and stepped away. "The godfather is on duty. Got to see to Joshua."

He was already at the door before she summoned breath enough to say, "Thanks, Jake."

"Any time. My shoulders are broad," he tossed at her good-humouredly, heading into his office to tend to his nephew.

Amy took several deep breaths to re-stabilise herself, then forced her legs into action. She picked up her handbag and strode off to the washroom, determined on being what she was supposed to be for Jake. She wouldn't forget his forebearance and kindness, either. Nor the moral support he'd given her. He almost counted as a friend, a solidly loyal friend.

On second thought, she shouldn't go overboard with that sentiment. Jake Carter was her boss. It was more efficient to get his personal assistant back in good working order than to train someone else to meet his needs. She was well aware of Jake's strong dash of pragmatism. Whatever it took to get the end he wanted was meticulously mapped and carried through.

All the same, she deeply appreciated his…well, his sensitivity…to her distress just now. He was also right. She *was* well rid of a man who cheated on her. She should stop grieving and start getting on with the rest of her life.

Though that was easier said than done.

At least she still had her job.

The black hole had closed up before she'd fallen right to the bottom of it, thank God!

Proving she was back in control again, her hand remained absolutely steady as she once more cleaned off her face and re-applied some masterly make-up. Then feeling more in command of herself, she hurried to Jake's office, determined to offer any assistance he required. After all, Joshua was not Steve's baby. She could handle looking after him.

As for Jake...well, she'd been handling him for the past two years. Nothing was going to change there. She just had to keep her head and not let him close to her body again. Business as usual.

CHAPTER FOUR

JAKE had left the door to his office ajar and Amy paused there before entering, amused by the crooning voice he was using for the baby.

"We're on a winning streak now, Josh. Oh, yes, we are, my boyo! We've got Amy Taylor right where we want her."

The smile was jolted off her face by those last words. Though hadn't she known not to trust his benevolence? Jake Carter always took advantage of what was handed to him. Always. If it suited him. One way or another he was going to capitilise on her lapse in professionalism.

"Well, not *precisely* where we want her," he went on.

Good! She'd show him she wasn't putty in his hands. One breakdown didn't mean she was a pushover. She knew where the line was drawn when it came to working with Jake Carter.

"Bit of patience needed, Josh. Bit of manoeuvring. That's a good chap. Hold it right there."

Unsure of how much of this speech applied to her, Amy stepped into the office to take in the scene. The capsule was on the floor and the baby laid out on the bunny rug which had been spread across the desk. Little legs and arms waved haphazardly as Jake triumphantly shoved a used disposable nappy into a plastic bag.

"Clean one coming up," he assured his nephew.

Deciding it was safe to interrupt without giving away the fact she'd been eavesdropping, Amy moved forward to offer the assistance she'd resolved to offer. "Would you like me to take over?"

Jake glanced up and shot her a grin. "Nope. I've got this all figured out." He grabbed Joshua's ankles, raised his bottom off the bunny rug and whipped a clean nappy into place. "Just a matter of getting the plastic tabs the right way around," he informed her.

Since Amy had never changed a nappy in her life, she was grateful Jake had acquired some expertise. It was quite fascinating, seeing the deft way he handled fastening the absorbent pad on the squirming little body.

"You could heat up his bottle for me." Jake waved towards the capsule. "Ruth said to stick it in the microwave for thirty seconds."

"Okay."

Glad to be given something positive to do, Amy quickly found the bottle in the Disney bag and raced off to the kitchenette where she usually made morning or afternoon teas for clients. She wasn't sure what temperature to set on the microwave, decided on medium, then watched the bottle revolve for the required time. A squirt of milk on her wrist assured her it wasn't too hot, and she carried it back to Jake with a buoyant sense of achievement.

Joshua was reclothed and clinging like a limpet to his uncle's shoulder as Jake patted his back. That makes two of us this morning, Amy thought ruefully. Guilt over her earlier refusal to have anything to do with the baby prompted her to offer full services now. Besides which, she didn't want Jake holding anything against her. Power came in many guises, and Jake Carter was a master of all of them.

"I can take him into my office and feed him," she said as *un*grudgingly as she could.

"It's my job," Jake insisted, holding his hand out for the bottle.

She passed it over, frustrated by his righteous stance. Paying *her* back, she thought. Rubbing it in.

"You can read me the mail while I take care of Josh," he added, granting her professional purpose. "I'll dictate whatever needs to be answered or followed through and leave that to you."

"Fine!" she agreed and darted into her office for her notebook, determined not to be faulted again. He already had too much ammunition against her...when he decided to use it.

The man was devilishly clever. She had never trusted him with personal information, suspecting he would somehow wield it to gain more power over her. All along, she had instinctively resisted his strong magnetism, perceiving it as a dangerous whirlpool that sucked people in. Especially women. Amy was in no doubt it paid to be wary around Jake Carter.

She deliberately adopted a business-like air as she seated herself in front of his desk, preparing to sort through the mail with him. However, despite her sensible resolution to take guard, she found the next half hour highly distracting to her concentration on the job.

Jake had settled back in his chair, feet up, totally re-laxed as he cradled the baby in the crook of his arm and tilted the bottle as needed for the tiny sucking mouth. He looked so natural about it, as though well practised in the task. He even burped the baby halfway through its feed, propping it on his knee and firmly rubbing its back. Amy herself wouldn't have had a clue how to do that, let alone knowing it should be done.

"Good boy!" Jake crooned as two loud burps emerged, then nestled the baby back in his arm to continue the feeding.

Amy was amazed. Maybe, however improbable it seemed, Jake Carter *was* a staunch family man when it came to his immediate family. Or maybe his self-assurance simply extended to anything he took on. It was all very confusing. She could have sworn she had her buccaneer boss taped to the last millimetre, but he was certainly adding several other shades to his character this morning. Unexpectedly nice shades.

When they'd dealt with the last letter, Amy felt reluctant to leave the oddly intimate little family scene. It was Jake who prompted her, raising a quizzical eyebrow at her silence.

"All finished?"

"Yes."

"Anything I haven't covered?"

"No." She stood up, clutching the letters with her attached notes.

Jake smiled at her, a genuinely open smile, nothing tagged onto it. "Let me know if you run into any problems."

"Okay." She smiled back. Unreservedly.

It wasn't until she was back in her own office with the door closed between them, that it occurred to Amy how much better she was feeling. The day was no longer so gloomy. Steve's betrayal had gathered some distance, making it less overwhelming. She could function with some degree of confidence.

Had she nursed unfair prejudices against her boss?

Had loyalty to Steve pushed her into casting Jake Carter as some kind of devil's advocate who could shake the foundations of a life she valued?

Only one certainty slid out of this musing.

She didn't owe Steve loyalty anymore.

Nevertheless, she'd be courting real trouble if she ever forgot the reasons she'd named her boss Jake the rake!

Amy spent the next half hour diligently working through his instructions, her concentration so intensely focused, she didn't hear the elevator open onto their floor. The knock on her office door startled her. She looked up to see a woman already entering, a tall, curvaceous redhead, exuding an air of confidence in her welcome.

Amy felt an instant stab of antagonism. Some of Jake's women had a hide like a rhinoceros, swanning in as though they owned the place. This one was new. Same kind of sexy glamour puss he usually picked, though—long legs, big breasts, a face that belonged on the cover of *Vogue,* hair obviously styled by a master cutter, very short and chic, designer jeans that clung seductively, a clingy top that showed cleavage.

"Hi! I'm Ruth Powell, Jake's sister."

Amy was dumbfounded. There was no likeness at all. If she hadn't been presented with Jake's nephew this morning, she would have suspected a deception. Some women would use any ploy to get to the man they wanted. Though on closer scrutiny, and with the help of the identification, Amy did see one similarity in the triangular shape of the eyes. The colour, however, was deeper, Ruth's more a sherry brown than yellow-gold.

She had paused beside the door, returning Amy's scrutiny with avid interest. "You're Amy Taylor?" she asked before Amy thought to give her own name.

"Yes," she affirmed, wondering about the testing note in the other woman's voice.

A grin of pure amusement flashed across Ruth's face. "I see," she said with satisfaction.

Perplexed, Amy asked, "See what?"

"Why you dominate so much of Jake's conversation."

"I do?" Amy was astonished.

"So much so that amongst the family we've christened you Wonderwoman," Ruth answered dryly.

Amy flushed, suddenly self-conscious of how less flatteringly she had privately christened Jake.

"Actually, we weren't sure if you were a fire-breathing dragon who kept his machismo scorched, or a stern headmistress who made him toe your line. Now I'll be able to tell everyone you're Irish."

"I'm not Irish," Amy tripped out, feeling more flummoxed by the second.

"Definitely Black Irish." Ruth started forward, gesturing her points as she made them. "You've got the hair, the eyes, and the spirit. You had me pinned like a butterfly for a minute there. Lots of power in those blue eyes."

"I'm sorry if you thought me rude," Amy rushed out, trying to get a handle on this strange encounter.

"Not at all. Call it a revelation. You must have Jake on toast." She laughed, bubbling over with some wicked kind of sibling pleasure as she strolled over to Amy's desk. "I love it. Serve him right."

Amy mentally shook her head. It was an absurd comment—her having Jake on toast. He had enough women to sink a ship. He was hardly dying of frustration because she refused to rise to his bait.

We've got Amy Taylor right where we want her...

The insidious words suddenly took on extra meaning.

With Steve written out of the picture...

Held in Jake Carter's seductive embrace...

But not *precisely* in his bed!

Amy almost rolled her eyes at the totally over-the-top train of thought. Imagination gone wild. Jake's sister obviously enjoyed teasing as much as he did. None of it was to be taken seriously and it was best to put a stop to it.

"I beg your pardon, but..."

"Oh, don't mind me." Ruth twirled one perfectly manicured hand dismissively. "Relief loosening my tongue. I thought Martin's injury was worse that it is. It was hell waiting around in Casualty, fretting over what was happening or not happening."

Martin... that had to be her husband. "His shoulder is all right then?" Amy asked, belatedly recalling it had been dislocated.

"They put it back in. He's sleeping off the anaesthetic now so I thought I'd pick up Josh." Her gaze swept the area behind Amy, frowning at not spotting the capsule. "Where is he?"

"With Jake." Amy nodded towards the connecting door.

Ruth looked her surprise. "You mean he didn't ask you to look after him?"

Amy grimaced. "Well, we had a little contretemps about that. As I understood it, you entrusted him with your baby, so..."

"You insisted he do it?" Ruth's eyes shone with admiration.

"I hope that was right," Amy appealed. "He does seem very good at it."

Ruth broke into laughter again, her eyes twinkling merry approval. "You are priceless, Amy. I'm so glad I got to meet you. As for Jake being good with Josh, he is. Dogs and children gravitate naturally to my brother. So do women. As I'm sure you've noticed," she added with arch understanding.

"Hard not to," Amy returned dryly.

"Too used to getting his own way, my brother."

She was right about that but Amy decided some loyal support was called for. "He does work at it. Not much is left to chance, you know. His background research on every project is very thorough."

"Oh, I wasn't besmirching his professionalism. Jake was always an obsessive perfectionist. A born achiever." Her mouth twitched sardonically. "But some things do tend to fall in his lap."

Like a pile of willing women, Amy silently agreed, but it wasn't her place to say so. She smiled. "Well, Joshua was in his lap, last time I saw him."

"Right! It's been fun talking to you, Amy. Hope to see you again someday," Ruth said warmly, taking her exit into Jake's office.

Fun... Jake's family seemed addicted to fun. Amy

wondered what it might have been like, growing up in that kind of atmosphere. She remembered her own childhood as being dominated by fear of her father. Not that he had ever stooped to physical abuse. He didn't have to. He could cut anyone down with a word or a look. In hindsight, she could identify him as a control freak, but at the time, he was the authority to be escaped from whenever it was possible.

Her mother had been completely cowed. The only escape for her had been in death, and it was her death that had released Amy from staying any longer in her father's household. Her two older brothers had already gone by then, driven away by their father's unreasonable demands. She hadn't seen them in years. She no longer had any sense of family.

What she did have was a strong belief in living life on her own terms. Which was probably why she hadn't pushed for marriage with Steve. The thought of a husband was too closely connected to her father. She didn't want to be owned like that. Ever. In fact, she'd found Steve's much quoted term of being "free spirits" very attractive. Until she found out what "free" meant to Steve.

What a stupid, blind fool she'd been!

Amy shook her head at herself and turned back to work. There was nothing to be gained by maundering over her mistakes. Her best course was to learn from them and move on. She was briefly tempted to pull out the magazine she'd bought this morning and read the article on exit signs. The thought of Jake catching her at it put her off. No more gaffes today, she sternly told herself.

We've got Amy Taylor right where we want her...

Amy didn't like that smug little boast. She didn't like it at all. She liked *not precisely* much better. She hadn't spent two years honing her defensive skills with Jake Carter for nothing. Whatever he had in mind, she was not going to be a patsy, falling into his lap.

It was Jake who'd made a gaffe, blabbing to the baby. She'd be on her toes from now on, ready to block whatever little one-upmanship game he was planning to play. This time she'd be one step ahead of him.

Yes...she was definitely feeling better.

Jake certainly had a knack of putting zest into her life. Which was a big improvement on the black hole.

CHAPTER FIVE

IT WASN'T long before Jake came in to check how Amy was doing. Ruth had apparently left through his door to the corridor since there was no sight or sound of her and the baby. "On top of it?" he asked casually.

"No problem," she answered, nodding to the printout of the work she'd done.

He picked up the sheets, then propped himself on the front edge of her desk to read them. As always, his proximity put her nerves on edge and she had to concentrate harder on keeping her fingers moving accurately on the keyboard. She was even more aware of him than usual, remembering how he'd held her earlier...his body, his touch. She wondered if he was a sensitive lover.

Her gaze flicked to his hands, the long tapered fingers wrapped around the sheef of paper. They'd stroked her hair so gently. She reminded herself Jake was very smooth at everything he did. Sexual sensitivity didn't necessarily mean he actually cared for the person. Stoking his own pleasure more likely. Though he had seemed to care about her this morning. Had it been entirely a pose for an ulterior purpose?

"Couldn't have worded this better myself," Jake said appreciatively. His smile had a caressing quality that almost made Amy squirm. "You have a great knack of filling out my instructions, Amy, applying the right

40

touch to get through to people without pushing too hard.''

She quelled the whoosh of pleasure at his praise. "I have been learning off a master the past two years," she pointed out, her eyes lightly mocking.

"And an apt pupil you've proved," he was quick to add, his admiration undimmed. "Don't know what I'd do without you. You're my right hand."

He was laying it on with a trowel. Amy instinctively backed off. "So what's next on the agenda?" He was probably buttering her up to land some task he didn't want to do himself in her lap.

"Two years, mmh?" he mused, ignoring her question. "You deserve a raise in salary. Ruth is right."

"About what?" This was very doubtful ground.

He grinned. "You're priceless."

Amy frowned. "Do you make a habit of discussing me with your family?"

He shrugged. "Perfectly natural. You are my closest associate. Don't you mention me to yours?"

"I don't have a family." It slipped out before she could catch it back.

His eyebrows shot up. "An orphan?"

The interest beaming at her was not about to be side-tracked. Amy sighed. All this time she'd worked with Jake Carter and managed to keep him at arm's length where any personal issues were concerned. Today she'd blown it in more ways than one.

"Not exactly," she muttered, telling herself her family was so far removed from her it didn't matter. "My mother died when I was sixteen. My father's remarried and we don't get on. I have one brother living in the

U.K., and another settled in Alaska. Hardly what you'd call close.''

Having rattled out the bare facts, Amy constructed a dismissive smile which she found difficult to hold when faced with Jake's appalled reaction.

''You mean you're alone? Absolutely alone with no one to turn to? No backup support?''

''I'm used to it,'' she insisted. ''I've been on my own a long time.''

''No, you haven't,'' he fired back at her. ''Which was why you were weeping on my shoulder this morning.''

Amy gritted her teeth and glowered at him. ''Must you remind me of that?''

''At least *I* was here for you. Just remember that, Amy. When your scumbag of a lover let you down, I was here for you.''

''You're my boss! You weren't here for *me,*'' she argued hotly. ''It was purely a matter of propinquity.''

''Nonsense! I took your side immediately. I know what you're worth. Which is a damned sight more than that fool did.''

She knew it! He just had to take advantage of any slip she made. He *revelled in it.* ''I do not wish to discuss Steve any further,'' she grated out.

''Of course not. The sooner he's wiped out of your life, the better. Eminently sensible. Though there are practical matters to take into consideration.''

''Yes. Like getting on with work,'' Amy tersely reminded him.

''You might need help in shifting to a new apartment.''

''I like the apartment I've got, thank you.''

"Not a good idea, keeping it, Amy. Memories can be depressing. I realise shifting would be another upheaval you might not want to face right now, but a clean break is the best medicine. Gets rid of the hangover."

"Well, I'm sure you'd know that, Jake," she said with blistering sarcasm.

The acid didn't make a dint. "I'll help you," he said, as though she'd conceded to his argument instead of commenting on his quick turnover in women.

"I don't need your help."

He smiled and blithely waved her protest aside. "Consider me family. It's times like these that family bucks in and picks up the slack. Since I'm the closest thing you've got to family..."

"I do not...remotely...associate you...with family," Amy stated emphatically.

"Well, yes..." One shoulder lifted and fell. Devilment danced into his eyes. "...That probably would be a bit incestuous, wouldn't it?"

"What?" she squawked.

"I can't lie to you, Amy," he declared loftily. "What zips between you and me could not be called sisterly...or brotherly...or motherly...or fatherly."

She flushed, biting her tongue so as not to invite more along this line.

"However, I am genuinely concerned about you," he said, projecting such deep sincerity it swallowed up the devilment and threatened to suck Amy in right after it.

She fought fiercely for a bank of common sense, needing some safe ground between her and Jake Carter. The danger of him infiltrating her private life felt very acute and every instinct told her it wasn't wise. He could bad-mouth Steve as much as he liked but was he any better? His record with women was hardly in his favour!

"I'll ask around," he burbled on. "Find you a nice apartment. Closer to work so you won't have far to travel. Bondi Beach isn't really suitable for you."

"I like Bondi," she protested.

He frowned at her. "Not good for a woman on her own. A lot of undesirables gather out there at weekends. You wouldn't be safe going out at night without an escort."

He had a point, but where was safe at night without an escort? Life without Steve was going to take some adjustment.

"Why not have a look around Balmoral if you want to live by a beach?" Jake suggested. "It's a respectable area. Doesn't draw any trouble."

She rolled her eyes at him and his big ideas. "It's also a very expensive area."

"No more than Bondi. And being on the north side of the harbour, it's much handier to Milsons Point. You won't have to drive across the bridge to work."

"I can't afford it. I can't afford where I am without a partner."

"I said I was upping your salary. Let's say another twenty percent. That should let you live decently."

Amy's mouth dropped open. Her mind flew wildly into calculation mode. "That's more than Steve earns!"

He grinned. "You're worth it. I'll just go and ring a few estate agents I know. See what they can come up with. In the meantime, send these off." He handed her the replies she'd printed out. "They're all fine."

He hitched himself off her desk and left her gaping

after him like a goldfish caught in a bowl, looking out at a foreign world. Jake Carter had always been a shaker and a mover, but never before on her behalf. Was it out of concern for her or did he have other motives up his sleeve?

Amy ran her fingers through her hair, trying to steady the mad whirl in her mind. What could she believe as irrefutable fact? Both Jake and his sister were into game-playing, scoring points. Nothing they said could be taken too seriously.

On the other hand, Jake always delivered what he promised. He wouldn't backtrack on the money. Her salary would now be more than she'd ever dreamed of earning, putting her on a financial level where she was truly independent. Which meant she had options she didn't have before.

A grin broke across her face.

Such a large salary would certainly make her life considerably brighter and it was wonderful to be valued so highly. This morning she'd felt her future had fallen into a black hole, but it wasn't true. There was life after Steve. And she was going to make the most of it, thanks to Jake.

Though if her devious boss was thinking he could attach personal strings to that big hunk of money he'd just handed her, he could think again!

CHAPTER SIX

AMY had just finished filing copies of the letters she'd sent when Jake erupted into her office.

"Grab your handbag," he commanded. "We're off."

"Where to?"

"I'll explain on the way." He checked his watch as he crossed her office to the door. "We've got precisely twenty-five minutes to make the rendezvous."

Amy grabbed her handbag and scooted after him. Jake had the door open for her. She strode into the corridor and summoned the elevator, glad they were going to be involved in some outside activity. Jake would be busy with other people who would take his focus off her and she could get back to feeling relatively normal in his company again.

She always enjoyed these meetings with clients, watching Jake work his brand of magic on them. "Who's the target?" she asked as they stepped into the elevator together.

"Not who. What," he said enigmatically, pressing the ground floor button.

"A new boat?"

He shot her a look of exasperation as the elevator descended. "We do not deal in boats, Amy. Only in yachts," he reminded her.

"Sorry. Slip of the tongue."

"Watch it," he advised darkly. "I want my P.A. to impress the man we're going to meet."

"What's his name?"

"Ted Durkin of Durkin and Harris. Big property dealers."

The name meant nothing to her but clearly it was well known to Jake. The elevator opened onto the reception area before she had time to question him. Jake steered her out and pointed her to the stairwell that led down to the back of the building where he parked his car in a private yard reserved for himself and clients.

"Kate," he called to his front woman, "we're out of the office. Take messages."

"When will you be back?"

"Don't know. If it's anything urgent I can be reached on my mobile."

He hurried Amy down the stairs and outside, using the remote button on his key to unlock the BMW M3 supercar which he currently fancied. Amy headed for the passenger side of the two-door coupe. Haste precluded courtesy. They both took their seats and Jake handed her a folded piece of notepaper as he switched on the ignition.

"What's this?"

"Where we're going. Better get out the Gregory's Street Directory and navigate for me. Haven't got time for wrong turns. I'm right to Military Road. After that, you direct me."

She extracted the guide book from the glove box and settled back for the ride. The scribbled list on the notepaper did not enlighten her as to their destination. In fact, it looked as though Jake had picked up the wrong sheet. What was written appeared to be information about a woman.

Her mouth curled. It seemed he did research on them, as well. "This says, 'Estelle, 26, 8, no smoking, no pets, no WP...'"

"Wild parties," Jake elaborated. "The address is 26 Estelle Road, Balmoral. Apartment 8. The rest are the conditions for rental."

Amy's sardonic humour dried up. Her heart performed a double loop. She waited until it settled back into seminormal rhythm, counting to ten in the meantime. "I take it this is for me," she said as calmly as she could.

"If you like it and if we can swing it."

"Jake, this is not your business." He'd been encroaching on her private life all morning. She had to put a stop to it before it got completely out of hand.

"I said I'd look into it for you," he replied, unshaken from his purpose.

"You said you'd make some calls, not escort me to view places during business hours. I cannot accept..."

"It's almost the lunch hour," he reasoned. "You're always obliging about working overtime in emergencies. The least I can do is this small favour in return."

"This is not an emergency, Jake," she argued, barely holding on to her temper. "I can look for an apartment—if I want to move from the one at Bondi—in my own time."

He frowned at her. "Why are you nit-picking? There's no harm in looking at a place you might like. It could be the ideal change for you."

Amy stubbornly stuck to her guns. "You could have given me the address and..."

"No good! You need me with you for this one. I'm your reference. I pressured Ted into showing it to you ahead of his listing it and he's on his way there now to meet us. He's a handy business contact, Amy. I wouldn't like to waste his time."

She heaved an exasperated sigh, accepting she'd been outmanoeuvred. He was her boss. It would be wrong for her to mess with his contacts. But a stand had to be taken. She didn't want him pulling strings on her behalf, entangling her in them without her knowledge or permission.

"You should have discussed it with me first. I haven't made up my mind on this." And she hated the feeling of being steam-rollered by Jake.

"There's no obligation to take it. Sounded like a great deal for you, though. Worth seeing if it's as good as Ted says. And I might add, he's proved spot-on in his advice to me in the past."

"What's so great about it?" she demanded tersely.

"Location for a start. Ted reckoned it was a pearl for the rent being asked."

"How much?"

He rolled out a sum that was only marginally lower than the rent for the Bondi apartment. Even with her new salary, it would take a bigger chunk of her income than she felt was reasonable for her.

"Ted told me it could command a much higher rent," Jake burbled on. "But the owner's fussy about getting the right tenant in and has scaled the rent to suit. The apartment was recently purchased and is in the process of being refurbished. The owner doesn't want any damage to it, so…''

"No smoking, no pets, no wild parties." Amy looked at the list again. "What does 'SCW' stand for?"

"Single career woman. Someone who respects property and has a tidy mind." Jake flashed her a teasing smile. "I said you fitted the bill. Never met a woman more intent on keeping things in order."

Including you, Amy thought darkly. He was such a tempting devil, too attractive for his own good, and he thought he could charm his way into anything. Not my life, she fiercely resolved. It was bad enough being dumped by Steve. If she let Jake get too close to her, she had a terrible suspicion he had the power to steal her soul. Then where would she be?

Every self-protective instinct screamed alarm in his presence and today the scream was louder than ever. Raw and vulnerable from the weekend's revelations, Amy admitted to herself she was frightened of Jake slipping past her guard, frightened of the consequences. She fretted over the knowledge he now shared that Steve couldn't be used as a barrier between them anymore.

Though that wasn't entirely right.

Steve had been much more to her than a barrier against Jake.

Much more, she insisted to herself.

She opened the Gregory's Street Directory and started plotting their course to Estelle Street, trying her utmost to ignore the man beside her. His power was threatening to swamp her; powerful masculinity, powerful car, powerful friends, and they were all being used on her. Or so it felt.

We've got Amy Taylor right where we want her.

Not precisely.

A bit of manoeuvring.

The provocative words clicked through her mind again, conjuring up another scenario. An apartment in Balmoral was Jake's idea. He'd given her a raise in salary so she could afford it. He'd found one for her, supposedly to order. He'd tricked her into his car so he could take her there, pressured her with the importance of a business contact.

Was it some kind of put-up job between him and his friendly property dealer, Ted Durkin?

But why?

What good would it do Jake to have her in Balmoral?

He was screwing her up again.

The only way to be sure of anything was to thwart him by making her own decisions her own way. In the meantime she'd play along like a good little girl. Which meant giving directions from the directory.

Amy had never lived on the north side of Sydney and didn't know the Middle Harbour area at all. Her only previous reference to Balmoral was an interview she'd read about a TV celebrity who lived there and loved it. Which undoubtedly meant it was very classy. And expensive. Any place on the harbour was expensive.

Having found Estelle Street on the map, Amy stared at its location with a sense of disbelief. It was only one block back from The Esplanade which ran around the beach. It faced onto a park that extended to The

Esplanade, giving residents a view of greenery, as well an uninterrupted vista of the water beyond it. This had to be a prime location.

She frowned over the rental Jake had mentioned. It was steep for her to pay alone, but it had to be amazingly cheap for an apartment on this street. Even the most run-down place would surely command double that amount, and Jake had said it was being refurbished.

"This doesn't make sense," she muttered.

"What?" Jake inquired.

"I've found Estelle Street. It's almost on the beach. The property there has got to be million dollar stuff. Even with the strict rules, the owner could ask a really high rent."

Jake must have made some under-the-table arrangement with Ted Durkin. She just didn't trust this sequence of events. Or coincidences.

"I did tell you Ted said it was a bargain. For the right person," Jake reminded her. "There is the catch of the six months' lease," he added in the throwaway tone of an afterthought. "But even if this is only a stopgap place for you..."

"What catch?"

She'd been waiting for a "catch." Jake was being altogether too persuasive about this wonderful chance for her. There had to be a "catch."

"Seems the owner plans to take up residence there. Only waiting on selling the current home. Doesn't want to hurry that." He sent her a wise look. "Always best to hang out for the asking price. It's a losing game, selling in haste."

"So it's only for six months."

"Mmh… more like a house-sitter than a tenant, according to Ted. Someone who'll value the place and look after it. Never a good idea to leave a property empty for an extended period of time."

It was beginning to make more sense. Maybe her suspicions were unwarranted. It wasn't beyond the realm of possibility that Jake might want to do her a good turn. If she hadn't overheard those words…was she reading too much into them?

Whatever the truth of the matter, it didn't make a great deal of sense for her to shift house if she had to shift again in six months' time. Changing apartments was a high-cost exercise what with putting up bond money and the expense of moving her furniture, not to mention the hassle of packing and unpacking. Nevertheless, she was curious to see the apartment now. Especially since Jake was investing so much time and talk on it. She still wanted to know why.

They were well along Military Road so she started giving him directions. Within a few minutes he'd made the turns she gave and they were heading down a hill to Balmoral Beach. Amy was entranced by the view. The water was a dazzling blue this morning. A fleet of small yachts were riding at anchor, adding their interest to the picturesque bay. The curved shoreline had a welcoming stretch of clean sand, edged by manicured lawns, beautiful trees and walkways.

This beach had a quiet, exclusive air about it, unlike the broad sweep of Bondi which invited vast public crowds. Even the populated side of The Esplanade looked tidy and respectable, no litter, no grubbiness, not a tatty appearance anywhere. Amy was highly impressed by its surface charm, wishing she had time to explore properly. She made a mental note to come here another day. After all, with Steve gone, she would have plenty of *free* days to do whatever she pleased.

They turned off into the street beside the park and found the address with no trouble at all. The block of apartments was on the next corner, a fairly old block in red brick and only four storeys high with garages underneath. Amy guessed Apartment 8 would be on the top floor, and found herself hoping it was on the corner with the balcony running around two sides, both east and north.

''There's Ted waiting for us,'' Jake pointed out, waving to the man standing by the entrance to the block.

As they cruised past in search of a parking place, Amy caught only a glimpse of the agent, a broad, bulky figure, smartly attired in a blue business shirt, striped tie, and dark trousers. Jake slotted the car into the kerb only twenty metres away. Amy checked her watch as they alighted. Twelve-thirty. They were on time. Ted Durkin had arrived early. No fault of theirs, but both she and Jake automatically covered the distance at a fast pace.

Amy was conscious of being scrutinised as they approached. It wasn't a sexual once-over, more a matching up to specifications. The agent looked to be in his late forties, his iron-grey hair thinning on top, making his slight frown very visible. It only cleared when Jake thrust out his hand to him, drawing attention away from her.

"Good of you to give us this opportunity, Ted," he enthused genially.

"Not at all. You've put business my way in the past, Jake. Appreciate it."

"This is my P.A., Amy Taylor."

"Pleased to meet you, Mr. Durkin," Amy chimed in, offering her hand.

He took it and gave her a rueful little smile. "To tell you the truth, Miss Taylor, I wasn't expecting someone quite so young."

Single career woman—had he been envisaging a spinsterish woman in her late thirties or forties, someone entrenched in her career with little else in her life?

One thing was suddenly clear. This had to be a *bona fide* deal or Ted Durkin wouldn't be raising questions.

Without pausing to examine her eagerness to dismiss objections to her possible tenancy, Amy rushed to reassure him.

"I'm twenty-eight, Mr. Durkin, and I've held a job since I was sixteen. That's twelve years of solid employment, working my way up to my current position."

"Very responsible," Jake slipped in emphatically.

Ted Durkin shot him a chiding look. "You didn't mention how very attractive your P.A. is, Jake." Another apologetic look at her. "No offence to you, Miss Taylor, but the owner of the apartment was very specific about..."

"No wild parties," she finished for him. "That's not my style, Mr. Durkin."

"Amy's been with me for two years, Ted," Jake said. "I really can vouch for her character. An ultra-clean living person."

"Uh-huh." He raised his eyebrows at her. "No boy-friend? I don't mean to get personal. It's a matter of satisfying the owner. Did Jake explain...?"

"Yes, he did."

Regardless if she was prepared to take the apartment or not, Amy bridled against the sense of being rejected, especially after the painful blow from Steve. She found herself pouring out a persuasive argument, uncaring that it was personal business. Jake knew it anyway and she felt compelled to convince Ted Durkin she was an appropriate tenant.

"Actually I'm looking for time to myself, Mr. Durkin. I've been in a rather long-term relationship which has just broken up." She grimaced, appealing to his sympathy. "No chance of a reconciliation, so I really am on my own and I don't intend rushing into socialising. Six months here would do me very nicely, right away from where I've been."

"Ah!" It was the sound of satisfaction. "Well, I'll take you up and show you around. It's not quite ready for occupation. Painters are in at the moment."

Won a stay of judgement, Amy thought, ridiculously pleased. She glanced at Jake as they entered the building, wanting to share the achievement with him since he'd helped. He wasn't looking at her but she caught a smug little smile on his face and then wanted to kick herself.

She'd ended up playing *his* game, showing positive enthusiasm for *his* plan to move her out of Bondi and to Balmoral.

I was only saving *his* face in front of Ted Durkin, Amy quickly excused herself. She could still say no to the apartment. There was no commitment until she signed the lease for it. In fact, if she decided to move— in her own good time—it was much more practical to find a place that didn't have a time limit on it.

Jake Carter hadn't won this round yet!

CHAPTER SEVEN

THEY rode a small elevator up to the top floor. It opened onto a broad hallway, lit by the multicoloured panes of glass which ran down the opposite wall, making an attractive feature for the stairwell next to it. Ted Durkin ushered them to an opened door on the left hand side. Amy's heart gave an excited skip.

It *was* the apartment with the east-north balconies.

They walked into a wonderfully light, airy, open-plan living area and for Amy it was love at first sight. To live here—if only for six months—it was irresistible—an incredible bargain!

The floor was covered with marvellous tiles, the pearlescent colour of sea-shells crushed into a wavy pattern that instantly suggested a seabed of gently undulating sand. The wall facing the bay was almost all glass, offering a panoramic view and a wealth of sunshine. Other walls were painted a pale cream. The kitchen was shiny new, all blonde wood and stainless steel, fitted with a dishwasher and a microwave oven, as well as a traditional one.

In the living room, two men in paint-spotted overalls sat on foldaway chairs, eating their lunch. A spread-sheet was laid out on the floor underneath them. Tins of paint stood on it in a tidy group.

"How's it going?" Ted asked them.

"One more coat on the skirting boards and architraves and we're finished," the older one answered.

These were being painted a pearly grey, picking up on some of the grains in the tiles and making a stylish contrast to the cream.

"Still wet?"

"Should be touch-dry by now. It's safe to move around."

"Fine." Ted turned to Amy. "The old carpet's been ripped out of the bedrooms for the carpenter to fit the cupboards properly. The new one won't be laid until later this week," he warned.

"There's more than one bedroom?" Amy asked, stunned by the spaciousness of the apartment.

"Two."

Jake wandered over to chat to the painters as the agent steered Amy towards an archway in the back wall of the living room. Apparently he didn't intend to participate in her decision, which made a mess of her line of logic.

She made a determined effort to shake off her pre-occupation with his influence, realising she must have misread the situation, possibly blowing it completely out of proportion. When all was said and done, he had only followed through on what he had advised her. Having her right where he wanted her could simply mean keeping her happy as his assistant.

Through the archway was a short hall with doors at both ends of it and two more doors facing the wall with the arch. The latter pair were opened first. "Laundry and bathroom," Ted pointed out.

The laundry held a linen and broom cupboard, washer, dryer and tub. All new. Amy was delighted to see the washer and dryer since Steve had taken those in the division of their property, leaving her with the refrigerator and the TV. She'd envisaged visits to a laundrette, an inconvenience she wouldn't have to put up with here.

The bathroom was positively luxurious. It had obviously been renovated, the same tiles in the living area being carried through to it and the same blonde wood in the kitchen being used on the vanity bench. Incredibly, it featured a Jacuzzi bath as well as a shower and everything else one could need.

"These old places were built to be roomy. Couldn't put a bath like that in most modern apartments," Ted remarked, probably noting her stunned expression. "You don't often see such high ceilings, either. All the rooms here have bigger dimensions than usual."

And there'd been an enormous amount of money poured into making the most of them, Amy thought. No expense spared. Little wonder that the owner didn't want it damaged by careless tenants.

The second bedroom was larger than average. The main bedroom was larger still, with glass doors that led out onto the north-facing balcony. "What colour is the new carpet?" Amy asked.

Ted shrugged. "Don't know. The owner picked it. I could tell you on Friday."

Amy shook her head. "It doesn't matter. I've never been in such a lovely apartment. Believe me, Mr. Durkin, it would be an absolute pleasure to keep this in mint condition. Do you think the owner will accept me as a tenant?" she pressed eagerly.

His face relaxed into an indulgent smile. His eyes twinkled at her in approval. "Why not? I can sell anything if I believe in it and I'm inclined to believe you, Miss Taylor.''

"I promise your faith won't be mislaid.''

"Well, I do have Jake's word for that, as well, so we'll call it a done deal.''

"Thanks a million, Mr. Durkin.'' She grabbed his hand and shook it vigorously, feeling as though she'd won a lottery.

His smile turned slightly ironic. "Guess you should thank Jake, Miss Taylor. He did the running.''

"Yes, of course. I will.''

Jake! He would probably be insufferably smug about it, but right at this moment Amy didn't care. He'd done her a great favour. A fabulous favour! She floated back out to the living room on a cloud of happy pleasure. The apartment was hers. Six months of blissful living in this beautiful place! It was better than a vacation! New surroundings, new people, new everything!

Jake turned from chatting to the painters and raised his eyebrows at her.

She couldn't help it. She grinned at him like a cheshire cat.

He grinned back.

Understanding zinged between them.

It was like a touch of magic, a fountain of stars showering her, lifting her into a new life. She barely stopped herself from pirouetting across the tiled floor and hugging Jake Carter.

"A done deal?'' he asked.

"A done deal,'' she affirmed exultantly.

"Then let's go to lunch and celebrate,'' he said.

"Yes," she agreed, too happy to worry about caution. Besides, he was part of this. Without Jake she wouldn't have got this apartment. It was only right to share her pleasure with him.

CHAPTER EIGHT

THE restaurant Jake drove her to was on the beach side
of The Esplanade, just along from the old Bathers'
Pavilion, which he pointed out in passing, informing her
it was a historic landmark at Balmoral. Amy smiled over
the name. It conjured up men in long shorts and singlets,
and women in bathing costumes with skirts and bloom-
ers.

The past, however, was wiped out of her mind as Jake
led her into an ultra-modern dining room that shouted
class with a capital C. "Table for Carter," he murmured
to the woman who greeted them, while Amy was still
taking in the huge floral arrangement in the foyer—a
splendid array of Australian flora in an urn. The waratahs
alone would have cost a small fortune.

Her heels clacked on polished floorboards as Jake
steered her into following the woman. Well-dressed pa-
trons sat in comfortable chairs at tables dressed in
starched white linen and gleaming tableware. They bypassed a bar that curved around from the foyer and
headed towards a wall of glass which seemed to rise
from the water beyond it.

This was an illusion, as Amy realised when she was
seated right next to the window. There was a strip of
beach below them, but they were so close to the water-
line, the sense of being right on top of it stayed. Outside,
a long wharf was lapped by waves and pelicans were

using it as a resting place. Inside, she was handed a menu and asked what she'd like to drink.

"Two glasses of champagne," Jake answered, and gave Amy a smile that fizzed into her blood.

"And a jug of iced water, please," she quickly added, telling herself she needed to keep a cool head here.

She'd been in classy restaurants many times with Jake and a party of his clients, but never before alone with him. The setting engendered a sense of intimacy, as well as a sense of special occasion. A glance at the prices on the menu left Amy in no doubt she was being treated to top class, and the dishes described promised gourmet standard from the chef. She wasn't sure it felt right to be sharing this much with her boss.

"Did you book a table before we left the office?" she asked.

He looked up from his menu, his golden eyes glowing warm contentment. "Yes, I did. Great forethought, wasn't it?" he said with sublime confidence in her agreement.

"There might not have been anything to celebrate," she pointed out.

"Then it would have been a fine consolation for disappointment. Besides, it's lunchtime. On the principle we have to eat, why not eat well? Superb food here. Have you chosen yet?"

"No. It all looks marvellous."

"Good! I figured you needed your appetite tempted. Can't have you pining away on me."

Relieved of any cause for battle, Amy returned her attention to the menu, satisfied she understood Jake's motives. This lunch was part of his program to push her into forgetting her grief and promote the attitude that life was still worth living. Put her in a new environment, lift her spirits with champagne, stuff her up with delicious comfort food, and Amy Taylor would be as good as gold again.

She smiled to herself as she made her choice, deciding on her favourite seafoods. Making the most of Jake's fix-it ideas was definitely the order of the day. He probably didn't have a clue about broken hearts. He never stayed in a relationship long enough to find out. Nevertheless, Amy had to admit he was positively helping her over a big emotional hump.

After this sinfully decadent lunch, they'd be dropping in at Ted Durkin's office to sign the lease on the apartment. She could take up occupation next Saturday. What had loomed as a long, miserable, empty week ahead of her would now be filled with the business of organising the move and coloured with the anticipation of all it would mean to her. To some extent, Jake was right with his practical solutions. Life didn't stay black when good things happened.

Their champagne arrived and their orders were taken. Jake lifted his glass, his eyes twinkling at her over it. "To the future," he toasted.

Amy happily echoed it. "The future. And thanks for everything, Jake. I really appreciate your kind consideration."

"What would I do without your smile? It makes my day."

She laughed at his teasing, then sat back in her chair, relaxing, allowing herself the luxury of viewing him with warmth. "I like working with you," she admitted. "It's never boring."

"Amy, you're the best assistant I've ever had. In fact, you're the perfect complement to me."

He was talking about work, nothing but work, she insisted to herself, yet there was something in his voice that furred the edges of sharp thinking and her heart denied any breakage by hop, skip, and jumping all over the place.

"Jake, darling!"

The jarring intrusion snapped Amy's attention to the woman who had suddenly materialised beside Jake. A blonde! A very voluptuous blonde! Who proceeded to stroke her absurdly long and highly varnished fingernails down Jake's sleeve in a very provocative, possessive manner.

It was like a knife twisting in a fresh wound. Amy could see Steve's blonde getting her claws into him, never mind that he belonged to another woman. A marauding blonde, uncaring of anything but her own desires. This one was insinuating herself between Amy and Jake, splitting up their private celebration party, stealing the lovely comfortable mood, demanding to be the focus of attention.

"What a surprise, seeing you here today!" she cooed to Jake, not asking any pardon for intruding.

Amy hated her. She wanted to tear that hand off Jake's sleeve and shove it into the woman's mouth, shutting off the slavering drool of words.

"An unexpected pleasure, Isabella," Jake returned smoothly, starting to rise from his chair, dislodging her hand.

Isabella! Of course, she'd have a name like that, Amy seethed. Something sexy and exotic.

"No, please stay seated." It was another excuse to touch him, to curl her talons around his shoulder. The blonde bared perfect teeth at Amy. Piranha teeth. "I don't think I've met your companion."

"Amy Taylor...Isabella Maddison," Jake obliged.

"Hi!" the blonde said, the briefest possible acknowledgement.

Amy met her feline green eyes with a chilly blue blast and nodded her acknowledgement, not prepared to play the all jolly friends game. She didn't want to know Isabella Maddison, didn't care to greet an uninvited intruder, and would not pretend to welcome a predatory blonde into her company.

Her and her "Jake, darling!" How rude could you get? It was perfectly obvious the blonde was putting in her claim in front of a possible rival and didn't care what it took to win. Never mind dimming Amy's pleasure, taking the shine off the day, pushing herself forward to block Amy out.

"Great party on Saturday night, Jake," Isabella enthused, giving it a sexy innuendo.

"Yes. A lot of fun," he replied.

Fun! The urge to have a bit of fun herself blew through Amy's mind. "What a pity I couldn't be there!" she said ruefully. "Jake and I have the best fun together, don't we, darling?"

His head jerked to her, eyes startled. He recovered fast, his mouth curving into his whimsical smile. "Ain't that the truth?" he drawled.

'Jake always says we complement each other perfectly,'' Amy crowed, buoyed so much by his support, she batted her eyelashes at the blonde bombshell.

"Then you should have been there, shouldn't you?'' came the snaky return comment, accompanied by a suggestively raised eyebrow.

"Oh, I don't know.'' Amy shrugged and swirled the champagne around in her glass as she gave Jake a smouldering look. "Some men like a bit of rope. I don't mind as long as I can reel him in whenever I want to.''

"Amy is very understanding,'' Jake said, nodding his appreciation.

"Well, perhaps another time, Jake,'' Isabella purred, undeterred from a future romp.

"Oh, I doubt it.'' Amy poured syrup into her voice. "He rarely dips into the same well twice.'' She bared her teeth. "Take a friendly word of advice. Best to move on to greener pastures. He is sort of stuck with me for the long haul.''

Isabella started to retreat. "If you'll excuse me…''

"With pleasure,'' Amy said to speed her on her way, then downed half the champagne to celebrate her going.

Jake's eyes were dancing with unholy amusement. "My wildest fantasy come true…you fighting another woman for me.''

"Huh!'' Amy scoffed. "That'll be the day.''

"Am I not to believe my ears?''

"She had the wrong coloured hair.''

"Ah!'' His wicked delight took on a wry twist. "The other woman.''

"Sorry if I've queered your pitch with her.'' She wasn't sorry at all, but it seemed an appropriate thing to say. After all, when all was said and done, he was still her boss. Though he could have stopped her roll if anything important was at stake. She would have taken her cue from him.

"No problem," he said carelessly.

"No, I don't suppose it is." Cynicism streaked through her. "If you snapped your fingers she'd come again."

"Isabella has no claim on me." It was a surprisingly serious statement, and his eyes held hers intently, as though he was assuring her he spoke the truth.

It was meaningless to Amy. No woman ever seemed to have a *claim* on him. "Is she your latest interest?" For some reason, she really wanted to know.

"No," he answered without hesitation.

"Just one of the hopeful crowd that trails after you," Amy said dryly.

He shrugged. "It hardly matters if I'm not interested, does it? To be blunt, Isabella doesn't appeal to me. She never will appeal to me. Any hope she might be nursing is therefore futile."

Goodbye, Isabella.

Amy was pleased that Jake had more taste than Steve. For both the men in her life to fall into the clutches of predatory blondes would have been altogether too wretched to bear. Not that Jake was an *intimate* part of her life, but he was a big chunk and she wanted to respect his judgement of character.

His quirky little smile came back. "You are quite a formidable fighter, Amy."

She shrugged. "You did encourage me, taking my side. If you'd clamped down on me…"

"And miss that performance?" His eyes sparkled admiration.

"The fact remains..." It felt really good that he'd supported her. "...You let me win, Jake."

He lifted his glass of champagne in another toast. "We're a team, Amy. A great team."

"A team," she echoed happily, and drank to the splendid sense of well-being flowing from being a solid team with Jake.

Their first course arrived.

Amy ate with gusto. Not only was the food fantastic, her tastebuds were fully revived from the weekend when everything she'd tried to eat seemed to have the texture of cardboard, indigestible. Maybe having a healthy appetite was a side effect from feeling victorious. Defeat was certainly the pits.

"More champagne?" Jake asked, seeing her down the last drops in her glass.

"No, thanks. I'd better move on to iced water. I think I've been hot-headed enough today."

He grinned. "Some things need letting out of your system. Especially the deep down and poisonous stuff."

"Well, I'm almost squeaky clean again."

"What a shame! So much volatile passion flying around. It's been quite an exciting experience watching it in action. Intriguing, too. Shows me a side of you you've kept under wraps. Not that I didn't suspect it was there."

Amy sat very still because her heart was fluttering extremely fast. Jake was regarding her with simmering speculation. The cat was out of the bag, well and truly, and she'd let it out with her wild flights off the rails. If she wasn't careful, the cat would feel free to pounce!

Twice she'd zoomed out of control, losing any semblance of the cool she'd kept with Jake. She could make excuses for herself. Jake was obligingly accepting them. But that didn't put things back the way they were between them.

"Anything else you'd like to spit out? Get off your chest?" he invited, clearly relishing exploring this newly revealed side of her.

Amy needed a safe topic fast, preferably focused on him instead of her.

"Yes. Since I've now been introduced to your sister, would you mind telling me about your family?" Her curiosity had been piqued by Ruth's revelations this morning.

"Not at all. What do you want to know?"

"Is there only you and Ruth?"

"Ruth is the youngest. I'm the next youngest. Above us are two older brothers, both very respectably settled down with families. Mum does her best to rule over us all and Dad lets us be."

"Do they all live in Sydney?"

"Yes."

"And you're the wild one."

He laughed. "They called me the adventurer when I was a kid."

He still was, Amy thought. "Tell me why," she prompted, eager to know more about him, to understand where he came from.

Again he obliged her, putting her at ease by regaling her with amusing stories from his childhood. Freed from the disturbing sexual pull he could exert on her, Amy enjoyed listening.

It was easy to imagine a little Jake trotting off on his own to explore the exciting things the world had to offer, worrying his mother, trying the patience of his older brothers who were sent to find him after they'd neglected to mind him properly. Ruth had become his partner in voyages of wonder when she was old enough, happy to be led anywhere by Jake.

The first course was cleared from their table. The main course was served and consumed. They were both persuaded to order the divine-sounding apple and brandy soufflé served with a lemon and kiwi fruit compote to finish off the meal.

The stories went on, eagerly encouraged by Amy. Hearing about a happy childhood, and a family that wasn't in any way dysfunctional, was something new to her, almost magical. She tended not to think about her own—no happy memories there—and Steve had been an only child whose parents had divorced when he was eight. He'd virtually lived in a world of computer games through his teens and they were still an escape for him whenever an argument loomed.

She wondered if his blonde knew that about the man she'd snaffled. Avoidance was Steve's answer to confrontation. Which was probably why Amy had been presented with his fatherhood and the date of his marriage, showing in one inarguable stroke there was no point in fighting.

Anything for a peaceful life. Steve's philosophy. She'd thought it was good but it wasn't really. Problems never got properly aired.

"I've lost you."

Jake's dry comment drew her attention back to him. She smiled. "No. I was just thinking how lucky you are not to have any fears. Or inhibitions. You were very blessed being born into your family, Jake."

He cocked his head slightly. The speculation in his eyes gradually took on the wolfish gleam that usually played havoc with her nerves. Maybe she'd been lulled by her good fortune, the champagne and fine food. Instead of alarm, she felt a tingling thrill of challenge.

"Everyone has fears, Amy," he drawled. "And inhibitions are placed upon them, whether they want them or not."

"Like what?" she said recklessly

"Well, take you and me. I'd like nothing better than to race you off to bed and make mad passionate love for the rest of the afternoon."

For one quaking moment, Amy was tempted.

Then Jake gave his quirky smile and added, "But if I had my wicked way, I'm afraid you might bolt out of my life, and I wouldn't like losing you. So here I am...hopelessly inhibited."

The soufflés arrived.

"Consolation," Amy said, doing her utmost to hide both the shock and the relief she felt.

Jake laughed and picked up his spoon. *"Bon appétit!"*

Off the hook, Amy thought gratefully. The temptation had come so swiftly and sharply, she was still quivering inside. She sternly bent her mind to reasoning it away.

It was because the physical attraction had always been there, and with Steve's defection, pursuing it was no longer forbidden. And it felt great having Jake at her side, fighting on her behalf against Steve, against the blonde, treating her as though she was precious to him.

But it would be crazy—absolutely crazy—to get sexually involved with Jake. She'd only be one of an endless queue—another little adventure—and how on earth would she be able to work with him afterwards? She'd hate it when he dumped her and took up with someone else. As he surely would.

Besides, she didn't really want to make love with him. It was just that he'd made her feel desirable, like a winner instead of a loser and a reject. It was simply a seductive situation. And he'd thought better of it, too, applying solid common sense.

Here she was on a winning streak and it would be really silly to spoil it. Today had brought her a wonderfully ego-boosting salary, and an apartment that was close to paradise. However tempting it might be to add a new lover to the list, it was best to get any thought of tangling with her boss in bed right out of her mind.

She put down her spoon and then realised she'd shovelled the soufflé down her throat without really tasting it. Wasted, she thought. Which was a pity. A delight missed.

A glance across the table showed Jake had finished his, too. She didn't know for how long but she suddenly felt him keenly observing her and had the awful sense he'd been reading her thoughts. She glanced at her watch, anxious to divert any further disturbing exchanges between them.

"Good heavens! The afternoon's almost gone!' Her gaze flew to his in sharp appeal. "We'd better leave, Jake.''

He checked his watch, raising his eyebrows in surprise. "You're right. Got to get that lease signed on our way back to the office." He signalled for the bill and smiled at Amy. "A good day's work."

She laughed, trying to loosen up. "We've played hookey for hours."

"There's a time and place for everything," he answered blithely.

And this wasn't quite the time and place...yet...for what he had in mind.

Amy tried to scotch the thought but it clung. "I'll just make a quick visit to the powder room," she said, rising from the table, hoping she wasn't appearing too skittish.

"Fine. I'll meet you in the foyer."

She had her armour in place when she emerged from the powder room. Jake was waiting, looking well satisfied with his world. He wasn't about to race her off, not without appropriate encouragement from her, anyway. She was safe with him as long as she kept herself under control.

"What's the name of this restaurant?" she whispered as they headed outside.

"The Watermark."

"Ah! Very appropriate. It was a wonderful lunch, Jake. Thank you."

"I enjoyed it, too."

No doubt about that, Amy thought. The teasing twinkle in his eyes was not the least bit dimmed. Jake Carter always lived to fight another day. He settled her in his car with an air of the man in possession.

But he wasn't.

Thanks to Steve, Amy *was* a free spirit.

The name of the restaurant lingered in her mind as they drove towards completing the business of the day. *The Watermark...* It made her think of tides. When one rolled out, another rolled in. High points, low points. She wondered if making love with Jake Carter would be like eating a soufflé—a delight and then nothing.

Sex without love.

Forget it, she told herself.

Missing it didn't hurt her one bit.

CHAPTER NINE

AMY did her best to carry a positive attitude home with her that evening. She didn't allow the emptiness of the apartment she'd shared with Steve swamp her with depression. Soon it would be empty of both of them, she told herself. This phase of her life was over. Another was starting and she was going to make the most of it.

She made lists of what had to be done; contact the agency that handled the Bondi apartment and give notice of moving, telephone and electricity bills to be finalised, look up removalists and get estimates, collect boxes for packing. She was mentally arranging her furniture in the new Balmoral apartment when the telephone rang, jolting her back to the present.

Amy felt reluctant to answer the call. It might be for Steve, someone who didn't know he was gone, and she would have to explain. Shock and sympathy would follow and she'd be forcefully reminded of her grief and humiliation. She glared at the telephone, hating its insistent burring, wanting to be left alone to pick up her new life.

The summons finally stopped. Amy sighed in relief. Maybe it was cowardly not to face up to the truth, but it was such a hurtful truth she just wanted to push it aside. To her increasing chagrin, however, she was not left in peace. The telephone rang on and off for the next hour, demanding an answer. She balefully considered taking the receiver off the hook, then realised that could instigate an inquiry from the telephone company since the caller was being so persistent.

In the end, the need to cut off the torment drove her to snatch up the receiver. "Amy Taylor," she snapped into it.

"Thank heaven! I was getting really worried about you, Amy. It's Brooke Mitchell here."

Brooke! Amy instantly grimaced. Her least favourite person amongst her acquaintances.

"When Ryan came home from work and told me what Steve had done, I just couldn't believe it at first," she blathered on. "Then I thought of you and how you must be feeling, you poor dear..."

"I'm fine," Amy interrupted, recoiling from the spurious gush of sympathy.

Gush of curiosity more like! Brooke Mitchell lived for gossip, revelled in it, and Amy had never really enjoyed her company. Brooke just happened to be married to Ryan who worked with Steve and the two men were both computer heads, moving their common interest into socialising occasionally.

"Are you sure? When you weren't answering the phone..."

"I've only just come in," Amy lied.

"Oh! I had visions of you...well, I'm relieved you haven't...uh..."

"Slit my wrists? I assure you I'm not the least bit suicidal, Brooke. No drama at all." *For you to feed off,* Amy silently added.

"I didn't mean...it's just such devastating news. And I can't say how sorry I am. I don't know how Steve could have done it to you. Infidelity is bad enough but getting the woman pregnant and deciding to marry her...after all the years you've been together..."

Amy gritted her teeth. Brooke was rubbing salt into the wound.

"...It's just terrible," she went on. "Though I've never thought living together was a good idea. You should have nailed him down, Amy. It's the only way to be sure of them."

It was the smug voice of a married woman. Amy refrained from saying divorce statistics didn't exactly prove Brooke right. It would have sounded like sour grapes.

"If you need a shoulder to cry on..."

The memory of Jake holding her brought a sudden rush of warmth, taking the nasty chill off this conversation. "I'm really fine, Brooke. In fact, I've had a lovely day. Jake Carter, my boss, took me out to lunch to celebrate my new freedom."

Which was almost true.

"You told him about Steve?" Real shock in her tone this time.

Caught up on a wave of bravado, Amy ploughed on in the same vein. "Yes, I did. And Jake convinced me I was well rid of him, so don't be concerned about me, Brooke."

"I see." Doubt mixed with vexation at this turn of events. "Didn't you tell me your boss was a rake?"

"Mmh. Though I'm thinking it might well be a worthwhile experience being raked over by Jake Carter."

"Amy! Really!"

"Yes. Really," she echoed, determined on wiping out

any image of her being thrown on the scrap heap, too crushed to raise any interest in another man.

"Well..." Brooke was clearly nonplussed. "I was feeling so awkward about bringing up next Saturday's party. I mean, when I invited you and Steve, I expected you to be together. Now...well, it is awkward, Amy. Ryan says Steve will want to bring..."

"Yes, of course," Amy rushed in, her heart contracting at the thought of the pregnant blonde on Steve's arm, queening it in Amy's place. And the plain truth was, Steve was far more Ryan's friend than she was Brooke's.

"But if you want to bring Jake Carter..." Her voice brimmed over with salacious interest.

"I was about to say I have other plans, Brooke. It was kind of you to be concerned about me and I'm glad you called. I'd forgotten about the party. Please accept my apologies. And I do wish you and Ryan a very merry Christmas."

She put the receiver down before Brooke could ask about her plans, which were none of the other woman's business. It gave Amy some satisfaction to think of Brooke speculating wildly about Jake, instead of pitying her, but it had probably been a rash impulse to use him to save her pride. The word would be quickly spread...

So what? Amy thought miserably. It would probably salve everybody's unease about excluding her from future activities. Brooke had been angling to cancel the party invitation and she wouldn't be the only one to dump Steve's ex-partner in favour of his wife-to-be.

When couples broke up, it forced others to make choices and the pragmatic choice was to accept a couple rather than a suddenly single woman who could either be a wet blanket at a social gathering or a threat to other women's peace of mind.

Depression came rolling in as she realised she was now a social pariah and she didn't really have friends of her own. The five years of sharing her life with Steve had whittled them away, and the past two years as Jake's personal assistant had kept her so busy, she literally hadn't had the time to develop and nurture real friendships. In fact, she felt closer to her boss than she did to anyone else at the present moment, and that brought home what a sorry state she was in.

Jake had filled the emptiness today but she knew how foolish it would be to let herself become dependent on him to fill her future. She had to take control of her own life, find new avenues of meeting people. The need-to-do list she'd made seemed to mock her. It would get her through the next week, but what then?

Amy couldn't find the energy to think further. She went to bed and courted oblivion. Being without Steve had to get easier, she reasoned. Everyone said time was a great healer. Soon she'd be able to go to bed and not think of him cuddled up to his blonde. In sheer defence against that emotional torment, she started visualising what it might be like to be cuddled up with Jake Carter. It was a dangerous fantasy but she didn't care. It helped.

Though it didn't help her concentration on work the next day. It made her acutely aware of every physical aspect of the man, especially his mouth and his hands. Even the cologne he wore—a subtle, sexy scent—was an insidious distraction, despite its being the same cologne he always wore. It didn't matter how sternly she berated herself for imagining him in Steve's place, the fantasy kept popping into her head, gathering more and more attractive detail.

It was terribly disconcerting. Thankfully, Jake didn't notice how super-conscious she was of him. He seemed totally tied up with business, not even tossing her teasing remarks. Certainly there was no allusion to any wish to race her off and make mad passionate love, nor any suggestion it was on his mind.

Amy hoped her stupid boast to Brooke Mitchell would never reach his ears. Not that she'd meant it. It was purely a reaction to circumstances, not a real desire. She knew better than to actually *want* Jake Carter in her bed. In the flesh.

The only personal conversation came at the end of the day as she was preparing to leave. Jake stood in the doorway between their offices, watching her clear her desk. "Are you holding up okay, Amy?" he asked quietly.

She flushed at the question. "I am *not* suicidal!" she snapped, the conversation with Brooke all too fresh in her mind, plus everything else that had flowed from it.

Jake's eyebrows shot up. "The thought never entered my mind."

"Then why ask?" she demanded, dying at the thought he'd noticed how jumpy she was around him.

His mouth quirked. "Guess you've already had well-meaning friends nattering in your ear."

"You could say that."

"Do you still plan to move house on Saturday?"

"Absolutely. Saturday can't come fast enough."

The quirk grew into a grin that seemed to say *That's*

my girl! and Amy's heart pumped a wild stream of pleasure through her body, spreading a warm, tingly feeling.

"You seemed rather unsettled today," he remarked with a shrug. "It made me wonder if there was too much on your plate. Moving can be a hassle if you intend to do it without the help of well-meaning friends."

"I've got it all lined up," she informed him, although it wasn't quite true. She had spent the lunch hour on the telephone, organising what she could.

"Fine! If you need some time off, just ask. If there's anything I can do to facilitate the resettling process…"

"Thanks, Jake." She smiled, relieved he'd put her edginess down to her emotional state over Steve. "I think I can manage but I'll let you know if I need some time off."

He nodded, apparently satisfied. "One other thing, Amy. You know we've sent out brochures and invitations to the New Year's Eve cruise on *Free Spirit*."

"Yes." The magnificent yacht came instantly to mind, pure luxury on water. The cruise, which would feature the fireworks display over the harbour on New Year's Eve, had a guest list of potential clients, all of whom could be interested in chartering the yacht for either business or pleasure. As Jake had it planned, New Year's Eve was the perfect showcase for *Free Spirit*.

"Well, if you're not tied up that evening, I'd really appreciate your hostessing for me on the yacht. I know it's work on a holiday night, but you would get a front-line view of the fireworks and they're supposed to be the best ever."

Amy barely heard his last words. Her mind was stuck

on *not tied up.* Steve would certainly be tied up. It was his wedding night. He and his blonde bride would be...

"I'll be happy to hostess for you," she rushed out, welcoming any distraction from those thoughts and the curdling that had started in her stomach.

"Thanks, Amy. It should be a most productive evening."

No, it won't, she thought. The production was already in place. The only difference would be the wedding rings, holding it together.

"And a fun time, as well," Jake went on.

Fun! Well, she could always fall overboard and drown herself. Except she wasn't suicidal.

"You can count on me," she said dully.

"Good!" He gave her a casual salute. "Happy packing."

It was more a case of ruthless packing, than happy. In sorting through the contents of drawers, Amy discovered Steve had left behind all the photographs of their life together, as well as mementos from their skiing trips and seaside vacations. She threw them out. Threw out the clothes that reminded her of special occasions, too. If he could walk away from it all, so could she.

When tears occasionally fell over silly, sentimental things, she dashed them away, determined on not faltering in her resolution. It occurred to her that death would be easier to accept than betrayal. At least you were allowed to keep good memories when someone died, but all her memories of Steve were tainted now. She could never again feel *good* about him. Best to let him go. Let the hurt go, too.

Unfortunately, however hard she worked at achieving

that end, she couldn't make the awful sense of aloneness go. Even the strong connection she felt with Jake Carter was not enough to dispel it. That couldn't be allowed to progress to real intimacy, so the pleasure of it was always mixed with a sense of frustration. Which added to her feeling of defeat, as though she was fated to be drawn to men who would never ultimately satisfy her.

She welcomed the weekend, eager for the move to Balmoral and the change it would bring to her life. No one except Jake knew about it. Easier to cut her losses, she'd argued to herself. Those who might try to contact her were all connected to Steve and she guessed that any caring interest would quickly fade once she was completely out of the picture. In any event, it was better for her to move on.

She did not regret walking out of the Bondi apartment for the last time on Saturday morning. It was a glorious summer day, an appropriate omen to leave gloom behind and fly off to the *wide blue yonder*. She smiled over her use of Jake's company name. It did have a great ring to it, promising an adventure that obliterated the greyness of ordinary day-to-day life.

As she followed the removalist's van across the Sydney Harbour Bridge, her spirits were buoyed by the sense of going somewhere new and exciting, and when she arrived at Balmoral, it was every bit as lovely as she remembered it. So was the apartment.

She did, however, have an odd sense of *déjà vu* on looking into the master bedroom. The new carpet was turquoise, almost the exact shade as used in the offices at Milsons Point. Then she realised the paintwork was similar, too. It felt uncanny for a moment, almost as if

Jake had left the imprint of his personality here. But the colours were easy to live with and an attractive combination. Anyone could have chosen them.

Having already planned where to place her furniture, Amy was able to direct the removalist men efficiently. They came and went in very short time. She spent the rest of the day, unpacking suitcases and boxes, exulting over how much space she had in cupboards and arranging everything to please herself.

When she was finally done, fatigue set in, draining her of the excitement that had kept her fired with energy. She was here, old shackles cut, bridge crossed, ready to write a new page in her life, yet suddenly it didn't mean as much as she wanted it to. There was no one to show it to, no one to share it with, and the black beast of loneliness grabbed her again.

She wandered around, still too wired up to relax. Watching television didn't appeal. She plumped up the cushions on her cane lounge suite, eyed its grouping with the small matching dining setting, and knew she'd only be fiddling if she changed it. The view should have soothed her but it didn't. Somehow it imbued her with the sense of being in an ivory tower, separated from the rest of the human race.

The ringing of her doorbell made Amy almost jump out of her skin. A neighbour? she wondered. Even a stranger was a welcome face right now. In her eagerness to make an acquaintance, she forgot to take precautions, opening the door wide and planting a smile on her face.

Jake Carter smiled back at her.

Jake, exuding his charismatic sexiness, looking fresh and yummy and sun-kissed in an orange T-shirt and white shorts, lots of tanned flesh and muscle gleaming at her, taunting her with its offering of powerful masculinity, accessible masculinity, his wicked, yellow wolf's eyes eating up her dishevelled state and his smile saying he liked it and wouldn't mind more.

Amy's impulses shot from wanting to hug him for coming, to a far wilder cocktail of desires running rampant. Or was it need clawing through her? It was madness, anyway. She felt virtually naked in front of him, clothed only in skimpy blue shorts and a midriff top that she usually wore to her aerobics class. Quivers were attacking her stomach and her breasts were tightening up. Indeed, she felt her whole body responding to the magnetic attraction of his.

It was scary.

Alarming.

And the awful part was she sensed he knew it and wasn't the least bit alarmed by it. He was positively revelling in it. And he'd come here at this hour, when she was so rawly vulnerable, having burnt all her bridges, making himself available to her, seeking entry...Jake, the rake.

The moment those words slid into her mind, sanity bolted back into it, repressing the urges that had been scrambling common sense. In sheer, stark defence, words popped out of her mouth, words she would have given anything to take back once they were said, but they hung there between them, echoing and echoing in her ears.

"I'm not going to bed with you."

CHAPTER TEN

"ACTUALLY, I was thinking about feeding other appetites," Jake drawled, holding up a plastic carrier bag that held takeaway containers and a paper bag bulging with bottles of wine.

Amy flushed scarlet. She knew it had to be scarlet because her whole body felt as though it was going up in flames. Even her midriff.

"First things first," Jake burbled on. "Moving is a hot, thirsty business and you've probably been run ragged today, too tired by now to think of bothering with a proper dinner, even if you did get provisions in."

Which she hadn't, except for absolute basics.

"And since you insisted on doing all this on your own, I thought you might welcome company at this point. Winding down at the end of the day, putting your feet up, enjoying some tasty food and a glass of wine..."

He was doing it to her again, pouring out a reasonable line of logic she couldn't argue with. Except he was here at the door of her home. And it wasn't business hours. And he certainly wasn't dressed for business. This was personal.

With Jake Carter, personal with a woman meant...

His eyes twinkled their devilish mischief. "But if you want to change your mind about going to bed with me later on in the evening..."

"There! I knew it!" she shot at him triumphantly, having worked her way out of the hot fluster.

"Whatever you decide is okay by me, Amy," he blithely assured her. "I wouldn't dream of going where I wasn't wanted."

"I didn't invite you here, Jake," she swiftly pointed out.

"Telepathy," he declared. "It's been coming at me in waves all day. Couldn't ignore it."

"I haven't thought of you once!"

"Subconscious at work. No one here to share things with. Low point coming up."

Suspicion glared back at him. "Sounds more like psychology to me." *Get the girl when she's down!*

"Well, you could be right about that," he grandly conceded. "I guess I was compelled by this sense of responsibility towards you."

"What responsibility?"

"Well, I said…Jake, my boy, you more or less pushed Amy into that apartment. There she is, without her familiars, and the least you can do is turn up and make sure she's okay."

"I'm okay," she insisted.

His mouth moved into its familiar quirk. His woman-trap eyes glowed golden with charming appeal. "I brought dinner with me."

No one, Amy reflected, knew the art of temptation better than Jake Carter. She could smell the distinct aroma of hot Chinese mixtures. Her stomach had un-knotted enough to recognise it was empty. More to the point, sparring with Jake had banished the black beast of loneliness. If she sent him away…

"Dinner does sound good," she admitted.

"I hate eating alone," Jake chimed in, pressing precisely the button that had Amy wavering.

"I wouldn't mind sharing *dinner* with you," she said with arch emphasis.

"Sharing is always better." He cocked an eyebrow in hopeful appeal. "Can I come in now? I promise I won't even ask you to show me the bedroom."

No, he'd just sweep her off there, Amy thought, and the awful part was, the idea had a strong attraction. But he didn't know that...couldn't know it...and she was making the rules here.

"Be my guest," she said, standing back to wave him in. "You know where the kitchen is," she urged, not wanting him to linger beside her.

He breezed past, never one to push his luck when the writing was on the wall. As Amy shut the door after him, it occurred to her she might be driving the loneliness beast out, but she'd let the wolf in, a wolf who'd huffed and puffed very effectively, blowing her door down, so to speak.

On the other hand, he wasn't about to eat her for dinner. He'd brought Chinese takeaway. She could manage this situation. But she wouldn't feel comfortable staying in these clothes. She was too...bare.

Jake was happily unpacking his carrier bag, setting out his offerings along the kitchen counter. His white shorts snugly outlined the taut curve of particularly well-shaped buttocks. When it came to cute butts, Jake Carter could line up against any gym buff. As for power-packed thighs... Amy took a grip on herself, wrenching her mind off the seductive promise of so much impressive male muscle.

Looks weren't everything.

So what if Steve had been on the lean side in comparison?

"Lemon chicken, sweet and sour pork, Mongolian lamb, braised king prawns, chilli beef, fried rice." Jake shot her a dazzling grin as he finished listing his menu. "All ready for a banquet."

"Good choice," she commented as blandly as she could.

He laughed. "I have acquired some knowledge of your preferred tastes, Amy."

It surprised her. "You noticed?"

"There isn't much I haven't noticed about you in the two years you've been at my side." His gaze skated over her skimpy clothes. "Though I haven't seen you look quite so fetching as you do this evening. Very *au naturel.*"

Amy instantly folded her arms across her midriff but she was acutely aware the action didn't hide the tightening of her nipples.

His eyes teased the flare of hard defence in hers. "Just as well I'm a man of iron control."

The need for evasive action was acute. "I was about to take a shower and clean up."

"Go right ahead." He waved expansively. "Make yourself comfortable. I'll get things ready for us here."

If he thought she was going to reappear in a sexy negligee, he was in for severe disappointment.

All the same, as Amy stood under the shower, soaping off the stickiness of the long, humid day, she couldn't help wondering how well she stacked up against Jake's other women. Thanks to her aerobics classes and a healthy diet, she was in pretty good shape, no flab or cellulite anywhere. No sag in her breasts.

She'd always been reasonably content with her body and normally she wasn't self-conscious about being nude. Not that she intended stripping off for Jake Carter. Besides which, he probably only fancied her because she remained a challenge to him. What physical attributes she had were really irrelevant.

With Jake it was always the challenge. Had to be. Which was why he lost interest once he'd won. At least, that was how it looked to Amy. Though she couldn't see there was much winning in it when women fell all over him anyway.

She decided to wash her hair, as well. It would do him good to wait. Show him she was not an eager beaver for his scintillating company. Besides, she felt more in control if she was confident of her appearance; fresh, clean, tidy, and properly clothed.

By the time she finished blow-drying her hair it was full of bounce and so was she, looking forward to keeping Jake in his place. She left her face bare of make-up since she wasn't out to impress. Jake could have that part of her *au naturel*.

Deciding jeans and a loose T-shirt would make a clear statement—demure and dampening—she tied the belt firmly on her little silk wraparound for the dash from bathroom to bedroom, opened the door to the hallway, and was instantly jolted from her set plan by a flow of words from Jake.

"She's in the shower, making herself comfortable."

He had to be talking to someone.

"Would you like a glass of champagne?" he burbled on, apparently having invited the someone into her apartment! "I've just poured one for Amy and myself."

"What the hell is going on here?"

The incredulous growl thumped into Amy's heart. It was unmistakably Steve's voice!

"Pardon?"

"Amy can't afford a place like this." Angry, belligerent suspicion.

The shock of hearing her ex-partner gave way to a fierce wave of resentment. How dare he judge or criticise!

"I gave her a raise in salary," Jake blithely replied. "She deserved it. Best P.A. in the world. Is it yes to the champers?"

"No. I only came to see that she was all right."

Guilt trip, Amy thought, writhing over how she'd been so hopelessly devastated last week.

"From the look of it I could have saved myself the trouble," he went on, the sneer in his voice needling Amy beyond bearing.

She whirled through the archway in a rage of pride, coming to a stage-stop as she took in the scene, Jake by the table he'd set for their dinner, brandishing a bottle of champagne, Steve standing by the kitchen counter, keeping his distance, obviously put out by her luxurious living area and Jake's presence.

His carefully cultivated yuppie image—the long floppy bang of hair dipping almost over one eye, the white collarless linen shirt and black designer jeans—somehow looked immature, stacked up against the raw male power so casually exhibited by Jake, and for once Amy was pleased Steve came off second-best in comparison. She fully intended to rub it into her ex-lover's ego. Let *him* be flattened this time!

"Good heavens! How on earth did you get here, Steve?" she trilled in amazement.

He gawped at her, making her extremely conscious of her nakedness under the silk and lace bit of froth, which, of course, he recognised as part of the seductive and sinfully expensive lingerie she'd bought herself for her last birthday, intending to pepper up their sex life. The outcome had been disappointingly limp, undoubtedly because he'd been bedding the blonde.

"Mmmh..." The sexy purr from Jake was meant to inflame. "I love your idea of comfortable."

"I'm so glad," she drawled, seized by the reckless need to prove she wasn't a downtrodden cast-off. Abandoning all caution, she ruffled her squeaky-clean hair provocatively as she sauntered towards Jake, knowing full well the action would cause a sensual slide of silk over her curves. "Champagne poured?"

"Ready to fizz into your bloodstream, darling."

The wicked wolf eyes were working overtime as he handed her a brimming glass. One thing she could say for Jake, he was never slow on the uptake. Right at this moment, his response was positively exhilarating. In the hunk stakes, Jake Carter was a star.

"Darling!" Steve squawked.

Hopefully he was feeling mortifyingly outshone! And very much the odd one out in *this threesome!*

"I've always thought she was," Jake tossed at him. "I should thank you for bowing out, Steve. It freed Amy up for me, got rid of her misplaced loyalty, opened her eyes…"

"I didn't do it for you," Steve chopped in, furious at finding himself upstaged by her boss.

"Which reminds me, where is your bride-to-be?" Amy asked silkily, having fortified herself with a fine slug of alcohol. "Lurking outside to see that you don't stay too long?"

"No, she's not!"

"Well, if I were her, I wouldn't trust you out of my sight. Not after working so hard to get a ball and chain on you."

Let his *free spirit* wriggle on that barb, Amy thought bitterly. She sipped some more champagne to dilute the upsurge of bile from her stomach.

Steve's face bloomed bright red. To Amy, it was a very satisfying colour. Much better than the pallid white he'd left on her face a week ago.

"She knows I'm here, I told her…"

"And just how did you know where to come, Steve?" she inquired with sweet reason. "I haven't given this address to anyone."

"Except me," Jake popped in, shifting to slide his arm around her shoulder in a man-in-possession hug. "We've moved so much closer in the past few days."

Amy snuggled coquettishly, getting quite a charge out of the hip and thigh contact.

Steve looked as if he was about to burst a blood vessel. Which served him right, having thrown a blonde and a baby in her face. He clenched his jaw and bit out his explanation.

"I went to the Bondi apartment this morning and saw our stuff being carried out to the removalist van..."

"*Our* stuff?" She couldn't believe he was backtracking on the division of their property. How crass could he get in the circumstances? "It was agreed this was *my* stuff."

"Mostly, yes. But there were little things I left behind. Overlooked in...well, not wanting to make things worse for you."

"Worse for whom?" she demanded with arch scepticism. "The great evader couldn't get out fast enough. That's the truth of it, Steve."

He flushed. "Have it your way. But I still want my things. And since you'd obviously packed up the lot, I followed the van here, then gave you time to unpack..."

"How considerate of you! What things?"

"Well, there were photographs and mementos..."

"I threw them all out."

"You...what?"

Amy shrugged. "Unwanted baggage. What's gone is gone," she declared and proceeded to drain her glass as though to celebrate the fact.

"One never enjoys being reminded of mistakes, Steve," Jake remarked wisely.

"You could have called me first," Steve spluttered accusingly.

"Sorry." She slid a sultry look up at Jake. "I've been somewhat distracted this week."

He instantly brushed his mouth over the top of her hair, murmuring, "Amy, I've got to tell you that scent you wear is extremely stimulating."

She wasn't wearing any scent. Unless he meant her

shampoo and conditioner. It occurred to her she was playing with fire but the warmth coursing through her felt so good she didn't care.

"Goddammit! I did my best to be decent to you," Steve bellowed.

"Oh? You call getting another woman pregnant being decent?" Amy flared.

"I bet you were already sneaking behind my back…"

"Amy sneak?" Jake laughed at him. "She is the most confrontationist woman I know. Sparks and spice and all things nice."

Steve glared furiously at her. "And I was fool enough not to believe Brooke when she told me you just couldn't wait to have it off with him."

"Well, sometimes Brooke does get things right," Amy fired back heedlessly.

"I feel exactly the same way," Jake declared with fervour. "In fact, I can hardly wait for you to leave."

"And you do have Brooke's party to go to," Amy pressed. "Apart from which, I'm sure your wedding will supply more suitable photos and mementos for your future." She lifted her glass in a mock toast. "Happy days!"

Unfortunately there was no champagne left in it to drink.

"Darling…" Jake purred "…let me take that empty glass." He plucked it out of her hand and set it on the table. "Bad luck you didn't get what you came for, Steve," he burbled on as he swept Amy into his embrace. "But as my girl here says, what's gone is gone. And it's well past time you were gone, too. Would you mind letting yourself out?"

"You know what she called you, Carter?" Steve yelled at him, his face twisting in triumphant scorn. "Jake the rake!"

"Well, fair's fair," Jake said, totally unperturbed. He whipped off his T-shirt and spread her hands against his bare chest. "You can do some raking, too, Amy. I'd like that. I'd like that very much." And his voice wasn't a purr anymore. More like the growl of a wolf with his dinner in view.

It should have frightened her. This whole scene was flying out of her control. Yet the fierce yellow blaze in his eyes was mesmerising and his skin had a magnetic pulse that compelled contact.

"You'll regret it," Steve jeered, but the words seemed to come to her through a fog, setting them at an irrelevant distance, and the door slam that followed them was no more than an echo of the throb in her temples.

"Let me rake you as you've never been raked before," Jake murmured, the low throaty sound hitting on some wild primitive chord that leapt in eager response, and his fingers were running through her hair, tilting her head back.

Then it was too late to pull away, even if she'd found the will to do it, because his mouth took possession of hers and she was sucked into a vortex of irresistible sensation from which there was no escape, nor any wish to. The desire to drown in what Jake Carter could do to her was utterly, savagely overwhelming.

CHAPTER ELEVEN

THE sheer passion of that first kiss blew Amy's mind. Conscious thought was bombarded out of existence. An insatiable hunger swept in and took over, demanding to be fed, to be appeased, to be satisfied.

He tasted so good, his tongue tangling with hers in an erotic dance, arousing explosive tingles of excitement across her palate, stirring sensations that streamed through her body which instantly clamoured for a bigger share of what was going on, a more intense share.

Her hands flew up to get out of the way and her breasts fell against the hot heaving wall of his chest, squashing into it, revelling in the rub of silk and firm male flesh and muscle. Her fingers raked his shoulders, his hair, his back, finding purchase to press him closer. She squirmed with pleasure as his hands clawed down her back to close over her buttocks and haul her into a sweet mashing contact with even more prominent and stimulating masculinity.

Clothes formed a frustrating separation.

They got rid of them.

Then everything felt so much more delicious, incredibly sensual, body hair tickling, hard flesh sliding against soft, mouths meshing, moving to taste everything, greedy, greedy, greedy, loving it, relishing it, feeding on each other in a frenzy of wanting, licking, sucking, hands shaping pathways, beating rhythms, wildly pushing for the ultimate feast of co-mingling, yet not wanting to forgo any appetiser along the way.

Exquisite anticipation, pulse racing, an urgent scream shrieking along nerve-endings, craving…and he lifted her up to make the most intimate connection possible and she wound her legs around his hips and welcomed him in, her muscles rippling convulsively, ecstatically as he filled the need.

And they were one—this wonderful man-wolf and the animal-woman he'd taken as his—as he went down on all fours, lowering her with him to some flat furry surface on the floor, and she tightened the grip of her legs around his hips, fearing the emptiness of losing him. But there was no loss. No loss at all.

With the purchase of ground beneath them he drove in deeper… oh, so soul-shakingly deep, the power of him radiating through her, waves and waves of it, building an intensity that rippled through every cell so it felt as though they were coalescing, melting, fusing with the thunder of his need to possess all of her, and she gave herself up to him, surfing the peaks he pushed her to, wallowing voluptuously in the swell of them, urging him on with wild little cries, exulting in the hot panting of his breath on her, the nails digging into her flesh, the pound of his heart, and the sheer incredible glory of this mating.

Even the ending of it felt utterly fulfilling, climactic in every sense, the shudder of his release spilling her into an amazing, floating, supernatural experience where all existence was focused internally and he was there— the warm, vital essence of him—and that part of him would always be part of her from this moment on.

Then his body sank onto hers, covering it in a final claim, imprinting the power, intoxicating her with it, lulling her into a peaceful acceptance of an intimacy which blotted out everything else because this had a life of its own and it was complete unto itself...like a primitive ritual enacted in a different world.

How long she lay in a euphoric daze, Amy had no idea. Somewhere along the line her mate had shifted both of them to lie on their sides, her body scooped against his spoon-fashion, one of his arms around her waist, the other cushioning her head. Gradually her eyes focused on the balcony she was facing and she became conscious of a strange reality.

Her two cane armchairs were sitting out there, along with the coffee table that served her lounge setting. She hadn't put them on the balcony. The glass doors were open and somehow those pieces of furniture had got out there without her knowledge. The table should be right in the centre of the mat in front of the lounge...except she was lying on the mat instead...and Jake Carter was lying right behind her...both of them very, very naked!

The slowly groping activity in Amy's mind stopped right there. A shock screen went up, forbidding any closer examination of how and when and why. A soft breeze was wafting in. It was pleasantly cool, certainly not cold enough to raise goose bumps, yet Amy's skin prickled with a host of them. Jake moved a big muscly leg over her thigh, nuzzled the curve of her shoulder and neck with a soft, seductive mouth, and slid his hand up from her waist to warm her breasts, his palm gently rotating over her highly sensitised skin.

"Getting cold?" he murmured.

"Yes." It was a bare whisper. Her throat had seized up, along with her shocked heart and frozen mind. She felt as paralysed as a rabbit caught in headlights.

"A hot spa bath should do the trick," he said, and before Amy could even begin to get herself into a semblance of proper working order, he'd somehow heaved them both off the floor and was carrying her to the bathroom, and she was staring over his shoulder at the mat where it had all happened.

Well, not quite all.

It had begun near the table. His orange T-shirt was hanging off one of the dining chairs. Her silk wraparound lay in a crumpled heap on the floor between the table and the lounge. A pair of white shorts had been pitched right across the room to droop drunkenly over the television set. She couldn't see what had happened to the sandals he'd been wearing.

Her view was blocked off as Jake moved through the archway and into the bathroom. He sat on the tiled ledge around the Jacuzzi, settled her on his lap and turned on the taps full blast. Amy didn't know where to look. Luckily he started kissing her again so she just closed her eyes and let him do whatever he liked.

Which he was extremely good at.

She certainly had to grant him that.

Though she was equally certain he had taken advantage of her...her susceptibility...to his...his manpower...which was stirring again and her body was riven by an uncontrollable urge to shift to a more amenable position, like sitting astride those two great thighs instead of across them.

As though Jake instinctively knew this was more appropriate, he rearranged her with such slick speed, it seemed like one lovely fluid movement with him sliding right back into the space that wanted him, filling it with a really delicious fullness.

It felt great. Even better when he started drawing her nipples into his mouth, tugging on the distended nubs, setting up a fantastic arc of sensation that zipped from her breasts to the deep inner sharing, driving her awareness of it to a kind of sensual madness that refused to be set aside.

The taps were turned off, the jets of water switched on and they slipped into the bath, still revelling in the erotic intimacy of being locked together. One part of her mind warned Amy she would have to face what she was doing with Jake Carter, but most of it just didn't want to think at all. Feeling was much more seductive and satisfying.

"Warm now?" he asked.

"Mmmh…"

He laughed, a low throaty gurgle coated with deep satisfaction. "Can't hold it in water, sweetheart, but let me tell you I've never had it so good."

She sighed over the inevitability of their connection ending, though she even found pleasure in his shrinking, feeling the relaxation of her inner muscles as the pressure decreased and tantalisingly slipped away. She peered through her lashes at the happy grin on his face and privately admitted she'd never had it so good, either, but she wasn't sure she should echo his words.

He was still Jake the rake.

Still her boss.

Letting him know he'd won first prize on the sexual

front might mess up things even worse than they'd already been messed up. Amy didn't know how to deal with this situation. Another bridge had been burnt and the future was now a lot murkier than it had been before. She pushed herself down to the other end of the bath and tried to get her mind into gear. Some straight thinking might help.

Jake raised his eyebrows at her in teasing inquiry while his eyes danced with the wicked knowledge that she couldn't ignore what they'd just shared.

Then she remembered the heart-sickening frequency of his sharing with other women. What if he told all of them he'd never had it so good? A charming ego-stroke to top everything off? And just in case he forgot their names in the heat of the moment…

"Don't call me sweetheart!"

The words shot out of her mouth with such vehemence, both of them were startled by their passionate protest. Amy was shaken by how violently she recoiled from having joined an easily forgotten queue, and Jake's good humour instantly lost its sparkle, his eyes narrowing, focusing intensely on her. His sudden stillness suggested he was harnessing all his energy to the task of perceiving the problem.

"I don't use that endearment loosely, Amy," he said quietly. "You *are* sweet to my heart. But if you don't like it…"

"I have a name. I'm not one of your passing parade, Jake. I'm your P.A.," she cried. "Just because I've committed the ultimate folly of going to bed with my boss, doesn't turn me into a no-name woman."

"You? Amy Taylor a no-name woman?" He threw

back his head and laughed. "Never in a million years!" A golden star-burst of twinkles lit his eyes. "And you know we didn't go to bed, Amy. You specifically said you weren't going to bed with me and I respected that decision."

Her insides were mush, churning with a million uncertainties, yet being hopelessly tugged by the sheer attraction of the man. Was she sweet to his heart? All she really knew was they'd done it, bed or no bed, and she was in a state of helpless confusion over what it meant or might mean to either of them.

Before she could think of any reply to him, he shook his head at her and offered a wry little smile as he made the pertinent comment, "Neither of us can blame our selves for spontaneous combustion."

This implied he hadn't planned what happened, any more than she had. An accident of Fate? Or a convenient excuse?

"Was it?" she asked suspiciously.

"What?"

"Spontaneous combustion."

"It felt like that to me." His brow puckered for a thoughtful moment. "I remember I was swinging in with all the support I could think of for your out-of-my-life act, socking it home to your ex, then...yes, I'd definitely have to call it spontaneous combustion. Mind you, the chemistry was always there. No denying it."

Amy had to accept the undeniable truth that she'd played with fire, tempted the devil, and the ensuing conflagration could not be entirely laid at Jake's door. She sighed, letting go the craven wish to dissolve in the bath. There was no escaping what had to be faced.

"So what do we do now?" she asked, looking for some signal from him.

He grinned at her. "I suggest we have dinner. Both of us need re-fuelling."

Pragmatic Jake. One appetite burnt out...might as well get on with feeding another.

Which could then re-ignite the first and... Amy clamped down on that thought. She had to get sex with Jake off her brain. More practical matters needed to be settled.

"Okay," she agreed. "You dry yourself off first and I'll follow."

He eyed her quizzically. "You're not going shy on me, are you, Amy?"

It triggered a nervous laugh. "A bit late for that. I just want the bathroom to myself while I tidy up."

In truth, Amy didn't want to risk tangling physically with Jake, with or without towels. She needed some clear space here to tidy up her responses to him.

"Fair enough," he said and whooshed out of the bath, the massive displacement of water almost causing a tidal wave.

He was a big man. Stark naked, there was a lot of him, all of it impressive. Amy couldn't help staring. In every male sense he was well proportioned, well muscled and most decisively well endowed. Very well indeed. Her vaginal muscles went into spasms of excitement just looking at him, remembering how he'd felt and what he'd done.

It was just as well she was still lying in the bath. Jake didn't even have to apply the art of temptation in the nude. He was *it*. He turned to reach for a towel and his backside scored a perfect ten beyond a shadow of a doubt.

Amy was struck by a powerful insight. Lust was not a male prerogative. Lust could hit a woman like a runaway train. She was left wondering how on earth it could be stopped.

A more urgent question was…did she *want* it to be stopped?

CHAPTER TWELVE

DINNER was good. Jake didn't press anything but food on her. He played the charming host, ready to serve her every whim, encouraging her to try everything he'd brought, pleased when she did, obviously resolved on giving her a breathing space and setting a relaxed mood.

Amy appreciated it. She appreciated the food, too. It seemed to stabilise her stomach and clear her head. Her confusion over the sexual element that had scrambled their relationship, gradually sorted itself out into various straight avenues of thought.

Of course, it helped that Jake was fully clothed again. And she felt...safer, protected...in the jeans and T-shirt she'd planned to wear before Steve's fateful intrusion. Probably her choice of clothes had alerted Jake to her nervous tension and reservations about any further intimate involvement. He was never slow on picking up signals.

Nevertheless, there could be no avoiding a discussion on where they went from here. As they cleared the dishes from the table, transferring them to the kitchen counter, Amy decided it couldn't be postponed any longer. She could only hope Jake would understand her position.

"Coffee on the balcony?" he suggested.

Her gaze zapped to the armchairs and coffee table he must have put outside while she'd been in the shower prior to Steve's arrival. "You thought of that before," she blurted out, flushing with embarrassment as she recollected precisely when she'd noticed their removal to the balcony.

He shrugged. "It seemed a pleasant way to finish off the evening."

She looked him straight in the eye, something she'd had difficulty in doing throughout dinner. "You didn't come here to jump me, did you, Jake?"

"No," he answered unequivocally. His face softened into a warm, whimsical smile. "I do genuinely care about you. I didn't want you to feel alone."

Her heart turned over.

Maybe caring made the difference.

"Besides, jumping isn't my style," he went on. "I'm only interested in mutual desire."

Desire...lust...he'd probably *cared* about all the others, too.

His eyes gleamed their dangerous wolf-yellow. "And it is very mutual, Amy. Don't put other labels on it."

Don't put *love* on it...that was certain.

Mutual desire was not going to lead anywhere good and it was no use wishing it might. Heat raced into her cheeks again as she tried to explain her spontaneous combustion away.

"Jake...it was just a moment in time...because of Steve...and..."

"No." He shook his head at her. "At least be honest, Amy. We're not ships passing in the night. What happened has been building between us for a long time. A progression..."

"But we don't have to choose it," she cried, agitated

by the way he was validating what had been madness on both their parts. "We work together, Jake. Please don't make it impossible for us to keep on working together."

He frowned as though he hadn't taken that factor into consideration.

"I'll make the coffee," she said, scooting off to the kitchen, hoping to keep the counter between them for a while.

Clothes didn't really help, not when he started radiating physical charm and reminding her of the desires they had indulged so…so wildly. If he reached out and touched her, she wasn't sure she could resist touching back. She had the feeling an electric current would sizzle her brain and her body would proceed on its own merry way to meltdown.

To her intense relief, Jake wandered out to the balcony. She stacked the plates and cutlery into the dishwasher as the coffeemaker did its job. The activity covered her inner turmoil as she clung desperately to what was the only sensible resolution to this volatile situation.

It couldn't go on. Couldn't! Jake's idea of a *progression* threw her into a panic. The sex had been good. Amazing. Incredibly marvellous. But it wouldn't stay that way. Moods and feelings were rarely recaptured. Lust did peter out. She had the evidence of Jake's many affairs to demonstrate how quickly it passed.

The article in the women's magazine which still lay in the bottom drawer of her desk came sharply to mind. If she indulged herself in more physical pleasures with Jake Carter, she'd be looking for the exit signs, every minute of every day, not trusting their togetherness to last long. Then how awkward would it be when he started looking for a fresh experience? How destroying it would be!

No, it was wrong for her. It would mess her up even more than she was already messed up. No matter what he said or did, she couldn't allow herself to be tempted. Now was the time to start building a hopeful future for herself, not plunge down a sidetrack to more misery.

The coffeemaker beeped. She filled two mugs, steeled herself for the stand she had to make, then set out to fight the man who was undoubtedly plotting a different scenario. Her hands shook so much the coffee slurped over. She put the mugs on the counter and walked slowly around it, clenching and unclenching her hands. Her chest was so tight, her heart felt as though it was banging against it, stifled for proper room. Nevertheless, she did manage to carry the mugs out and set them on the coffee table without further spillage.

Jake was leaning on the balcony railing, apparently taking in the night view. He didn't turn even though he must have heard her. Having got rid of the mugs from her nervous hands, Amy fidgeted. Sitting down didn't feel right. It was impossible to relax enough to make it look natural. Yet to join Jake at the railing in the semi-darkness...

"Tell me what you want, Amy."

The soft words caught at her heart, turning her doubts and fears into silly trivialities. Jake had moved on to the big picture. He was simply waiting for her to paint in how she saw it.

Without any further hesitation, she stepped over to the railing and took a deep breath of fresh sea air. The winking myriad of lights around the bay assured her of life going on in a normal fashion, despite the ups and downs everyone was subjected to from time to time. It was normality she needed now.

"I want to keep my job," she said simply.

He didn't move, not even to glance at her. She had the sense of him being darkly self-contained, waiting and listening, biding his time until he had what he needed to work with.

"There's no question of your losing it," he assured her.

"I want to feel comfortable in it. I need to feel secure in it," she explained further. "It's my anchor right now. If you take that away from me..."

"Why on earth would I?"

He sounded genuinely puzzled.

"You could make it too difficult for me to stay."

"You think I'm going to chase you around the office?" he asked, the dry irony in his voice mocking such a notion. "It's a fool's game, mixing business with pleasure, Amy. Have I ever seemed that much of a fool to you?"

"No."

"I respect you far too much to press unwanted attention on you anyway."

"I'm sorry. I...maybe I've got this wrong," she rushed out in an agony of embarrassment. "I shouldn't have assumed you'd want to..."

"Oh, yes, I want to, Amy. I really would be a fool not to want to make love with you whenever I can. Outside of office hours."

He spoke matter-of-factly yet Amy was left in no

doubt he meant every word of it. One taste was not enough for him. He wanted more, and just the thought of him wanting more aroused all the sensitised places in her body that craved the same.

"But I'd hate you to feel...under duress," he added, his voice dropping to a low rasp of distaste.

The choice was hers, he was saying, and she should have felt relieved, except she was so twisted up inside, her mind couldn't dictate anything sensible.

"It has to be freely given," he went on. "As it was tonight." He half turned to her, a lopsided smile curving his mouth. "You did want me, you know. Not because of Steve. You wanted *me.*"

Amy was further shaken by the passion creeping through the quiet control he'd maintained. "Any woman would want you, Jake," she blurted out.

"You're not...any...woman." He flashed her a scathing look. "For God's sake, Amy! Do you think it's like that every time I turn around?"

"How would I know?" she flared back at him, losing the sane control she'd tried so hard to hold on to. "You turn around so often..."

"Because once I know it's not going to work I don't string a woman along as a convenient backup while I cheat on the side, as your precious Steve did," he shot at her.

Pain exploded through her. "Fine!" she fired back at him. "Just don't expect me to give repeat performances until you decide it's not working for you anymore. I'd rather choose my own exit, thank you very much."

He straightened up, aggression emanating from him in such strong waves, Amy almost cringed against the railing. Pride stiffened her spine. She was not going to be intimidated. The memory of her mother being cowed by her father flashed into her mind. Jake had that kind of power but she would not give in to it. Never! She would stand up for what was right for her, no matter what the consequences.

Maybe he sensed her fierce challenge. Something wrought a change. The aggression faded. She felt him— the strength of his will—reaching out to her even before he raised a hand in a gesture of appeal.

"It could be something special for both of us, Amy," he said in soft persuasion.

The fire in her died, leaving only the pain. "It *was* special. Please...leave it there," she begged. "I don't want to fight with you, Jake."

He sighed and offered a wry smile. "I don't want to fight with you, either. Nor do I want you to regret tonight."

She had a hazy memory of Steve yelling, *you'll regret it,* and everything within her rebelled against his mean-minded prediction. Besides, *he* had never once given her so much intense pleasure, never once swept her into such an all-encompassing sensual world. That belonged to Jake and she would never forget it...surely a once-in-a-lifetime experience which had exploded from a unique set of circumstances.

"I'll never regret it, Jake. It was something very special," she reiterated, because it was the truth and it was only fair to admit it to him.

His smiled widened, caressing her with his remembered pleasure. "Then you'll keep it as a good memory?"

He was giving in…letting go…

"Yes," she cried in dizzy relief.

"Of course, if you ever want to build on the good memory, you will keep me in mind," he pressed teasingly.

She laughed, the release of tension erupting through her so suddenly she couldn't help but laugh. It was the old Jake back again, the one she was used to handling, and she loved him for giving him back to her.

"I couldn't possibly consider anyone else," she promised him.

"I can rest content with that," he said, sealing the sense of security she'd asked him for. "And just remember, Amy, you're not alone. You do have me to count on."

Unaccountably after the laughter, tears swam into her eyes. "Thank you, Jake," she managed huskily, overcome with a mixture of sweet feelings that were impossible to define.

"It's okay," he assured her, then stepped over, squeezed her shoulder in a comradely fashion, gently pushed her hair aside and dropped a kiss on her forehead. "Goodnight, Amy. Don't you fret now. It's back to work on Monday."

She was swallowing too hard to say anything. He touched her cheek tenderly in a last salute, and she could only watch dumbly as he walked away from her. All the way to the door she felt the tug of him. Her body churned with need, screaming at her to call him back, take him into her bed, have him as long as she could.

But she stayed still, breathlessly still, and listened to the door closing behind him.

"Goodnight," she whispered.

It had been good.

Best that it stayed good.

CHAPTER THIRTEEN

DESPITE Jake's assurances, Amy's nerves were strung tight as she walked down Alfred Street on Monday morning. Resolutions kept pumping through her mind. She was not going to look at Jake and see him naked. She had to focus every bit of her concentration on the job. And act naturally.

Acting naturally was very important. No overt tension, no signs of agitation, no silly slips of the tongue. Think before you speak, Amy recited over and over again. Pretend it's last week. Pretend it's next week. No matter what she felt in the hours ahead of her, it would pass.

Determined not to falter, Amy pushed past the entrance doors to their office building and strode down the foyer to the elevators. "Hi, Kate!" she called to the receptionist, and practised a bright smile.

"Well, that's a happier start to the week," Kate remarked, smiling back. "No Monday blues. Things must have picked up for you."

Had it only been a week since Steve dumped her? Amy felt as though she'd shifted a long way since then. And she had. All the way to Balmoral. Which was absolutely lovely.

"Feeling good," she declared, pressing the Up button with blithe panache. Positive thinking had to help. "Boss in?"

"Up and running."

"How did your weekend go?" Amy asked, wondering if she could make a friend of Kate.

"I Christmas shopped till I dropped," she replied with a mock groan.

Christmas! Barely three weeks away. And she had no one to share it with this year. No one to buy presents for. But that didn't mean she couldn't celebrate it herself, buy a Christmas tree for the apartment and think of different things to do. She was not going to feel depressed. She had her composure in place and she simply couldn't afford to let anything crack it.

The elevators doors opened and Amy stepped in, throwing Kate a cheery wave. "See you later."

The ride in the elevator was mercifully short. Amy carried the power of positive thinking right to Jake's office. Their connecting door was open. She gave a courtesy knock and stepped inside, exuding all the confidence she could muster.

"Good morning," she trilled, smiling so hard her face ached.

Jake was reading a brochure on planes, chair leaning back, feet up on the desk. He looked over it, cocked an eyebrow at her and said, "The top of the morning to you, too."

"Start with the mail?" she asked.

"I've already looked at the E-mail messages. Go and read the inbox and get up to date. We'll deal with the Erikson inquiry first. And check the diary, Amy. We'll have to set up a meeting with him."

"Right!"

She was almost out of his office when he raised his voice in command.

"Hold it!"

Amy's heart jumped and pitter-pattered all around her chest. She held on to the door and popped her head around it. "Something else?" she inquired.

Jake had swung his feet off the desk and was leaning forward, beetling a frown at her. "You're wearing black. Didn't I specifically tell you my P.A. was not to wear black?"

It was true. He had. "I forgot," she said. Which was also true.

"Black does not fit our image, Amy," he said sternly. "Black is safe. Black is neutral..."

Which was precisely why she had chosen it this morning, having dithered through her entire wardrobe.

He wagged a finger at her. "Black is not to be worn again."

"Right!" she agreed.

"Just as well we don't have any important client meetings today," he muttered, then shot her a sharp look. "You're not in a black mood, are you?"

"No!" she denied swiftly.

"Good!" His expression brightened. The familiar teasing twinkled into his eyes as he lifted his feet back on the desk. "You can wear red anytime you like. You look stunning in red."

He picked up the brochure again and Amy skipped out to start work, her heart dancing instead of pitter-pattering. Everything was normal. Everything was fine. Jake was as good as his word. Life could go on as it had before.

Almost.

Amy found the to-and-fro between them wasn't quite

as easy as the day wore on. Not that she could lay any
fault at Jake's door. Not once did he do or say anything
to discomfort her along intimate lines. The problem was
all hers.

When Jake bent over to pick up some papers he'd
dropped, and the taut contours of his backside were
clearly outlined, his trousers just disappeared and she
could see him stepping out of the bath in all his natural
glory. When he sat down and crossed his legs, the bulge
of his powerful thighs vividly reminded her of their
strong, bouncy support when she'd sat astride them. His
mouth generated quite a few unsettling moments, too.
She hoped Jake didn't notice these little distractions.

Lust, she decided, was not a runaway train. It was
more like a guerilla soldier who could creep up and capture you before you even knew he was coming. But the
memories of that *special* time with Jake were still very
fresh, she told herself. Given a few days, they wouldn't
leap to the forefront of her mind quite so much.

As it turned out, by the end of the week, Amy was
really enjoying her job again, feeling a sense of achievement in meeting the challenges Jake regularly tossed at
her, countering his bouts of teasing with the occasional
smart quip, helping with the deals he set up and made
for their clients. Best of all, without her old hackles rising all the time, she was open-minded enough to realise
Jake truly did value and appreciate her contribution to
his business.

He showed it in many ways, generous with compliments if what she'd done warranted them, giving consideration to her opinions and impressions of clients,
readily taking suggestions if he thought them effective.

She was also more acutely aware of the close rapport they shared, where just a look conveyed a message which was instantly understood. Two years of familiarity did build that kind of knowledge of each other, she reasoned, yet she was beginning to feel she was more attuned to Jake's way of thinking than she'd ever been to Steve's, so the longevity of a relationship did not necessarily count.

As she left the office on Friday, she was wishing there was no weekend and it would be work as usual tomorrow. Which showed her she was becoming too dependent on Jake's company. Get a life, she sternly told herself.

On Saturday she canvassed several gyms between Balmoral and Milsons Point to see what equipment and classes they offered, comparing their fees, chatting to instructors, appraising their clienteles. She did some research on dance schools, as well, having always fancied learning tap-dancing. Wait for classes to be resumed in the new year, she was advised.

Saturday night proved difficult. It didn't matter what she tried to do, her mind kept wandering to Jake. She couldn't imagine him sitting at home by himself. He'd be involved in some social activity—a party, a date—and one or more women would be enjoying his charm and attention, beautiful sexy women who wouldn't say no to an experience with Jake Carter.

Envy frayed any peace of mind over her decision to cut any further intimate involvement with him. But it was the right decision, she insisted to herself. At least she was saved from the bitterness of becoming his ex-lover when he started favouring someone else. And her job was safe. No risk of a nasty blow-up there. But "the good memory" lingered with her a long time when she finally took herself off to bed.

She spent Sunday on the beach, determined to relax and enjoy what she had within easy reach. It passed the time pleasantly. She succeeded in pushing Jake to the edge of her mind for most of the day. On Monday morning, however, her hand automatically reached for the scarlet linen shift. She told herself it was stupid to want to look "stunning" for him, but she wore it anyway.

"Ah!" he said when she walked into his office to greet him. It was a very appreciative "Ah!" and the wolfish gleam in his eyes as he looked her up and down put a zing in her soul.

"Image," she said pertly. "We're meeting with Erikson today."

"Of course," he said and grinned at her.

She felt ridiculously happy all day.

The buoyant mood continued for most of the week.

The first niggle of worry came on Friday.

She'd finished the monthly course of contraceptive pills she'd been taking for years and her cycle always worked with clocklike regularity. Her period should have started today. So why hadn't it?

Her mind kept zinging to the night she'd forgotten to take a pill, but she'd taken two the next day to make up for it. Though it was actually the next night—not the morning or the day—when she'd discovered the error and taken double the dose. One missed night. It wouldn't matter normally. She had doubled up before, when she'd accidentally missed one over the years, and nothing had gone wrong.

But this time…this time…

Impossible to forget which night it was…she and Jake losing themselves in spontaneous combustion…and the deep, inner sense of mingling…melding inextricably.

Had their mating…such a terribly evocative word— borne fruit?

It was a nerve-shattering thought. Amy kept pushing it away. It would be the worst irony in the world if she'd fallen pregnant, just when she was trying to get her life in reasonable order after her long-term partner had taken off because he'd got another woman pregnant. Not that she wanted Steve back. That was finished. But Jake…as the father…it didn't bear thinking about.

Her cycle was messed up a day. That was all it was. Any minute it could correct itself. Tomorrow she'd be laughing about this silly worrying. One missed pill…it was nothing in the big picture. Her body wouldn't play such a dirty trick on her when she'd been protecting it against such a consequence for years.

Saturday brought her no relief. By Sunday afternoon Amy was in full panic. She bought a pregnancy test kit from a twenty-four-hour pharmacy. She couldn't bear the uncertainty.

The uncertainty ended on Monday morning.

It didn't matter how much she wanted to disbelieve the results of the test, two deadly pink lines were looking her in the face, not changing to anything else, and according to the instructions with the test kit, this meant she was pregnant. She checked the instructions again and again. No mistake. Pink was positive.

Just maybe, she thought frantically, the kit was faulty. Best see a doctor. Get a blood test. She looked through the telephone directory, found a medical centre at Mosman along the route she drove to work, then considered what lie she could tell to cover her late arrival at the office.

Impossible to say she needed to see a doctor. Jake would ask why. Jake wouldn't leave it alone until he found out. A flat tyre on her car, she decided. It could happen to anyone.

The visit to the doctor was a nightmare. Yes, missing a pill at a critical time could result in pregnancy. Test kits were usually reliable but a blood test would give absolute confirmation. Amy watched the needle going in and almost fainted as the blood started filling up the tube, blood that was going to tell her the awful truth. A baby! She closed her eyes. No, no, no, she begged. Having a baby—Jake's baby—made life too impossible.

She'd have the results in twenty-four hours, the doctor said. All she had to do was telephone the surgery and ask for them. She checked her watch. Nine-thirty. Twenty-four more hours of hell to get through, a third of those hours with the man who'd done this to her.

Not intentionally.

Though he should have used protection...should at least have asked her if she was protected. In which case she would have said yes, so there was no point in blaming him. Nevertheless, she might have remembered to take the wretched pill if he'd asked. Spontaneous combustion might be a very special experience but the "good memory" was swiftly gathering a mountain of savage regrets.

Jake, the rake... How would he react to being told he'd sown one too many oats? With his P.A., no less.

But she didn't have to face that yet.

Not yet.

Twenty-four hours.

Amy didn't know how she got through the day with Jake. He asked about the flat tyre and she blathered on about it, excusing the time away from the office. She was aware of him frowning at her several times. It was almost time for her to leave when he asked, "Is something wrong, Amy?" and her glazed eyes cleared enough to see he was observing her very keenly.

Would their child have those wolf eyes?

Her stomach cramped.

"No," she forced out. "Everything's fine." *Except I'm probably pregnant.*

"You haven't been with me, today," he remarked testingly.

"Sorry. I have been a bit scatter-brained. Christmas coming on..."

"Planning anything special?"

The excuse had popped into her mind but she was totally blank about it and had to grope for a reply. "No. Not really. Just...well, I guess I was thinking about the family I don't have. Kate Bradley was saying she'd shopped till she dropped and..." Amy shrugged, having run out of ideas to explain herself. "At least I'm saved that hassle."

Christmas...celebrating the birth of a child...

Dear God! Please don't do this to me.

"Uh-huh," Jake murmured noncommittally. "Not a good thing, spending Christmas alone. No fun in all. I'll speak to my sister about it."

"What?" Amy didn't understand what his sister had to do with it.

"Leave it to me," he said and went back into his office.

Amy shook her head in bewilderment. She simply wasn't in tune with Jake's thought processes today. But at least he'd stopped questioning her and she wasn't about to chase after him and invite more probing into her own thought processes, which were hopelessly scrambled by the waiting to know.

The next morning, she wasn't free of Jake's presence until ten-thirty. Almost sick with apprehension, she pounced on the telephone and called the surgery, all the while watching the door she'd closed between Jake's office and hers, desperately willing it to stay closed. Which it did, thankfully, because the news she received, although expected, still came as a shock.

No doubt about it anymore.

She *was* pregnant.

To Jake Carter.

And she had no idea in the wide world what to do about it.

An abortion?

Instant recoil.

Tell Jake.

No, she wasn't ready for that. She needed time to armour herself against...whatever she had to armour herself against.

An unworthy thought flashed through her mind. Steve's blonde had used her pregnancy to pull him into marriage. Would Jake...

No, Amy fiercely decided. She couldn't—wouldn't—

go down that road. Marriage could be a trap, as she well knew, and using a baby to seal the trap would be a terrible thing to do to all three of them. Jake wasn't the marrying kind. He was the perennial bumblebee flitting from flower to flower.

He'd probably be appalled at the prospect of fatherhood being thrust upon him…a long-term relationship he couldn't get out of. Unless she had an abortion. Would he ask it of her?

She'd hate him if he did.

She remembered the lovely, natural way he'd handled his baby nephew, Joshua. Surely, with his own child…

The telephone rang.

Amy picked up the receiver, struggling to get her wits together to handle a work-related call.

"Good morning…"

"Amy, is that you? Amy Taylor?" an eager female voice she didn't recognise broke in.

"Yes…"

"Good! It's Ruth Powell here, Jake's sister."

"Oh?" The coincidence of having just been thinking of Ruth's son dazed Amy for a moment. "How can I help you?"

"We'd all love you to come for Christmas Day, Amy. It's at my house this year. Well, mine and Martin's, naturally. The rest of the family will be here and they're dying to meet you. Jake said you didn't have family of your own to go to, so how about joining us? It'll be such fun!"

This was rattled out at such high speed, Amy was slow to take it in. "It's…very nice of you, Ruth…"

"Please say you can. It's no trouble, I promise you.

We'll have food enough for an army. Mum's bringing the turkey and my sisters-in-law are providing the ham and the pudding, and Jake, of course, is in charge of the drinks. We've told him, nothing but the best French champagne…''

Which had probably contributed to the mess she was in, Amy thought miserably.

''So you see,'' Ruth went on, ''we'll have the best time. All the festive stuff has been thought of and you must see my tree. It's Joshua's first Christmas and Martin and I bought the most splendid tree you can imagine. Fabulous decorations. Please say you'll come, Amy.''

She never had got around to buying a tree. Too much else on her mind. Jake's baby. And this was his family— her baby's family—inviting her to meet them. Suddenly it felt important to do so, to see Jake in action with his family, to see him with children…

''Thank you, Ruth. It's such a kind thought…''

''You'll come?'' she cried excitedly.

''Yes. I'd like to.''

''Great! Jake will pick you up at…''

''No, please, I don't want that. He should be with you.''

''He won't mind.''

''Ruth, *I'd* mind.'' She could cope with him in office hours. Outside of them…her stomach quivered. ''I'd rather come and go by myself,'' she stated firmly.

Ruth laughed. ''Still keeping him in line. Good for you, Amy! Does eleven o'clock Christmas morning suit you?''

''Yes. Where do you live?''

The address was given and the call ended, Ruth sounding triumphantly satisfied with the arrangements.

It was really Jake's doing, Amy realised, remembering how he'd questioned her about Christmas yesterday.

He didn't like the idea of her being alone.

The irony was the last time he'd acted to save her from being alone, he'd left her pregnant, ensuring she wouldn't be alone in the future.

But where was he going to stand in her future?

He did care about her.

But how much? …How much?

Christmas…

Maybe that would be the day she'd find out.

CHAPTER FOURTEEN

CHRISTMAS day with the Carter family was happy chaos. From the moment Amy arrived at the Powell home, Ruth linked her arm with hers in warm welcome and whizzed her into a wonderfully large family room which opened out onto a lovely patio and pool garden area. People were scattered everywhere and introductions were very informal.

"Amy, this is my dad, trying to clear the room of wrapping paper."

"Hi, Amy!" An elderly version of Jake grinned at her over the mountain of brilliantly printed Christmas gift wreckage he held in his arms. "I'm sick of wading through this stuff. Might stub my toe on something."

She grinned back. "I can see it might be a problem. Nice to meet you, Mr. Carter."

"And this is our tree," Ruth went on proudly, not giving Amy time to get into conversation. It didn't really seem expected. Which was totally unlike any visitor's encounter with *her* father, who would have demanded full and absolute attention.

The tree was, indeed, fabulous—three metres tall, at least, towering up towards the cathedral ceiling, a green fir draped in red and purple and silver ornaments and hundreds of fairy lights.

Amy was swept into the adjoining kitchen where two women were gathered around an island bench loaded with festive food. "Grace, Tess, here she is. These two busy bodies are my sisters-in-law, Amy."

She managed a "Hi!" before being interrupted.

"At last!" Grace, a plump and very pretty brunette exclaimed, brown eyes twinkling triumphant delight. "You're making our day, Amy. We can really henpeck Jake about you now."

"Pardon?" The word tripped out as alarm shot through Amy. She didn't want to be a target of teasing, no matter how good-natured it was. The situation was too serious for her to respond light-heartedly.

Tess laughed. She was a honey-blonde and obviously pregnant, making Amy even more conscious of her own condition. "Don't worry, Amy," she was quick to assure. "We won't embarrass you. It's just that our brother-in-law is such a slippery customer when it comes to women, it's nice to hang one on him."

"I am only his P.A.," she reminded them.

"Don't say *only*," Ruth instantly expostulated. "We think you're marvellous. The only constant female in Jake's life, apart from his family."

"And he cared enough to want you here," Grace put in.

"Which proves he *can* care," Tess declared. "We were beginning to doubt he was capable of it. You're the only one he's ever wanted to share his Christmas with, Amy."

"Well, we do share a lot of days," Amy explained, trying to hide the flutter of hope in her heart. "I guess he thought this was just another."

"Nope. It's definitely caring," Grace insisted.

"Trust, too," Tess said decisively. "You've given us

hope for him, Amy. He actually trusts you to survive meeting his family. Obviously a woman of strength.''

Amy smiled at their free flow of zany humour. ''Are you so formidable?''

''Dreadful en masse,'' Ruth said, rolling her eyes to express the burden of belonging to them. ''Loud and competitive and opinionated and everyone tells horrible stories. You'd better come and meet the rest so you can sort them out.''

Ruth's husband, Martin, Jake and his two older brothers, Adam and Nathan, were all in the pool, playing water games with five children. ''Hannah's the eldest at ten. Olivia's eight. Tom's seven. Mitch is four and Ashleigh's three,'' Ruth rattled out. ''It's a rule in this family that everyone has to learn to swim before they walk.''

They all yelled out, ''Happy Christmas!'' and Amy was struck by their happiness and harmony as they continued their fun. Jake was holding a big plastic ball, ready to throw, and the cries of ''Me, Uncle Jake, me!'' rang with excitement and pleasure.

She would have liked to stop and watch him frolicking with his nieces and nephews but Ruth steered her to where an elderly woman sat in the shade of a vine-covered pergola, nursing a wide awake Joshua on her lap. ''Mum, this is Jake's Amy,'' she announced.

''Ruth, do try to introduce people properly,'' her mother chided, and Amy instantly had a flash of Jake saying, ''Mum does her best to rule over us all.''

''Amy Taylor, please meet Elizabeth Rose Carter,'' Ruth trotted out in mock obedience.

Her mother sighed. She was still a striking woman,

however old she was. A lovely mass of white wavy hair framed a face very like Ruth's, but her brown eyes were more reserved than openly welcoming.

"It's very kind of you all to include me in your family Christmas, Mrs. Carter," Amy said, aware she was being given a keen scrutiny by Jake's mother during this mother-daughter exchange. "It's a great pleasure to meet you."

"And you, my dear," came the dignified reply. "Jake has spoken so much about you."

"I enjoy working with him," was the only comment Amy could think of.

It was rather disconcerting being measured against whatever Jake had said about her, and being visually measured from head to toe, as well. It was silly to feel self-conscious in her white pantsuit since the other women wore similar casual clothes, but she suddenly wished she'd worn a loose shirt instead of the figure-moulding halter top. *I might be pregnant to him but I'm not a brazen hussy out to trap your son,* she found herself thinking.

"I understand you have no close relatives," Elizabeth Carter remarked questioningly, making Amy feel like a reject of the human race.

"My parents emigrated from England and my brothers now live overseas," she answered. "This kind of gathering is quite remarkable to me. You're very lucky, Mrs. Carter."

"Yes, I suppose I am. Though I tend to think one makes one's own luck. I did bring my children up to value the close bonds of family."

"Then they were very fortunate in having you as their mother."

"What of your own mother, Amy?"

"She died when I was sixteen."

"How sad. A girl needs her mother. So easy to go off the rails without good advice and support."

"I suppose so," Amy said noncommittally, feeling she was being dissected and found wanting. No solid family background. No wise maternal guidance in her life.

"Mum, do you think it's kind to ram that stuff down Amy's throat on today of all days?" Ruth demanded in exasperation.

"Amy!"

Jake's shout saved the awkward moment. They all looked to see what he wanted. He'd hauled himself out of the pool and was striding towards them, rubbing himself vigorously with a towel. Amy's heart caught in her throat. He was so...vital...and stunningly male.

She forced her gaze to stay fixed on his face as he neared them. The rest of his anatomy held too many pitfalls to her peace of mind. Not that she had any peace of mind, but her knees suddenly felt very shaky and if there was ever a time to appear strong it was now, especially in front of his mother's critical eye.

"Sorry I wasn't out of the pool to greet you when you arrived," he said, his smile aimed exclusively at her, a smile that tingled through her bloodstream and made her feel light-headed.

"No need to apologise. Ruth is looking after me," she said, struggling to be sensible. "Go back if you like. I don't want to interrupt the game."

He shook his head. "You look great in that white outfit. Why haven't I seen you in white before?"

"You would have said it's a neutral, not fitting our image," she said dryly.

He grinned, the yellow wolfish gleam lighting his eyes. "Definitely a positive. Give me five minutes to get dressed and I'll be at your side to protect you from the hordes."

"Well, if you're going to poke your nose in, I'm taking Amy back to the kitchen so we women can get some chat in first," Ruth informed him archly.

He laughed. "I can feel the knives in my back. Take no notice of them, Amy. The women in this family have mean, vicious hearts."

"Oh, you..." Ruth tried to cuff him, but he ducked out of reach and was off, still laughing.

"Are you still okay with Joshua, Mum?" Ruth asked.

"Yes, dear." The dark eyes pinned Amy purposefully. "Perhaps we'll have time to converse later."

"I'm sure we will," she answered, forcing a smile she didn't feel. The impression was too strong that Elizabeth Rose Carter did not consider her a suitable person to be the one woman her youngest son chose to share Christmas with his family, let alone be the mother of his child.

It hurt.

And the natural acceptance given her by all the others as the day wore on, didn't quite overlay that initial hurt. It preyed on her mind more and more as she watched the Carter family in action over the long and highly festive Christmas luncheon.

They connected so easily and they had no fear of saying anything they liked to each other. There was no tension. Laughter rippled around the table. Children were lovingly indulged. Good-natured arguments broke out and became quite boisterous but there wasn't a trace of acrimony, merely a lively exchange of opinions accompanied by witty teasing. It was interesting, amusing, and most of all, happy.

Jake didn't allow her to be simply an observer. Neither did his siblings nor their partners. It seemed everyone was keen to draw her into being one of them, inviting her participation, wanting it, enjoying it. Occasionally Jake's father would stir the pot with provocative remarks, then sit back, his amber eyes twinkling like Jake's as comments bounced around the table.

They knew how to have fun, this family. To Amy it was a revelation of how a family could be, given a kindly and encouraging hand at the helm. She wished her baby could know this, know it from the very beginning...to grow up without fear, with an unshakable sense of belonging to a loving circle. Maybe she was idealising it, but the contrast from what she'd come from was so great, it all seemed perfect to her.

The rapport she shared with Jake was heightened in this company. There were times when their eyes met, the understanding felt so intimate she was sure she could tell him she was pregnant and it wouldn't cause any problem between them. He would want his child. He would love it. Family was natural to him.

Then she would catch his mother watching them and knew there was no easy solution to her situation. Elizabeth Carter did not approve of her. Besides, the sense of intimacy was an illusion, generated by the special harmony of a happy Christmas day. Jake might care for her and trust her. It didn't mean he would want to be bound to her through their child.

She was his P.A.

He wasn't in love with her.

He probably wasn't the type to fall in love since he'd never brought any other woman to a family Christmas. Brief affairs was his style when it came to women. She probably wouldn't be here if she was still one of his "brief" affairs. He undoubtedly thought she was *safe*, not expecting anything of him.

After the feast had been devoured to everyone's satisfaction, they drifted out to the patio. Nathan had set up a badminton net beside the pool, and the two older brothers challenged Jake and Ruth to a game. The rest of the family took up spectator positions, ready to barrack for their team. The children sat around the pool, making up their own competition about diving in to retrieve the shuttlecock should it be hit into the water. Elizabeth Carter invited Amy to sit with her under the pergola.

Here comes *the conversation,* Amy thought, and wondered why Jake's mother was bothering. Didn't she know her own son?

"I hope you've been enjoying yourself," she started.

"Immensely," Amy returned with a smile.

"This badminton match is something of a tradition. Jake started it years ago. They'll play on for a while. It's the best of five games."

"Closely fought, I'd imagine."

She actually unbent enough to laugh. "Very. And

they use outrageous tactics. Which is why their father has to umpire.''

"But all done in the spirit of fun, I'm sure,'' Amy commented.

"Oh, yes.'' The amusement faded into a shrewd look. ''Though life isn't all fun. I've found it's a lot less complicated if one follows a straight path.''

"How do you mean?'' Amy prompted, thinking they might as well get to the meat of this talk.

"Well, as I understand it from Jake,'' she started tentatively, ''You've been...attached...to a relationship for many years.''

"Most people do get attached,'' Amy said dryly. Not counting Jake, she could have added even more dryly.

Elizabeth Carter gathered herself to spit out what was on her mind. ''I must say I don't hold with this modern custom of moving in together,'' she plunged in, her expression implying she was giving Amy the benefit of her wisdom. ''I don't think it does anyone any good in the long run. No clear-cut commitment to a shared future. No emotional security. It's not the right way to go, Amy. Your mother would have told you that,'' she declared with confidence.

"You didn't know my mother, Mrs. Carter,'' Amy said quietly. ''Nor what she suffered in her marriage. What we all suffered. You may see marriage as a safe haven where people can grow happily. It's not always so.''

Silence.

Amy watched the badminton game, her stomach churning over the judgement Jake's mother had made on her—a loose-living woman without commitment. It wasn't fair. It wasn't right. And her defences were very brittle today. She didn't need this. She needed...support.

"I'm sorry. I can only assume your mother made a bad character judgement in her husband," came the gentle rejoinder.

The criticism hit Amy on the raw. One didn't have a clear-minded choice over everything. She hadn't chosen to get pregnant. Especially to a man who didn't love her!

"Perhaps you'd like to give me a reading of Jake's character, Mrs. Carter." Amy swung a hard gaze on her, giving no quarter. "From where I've sat over the past two years, he's a rake with women. A very good boss, a very charming man, but not someone I'd trust to make me happy in the long run, as you so succinctly put it. His turnover rate hardly makes him a good choice, does it? Or do you see it differently?"

The recoil of shock was written all over Elizabeth Carter's face. Being hit by a such a direct and pertinent challenge had certainly not been anticipated. Do her good, Amy thought grimly. Stop her from thinking her youngest son was a glittering prize any woman would love to snatch.

Shock was followed by bewilderment. "Why did you come here today, Amy?"

"I wanted to see what Jake's family is like," she answered bluntly. "It can tell you a lot about a person."

"Then you must understand Jake is looking for the complement to what we have here. He'll keep on looking for it because he won't settle for anything less."

Amy gave her an ironic look. "He's been looking a long time, Mrs. Carter, without success. I may have *moved in* with a man but at least I was constant for five years, which I'm sure Jake told you, and it was my partner's infidelity that broke up the relationship. Infidelity does not appeal to me.''

She frowned. ''I did not mean to offend you, Amy.''

In that case, tact certainly wasn't her strong point, Amy thought.

The frown deepened. ''I know Jake wouldn't cheat on anyone. It isn't in his nature.''

He'd said as much himself, on the balcony after…but that didn't mean he'd stay with one woman for the rest of his life. And Amy suddenly realised it was what she'd want of him…a commitment to her and their child…and it wouldn't happen…so to tell him she was pregnant would almost certainly result in an intolerable situation for both of them. It wouldn't be happy families. It would be emotional hell.

''Don't worry, Mrs. Carter,'' she said ruefully. ''I will not embroil your son in a relationship you wouldn't like.''

''Amy…'' She shook her head in distress. ''Oh, dear… I just wanted to help. I know you've been hurt. Sometimes people just don't see straight and they keep repeating their mistakes instead of learning from them. Moving in together is so…so messy.''

So is divorce, Amy thought, but she held her tongue. The couples in the Carter family looked far too solid for her to make that sour comment.

''I have no intention of moving in with your son,'' she stated flatly. ''I work for Jake. We get on well. This invitation to join you for Christmas was a kindness on his part. It's unnecessary to make more of it than that, believe me.''

And I won't intrude again.

''Jake is kind,'' his mother said, as though preparing to build a case for her son's *good* character.

''Yes, he is,'' Amy agreed.

''Underneath all his wild ways, he has a heart of gold. He wouldn't hurt anyone. He goes out of his way not to hurt anyone.''

Amy sighed. ''You don't have to defend him to me, Mrs. Carter. I guess I don't like being put in a position where I'm pushed to defend myself. Shall we leave it at that?''

She knew she sounded hard, but she was in a hard place and Jake's mother hadn't made it any easier. Not that anything would, she thought despairingly.

Elizabeth Carter was clearly upset by this outcome. ''I'm sorry...'' she began again.

''It's okay,'' Amy rushed out dismissively, wanting the conversation dropped. She couldn't bear it on top of everything else. ''Let's just watch the match through and then I'll go.''

''Jake won't want you to go.''

''I make my own decisions, Mrs. Carter.''

She had for a long time. A very long time. Starting when she'd decided independence was the only way to survive intact in her father's household, not to care, not to want, not to need what she didn't have. And now she looked out over Jake's family, feeling like a disembodied outsider, watching a magic circle she could never hope to join. Not freely.

Her baby might be a passport to it in a limited sense—

Jake was kind—but that kindness could be a terrible cruelty, too—to be given a taste while not truly belonging. The only way she and their child could properly belong would be if Jake were her husband, and she couldn't trap him into marriage like that. Marriage should not be a trap. For anyone.

It hurt to watch him. She tried to move her attention to the others but her gaze kept being drawn back to him…the father of her child…the accidental father…unaware that part of him was growing inside her. Was it right not to tell him? Was it best, in the long run, to just disappear from his life?

She didn't know.

She felt as though she didn't know anything anymore.

She was in chaos. It wasn't the happy chaos of a Carter family Christmas. It was the dark chaos that came with the constant beating of uncertainties.

Finally the game was over, Adam and Nathan conceding victory to Jake and Ruth, and Jake was coming for her, wanting her to play.

And she had to find an answer.

CHAPTER FIFTEEN

"WINNER'S choice now," Jake crowed. "Amy and I challenge Ruth and Martin."

"You can have it, boyo," the oldest brother, Nathan, groaned. "I'm for a long cool drink."

"Me, too," Adam agreed. "Preferably in the pool."

"Ah, the frailties of age," Jake teased.

"You'll get yours," Nathan retorted. "Martin will wipe you off the court."

"Huh! You don't know my Amy."

My Amy…and the glorious grin he aimed at her…she couldn't take any more turmoil.

"Not me, Jake," she quickly protested. "Take Grace as your partner. I really must be going now." She stood up, preparing to make her farewells.

"Going?" He looked incredulous.

"It's been a wonderful day…"

"It's not over yet," he argued. "We light up the barbecue at about seven and…"

"I'm sorry. I can't stay."

"Why not?" Ruth demanded, getting in on the act. "We need you to balance up the party, Amy."

She forced a smile. "The truth is I have a raging headache. Too much champagne over lunch, I guess. Please don't mind."

Elizabeth Carter leapt up from her chair. "You should have said, Amy. I'll get you some pills to take."

"You could lie down for a while," Ruth suggested.

"No, please…" Amy reached out to stay Jake's mother, unaware her eyes filled with anguished appeal. "Just let me go. All right?"

The older woman hesitated, then blurted out, "I'm so sorry…"

"For what, Mum?" Jake asked sharply.

"That I'm not up to more fun and games," Amy hastily explained. She forced another smile. "I'd like to say my goodbyes, Jake."

He searched her eyes, obviously sensing something wrong beyond the headache. However, much to Amy's intense relief, he decided not to press the point. "You're the boss today," he said with his quirky smile. "Mum, would you mind getting the headache tablets for Amy to take before she goes?"

"Of course, dear."

"Can't have you driving in pain," he said, then raised his voice. "Hey, everyone! Amy has to leave now so come and wish her well."

They all bunched around, shaking hands, kissing her cheek, saying what a pleasure it was to have met her. It passed in a blur to Amy. She hoped she made suitable responses. Jake's mother handed her a glass of water and two pills. She took them. The raging headache was very real. The crowd around her receded. So did the noise. Finally, there was only Jake who took the glass from her, set it down on a table, then wrapped her arm around his.

"Are you sure you're fit to drive, Amy?" he asked in concern as he walked her into the house.

It was all she could do not to tremble at his touch, his

nearness. He didn't realise the effect he was having on her, the sheer torture of being so closely linked, yet impossibly far from what she wanted of him. "I'll be fine," she insisted huskily.

He paused her in the family room. "I'll sit with you for a while if you like. Some quiet time won't go amiss."

"No. I don't want to be a trouble." It was hard to keep a frantic note out of her voice. She broke away from him to pick up her handbag which she'd left on a chair by the Christmas tree.

Christmas...peace, hope and goodwill...it was a joke... a wickedly painful black joke!

"It's no trouble," Jake assured her.

"I'll be fine," she insisted more firmly, and having collected her bag, she headed for the foyer, every step driven by the need to get away from the torment he stirred.

He followed. "Amy, did Mum say anything to upset you?" Urgent concern in his voice now.

"Why should she?" she flipped back.

"Because my mother has a habit of thinking she knows best," he grated out.

"Most parents do." *Except me,* Amy thought, in helpless panic. Here she was, a parent in the making, with no idea what was best.

"You're not answering my question," Jake persisted.

"It doesn't matter."

He halted her by stepping in front of her, right in the centre of the foyer which served the front door. "*You* matter," he said with quiet force. "You matter to *me.*"

Do I?...Do I?

The words pounded through her mind as she lifted her head to search his eyes for how much she mattered to him. Golden eyes, burning fiercely. But what did it mean?

She didn't see him lift his hand. Her cheek quivered under its tender touch, a touch that was only there fleetingly, because fingers were suddenly raking through her hair and his head bent closer and his mouth claimed hers.

Amy completely lost track of what happened after that. The pain in her head was pushed to some far perimeter, her mind filling up with a host of clamouring needs, every one of them chorusing yes to the connection being forged…yes, to the sweet caress of his lips, yes to the seductive slide of his tongue, yes, yes, yes, to the passionate plunder that followed, a wildly exhilarating, intensely evocative reminder of sensations she'd known before with this man…only this man.

She wasn't aware of moving her body to meet his, of clinging to him, of basking in the heat he generated, the strength emanating from him, surrounding her, cocooning her in a place that felt safe and right. Her whole being was swimming in a sea of bliss, feeling—knowing on some deep subconscious level—this was the answer, the answer to everything.

"Uh-oh…"

Ruth's voice…intruding, jarring.

"…Slice of Christmas cake for Amy… I'll just leave it here."

The pain in Amy's head crashed through the wall of sensation that had held it at bay. The realisation of what she was doing—what Jake was doing—exploded through her mind. This physical compulsion…sexual attraction…*didn't answer anything!*

She tore her mouth from his. Her hands were buried in his hair. Her body was plastered against his, his arms, hands, ensuring she was pressed into maximum, intimate contact, and she'd not only allowed it, she was actively *clinging,* as though he was the only rock that could save her from going under.

Clinging…like's Steve's blonde…for whom she'd felt contempt.

Such a wretched lack of understanding on her part.

Yet she was appalled at her own weakness.

"It's the same," Jake murmured near her ear, his voice furred with satisfaction.

She jerked her head back. Her hands scrambled out of his hair to push at his shoulders, frantic to make some space between them. "You shouldn't have done this. You agreed!" she cried, her eyes meeting his in agitated, anguished accusation.

"It *is* out of office hours," he reminded her in mitigation of the offence. His mouth—his damnably mesmerising mouth—curved into a soft, sensual smile. "And I'd have to confess the temptation to refresh the memory got the better of me."

The memory…still physically surging between them. Flustered by her own complicity in reviving it, Amy broke his embrace, her hands fluttering wildly over his chest as she forced a step back from him, her eyes begging for release.

"You took advantage." Blaming him didn't excuse herself, but she had not invited this. He couldn't say she had.

"Mmh..." He was not the least bit abashed. The smile still lingered on his lips and the molten gold in his eyes remained warm, twinkling with the pleasure of a desire fulfilled. "Look up, Amy."

"What?" She *was* looking up, her gaze trained directly on his, desperately seeking the heart of this man.

"Right above your head is a bunch of mistletoe hanging from the light fitting."

She looked up. There it was, just as he said.

"A man's entitled to kiss a woman standing underneath the mistletoe on Christmas day."

Fun, she thought despairingly. He was having his wicked way with her, out of office hours, just because he wanted to. Never mind how she felt or what it would do to her. Jake, the rake, couldn't resist an opportunity to satisfy himself. Fury swept through her, a fury fed by fear and frustration.

"You deliberately stopped me here," she hurled at him, her hands dropping from all contact from him, curling into fists, her whole body bristling with fierce aggression. How dare he touch her *in fun!* It was monstrous, without care or conscience.

He frowned, perceiving her sense of violation and not liking it. "I'm simply letting you know there's no reason to be fussed by it, Amy."

Fussed! It was the most contemptible word he could have used, making light of what he'd done when it wasn't light at all. Nothing about her situation was *light*. She hated him in that moment, hated him with a passion.

"That was not a Christmas kiss," she bit out, her eyes furiously stripping him of any further attempt at levity.

Any trace of a smile was wiped from his face. His

eyes suddenly gathered an intense focus, gleaming more yellow than gold. A wolf on the hunt, Amy thought wildly, determined on tracking through anything to get to her.

"No. It was much more," he quietly agreed.

Her heart squeezed into a tight ball. He was going to close in on her no matter what she said or did. She could feel the power of his purpose, and couldn't move away from it.

"Don't you find that curious, Amy?" he asked.

She had no answer. Her mind had seized up on the idea of his being an irresistible force.

"How well we get on now that Steve's out of the way?" he went on, the words seeming to beat at her in relentless pursuit. "How perfectly we click when we come together?"

Perfectly!

That triggered a rush of hysteria which was impossible to contain. The words bubbled out of her mind and spilled into irretrievable sound.

"Oh, so *perfectly* I'm pregnant, Jake!"

Her hands flew up in dramatic emphasis.

"How do you like that for perfect?"

CHAPTER SIXTEEN

Sнock!

Amy saw it, felt it reverberating through Jake just as it quaked through her. It was like a live thing, with writhing tentacles, reaching and changing everything. She couldn't believe she'd done it...set this irrevocable happening in motion without any rational planning for consequences...just blurted it out...here it is...

"Pregnant."

The word fell from Jake's lips as though there was too much to take in and he couldn't quite cope with it.

Amy flapped her hands helplessly. "I'm sorry... I'm sorry... It was that night you came to my apartment and...and I forgot to take the pill after...after you'd gone. I took two the next day but..."

Her voice faltered as she saw the shock clear from Jake's face, to be replaced by a strange, wondrous look.

"You're pregnant to me," he said.

Amy didn't understand. He sounded as if he liked the idea. Maybe his thinking had been knocked haywire. "Jake..." It was of paramount importance to get through to him. "...It wasn't meant to happen..."

"But it did." He grinned from ear to ear.

Amy started to panic. His reaction wasn't right. He certainly wasn't thinking straight. "Are you listening to me?" she cried.

"You're carrying my child...mine!" He spoke as

though he'd won the best lottery in the world. "For a moment there, I thought it was Steve's, and that would have been hard, Amy. A hell of a reminder..."

"Jake, this is not okay!" she hurled at him, desperate to get the conversation on some kind of clear track. "It was an accident. I didn't want to hang it on you."

"Hang it on me! Hang it on me!" He repeated in a kind of dazed incredulity. "I'm the father. You're not hanging anything on me. The biological fact is..." He paused, apparently having been struck by a different thought. "How long have you known?"

"What?" Amy just couldn't get a handle on how Jake's mind was working. It was totally incomprehensible to her.

"About the baby."

"Oh!" She flushed. "I got the results of the blood test two days ago."

He grinned again. "So it *is* absolutely certain."

"Will you stop that?" she cried in exasperation.

"Stop what?"

"Looking so damned pleased about it!"

"I can't help it. It's not every day a man gets told he's going to be a father. We're talking about our first child..."

"Jake! We're...not...married," she almost shouted at him.

"Well, we can soon fix that," he said, his delighted expression moving swiftly to purpose.

Amy glared at him in helpless frustration. The man did not have his feet on the ground at all. Maybe he was besotted with the idea of being presented with a child of his own, having been surrounded by his siblings' children all day. Whatever the reason, there was no sense coming from him. He probably needed a few days to think about it, do some sober reflection on their situation.

"I'm going home," she stated firmly. "I've got a headache."

As she started to step past him his arm shot out to prevent it.

"Wait! Please…"

It was too much. Tears welled into her eyes. She was too choked up to speak, too distressed to look at him.

"I'm sorry. I'm not getting this right, am I?" he said softly, apologetically.

She shook her head.

"Don't cry, Amy. I'll do better, I promise."

The tears flowed faster.

Then his arm was around her shoulders, hugging her close for comfort. "I'll take you home."

She swallowed hard, struggling to get control of her voice. "Your family…"

"You're my family now, Amy. Let me at least take care of you."

That did it, speaking to her so gently, saying what she'd been secretly craving to hear. The tears were unstoppable now and he was already urging her to the front door, opening it for her. She didn't have the strength to fight him, didn't have voice enough to argue. They were out of the house and walking down the path to the street before he spoke again, his sympathetic tone soothing some of the turmoil inside her.

"It must have been rough on you the past two days, worrying about what to do."

"Yes," she managed to whisper.

"You're not...umh...thinking of a termination, are you, Amy?"

"No."

"Good!" His sigh expressed deep relief. "I'm not sure I could have borne that, either."

This was muttered more to himself than to her and Amy briefly puzzled over it. She was the one who had to do the bearing. Jake seemed to be off on another plane again. Though it was clear he wanted her to have the baby. He hadn't left her in any doubt about that. Though she had a mountain of doubts surrounding what would eventuate from it.

"The car key?" he prompted.

They'd reached the sidewalk where her car was parked at the kerb. She fumbled in her handbag and found the key, found a tissue, too, and wiped her weepy eyes. She was feeling slightly more in control, though still very shaky on how to proceed from here with Jake.

He held out his hand. "Better let me drive, Amy. I don't think you're in a fit enough state to concentrate on it."

Taking care of her...being kind. Jake *was* kind. For a moment Amy wallowed in the warm reassurance. He wasn't going to make this hard for her. He was prepared—more than prepared—to take responsibility. Which reminded her of other more immediate responsibilities.

"What about you? The champagne?" she asked, unsure how many glasses he'd consumed over lunch. The last thing she needed was to end up today in a police station with Jake charged for drunk driving.

"No problem." He gave her his quirky smile. "Sober as a judge."

Somehow that typical little smile put things on a more normal footing. She sighed, trying to loosen the tightness in her chest, and handed over the key, relieved he could take care of the driving, relieved also that he appeared to be more himself now.

Despite her headache, Amy decided it would be good to get a few things settled so she had some idea where she stood with him. And with her job. There was no longer any escape from the truth, so the sooner they talked it over, the better.

Jake unlocked the car, saw her settled in the passenger seat, then moved quickly to the driver's side, sliding in behind the wheel and closing them in together. *Together* was the operative word, she thought ruefully. They'd made this baby together and now they were stuck together until something was sorted out.

"One thing I want to say, Amy, before you do any more thinking."

She could feel him looking at her with urgent intensity but she couldn't bring herself to let him see just how vulnerable she was to whatever he had to say. It was easier to stare straight ahead, easier for steeling herself to face the difficulties he would certainly bring up.

"Go on," she invited, hoping she could cope with the outcome.

"Don't rule marriage out," he said quietly. "I want to marry you, Amy. I think we could have a good life together. So please give it your serious consideration while I drive you home."

He didn't wait for a reply, which was just as well,

EMMA DARCY 155

because Amy was too poleaxed to speak. He switched on the engine and got on with driving.

She didn't really notice the journey home, wasn't aware of time passing. Her mind was in a ferment. How could she give marriage to Jake Carter serious consideration? What was he thinking of? It was time to take a wife and have a family and she'd do as well as anyone else, especially since she was already pregnant to him? The good old chemistry spark was there so why not?

Never mind that the spark might go out before she even had the baby! There was always a host of other available women to have on the side when that happened. Did he think he could fool her when she knew so much about him? It was true they got on well together, but how long would that last under pressures they'd never had before? She could not live with infidelity for a start!

It was all very well for his mother to say it wasn't in Jake's nature to cheat. Without love, they'd be cheating each other anyway if they got married. Besides, Elizabeth Rose Carter certainly wouldn't welcome her as a daughter-in-law. Though Jake could probably charm his mother into accepting anything if he worked at it.

Amy was only too aware of how charming he could be. She couldn't let it work on her. There was too much at stake here. Her happiness. Their child's happiness.

Their child…

Misery swamped her. It wasn't right to bring a child into the world when neither parent had planned for it. What was she to do? What did she want Jake to do?

Dazedly, she looked around for landmarks and realised they were heading down the hill to Balmoral Beach.

It reminded her of the day Jake first drove her here, the day she'd told him Steve was going to marry his pregnant blonde.

Pregnancy...marriage.

Did all men think like that?

No, of course they didn't. If men were so committed to their children there wouldn't be so many single mothers. Not that she wanted to be a single mother. That would be a very hard road. But getting married because of a baby...the thought of an oppressive prison loomed darkly on the edges of what looked like an easier road. Becoming dependent on a man who didn't really want to spend his life with her...

We could have a good life together.

Amy rubbed at her temples.

Did Jake really believe that?

"Headache worse?" he asked in concern.

"No. Just trying to think."

"Leave it until we get home," he advised. "Almost there."

It wasn't his home, Amy thought crossly. He was going to invade it again, as he had before...invading her life...but they did have to talk. He was the father of her child and there was no locking him out of their future. One way or another, he would always be in it. Especially if he kept up his current attitude.

He parked the car in her garage slot underneath the apartment block. She vaguely wondered how he knew which slot was hers. Probably a lucky guess.

As they rode up to the top floor in the elevator, Amy became acutely aware of Jake's physical nearness. She started remembering the kiss underneath the mistletoe and how she'd clung to him...how he'd felt, how much he could make her feel, the sheer power of his sexuality drawing on hers. If he started that again...tried to use it...she must not let him.

He held out her car key. She snatched it off his palm, frightened of any skin-to-skin contact with him. For a moment Jake's palm hung there empty and her graceless behaviour shot a wave of heat up Amy's throat.

Thankfully Jake made no comment. He lowered his hand to his side and Amy busied herself with her hand-bag, putting away the car key and finding the one for her front door.

Her inner tension increased, screaming along every nerve in her body as Jake accompanied her out of the elevator. Fortunately he had the good sense not to touch her. She would have snapped.

Once the door was unlocked, Jake gestured for her to precede him into the apartment, so she went ahead and left him to follow, grateful he was tactful enough not to crowd her and she had the chance to establish a com-fortable distance. Having dropped her handbag on the kitchen counter, she walked straight across the living room to open the doors to the balcony.

The instant waft of fresh sea air on her hot face felt good. Unbelievably, despite her fevered thoughts, her headache had eased. If she could just keep enough cool to handle Jake in a calm and reasonable manner, maybe they could come to some workable agreements.

"Can I get you something, Amy? A cup of tea or..."

"No."

His voice came from the kitchen area. He'd probably paused there, watching her. She took a deep breath and turned to face him, forcing an ironic smile to ease the concern he was expressing. He was behind the counter, hands resting on it, poised to minister to her needs, but he was no more relaxed than she was.

His shoulders looked bunched, his facial muscles were taut, a worry line creased the space between his brows, his triangular eyes were narrowed, sharply scanning, weighing up her body language.

"Thank you," she added belatedly, "but I doubt anything would sit well in my stomach right now. I wasn't ready for this, Jake. Telling you, I mean."

He nodded. "Better done than churning about it, Amy."

"Yes. Though I didn't mean to mess up your Christmas day with your family. I only went to see..." She trailed off, finding it too difficult to describe all the nuances of her observations.

"What it might be like if you joined it?"

His quick perception jolted her. "I can't marry you," she blurted out more baldly than she had meant to.

He frowned. "Because of my family?"

"No...no..." She shook her head, berating herself for being as tactless as his mother. "You have a great family. It must be wonderful to belong to them. For you, I mean. For them. All of you..."

Now she was blathering. She stopped and took another deep breath. Her heart was fluttering. She couldn't seem to keep two coherent thoughts in her head.

"There's no reason why you couldn't belong, Amy," Jake said with serious intent. "And our child certainly would, as naturally as all the other children. You met

Tess and Grace and Martin today. You must have seen how they…"

"Please…" She waved an emphatic dismissal. "That's not the point, Jake."

"What is the point?"

"I wouldn't be living with them day in and day out. I'd be living with *you*."

"So?"

Living with anyone wasn't simple. Amy knew from living with Steve…the adjustments, the compromises. It was hard enough *with love*. Without it…and always worrying about Jake connecting with other women, beautiful women running after him all the time…

She shook her head. "I can't do it."

"Why not?"

The need for this torment to be ended formed her answer. She looked at him squarely, defying any further persistance on this question, sure there was no way of refuting what was necessary to her.

"I don't love you, Jake."

He stiffened. A muscle in his cheek contracted. It was as though she'd hit him physically and Amy had the strangest feeling—a strong, unshakable feeling—that she'd hurt him. Hurt him badly. Which rattled her. She hadn't considered Jake would be hurt by her rejection. Frustrated at not getting his own way, but not hurt.

She stared at him in wretched confusion and was caught by the changing expression in his eyes, the sharpening of his focus on her, the gathering of an intensity that felt like a powerful concentration of his will and energy, burning a challenge straight into her brain…a challenge that denied the knowledge she thought she had of him, denied even her knowledge of herself.

For a few riveting moments he seemed like a total stranger to her...or he took on dimensions she had not been aware of before. It gave her the scary feeling she was dealing with much more than she had anticipated, and she was suddenly riven with uncertainties. She almost jumped when he spoke.

"There is such a thing as a marriage of convenience, Amy. I believe it could work very well," he said quietly.

One certainty instantly exploded from all the thinking she'd done and because he'd unsettled her so deeply, she answered with fierce emphasis. "I will not be a *convenient* wife to you. That might suit you, Jake, out and about your life, but I don't see myself as the little woman at home, subservient to your needs."

"Subservient! Since when haven't I considered your needs?" His tone was harsher, edged with angry disbelief. "I've spent most of my time with you, putting your needs above my own. Can we have a bit of fair-mindedness here, Amy?"

She flushed, unable to pluck out one pertinent example of inconsideration on his part, and he'd been especially sensitive to her needs since Steve had dumped her. The long shadow of her parents' marriage crossed her mind...her mother serving her tyrannical father like a slave...but there was nothing tyrannical about Jake. He was more like a free-wheeling buccaneer, happy to lead anyone into adventurous fun.

"I want a marriage of sharing, Amy," he pressed. "We happen to do that well."

"Am I supposed to share you with all the women you

fancy?'' she flared, fighting her way out of being in the wrong.

''That's enough!''

He slammed his hand down on the counter, the angry frustration he'd repressed erupting with such force, Amy shrank back against the door. Then was angry at herself for being intimidated.

''Don't like the truth, Jake?'' she challenged, her chin lifting into fighting mode.

''You want the truth?'' he flung back at her, too incensed to back down this time. ''I'll give it to you. The high turnover of women in my life can be placed entirely at your door.''

''Mine?'' she retorted incredulously.

''Yours!'' He stabbed a finger at her. ''So try swallowing that for a change instead of spitting out slurs on my lack of staying power.''

''And just *how* can it be my fault?''

''Because what we sparked off each other—and don't you deny it, Amy—was stronger than anything I felt with the women I tried to relate to. Tried, because you made yourself inaccessible to me and it seemed pointless to wait for something that might never happen.''

The sheer passion in his voice rocked her into silence.

His eyes flashed with savage mockery. ''Oh, you did your best to block it out...the natural connection that was always there between us. With two long years of blocking it out, it's become a habit, hasn't it? Keep Jake at a distance. Don't let him close because something big might slip out of your control.''

A fierce pride hardened his features. ''Which it did.

The night we made a baby was bigger than anything I've felt in my life. And I'll bet my life it was for you, too.''

His mouth twisted into a bitter grimace. ''Two years wasted while I was fool enough to respect your commitment to a guy who ended up cheating on you. Two years…and now you want to waste the lot, clinging to some prejudicial rubbish.''

His eyes glittered derision at her. ''Give her more time, I told myself. She's still getting over that bastard. You'll win her in the end, Jake.''

He shook his head. ''You're not even prepared to give me a chance for the sake of our child.''

The indictment he was delivering was so devastating, Amy could do nothing but listen, absorbing shock after shock as he forced her to recognise and acknowledge a different perception from what she had allowed herself. And the worst of it was, there was ample evidence to back up all he was saying.

She *had* used Steve as a barrier between them, no denying it if she was truly honest.

Once the barrier was gone…

She remembered Jake rattling on to baby Joshua after he'd learnt Steve was out of her life… *We've got Amy Taylor right where we want her…well, not precisely.*

Then later when she'd said she was on her own, Jake reminding her…*I was here for you. When your scumbag of a lover let you down, I was here for you.*

You do have me to count on.

Ruth's attitude to her…the Wonderwoman in Jake's life ever since she'd begun working for him. Even his mother saying Jake had talked so much about her… And they'd all told her she was the only woman he'd ever wanted to share his family Christmas.

The night of their *mating* flooded back into her mind... Jake asking her not to forget it, a special memory...uniquely special...and it truly had been...but she'd twisted it all to fit a different picture to the real truth...the truth he'd just forced her to see...the truth that damned everything she'd said and thought.

She saw the anger drain out of him, saw the passion give way to sadness, and had the sinking feeling she had dug her own grave and there was no way out of it.

"One day you'll have to explain to our child why you wouldn't marry me," he put to her, his eyes dull and opaque, blocking her out of his heart. "If you have to keep lying to yourself...well, I guess that's your choice. But don't lie to my child about me, Amy. I don't deserve that."

Her heart felt like stone. She had done him so many terrible injustices. And for what? To ensure she was protected against her own natural impulses, her own instincts? Jake was twice the man Steve was. More. She'd always known it. Of course she had. And told herself he was too much to handle, too risky to take on. He was too handsome, too attractive, and there was too much competition for him. She wasn't good enough to hold him.

Not good enough...

It was what her father had always said to her.

So she'd stayed with less, chosen safety, and told herself it was sensible, right, for the best.

Jake stepped back from the counter, stood very straight and tall, a man who'd fought and lost but not without dignity, not without courage and fire and belief in himself.

"Ask whatever you want of me and I'll give it to you," he said flatly. "But let's leave it for a few days. When you come back to work will be soon enough. I'll listen to your plans then. I've lost any taste for them right now."

He nodded to her. "If you'll excuse me..."

Without waiting for a reply, not expecting one, he moved out of the kitchen and headed for the front door. For several seconds, Amy was completely paralysed. The click of the knob being turned snapped her out of it.

"Wait!" Her voice was little more than a hoarse croak. She rushed to the far edge of the kitchen counter, desperately calling, "Jake, please wait!"

He stood at the end of the short hall, his back turned to her, his hand still on the doorknob, his shoulders squared, but his head was thrown high as though in acute listening mode.

He *was* waiting. Not inviting any more from her, but prepared to hear why she wanted to stop him from going. If she didn't get it right, he would go. She knew he would.

"What is it?" he rasped, impatient with her silence.

What could she say? Amy only knew she had to stop him from walking out of her life. Then the words came, sure and true.

"I'll marry you. I will. If you'll still have me."

CHAPTER SEVENTEEN

TENSION racked Amy as she watched Jake's shoulders rise and fall. It had to be a deep, deep breath he was taking and she had no idea what emotion he might be fighting to control.

Then he turned.

Slowly.

Amy *held* her breath.

He looked at her as though he didn't know her, scanning for a recognition which should have been there, but had somehow slipped past him. "Why, Amy?"

"Because..." The grave she'd dug for herself was so huge, so deep, she quailed at the task of climbing out of it. Her stomach contracted in sheer panic. Her mind skittered all over the place, finally grasping a hook Jake had given her. "What you said is true. I've lied and lied and lied, to stop myself...to stop *you* from getting too close to me."

His face tightened. His eyes gleamed yellow, hard and merciless. "That hardly makes marriage desirable for either of us," he bit out derisively.

Her hands fluttered out in desperate appeal. "I don't know how to explain it to you."

"Try!" It was a harsh, gutteral sound, scraped from wounds too freshly delivered for him to accept any evasion from her.

Amy knew it was a demand she had to meet, yet

where to start, how to make him understand? She hadn't understood it herself until he'd started putting it together for her.

"No backward steps now, Amy," he warned.

"You once asked me about my family," she plunged in, her eyes begging his forebearance. "I glossed over it, Jake."

Impatience exploded from him, his hands cutting the air in a sharp-scissor motion. "What can your family possibly have to do with us? You told me they've been out of your life for years."

"Control," she answered quickly, frantic to capture his attention and keep it. "With your upbringing, you couldn't imagine what my childhood was like...the constant emotional abuse from my father...having to wear it...trying not to be crushed. When I left home at sixteen, I swore never to let anyone have control over me again...not...not in an emotional sense."

"You expect me to accept that? After all the emotion you spent on your ex-lover?" he hurled at her in disgust. "Was it five years of nothing? Is that what you're telling me?"

"It wasn't like that!" she cried.

"You're not making sense to me, Amy."

"With Steve...there was never any talk of marriage between us. He called us *free spirits*. I felt...*safe*...with him."

"Safe!" Jake jeered.

"Yes, *safe!*" she snapped. "If you don't want to hear this, just go," she hurled back at him, driven to the end of her tether.

"Oh, I wouldn't miss this story for anything," he retorted scathingly. "Do go on."

Amy paused, taking a deep breath to calm herself. Her heart was thundering. The pulse in her temples was throbbing. There was no escape from this pain. It had to be faced, dealt with. Then the choice of what to do would be Jake's.

"If you want to understand anything about me instead of leaping to your own coloured judgements, then you'll listen," she told him as forcefully as she could. "If only for the sake of your child, you should listen."

The mention of the baby visibly pulled him back from the more personal issues between them. He took on an icy demeanour. "I'm listening."

They were so cold those words, Amy shivered. Nevertheless, she stuck grimly to her course, determined now to lay out the truth, whatever the consequences.

"To get back to Steve. He came from a damaged family, too. It effects people, Jake. You want someone—no one likes being alone—but you don't want to be owned. Because that's threatening."

He frowned, assessing what she was saying.

Encouraged, Amy rushed on to the vital point. "You threatened my sense of safety, Jake."

It startled him. He cocked his head on one side, considering this new perspective, his eyes still reserved but intensely watchful.

"You had the power to get at me, no matter how guarded I was against it. I guess you could say Steve was my bolthole from you."

Another jerk of his head, seemingly negative to Amy's view.

"Call me a coward if you like," she offered, feeling a heavy load of self-contempt for all the running away she'd done. "I *was* a coward with you."

"No." His eyes flashed hard certainty. "You always stood up to me."

"That wasn't brave. It was the only way to retain control," she pressed, trying to reach him on what she saw as the crux of everything. "I lost it the night you came here. I didn't listen to what you were saying afterwards. I was fighting to regain *control,* fighting your power to…" She paused, trying to get it right for him. "…To take over my life and do whatever you wanted with me."

He shook his head, patently appalled at how she had thought. "Amy, you'd always have a say in it. I've respected your wishes. I'd never not respect them," he argued, fiercely dismissing what probably seemed to him a gross allegation.

"I realise that now," she acknowledged. "But I was too frightened to see it then. I kept pushing you away from me, trying to protect myself. I tried to cling to the idea of *spontaneous combustion.* It was like an excuse. But you said it more truly a few minutes ago… *something big slipping out of control.*"

"But our child…" he burst out in angry confusion. "Didn't the baby we made…and its future…deserve some re-thinking?"

"I've been frightened of that, too, pushing it away from me," she confessed.

"But you want the baby. You said…you assured me…"

"That I wasn't thinking of a termination," she finished for him, leaping ahead, anxious to get it all out now. "I couldn't, Jake. Not because it was my baby. This will probably sound unreal to you, but from the moment the pregnancy was confirmed, I thought of the baby as *yours*."

"Blaming me?"

"No...no..." She shook her head vehemently, anguished by his misunderstanding. "I meant...you have this power, Jake. It...it clouds everything. I didn't think of it as *my* baby. Not even an entity by itself. It was like a bond you'd made with me. A tie. And I see-sawed between wanting the link with you and being frightened of what it might mean to me."

"Frightened... you're *frightened* of marrying me?" He looked repelled by the idea.

"I was. I'm not anymore," she cried in a fluster. "Don't you see?" she pleaded. "There was no way out because of the baby. And if you hurt me...it's like a trap. I can't bring myself to let you go...yet you have the power to damage me far more than my father ever did. For far longer."

"You have the same power over me," he said tersely. "Don't you realise that?"

It jolted her. She hadn't realised it. Hadn't even thought of it. Yet she'd seen the hurt she'd given him, was watching the pain of her rejection working through him now as she pleaded her case.

"The power goes both ways," he said less harshly. "It's up to both of us not to abuse it."

She rubbed at her forehead. "I don't know what to do. The baby..." She looked down at her stomach, touched it tentatively. "It's still unreal to me as mine.

Maybe I'm not maternal. I wanted it to belong to your family. I don't think I know how to be a mother. My own mother…'' She raised anguished eyes. ''…She was too frightened of my father to stand up for us.''

''It only takes love, Amy. Freely given.'' He grimaced. ''Maybe your mother didn't feel free to give it. But there's no reason you can't. At least to our child.''

Freely given…he'd said that to her before…the night they'd made the baby…their baby. She wished she could feel good about it, that it wasn't some kind of a trap for either of them. Maybe that would come. She hoped so. She needed to feel good. Good enough, anyway.

Jake still didn't know all he had to know, and she had to tell him. No more lies. No evasions. Her eyes ached with the need to reach him as she said, ''I do want you, Jake. I've wanted you for so long… I said I didn't want to go to bed with you but that was another lie. I lied because I didn't want you to know how much I had thought about it, how much I wanted it. Wanted you…''

She could read no reaction from him. He was completely still. Whether he was absorbing what she said or shutting it out she couldn't tell. She felt drained from the effort of unburdening herself to him, yet the compulsion to draw him back to her would not let her rest.

''Today, when you kissed me under the mistletoe… I wanted to believe what you made me feel was forever. It meant…too much. It scared me again. And then you said…it was only a Christmas kiss…''

''No,'' he denied vehemently. ''I said a man was entitled to kiss a woman standing under a mistletoe on Christmas day.''

"So I screwed that up, too," she said helplessly. "I guess I've made it too hard for you to believe me now."

"What's too hard for me to believe, Amy?"

Not too hard. Impossible. But she said it anyway.

"I love you, Jake."

It was true. She loved everything about him, loved him so much it hurt. Her heart was bleeding with all she felt for him. And it hurt all the more because he hadn't said he loved her. He wasn't saying it now, either. He just stood there, staring at her with seemingly unseeing eyes.

Maybe he didn't love her and was shocked by her confession. She'd assumed...but it could have been his ego hurt by her blanket rejection, not his heart. Why hadn't she thought of that? Because she needed... Dear God! She *needed* his love. *She couldn't marry him without it.*

"Jake..." His name scraped out of her convulsing throat. She swallowed hard. Her hands lifted in agitated appeal. "...If you don't love me..."

He moved then. Before Amy could take a breath she was wrapped in his arms and held so close she could feel his heart beating and his warmth flooding through her. She wrapped her own arms around his neck, buried her face against his broad shoulder, and hung on for dear life as tremors racked her body and her mind slipped into meltdown, knowing only that Jake had taken her back, he was holding her safe, and they were together again.

He rubbed his cheek against her hair, tenderly soothing. "Don't be frightened of me. Not ever, Amy," he said, his voice furred with passionate feeling. "If you'll just open your heart to me, I'll listen. We'll work things out together. That's how it should be.''

He'd forgiven her. The relief of it went through her like a tidal wave.

''Maybe I should have spoken…instead of holding back,'' he went on, his own torment pouring out. ''I guess we all try to protect ourselves from hurt. You'd been with Steve for so long… I was wary of a rebound effect. I wanted you free and clear of him, Amy, before I told you how I felt.''

How could she blame him? She'd given him so little to work on.

He sighed, his warm breath caressing her ear. ''I've loved you for a very long time. I can't imagine not loving you.''

He loved her.

It wasn't just for the baby.

It wasn't only the pull of physical chemistry.

He loved her.

The wonderful surge of energy that shot through Amy pushed her head up. She wanted—needed—to see. There was no mistake this time. No misreading. The molten gold in his eyes glowed with such rich depth of feeling, she knew instinctively this was only the tip of a river that flowed through every part of him.

''But I do need some love back from you without having to fight for it,'' he pleaded, searching her eyes for it. ''Do you understand?''

''Freely given,'' she whispered, awed by the strength of his giving.

''Yes.''

She didn't hesitate. She went up on tiptoe, pulled his

head down to hers and kissed him with all the passion his giving had released. A storm of passion. Years of pent-up feeling, freed at last, to be expressed, revelled in with joy and love and the deepest, most intense pleasure. No fear. Not the tiniest hint of fear or worry or doubt about anything. He loved her. She loved him. And the baby made a beautiful bond between them.

She took him to bed with her, showing him it was her choice, her desire, her wish to share everything with him, openly and honestly, and they made love for a very long time. There was no need to stop and every need to experience and learn all they wanted to learn of each other. The wonder of touching—touching without any inhibitions—was incredibly marvellous.

Jake was the most magnificent man. In every way. She adored him. And he adored her right back…sensually, sexually, emotionally. And when he kissed and caressed her stomach so lovingly, and she saw the happiness and pleasure in his eyes at the thought of her carrying his baby inside—their baby—she suddenly felt an intense wave of love for the life they had created, Jake and her together…their child…who would be brought up with love…freely given.

Instead of being dark and fearful and threatening, the future now shone with so much glorious promise.

Except…

"Jake!" In a rush of agitation, she lifted his head up.

"Mmh…" He smiled at her, his eyes dancing with teasing wickedness. "Can't I do what I want with you now?"

"Yes, but…" She sighed. "Your mother doesn't like me, Jake. She won't approve of us marrying."

"Ah!" He sobered into serious speculation. "I suspected something had gone on between you today. So what did?"

Amy grimaced at the unpleasant memory. "Your mother thinks I'm loose...living with Steve...not marrying him. She said my mother would have advised me it wasn't good. Wasn't right."

"She spoke out of ignorance, Amy," he said soothingly. "That can easily be fixed."

"It was like she was warning me off you, Jake."

"No." He gave his quirky smile. "Just warning you off living with me. She got upset about me giving you the apartment."

"What?"

"Okay..." He rolled his eyes. "I've been a bit devious, but it was for your own good, Amy."

"This is your apartment?" she squeaked. The colours used in the decor...his knowledge of her garage...

"I just wanted you away from any memory of Steve, so I fixed it with Ted Durkin and..."

"You made up all those conditions?"

"Well, the rent was too steep so I had to bring it down in a way you'd accept."

"And Ted Durkin was in on it?" She remembered her suspicion at the time, the suspicion she'd dismissed because of Ted Durkin's manner.

"He helped me make up a credible cover story."

"Oh!" She didn't know whether to feel outraged or...beautifully taken care of.

"Anyhow, Mum thought I was plotting to set you up as my mistress. But I wasn't, Amy. I truly wasn't. Marriage was always on my mind."

She laughed, suddenly remembering something else. "You just wanted to get me where you wanted me." Her eyes danced back at his.

"Precisely," he agreed, completely unabashed.

And she laughed some more, all the doubts of the past behind her.

"Mum probably thought, because you'd lived with Steve, you might choose to do that with me, too, so she was trying to steer you straight." He heaved an exasperated sigh. "She just can't keep out of things."

Amy sobered up. "I'm afraid I said some harsh things to her, Jake. About you and your women. Sorry, but…" She shook her head regretfully. "I was really quite rude, cutting her off when she tried to defend you."

He shrugged. "All's well that ends well, Amy. I'll call her now, fix it up."

His confidence amazed her. He leaned over, picked up the bedside telephone, dialed, listened, then said, "It's Jake, Ruth. Is Mum still there?"

He sighed as his sister apparently rattled on.

"Never mind that, get Mum for me." He smiled at Amy. "Ruth's all excited about seeing us kissing. She knows how I feel about you."

"Do they all?" Amy asked curiously.

"More or less. I'm no good at hiding things from my family," he confessed.

Then he'd be no good at hiding things from her anymore, either, Amy happily decided. Not that he was trying to. She thought fleetingly of Steve who'd clam up like an oyster whenever she'd tried to dig anything out of him. It was so different with Jake, ecstatically different.

"Mum?"

Apparently his mother rattled on to him, too. His family were certainly great talkers. Which was good. Great! Nothing repressed or suppressed.

"No, you haven't ruined everything." His eyes twinkled at Amy. "In fact, things couldn't be better. Amy loves me and she wants to marry me. Except she thinks you don't approve of her."

Another long speech which Jake interpreted for Amy as it went on.

"Mum is very sorry...she didn't mean to give that impression...she thinks you're beautiful...she thinks we're well suited...and you obviously have good sense and taste to choose me as your husband...she's relieved she didn't upset the applecart, so to speak...we're invited to lunch tomorrow...so she can show you how happy she is about us...is that okay, Amy?"

She nodded.

"We'll be there, Mum." He grinned as he put the receiver down. "She says this is the best Christmas ever. The last one of her brood finally settling down." He laughed, all his shadows gone, too. "It certainly is the best Christmas for me, Amy."

"Me, too," she agreed, her heart brimming over with happiness.

Jake gathered her close and kissed her, and she stretched against him languorously, provocatively, wanting all of him again. He was not slow to oblige, and Amy exulted in the sense of belonging to him, not Jake the rake, *her* Jake, always and forever.

And she'd belong to his wonderful family, too.

No more being alone.

Not for her nor her baby.

Their baby.

The miracle of love, she thought, and gave herself up to it.

Freely.

CHAPTER EIGHTEEN

NEW Year's Eve...

Amy watched *Free Spirit* gliding through the water to the wharf. It was a beautiful yacht, long sleek lines, exuding luxury, glamour, no expense spared in design or amenities. Murmurs of excitement and pleasurable anticipation ran around the select group of Jake's clients as they waited to board.

Free Spirit...

The name reminded her of Steve. And his blonde. Tonight was their wedding night. But she was not going to drown herself. No way. She was going to have a wonderful night with Jake, a wonderful life with him, too. In fact, she was more free with Jake than she'd ever felt before.

The men in the group wore formal dinner suits, adding style and class to the festive evening. Amy couldn't help feeling pride in the fact that not one of them looked as handsome as Jake. He outshone them all. The strange part was, she didn't feel the least bit insecure about it. Jake had only to glance at her and she knew no other woman here—regardless of beauty or finery—held a candle to her, not in Jake's mind.

She smiled to herself, remembering the women's magazine with the article on exit signs. It was still in the bottom drawer of her desk at the office, still unread. No need to read it now. Or ever. Jake believed implicitly in the marriage vows. Absolute commitment. For better, for worse...until death do us part.

Since Christmas, she had seen so much more of his family, and they all shared the same attitude. They'd been brought up to view a good marriage as the most desirable state in life, with children as the blessed bonus. Not one of them had anything negative to say when Jake had made the announcement about the baby. Expressions of delight, congratulations, offers of help from all the women were instantly forthcoming. And Jake's mother could not have been nicer, only too happy to push wedding plans.

Amy shook her head over her initial impression of Elizabeth Rose Carter. Jake's mother was really a very generous person, wanting everything to be lovely and possibly a little too concerned that it be so. His father had more of an optimistic, let-it-be outlook, confident his children would work out what was best for themselves. Amy considered him a real darling.

As the yacht docked and two of the deckhands started sliding out the boarding ramp, Jake hooked Amy's arm around his and smiled at her. "Ready to start hostessing?"

"Lead on." she replied happily.

His smile turned quirky. "Actually you don't have to hostess. I've hired people to do the necessary."

"But you said..."

"I needed some excuse to get you on this cruise with me." His eyes sparkled wickedly. "It was my seduction plan. And I see no reason to change it."

She laughed, hugging him closer to her as they walked to the ramp.

"You know, Amy, you look stunning in red but I've got to say, that blue you're wearing completely knocks me out." he declared decisively.

"You really like this outfit?" It was a long skirt and tunic in a soft, slinky, royal blue fabric, to which she'd added an ornate silver belt, silver shoes and silver jewellery.

His eyes gleamed gold. "You give it the magic of the night, my love."

"Mmh...keep up that seductive talk and who knows where it may get you?"

He laughed.

They were both of them bubbling with good humour as they preceded their party onto the yacht. A flight of steps led up to the main sundeck, an outdoor entertainment centre with a long bench lounge, table, chairs. Two hostesses hovered by a bar table which had been set up with wines, beer, fruit juice, iced water.

"Champagne, sir?" one of them instantly asked Jake, her eyes feasting on his every feature.

"Two, thank you." he replied, indicating Amy be served first.

Jake in control, and not the least bit interested in other women's interest, Amy observed. As he'd once said to her, any amount of interest was futile when it wasn't returned.

They moved to a position by the door leading in to the formal saloon, ready to greet everyone as they passed through to check out the luxurious appointments of the yacht.

In the saloon, three long deeply cushioned sofas, their cream upholstery trimmed with terracotta piping, were positioned around a polished granite coffee table, graced by an artistic floral arrangement. Beyond it was the formal dining room, its black lacquered table surrounded by black leather chairs.

Below, there were two queen-size staterooms with full ensuites and two twin bedrooms with ensuites, as well, all of the rooms designer decorated. The rear deck featured a spa-pool, and the bridge deck above them provided more lounging space for a topside view of their cruising around the harbour.

Amy was ready with all the facts and figures about the yacht should anyone ask. Mostly, the clients and their guests wanted to see for themselves, passing by her and Jake after a few words, happy to explore and assess everything on their own.

"Jake, darling!"

Amy glanced back from chatting to one couple to find the voluptuous blonde who'd fallen on Jake at *The Watermark,* coming on strongly again... Isabella Maddison...red talons raised ready to grab and dig in.

The sight of Amy stepping back to Jake's side stopped her in mid-pounce. The feline green eyes flashed venom.

"Oh! I see you have your companion with you."

"More than that, Isabella." Jake informed her, sliding his arm around Amy's shoulders and bestowing a smile lit with very possessive love on her. "My wife-to-be. Amy has finally agreed to marry me."

"Finally?" Isabella echoed in shock.

"Yes." Amy confirmed, ostentatiously holding up her left hand where Jake had placed a magnificent solitaire diamond ring on her third finger. She wriggled her fingers to make it flash under Isabella's catty eyes. "I decided to haul him in for good. It's time we had a family."

"Well...congratulations." came the weak rejoinder.

"Do help yourself to champagne." Amy invited sweetly. "This is a cruise to really enjoy."

"Yes...thank you."

Off she moved in a daze and Amy couldn't help grinning at Jake.

His wolf eyes gleamed. "You *were* jealous of her that day at *The Watermark.*"

"I could have scratched her eyes out." Amy admitted.

"I should have raced you off to bed that afternoon."

"You can do it tonight instead."

"Oh, I will. I will." he promised her. "Though I doubt we'll make it as far as the bed."

Which put Amy in such a high state of sexual arousal, she barely tasted the gourmet food circulated by the hostesses; smoked salmon with a sprinkling of caviar, swordfish wrapped in Chinese spinach, little cups of sweet lamb curry and rice, deep-fried corn fritters, tandoori chicken kebabs. She tried them all, wanting to experience everything about tonight, but her awareness of Jake was uppermost.

It was a beautiful evening, a clear sky filling with stars as it darkened, only a light breeze ruffling the water, the warmth of the long summer day still lingering in the air.

The harbour was almost a maze of yachts, all sorts of small crafts, pleasure boats, the tall ships that had sailed in from around the world, ferries trying to weave through them all.

Crowds had gathered at vantage points around the foreshores, some of them virtually hanging on cliffs, clinging to rocks, waiting to see the fireworks display. It seemed as though all of Sydney had come out to watch the spectacle and celebrate New Year's Eve together.

The captain positioned *Free Spirit* mid-harbour, quite close to Fort Denison, giving a centre-stage view of the Opera House and the great Coat-hanger bridge which would be highly featured by the fireworks. As twilight sunk into the darkness of night, most of the guests moved up to the top deck, Jake and Amy with them. The display was scheduled to begin at nine o'clock, so families could enjoy it before children became too tired.

Amy leant against the waist-high railing. Jake stood behind her, his arms encircling her, holding her close, letting her feel his arousal, exciting her with it. There might have been only the two of them, alone together. Everyone was looking skywards, waiting for the darkness to light up with colour.

Then the fireworks began, shooting up from the great stone pylons that supported the bridge—huge explosive bursts of stars, balls of brilliant colour growing bigger and bigger before showering the sky with a brilliant rain of sparks, the whole skyline erupting in a wildly splendid mingling of reds and blues and greens and gold and silver. It was magical, glorious, totally captivating. It went on and on, becoming more and more surprising, stunning, fantastic. The whole span of the bridge came alight, streams of gold pouring down to the water far below it.

"What are you thinking?" Jake murmured in her ear.

"I was thinking of our wedding night and how it will feel." Amy whispered.

"How do you imagine it will feel?"

"Like this, Jake. Like this."

Suddenly, flashing across the huge coat hanger arch were the two curved lines of a smiling mouth, outlined in brilliant gold.

"Yes." Jake breathed in awe. "Just like that."

Amy's heart swelled with love and happiness and wonder.

A smile...

The smile of fulfilment...

On their wedding night.

THEIR WEDDING DAY

Emma
DARCY

CHAPTER ONE

ROWENA COULDN'T LET go without putting up a fight. A seven-year marriage didn't end overnight. There had to be some way to fix it, some way to stop what was happening. She had to see for herself this woman who had turned Phil's heart so cold to her and their children. She had to know what she was up against.

Despite the steady determination she had fostered from their home in Killarney Heights to Phil's work place at Chatswood, nerves fluttered sickeningly through Rowena's stomach as she drove into the basement car park of the Delahunty building. Her eyes quickly scanned the row of reserved spaces for staff. She didn't want Phil to be here. If someone told him she had come, he might try to prevent her from confronting the situation head on.

His red Mazda convertible was nowhere in sight. Rowena breathed a long, tremulous sigh of relief. As she manoeuvred the family Ford sedan into a parking bay, it suddenly slid through her mind that Phil might have lied to her about the flashy sports car being an impulse buy. Had he been re-imaging himself to impress the other woman? If so, what kind of love needed sexy status symbols?

Rowena wouldn't concede it was love, no matter what Phil said. This was another one of his flirtations, an ego boost that had somehow gone too far, probably pushed by the woman. Phil was a very attractive man. He earned a high income as Delahunty's chief property buyer. He was a catch in most women's eyes.

But she was his wife, and the flirtations had never meant anything before. A bit of fun. Phil had always assured her of that. Although it hadn't been fun for her, and it certainly wasn't fun now.

The shock announcement last night that he was leaving her for another woman, leaving her and their children and their home, had been so devastating she had barely been able to think, let alone try to change his decision. She hadn't even suspected their marriage was at risk.

It shouldn't be. Not when they had shared so much together, had so much together. Rowena would not accept what was happening. Not without a fight.

Some shallow infatuation…that was all it could be. Propinquity at the office. She had to believe that. She had to. Or seven years of her life lost their meaning.

She switched off the engine and checked her reflection in the driving mirror. Hours of weeping had robbed her green eyes of any sparkle, but at least the skilfully applied make-up concealed the shadows under them. Her eyelashes were long enough and thick enough to veil the slightly puffy lids.

The ruby-red lipstick looked rather stark against her pale skin but she had read in last Sunday's newspaper that vibrant shades were part of power dressing and gave a woman clout. Rowena was not about to appear wimpish to her rival. She might be a housewife but she was no walkover.

She brushed her fingers across the fringe that kept the thick curtain of her black hair from falling over her face. It needed a trim. Maybe she should have done something dramatic like getting her hair cut into a short-cropped style, make Phil take a second look at her, but he had always said he liked her hair long. The shoulder-length bob with the soft, razor-cut wisps that framed her face did suit her, and she had washed and blow-dried it to shiny perfection.

She fiddled with the red and green silk scarf she had tied around her neck to add some bold colour to her navy suit, then told herself she was dithering for no good reason and alighted from the car. She looked as good as she could in the circumstances. She hadn't let herself go. Her figure was slightly more rounded, more womanly than it had been before she had had children, but she certainly wasn't sloppy.

Whatever Phil had told his other woman about her, she was about to come face to face with the truth, Rowena thought, holding grimly to her purpose as she locked the car and turned to walk to the elevators. She checked her watch. Eleven-thirty. Time enough to say all she wanted to say before the lunch break.

A classy BMW swept into the car park and took the space beside the elevators. Rowena froze. It had to be Keir Delahunty, the one man whose path she least wanted to cross, especially today of all days!

It was difficult enough to come to terms with the fact that Keir was Phil's boss and always being mentioned when Phil talked about his work. She wished the job at Delahunty's had never come up. Or been won by some other applicant. Anything to be spared the connection to Keir and the memories he evoked.

No matter how better off they were financially from Phil's move to Delahunty's, it had been disastrous in every other sense, Rowena reflected miserably. First the unsettling effect of having Keir on the fringe of her life, and now this woman threatening her marriage. Having to face

both of them was too much this morning. Better to go back
to her car and wait until Keir had gone.

His car door opened, head and shoulders rising above
the bonnet. There was no mistaking those broad shoulders
and the thick dark hair. She started to turn away, feeling
agitated at the loss of time, but more agitated at the thought
of being caught with Keir Delahunty and having to share
an elevator with him. Did he know what was going on between Phil and another one of his employees?

"Rowena…"

Her heart stopped. No avoiding him now. He'd seen
and recognised her. He'd recognised her instantly at the
company Christmas party a year ago, despite not having
seen her since she was seventeen. Their association had
been too long, too close—all her childhood and adolescent
years—for him to forget her face. And, of course, there
were other things that were unforgettable, however much
one might want to block them out.

But she mustn't think about that now. She had to come
up with some bright small chat to get her through the next
few minutes. She took a deep breath to steady herself and
turned to him with what she hoped was a surprised smile.

"Keir…" She forced her legs into resuming their walk
towards the elevators. He remained by his car, clearly waiting for her and expecting some polite exchange between
them. "How is everything going for you?" she asked.

"Fine! And you?"

She ignored that question in favour of concentrating
on him. A brilliant architect and an astute property de-
veloper, Keir Delahunty had not let the grass grow under
his feet over the last few years. While he'd established
a highly reputable name on the northern side of Sydney
Harbour, he was now spreading his business interests to
other parts of the city.

"I loved your design for the town houses at Manly," she said with genuine admiration. "Phil showed me through them. They've all been sold already, haven't they?"

"Yes. They went quickly." He smiled, and in his eyes was the warm appreciation of a man who liked what he heard. It surprised her when he remarked, "You look very chic this morning."

"Thank you. It's kind of you to say so."

It was a boost to her confidence. If Keir Delahunty thought her attractive today, she had certainly covered up the ravages of last night's despair. Not that she welcomed such a personal comment from him. It was far too late, with far too much water under the bridge for her to want to be reminded of the attraction—the love on her side—that had been so cruelly severed eleven years ago.

He'd been handsome at twenty-four but he was even more impressive now, exuding the kind of effortless assurance and authority that came with a long line of successes in his chosen field. The terrible injuries he'd sustained in the accident that had killed her brother had left no lasting mark on him. He stood tall and strong and moved with the easy coordination of an athlete in top condition. Not for him the consequences that had torn her family apart.

Was he aware that she was facing a more immediate, more personal family break-up? Had Phil been indiscreet in pursuing this office affair? Why had Keir made a point of stopping to speak to her?

"I'm afraid you're in for a disappointment if you've come to see Phil. I left him to do a valuation of a warehouse at Pyrmont. He won't be back until well after lunch."

The information was welcome. "Thank you, but it's someone else I want to see," she said, her inner tension bringing a brittle tone to her voice.

Keir's deep brown eyes scanned hers sharply as she

drew level with him. Had he sensed something wrong? She quickly moved towards the closest elevator, acutely conscious of him falling into step beside her. He pressed the up button. The doors slid open immediately, much to Rowena's relief. Another minute at most and she could escape from his disturbing interest.

A Christmas holly decoration was pinned to the back wall of the elevator. Christmas only ten days away. How could Phil leave her and the children at such an important family time? And the woman... She must be young and thoughtless and selfish to ask it of him. Or didn't she know about the children? She soon would, Rowena vowed.

"It's been a year since we last met," Keir remarked casually, gesturing for her to enter the compartment ahead of him. "I was looking forward to seeing you at the company Christmas party last Friday. Was there a problem with the children?"

A tide of heat swept up Rowena's neck and scorched her cheeks. Phil had lied to her about that, too, telling her the party was limited to staff only this year. She moved slowly to the rear of the elevator, hoping Keir hadn't noticed her embarrassment.

"I had another engagement," she said, instinctively covering up her husband's deception. It was too humiliating to admit. She didn't want to encourage any enquiries about the children, either. That was too close to all she had to contain.

"I wondered if you were avoiding me," Keir said quietly.

Such loaded words.

They pressed on Rowena's heart and constricted her chest. Why now? she railed desperately. She didn't need this on top of everything else she had to contend with. Pride forced her to swing around and face him as he followed her into the compartment.

"Why on earth should you think that?" she asked with what she hoped was credible astonishment.

His swift scrutiny was offset by a shrug. "Because of Brett's death. You could have ended up blaming me, as your parents did."

"You know I didn't. I visited you in hospital."

His eyes seemed to take on a piercing intensity. "Did you receive my letter, Rowena?"

She stared at him in confusion. Only days after Brett's funeral Keir had been flown to the United States for highly specialised corrective surgery, and that had been the end of any contact between them.

"When?" The word sounded like a croak from her throat.

"I wrote from the clinic in California. You didn't reply."

She shook her heard. "There was no letter."

He frowned. "I thought...assumed..."

"Well, it doesn't matter now, does it?" she cut in.

There was simply no point in a post-mortem over what might have been. Keir could have written again if she'd been really important to him. Or looked her up when he came home all repaired and fit to pick up his life. The past was gone. To open that sealed compartment and invite the old pain out into the open was more than she could handle. It was the present she had to deal with, and Keir was delaying her for no good purpose.

She forced a smile to mitigate any offence in the abrupt snub. "Would you press the button for reception, please?"

With a look of ironic resignation he turned to the control panel, lifted a finger, then unaccountably hesitated, passing over the button she had requested and pressing the one for Close Doors. He then faced her with a direct inquiry.

"Whom have you come to see, Rowena? I know all my employees and the departments in which they work.

There's no need for you to stop at reception. I can direct
you to the floor you want."

It sounded friendly and helpful, but Rowena wished
she could die on the spot. She wanted to say it was none
of his business. The expression in his eyes told her it was
his business. Everything that happened in this building
was his business.

It was a bitterly capricious stroke of fate that her arrival in the car park had coincided with his. Here she was,
trapped with him in a confined space, his eyes asking her
for a direct reply. Even as she frantically sought some evasive explanation for her visit, the certainty came to her
that he knew why she had come and what she meant to do.

Maybe the affair had been carried on so blatantly it
was common knowledge throughout the whole building.
Rowena inwardly cringed at the thought. Then pride
clawed through the miserable weight of humiliation, pride
and a fierce maternal need to fight for her children's emotional security. She had done nothing wrong. What other
people thought did not matter when so much of real importance was at stake.

She aimed a direct appeal at the man who had the power
to stop her. "I've come to talk to Adriana Leigh."

He held her gaze for several fraught moments, then
slowly nodded. "Adriana works in an open floor area,
Rowena," he said gently. "I'm sure you'd prefer complete
privacy for your talk to her."

"I'm not exactly overwhelmed with choices," she confessed, her courage deflating at the idea of a public audience.

"May I suggest you use my office? I can call Adriana
to come there, and I guarantee you'll both be left alone
together to say whatever you wish to say."

Once again unruly heat burned into Rowena's cheeks.

His sympathy to her plight was somehow shaming, yet to reject it was self-defeating. "Does everyone know?" The painful question slid off her tongue before she could clamp down on it.

"There's been gossip."

She closed her eyes, swallowed hard. "How long...how long has it been going on?"

"I don't know, Rowena." He paused, then quietly added, "More than three months."

Phil had bought the sports car three months ago. Last night's despair pressed in again. But she had come to try for a different outcome, to salvage what might not be a total wreckage. She had to try. She would try. She mentally constructed a protective shell around herself and opened her eyes. Keir was watching her, waiting for her decision, his expression carefully neutral.

"Your offer is...very kind," she said with as much dignity as she could muster. "Thank you. I'll take it."

He turned to the control panel. The elevator started to rise. Rowena fought to keep her composure and her resolve. She watched the floor numbers light up above the doors. They were travelling to the top level of the building. Keir's eyrie, Phil called it. She would soon find out why.

"Why are you doing this for me, Keir?"

It was an irrelevant question. Silly to ask it, really. It put the situation on a personal footing, which was the last thing she wanted to invite or encourage with Keir Delahunty. Yet something inside her had wormed past common sense...perhaps a need for comfort from someone who cared about her. Although Keir was probably only thinking of saving his other employees on the open floor area from what could be an ugly, disruptive scene, causing more gossip and stopping work.

He looked at her, his face grave, his dark eyes intensely

focused on hers. "We were friends for a long time, Rowena. I remember it, even if you don't want to."

Friends…and lovers at the end. Did he remember that? Or had concussion from the accident wiped out the memory of the night before Brett was killed? She hadn't spoken of it when she'd visited him in hospital. They'd both been in shock over what had happened. She wondered what had been in the letter she hadn't received.

She searched his eyes for some hint of knowledge of the intimacy they had once shared. It didn't show. Maybe he had no recollection of it at all. Maybe that was why he had never come back to her. Maybe he simply remembered her as Brett's younger sister, who had once had a school-girl crush on him.

The elevator stopped. The doors opened. He waited for her to exit first. Courtesy. Consideration. A friend. Brett's best friend all those years through school and university. Like another brother to her until… But she mustn't think about *until*. She had to think about Phil. And this imminent encounter with Adriana Leigh.

She forced her legs to move. She was extremely aware of Keir at her side as he directed her to his private office. A friend. She needed a friend. It was so hard…so very hard…to stand alone.

CHAPTER TWO

KEIR'S OFFICE WAS an architectural wonder in itself. The outside wall was constructed of massive glass panels, which were angled to extend over half the rooftop. The room was flooded with natural light.

At one end was Keir's workstation—desk, computers, library, several big drawing boards on stands made of round metal tube with hydraulic lift for height adjustment. Rowena was familiar with the latter. Her brother, Brett, had owned one. She remembered her father getting rid of it, getting rid of everything that connected Brett to Keir Delahunty, photographs, books, postcards, university lecture notes.

Then there was the burning of the sympathy cards and letters that so traumatised her mother. Had Keir's letter from California been burnt, too? It had been impossible to even mention his name in those dark months after Brett's death.

Tears blurred her eyes, and she quickly turned to look at the display of models featured on shelves running along the inner wall. These were the buildings Keir had designed, an impressive testament to what he had achieved by himself. It made Rowena wonder if his work took first place in his life and that was why he hadn't married. Marriage didn't seem to be popular with high-powered career people. Easy-come, easy-go relationships probably suited their lifestyles better.

How different all their lives might have been if Brett had lived. He and Keir in the partnership they had planned, she and Keir...but that might not have happened anyway. Dreams didn't always come true.

At the opposite end to Keir's work area was a round table, furnished with contoured leather armchairs set on swivel bases. He ushered her to one of these seats, then excused himself to speak to his secretary, whose office they had bypassed.

Rowena was glad of the opportunity to sit down and re-concentrate her mind on the problem of Adriana Leigh. Yet it was difficult to come to grips with the idea of a woman she had never met, never seen. *I'll know more when she walks into this room,* Rowena assured herself, trusting instinct more than unsubstantiated guesses.

Her gaze drifted to the window view on the other side of the table. It was nothing dramatic, just blocks of homes on tree-lined streets stretching out over the suburb of Chatswood, streams of cars taking people to their chosen destinations, everyday lives going on as they invariably did, regardless of death, births, marriages.

And divorces.

Would it come to that for her?

An underlying sense of panic started churning through her stomach again. She didn't want to bring up three children alone. She remembered how hard it had been without a helpmate when Jamie was little. Phil had been so kind and generous, taking them both into his heart and life.

She had tried to be the best of all possible wives to him, although in her heart of hearts she had known she didn't feel for Phil what she had once felt for Keir. It was a different kind of love, less passionate, almost motherly in some ways. Despite being five years older than her, Phil could be boyish at times, wanting to show off, to be the centre of attention.

Looking back over the past year, Rowena had to acknowledge their marriage had become rather flat and routine. But surely every relationship had its highs and lows. It was a matter of working at it, being committed, trying to make it as good as it could be. Both parties were responsible for that. She didn't understand why this was happening to her. What had she done that was so wrong?

The sound of the office door opening snapped her mind to the immediate present. Keir returning, having summoned the woman she would soon be facing. He looked so big and powerful, a rock to lean on, and Rowena ached for the support that his caring seemed to offer, yet she knew she couldn't afford to let Keir close to her. It could only muddle everything far more than it was already muddled.

Keir didn't know he had left her pregnant eleven years ago. He knew nothing of the son she had given birth to nine months after the fatal accident that had destroyed so much. She had come to believe he didn't want to know, long before she had married Phil.

Whether that was true or not, it was not possible to change the course of events that had taken place. Phil had legally adopted Jamie. To all intents and purposes, Phil was Jamie's father. It was best for everyone if it stayed that way.

Nevertheless, Rowena allowed herself the indulgence of really studying Keir for the few seconds it took him to walk down the room, noting the likenesses to her son...*his* son.

Deeply socketed eyes, although Jamie's irises were hazel, a mixture of her green and Keir's brown. The hairline was strikingly similar with a cowlick at the left temple. Jamie's upper lip was softer, fuller, more like hers, and the shape of his face was rounder, less hard-boned. Perhaps as Jamie got older, his jawline would firm into the same mould as Keir's, but that was not obvious yet.

Her gaze skated down the perfectly tailored grey business suit to the stylish leather shoes on Keir's feet, feet she knew had longer second toes than the big ones. The mark of a fast runner, Keir had laughingly told her. Jamie had them, too, and he was the best sprinter in his age group at school.

"Rowena..."

She sighed and lifted her gaze.

"Would you like coffee brought in?"

She shook her head.

"Is there anything else I can do for you?"

"No. I'm grateful to you for this chance to get things straightened out, Keir. This is all I want. I won't be making a nuisance of myself."

"I'd never consider you a nuisance, Rowena," he said seriously.

"You know what I mean." She grimaced. "I don't intend to subject Delahunty's to a series of hysterical scenes."

"If I can be of any service to you, at any time, please call me, Rowena. I'll do all I can for you," he assured her.

She could see the deep sincerity in his eyes, and it hurt. Unbearably. *Where were you when I needed you?* she cried in silent anguish. *It's too late now. Our lives have moved on.*

A courtesy knock on the door heralded its opening. Rowena shot to her feet and stepped away from the table, inadvertently moving close to Keir, who merely turned to greet the newcomer. She wasn't seeking his support or protection, and wasn't aware of how they looked together as Adriana Leigh entered the office.

"Good morning, Mr. Delahunty," she said with a bright, winning smile. Her elegance, sophistication and complete self-assurance were heart-joltingly evident. Not a younger woman. Very much a woman of considerable worldly experience. Rowena was spared a flick of curiosity, but the full beam of Adriana Leigh's concentration was on Keir as she added, "What can I do for you?"

She was the kind of woman who was always aware of men and knowingly watched for her impact on them. Rowena recognised that instantly. She also knew instinctively there would be no tapping any vein of sympathy or guilt. In a roomful of women, this woman would be bored.

"I'd be obliged if you'd give some time to Mrs. Goodman, Adriana," Keir answered, his clipped tone making the request more of an order. "Rowena, this is Adriana Leigh."

The bright smile was only briefly jolted. She batted her eyelashes at Rowena. "How do you do, Mrs. Goodman?" A honeyed voice, dripping with confidence. With barely a pause, she inquired, "Did Phil ask you to come?"

It was a bold and subtle sliding in of the knife.

"No. It was my decision," Rowena replied, silently challenging the other woman to make something belittling of that.

Adriana Leigh raised perfectly arched eyebrows at Keir. "This is rather different from the usual bounds of work requirements, Mr. Delahunty," she pointed out, maintaining her decorum while questioning the propriety of his authority in what they all knew to be a personal matter.

"Sometimes extraordinary situations arise," Keir answered smoothly. "I understood your position as personal secretary to one of my executives requires an ability to handle delicate matters with courtesy and patience." He paused. Was there a threat left hanging? "However, if you feel unable…"

"Not at all, Mr. Delahunty. As you say, I am used to dealing with such situations."

"I thought you would be." A touch of dry irony.

"I'll do my best to give Mrs. Goodman satisfaction," she said with her own touch of irony as she started forward, showing no further reluctance to join them by the table. A smart, intelligent career woman would do no less after Keir had put her skills in question.

Rowena concentrated on assessing everything about Adriana Leigh before they were left alone together. She had long, toffee-coloured hair, liberally streaked with blonde and deliberately styled in a casually tousled look. It was not only suggestive of a recent tumble in bed but a ready receptiveness to repeating the pleasure at any time.

She wore a long-sleeved, transparent cream blouse with a lace-trimmed, silk camisole underneath. Her full breasts jiggled freely. Her hips swayed, their voluptuous curve from a small waist emphatically outlined by a tan gaberdine figure-hugging skirt that was buttoned down to thigh level and left free to swing from a side split. She wore high heels. High, high heels.

This woman exuded sexuality, flaunted it, and Rowena doubted any man would be a hundred percent proof against it. There was no problem in understanding the attraction for Phil. The question was how deeply did Adriana Leigh have her claws into him?

"Rowena." Keir took her hand, pressing it to pull her attention to him. "I'll be in my secretary's office. You have only to call me."

Part of Rowena's mind registered his earnest concern and caring. She felt the warmth and strength of his touch. She had a craven urge to cling to it, but the purpose that had brought her here made it inappropriate. Badly inappropriate. Didn't he realise that?

"I'm all right, Keir. Thank you," she said in deliberate dismissal.

He gently squeezed her hand before letting it go. Adriana noticed it. Her amber eyes gleamed feline derision at Rowena before she turned her gaze to watch Keir make his departure. The moment the door was closed behind him, she opened hostilities.

"How did you come to be so cosy with our Mr. Delahunty?"

Rowena ignored the dig. "Do you love my husband, or is he simply another conquest to you?" she asked with quiet dignity.

It won a flicker of surprise. "Well, you're certainly direct."

"I'd appreciate a direct answer."

Adriana led from the chin. "I love Phil and he loves me and there's nothing you can do about it."

"You must have known he was married."

"So what? *He* knew he was married, too. I didn't take anything from you. You'd already lost it. Phil came to me." Gloating triumph. Power. No sense of guilt whatsoever.

"Are you married?"

"No."

"Divorced?" Perfect and obviously expensive make-up gave Adriana Leigh's face a youthful glow, but Rowena had no doubt this woman was in her thirties, possibly older than Phil, who was thirty-three.

"No." She was amused by the questioning.

"Children?"

Her laughter was mocking. "Two abortions." There was a hardness in her eyes as she added, "I won't go down that road again."

It made Rowena wonder if previous lovers had let Adriana down, and she felt a twinge of sympathy, remembering the pain of being left without Keir's support when she was pregnant with Jamie. The sympathy was short-lived. There was none coming from Adriana for the situation Rowena faced.

"Has Phil ever mentioned our children?"

She shrugged. "Emily is five and Sarah is three. They're young enough to get over the separation without any lasting trauma. The boy is old enough to look after himself. It's not as though their father has played a great role in their lives."

"Is that what Phil told you or what you want to assume?"

"I know the hours Phil works," she said smugly.

"Since *you* entered his life." That truth was obvious now. Rowena silently castigated herself for not realising Phil's long hours and overnight trips could have another purpose besides work. How complacent she had been to attribute it to ambition!

"Doesn't his desire to stay with me tell you something?' Adriana taunted.

Rowena hated her mocking amusement. She might be guilty of complacency, but she hadn't gone out hunting another woman's husband to fill in the lonely hours. It took all her willpower to keep her voice steady, her demeanour unruffled. She would not give her antagonist the satisfaction of goading her out of control.

"I suppose you think you've rearranged his priorities. For the short term," Rowena emphasised, wanting to shake Adriana Leigh's complacency. "Passion does tend to burn out."

"You don't know much about men, do you?" Pitying condescension. "They have two brains. Keep the one below the belt satisfied and you can bend the other any way you like."

Such heartless calculation sickened Rowena. Phil preferred *this* woman to her? "If that's the case, I find it odd that you haven't been able to hold onto one of the many men you've obviously had in the past," she retaliated.

"I haven't wanted to until now."

"Then your theory hasn't exactly been tested, has it?" Rowena pointed out, to no effect whatsoever.

"Face it, darling, you're beaten. You've never satisfied Phil as I do. That's a fact." The cat's eyes glittered down Rowena's classic navy suit and up again. "I daresay you're too much of a lady."

"There's more to a relationship than sex," Rowena declared with conviction.

"What?"

"Companionship, sharing goals and achievements, caring about each other, understanding…"

Adriana laughed. "Tell that to a sex-starved man. And there's so many of them around. Especially fathers."

The unexpected singling out of fathers bewildered Rowena. She stood, speechless, as enlightenment came in a shower of scorn.

"You dedicated mothers tend to focus all your energy on your children. Your attention is divided. You get tired. You have headaches. And the door opens for another woman to give a man back what his children have taken from him. Quite suddenly he doesn't give a damn about his children any more. He wants a woman in his life, not a mother."

"I'm sure that's what you'd like to think," Rowena said tersely, disturbed by Adriana's knowingness. Had Phil complained to her that his wife ignored his needs?

"I'm giving you some good advice for the next time around. The world is full of discontented married men."

"Why pick on Phil?"

"He was here. He's what I want. I'll keep him happy." Rowena dearly wanted to rattle Adriana's mind-battering confidence. A flash of intuition came to her. "Phil wasn't your first choice, though, was he?"

A pause. A flicker of wariness. Then a return to aggression. "He's my last choice, and I'll make it stick, so don't think you can muddy the issue."

Rowena pressed further. "You got a job here so you could be around Keir Delahunty and try to catch his interest. He's the bigger prize, isn't he? Only he didn't take the bait."

Her eyes narrowed with anger. "Did he tell you that?"

"You were still flashing availability signals at him when you came into this office. You'd drop Phil if Keir gave you any encouragement."

Adriana snorted. "That man is made of stone. Phil's much more my style, and he knows it. You can't put Keir Delahunty between us."

That was probably true, Rowena thought in painful frustration. It didn't matter how right her observation was about Adriana's motivations, Keir obviously had a fine sense of discrimination in judging women on the make and wasn't interested. Why on earth couldn't Phil see... But maybe Adriana was right about him feeling neglected, overlooked in favour of the children's needs.

What was the best balance for being both a wife and mother? And why was the onus on her? Shouldn't a good marriage be mutually supportive?

Her head spun between a confused sense of guilt and a sickening sense of having all her ideals betrayed. Coming here, speaking to this woman, was worse than futile. There was no help in it. None at all. If Phil wanted Adriana Leigh, then let him have her, she thought, resolution undermined by a tidal wave of deep hurt and disillusionment.

But what about the children?

"I take it you're not overly keen about the role of step-mother," she said flatly, trying to think of anything that might change the situation, might give Adriana pause for second thoughts about a future with Phil.

"You chose to have kids. They're your responsibility. Not mine."

"You honestly believe Phil will be happy about shutting them out of his life?"

"Put it this way. You needn't worry about any fight over custody. Phil may want to see the girls now and then, and I'll be happy to go along with that."

"You're forgetting Jamie."

Again she shrugged, as though the burden was not hers to shoulder. "Well, he's not really Phil's, is he?" she drawled meaningfully.

"Phil is the only father Jamie's known."

"Whose fault is that?"

Angry heat crept into Rowena's voice despite her resolution to keep cool. "Phil adopted Jamie as his son."

"When he was how old? Four?"

"Three."

"No difference. He was a little boy, not a baby. The feeling's not the same no matter how you want to dress it up. The boy is yours, not Phil's, and at his age, he's bound to be a sulky troublemaker."

Rowena could not trust herself to suppress her outrage at these callous sentiments. Her body was beginning to tremble. "Thank you," she said tightly. "I won't take up any more of your time."

"Thank you," Adriana returned snidely. "It's always interesting to meet the wife."

CHAPTER THREE

"MRS. GOODMAN HAS said all she wishes to say to me, Mr. Delahunty."

Adriana's light, almost flippant tone made Keir grit his teeth against an unwise snap. It would be unprofessional to reveal the strong antipathy he felt, knowing as he did that it was aroused by his sympathy for Rowena. He had no right to any personal involvement with this affair. It behove him to maintain some objectivity.

He unhitched himself from the edge of his secretary's desk in deliberate slow motion. The report he'd been trying to read was still in his hands, and he used it as a point of dismissal. "Thank you for your cooperation, Adriana."

"My pleasure."

"To give pain?" The biting, judgmental words were out before he could monitor them. At least he had the satisfaction of wiping the smug look off her face.

"I didn't ask for this meeting, Mr. Delahunty," she coolly reminded him.

"A matter of opinion, Adriana. It's my experience that changing people's lives incites retaliation, even when the change is innocently caused."

Rowena's parents had taught him that. Not that this self-obsessed woman would care what damage she wreaked in going after what she wanted. They were empty words to her.

"I don't want more company time wasted on gossip, Adriana," he went on, chilling her out of any further comment. "I'd advise you to keep your meeting with Mrs. Goodman entirely private. Do I make myself clear?"

"Perfectly, Mr. Delahunty. I appreciate your tact."

He nodded.

She left.

He turned to his homely, middle-aged secretary. "Same for you, Fay. No talk about this."

"Locked box," she replied, giving him her owl look.

The tense muscles in his face relaxed into a smile. He liked Fay Pendleton. She not only delivered everything he asked of her with a minimum of fuss and maximum efficiency, her wonderfully expressive face and dry sense of humour always amused him. As did her hair, which was burgundy with wide, blonde streaks at the moment. Every three months she experimented with a new colour combination. Grey, she had declared, was too dull for her.

"I'll check this later," he said, dropping the report she had prepared for him on her desk. "Would you make some coffee, Fay, and bring it in with the sandwiches as soon as they're delivered?"

"Will do."

He wasn't about to let Rowena go without any sustenance. She had probably been too wrought up to eat breakfast, and Adriana had undoubtedly gone for the kill. Rowena would be in no fit state to drive. She shouldn't be alone, either.

Keir reached the office door in a few quick strides. He didn't know if Rowena would welcome his company or not. He remembered the polite barrier she had maintained between them at last year's staff Christmas party. He had felt then that she wanted no part of him, and he had reluctantly respected her wishes. It was probably only the shattering effect of knowing her marriage was on the rocks that had allowed the old sense of familiarity to break through this morning. He hoped....

Well, he could only try.

As he entered the office and closed the door quietly behind him, he was intensely aware of the need to tread very carefully. Rowena had come to do what she could to save her marriage. She wanted—loved—Phil Goodman. She was not looking for another man in her life, certainly not in any close capacity.

She sat with her elbows on the table, her head in her hands, fingers pressed tightly to her temples. Pain, defeat...and there was nothing he could do about either. It flitted through his mind that Brett would have pummelled Phil Goodman, inflicting hurt for hurt to his little sister. Keir knew it would do no good in these circumstances, yet he found himself empathising with the urge to do violence. Rowena deserved to be valued. To be cast aside for a woman like Adriana Leigh...

Keir took a deep breath, unclenched his hands and headed down the room to offer what comfort he could. Maybe she would accept a shoulder to cry on. Maybe she would let him drive her home. Maybe there would come some time in the future when she could view him as a friend again. More than a friend.

He was acutely conscious of the hole in his life, the emptiness that no one had been able to fill since Rowena and Brett had been lost to him. A bond of long sharing and understanding had been broken, and the years since had only hammered home how precious and rare it had been. It was impossible to get Brett back, but Rowena...

Dared he lift her from that chair and enfold her in his arms?

She looked up.

Her beautiful green eyes were awash with tears.

There was no decision-making.

He simply did it.

CHAPTER FOUR

IT HAPPENED SO fast, Rowena was scooped from the chair and wrapped in Keir Delahunty's embrace before she could even begin to think it was wrong to have such intimate contact with him. Then the impact of his body against hers threw her into confusion.

She wasn't used to being held closely by any man but Phil. It had been so long since Keir had made love to her, yet she was instantly reminded of how it had felt with him. It made her acutely aware of both her sexuality and his.

Images of their youthful nakedness flashed into her mind. Her breasts, pressed flat to his broad chest, started prickling with disturbing sensitivity. Her thighs trembled with the shock of recognising the virile strength of his. Her back burned under the cocooning warmth of his arms. All normal thought processes were paralysed by sensations she was utterly powerless to stop.

One hand slid up to her neck, his fingers splaying through her hair as he gently pressed her head onto his shoulder. Her heart seemed to pound in her ears. The scent of some tangy aftershave lotion assaulted her nostrils. Her stomach contracted in sheer panic at the memories evoked.

"You don't have to fight the tears, Rowena," Keir murmured, his cheek resting against her head. "You can let out the grief with me. Just as you would with Brett if he were here."

Guilt that she no longer had a big brother? Sympathy for her pain? The tears were gone, shocked back to the well of despair that Keir's action had suddenly submerged. She shouldn't be feeling other things, but she was. And it was wrong. Terribly wrong!

Her mind shifted from one turmoil to another. Was Keir remembering other times when he'd held her, not as a surrogate brother but as a man who wanted her, needed her to be a woman with him?

She was not seventeen any more. She was well and truly a woman, an experienced woman who was in a highly vulnerable state, with her marriage on the rocks and her husband in love—or lust—with someone else. Did Keir think that made her available to him?

Why hadn't he married? What kind of man was he now? She didn't know. The meeting with Adriana had left her feeling she was a naive fool who didn't know anything!

It was as though all the foundations of her life had been ripped away. Was Keir a steady rock that she could cling to? Confide in? Or was there danger in trusting him, danger in trusting anybody?

His cheek moved, rubbing over her hair. His mouth—surely that was his mouth—pressing warmth…kisses! Her heart kicked in alarm. She jerked her head back and looked up. It wasn't brotherliness she saw in Keir's eyes. There was no soft sympathy. She caught a darkly simmering passion that triggered a tumultuous eruption of the doubts and fears Adriana had raised.

"Let me go!" she cried, pushing herself free of his embrace as he loosened it.

"Rowena…"

The gruff appeal fell on closed ears. Her eyes flared a

fierce and frightened rejection as she backed away from his trailing touch. "Adriana's right. Sex is all that matters with men."

"No," he denied strongly.

But Rowena took refuge in walking over to the glass wall beyond the table, putting a cold, safe distance between them, wrapping her arms around herself, hugging in the pain of hopeless disillusionment.

She was a married woman. It was wrong of Keir to pretend to offer brotherly comfort and then use the opportunity to change it to something else. Even though Phil... But that didn't excuse it. Keir must realise she had come to save her marriage if she could. For him to take advantage of her weakness at such a time placed him on the same moral level as Adriana Leigh.

"*She* would have had you." The words burst from her, the bitter irony of his behaviour being similar to Adriana's striking her hard. "Why didn't you take her on, Keir? She was handy, available..."

"Rowena, I care about you. I always have."

The soft answer stirred more turmoil. She clutched wildly at the first reason she could think of to disbelieve him. "Then why didn't you stop what was happening between Adriana and Phil?"

No answer.

She swung around to probe further. "Don't tell me you didn't know she fancied you, Keir. Even I saw the signals when she walked into this room."

His face tightened as though she had hit him, yet there was no backward step in the dark blaze of his eyes. "You want a husband that needs to be rescued from another woman?" he challenged, a sting of contempt in his voice. "Face it, Rowena. Phil isn't worthy of your love. If he really cared for you, Adriana wouldn't have had a chance with him."

Phil *had* cared for her. Rowena was not about to forget he had cared when Keir's so-called caring wasn't anywhere in touching distance. "Who are you to judge that? Maybe it's my fault. Maybe I didn't give him enough...enough——"

"Sex?"

Heat flooded up her neck and scorched her cheeks. It was too shaming to concede she must have left Phil dissatisfied in that area, yet it had to be true. She bit her lips, wishing she hadn't started this tasteless argument. Even Keir's mouth was curling in disgust.

"Sex isn't the glue that keeps a man and woman together, Rowena. It helps, but if other things are missing..." He paused, compelling her full attention. "You have so many desirable qualities, any man should consider himself fortunate to have you in his life."

Desirable. Is that how Keir saw her? Still? But he had no right. And she mustn't let herself get confused and distracted.

"The evidence is against it," she reminded him. "Phil wants to be with Adriana. Everything we've shared means nothing against what she gives him."

"She strokes his ego, Rowena," he said flatly. "Phil likes to be stroked. He can't have enough of it. He never will have enough of it. Surely you've recognised that weakness over the years."

"Then why did you hire him?" she demanded, trying to reject his clear-sightedness about Phil's vulnerability to flattery. It went against her ingrained sense of loyalty to accept it.

"He's good at his job."

"Why did you hire her?"

"I didn't. Phil did. He's entitled to choose the staff

that work with him. Usually it makes for a more effective team."

All perfectly reasonable. Rowena was left floundering in a quagmire of emotions with no outlet for them. A knock on the office door provided a welcome distraction.

A woman entered, pushing a traymobile. Either the silence or the palpable tension got to her. She paused, her eyes darting from Keir's rigid back to Rowena's face, obviously gauging the weather in the room and finding it dangerously volatile. She winced apologetically and started to retreat.

"It's all right, Fay. Bring it in," Keir commanded quietly. He turned to wave encouragement. "This is my secretary, Fay Pendleton. Mrs. Goodman, Fay."

"Pleased to meet you, Mrs. Goodman." The quick greeting was accompanied by a tentative smile.

"Yes. Thank you," Rowena returned jerkily, surprised by Keir's choice of secretary. Far from being a slickly sophisticated front person for him, this woman looked more like a homely pudding. Except for her hair. The rich burgundy colour with wide blonde bands had a definite touch of eccentricity.

The traymobile was swiftly wheeled to the table, and cups, saucers and plates were set out with deft efficiency. Black coffee was poured, milk and sugar placed handily, and a plate of artistically arranged sandwiches completed the service.

"Smoked salmon, turkey and avocado, ham and—"

"Thank you, Fay." Keir cut her off.

She gave Rowena a motherly look, her lively brown eyes kind. "Do try to eat."

"Fay..." Keir warned.

Rowena watched her leave, instinctively liking the woman and oddly comforted by the fact that she didn't emanate competitive sexiness. Not that it should matter what kind of woman Keir had close to him at work. It didn't, Rowena told herself. The contrast to Adriana Leigh was simply a relief.

The click of the door shutting behind Fay Pendleton jolted Rowena into realising she should have left, too. This brief hiatus didn't change anything. Coffee and sandwiches did not fix anything. In fact, they lent an absurd cloak of normality to a highly charged situation, one she should get out of right now before it developed into something worse.

She steeled herself to look at Keir again, thank him for the use of his office and escape from being alone with him any longer. With slow deliberation, she shifted her gaze from the door and met his squarely, determined to put an end to whatever he had in mind.

No matter what Phil had done, she was still married to him, and Keir had no right to be stirring feelings that should have been buried long ago. Buried along with her brother, Brett, because that had been the end of what they had shared together.

Whether he read her intention or not, Keir instantly forestalled any speech from her. "To answer your earlier question," he said in a tone of relentless pursuit, "I had no interest in Adriana because I don't care for manipulative people. I don't want to be with a woman whose responses aren't genuinely felt. It's a complete turn-off, regardless of how physically attractive and available she is."

"And I'm suddenly a turn-on?"

The tense words hung between them, loaded with too much to back away from. Rowena was appalled at having been goaded into such a provocative retort. Somehow Keir's supreme confidence in who and what he was diminished Phil as a man, and she resented it. She resented even more the idea that Keir might think he could just

step in and take advantage of her vulnerable state, letting
her know he found her desirable even if her husband no
longer did.

"No. Not suddenly," he answered quietly. "I doubt that
many people forget their first love."

The yearning for that simpler time was in his eyes, and
it hurt. It hurt because if he hadn't forgotten, he should
have done something positive about it when it had really
mattered. It hurt because it reminded her how naive and
trusting she had been, the faith she'd had that he would
come back to her and they'd make a life together.

It was he who had broken that faith, he who had dismissed his first love and put it behind him, and he had no
right to call on it now. It was Phil who had brought love
into her life again. Yet Phil was betraying that love, just
as Keir had.

"It doesn't mean anything," she said desolately.

"It does to me."

She couldn't believe him, not after all this time. He
might still be able to stir treacherous feelings in her, but
his feelings could only be shallow, a response to present
stimulus, nothing deep and lasting.

"How many years have we led separate lives, Keir?"

"We're still the same people, Rowena."

The burning conviction in his eyes riled her. "No, we're
not. I'm not," she stated very deliberately, her conviction
rising out of the pain of too many losses. *I'm scarred,* she
wanted to yell at him, but pride held her tongue.

There was a shift in his expression. A frown. A doubt.
"Do you really want Phil back, Rowena? Knowing what
you now know about him and Adriana?"

It stung raw wounds. "He's my husband. He married
me." *When you didn't.* "He's the father of my children,"

she added, then wished she had cut out her tongue before uttering those last words.

His face tightened. The sudden bleakness in his eyes smote her heart, awakening a painful guilt over the secret she had kept from him. His child…his son. But Keir had forfeited any right to Jamie. Phil was the only father Jamie had known, and Phil had been there for him, good to him. Only now… What should she do now? What if Adriana got her way and Phil didn't want to be bothered with Jamie any more?

Keir's gaze dropped to the table. He stepped over to it and lifted the milk jug. "Do you still have white with one sugar?" he asked without looking up.

"I don't want coffee," she said flatly, wishing he hadn't remembered how she liked it. The familiarity hurt. Everything hurt. She should go. Why did she feel this heavy reluctance to move? What could be gained by continuing such a disturbing dialogue with Keir?

He slowly returned the jug to the table, then lifted his gaze directly to hers, his eyes having gathered a piercing intensity. "Do you want me to try to take Adriana away from Phil?"

That he should even think of making such a move for her stunned Rowena. "You said you didn't like manipulative people."

"I don't. Sometimes fire can only be fought with fire." He shrugged. "If it means so much to you to get Phil back…"

"No. Not that way." She inwardly recoiled at the awful dishonesty of it.

"If you really believe your happiness lies with him…"

"It wouldn't work anyway. Adriana's not stupid, Keir. You shouldn't have taken my hand."

Hand…body… She flushed again at the response his

embrace had drawn from her. It wasn't fair that he could still affect her so deeply, so shatteringly.

"I'm sorry. I didn't mean to upset you," he said softly. Then with dry self-mockery, he continued, "I should have curbed my natural impulses."

"Maybe you meant no harm, but people put their own interpretations on things and reputations can be tainted. I don't want more trouble than I've got, Keir." She nodded to the door. "Your secretary could have come in while you were holding me. How would that have looked?"

She saw his eyes harden with weighing calculation. "You want Phil back," he said, as though planning how to achieve that end.

"I don't know what to do," she said miserably. She honestly didn't know how their marriage would work with the undermining spectre of adultery hovering between them, yet for the children's sake...

"It could do some good to jolt him out of taking you for granted."

"How?" she asked without hope. Adriana had left her with no hope.

"I'm his boss. Most people would consider me a highly eligible bachelor. Adriana certainly saw me in that light," he said sardonically.

"What has this to do with me?" She didn't follow his train of thought at all.

"Sometimes people don't appreciate the value of what they have until someone takes it over, especially someone in a higher position than themselves. If we make a point of being seen together, you could use me to make him jealous, Rowena," Keir suggested without batting an eyelid. "You might find that Phil will suddenly want you again."

"If you think I'd start an affair with you..." She was

shocked speechless. It simply wasn't in her to play tit for tat in the adultery game. And Keir thought he knew her?

"I don't expect you to jump into bed with me. We could obviously spend some time together. We used to be friends, Rowena," he pressed, giving her an appealing smile.

She stared at the smile. No, she thought, they couldn't be friends. They had moved beyond friendship. There was no doubt now that he remembered making love to her. And his attraction was far too potent. She'd be aware of him all the time. It would muddle her up. Hopelessly. And for what gain?

"I don't want to make Phil jealous. If he loses faith in my commitment... Don't you see? It all becomes too destructive. We'd have nothing left."

The smile died, swallowed up by a dark, blazing anger. "He doesn't deserve you."

"And you do?" The bubbling quagmire of emotions inside her erupted. "What about the women who've been in your life, Keir? The intimate relationships from which you've moved on. And on. Why didn't any of them stick? Did they mean as little as Adriana would if you seduced her away from Phil?"

"No." Hot colour raced across his cheekbones. He made a slashing gesture with his hand. "I wouldn't have touched Adriana. I was only trying to see what you wanted, Rowena."

"What about the others?" she pressed, wanting to know, needing to know how he treated the women he had made love to. "I won't believe you've been celibate all these years."

"Of course I've sought what I needed. No one wants to be alone," he justified with passion. "I tried. I tried," he repeated, then shook his head in anguished hopelessness. "There was always something missing."

"So you dismissed them from your life."

"No. They're still friends."

You dismissed me. "Well, I won't be your friend, Keir. I'll never be your friend," she decided, her hurt deepened by the thought she had been the least of his women, someone he hadn't bothered to contact after the trauma of the accident had come between them.

"Rowena, please." He stepped towards her, hands reaching out.

"Don't come any closer, Keir," she fiercely warned. "Don't touch me. Ever again."

"I want to help. I want to—"

"No! I suppose it's some kind of compliment that I'm still desirable to you, but that's all it ever was. Only sex. You don't know the meaning of the word love. Or commitment."

"That's not true." His eyes burned into hers as though he was focusing his whole life force on her heart and mind. "Is it my fault that the woman I loved married someone else? That the children I wanted with her are Phil Goodman's?"

Her heart stopped. Her mind reeled. The world tilted, then slowly straightened. Her path was deadly clear. In a voice that shook with the strength of irrefutable knowledge, with all the pain she had once suffered for him, she delivered her judgment on Keir Delahunty, her eyes green daggers, stabbing home the fatal truth.

"I waited years for you. Years of faith and hope that gradually crumbled into the inevitable reality that what we'd shared was not important to you. Years, Keir. Years before I married Phil Goodman. Who gave me what you didn't give."

That stopped him. There was no comeback to those blunt facts. With a sense of having put the record absolutely straight and with adrenaline running high, Rowena moved forward, scooped her handbag from the chair where it had rested since before Adriana had arrived, skirted the shell-shocked figure of her first love and headed for the door into the corridor that bypassed the secretary's office.

"Rowena, stop! For God's sake! This doesn't make sense."

She whirled as she reached the door. "Liar! Liar!" she hurled at him.

It silenced him.

She opened the door and left him behind.

If she had to leave Phil behind her, she would do that, too. She didn't need a man in her life whom she couldn't trust.

But what about the children?

CHAPTER FIVE

"WHEN IS DADDY coming home, Mummy?"

The unanswerable question. "I don't know, Emily," Rowena murmured as she bent to kiss her five-year-old daughter good night. Phil had not called her since he had left late last night, reinforcing his announcement that their marriage was over by walking out on her and going to Adriana Leigh.

"If it's soon, could I get up again? I want to show him my painting."

Emily was very much Daddy's girl, being Phil's first-born and favouring him in looks. Her fair hair was long, as her father liked it, and her blue eyes looked hopefully at Rowena, making her heart ache with the uncertainties that lay ahead of them.

"Darling, your painting is pinned to the corkboard," Rowena reminded her. "Daddy will see it when he comes home. Go to sleep now."

She dropped a soft kiss on her forehead. Emily sighed, disappointed, and Rowena wondered how scarred her young life would be without the father she adored on hand to provide her with the ever-ready support children needed.

Then Emily's little arms wound around Rowena's neck and she planted a big wet kiss on her cheek and said, "I love you, Mummy," and Rowena's heart turned over. Perhaps having a mother was enough if the bond was kept strong. In today's world there were many single parents coping successfully with the problems she would face if Phil didn't come back.

"I love you too, Emily," she whispered. "Good night."

Emily snuggled into her pillow, and Rowena tucked the bedclothes around her, fighting back the tears that pricked her eyes. She quickly crossed the room to check Sarah, who had dropped asleep during their bedtime story. It was fortunate that today had been one of her two days a week at a local playgroup. Sarah was quite a precocious three-year-old, and Rowena had been grateful to have her bright little girl occupied with other children while she grappled with grim realities.

A strand of long brown hair was still curled around the finger that habitually twiddled with it. Her thumb rested slackly in her mouth. Still a baby, despite her surprising astuteness. Very gently, Rowena removed the thumb and untwined the hair. Sarah didn't so much as twitch, tired out from playing games all day. Would she miss her father as much as Emily would?

It was easy for Adriana Leigh to say the girls were young enough to get over the separation without any lasting trauma. She was far enough removed to neither know nor care. What worried Rowena was how much Adriana was influencing Phil's thinking about it.

Yet how could Phil not miss his family? He hadn't been the kind of man who ignored his children. If anything, he had been on the indulgent side, leaving any disciplinary measures to her.

Best Daddy in the world.

Had that stroked his ego?

She shook off Keir's insidious criticism of Phil's character and walked quickly to the door. She cast one last maternal look over her daughters settled peacefully in their twin beds. They didn't have to be told anything yet. Phil might change his mind.

Two more days and school was finished for the year. Then Christmas only a week later. There wasn't much time for Phil to have second thoughts. How could she possibly explain his absence to three children who expected their father to be with them for Christmas?

Having quietly closed the girls' bedroom door, Rowena took a deep breath, hoping to lower her anxiety level before facing Jamie again. Being ten, he stayed up later than the girls, and he'd been unnaturally quiet over dinner, watching her as though he sensed something wrong. She hadn't given him much attention. He reminded her too painfully of Keir tonight. And the memories that had been evoked earlier today.

She had to shut that out of her mind, concentrate on other things. No good could come from thinking about Keir and what he'd said and how he had reacted to her. She could not delude herself with might-have-beens. If he hadn't lied to her... But he had, and she couldn't forgive him that patently false declaration. She had to be strong now, strong enough to stand alone if need be.

She had left Jamie watching television in the family room. As she headed for the kitchen she realised the house was quiet, no noise at all. Perhaps Jamie had his head in a book. He loved reading. Rowena hoped that was the case. It would leave her free to ponder what course she should take next.

He was sitting on a bar stool at the counter that divided the kitchen from the family room. A book was open in front of him, a glass of milk half-drunk at hand. He looked up as Rowena entered the room, and she had an instant flash of Keir, assessing her with weighing calculation. The expression was shockingly the same.

"Good book?" she forced herself to ask lightly, crossing to the sink to fill the electric jug for coffee.

No reply.

She flicked him an inquiring look as she reached for the jug. "What's going on, Mum?" Serious, direct and determined.

Rowena's heart fluttered. She swiftly switched her attention to the tap, turning it on, running water. "Well, the girls are settled for the night."

"I mean about Dad."

Rowena's heart squeezed tight. How could Jamie guess that something was wrong? She thought she'd covered up reasonably well so far. "What do you want to know, Jamie?" she asked, evading his keen gaze by putting the jug on to boil and spooning coffee into a mug.

"I heard you crying last night. It sounded awful. I didn't know what to do. I thought Dad was with you and I shouldn't butt in. But when I got up this morning he wasn't here. And he hasn't come home tonight, either."

The blunt statement of facts was recited in a tightly controlled voice that tried so hard to be calm and sensible it moved Rowena to tears again. Jamie was only ten, yet here he was, manfully taking the bull by the horns in his concern for her. He must have been worrying all day, poor darling, and she hadn't wanted to see it.

Well, there was no hiding the truth now. Jamie wouldn't be fobbed off with soothing platitudes. Yet to tell the whole truth might damn Phil in his eyes for a long time. A surge of white-hot anger helped restore her composure. Did Phil even begin to comprehend what damage he was doing, getting his ego stroked by that woman?

"Mum?"

Jamie had to be answered. What was the best line to tread? She put down the coffee spoon and turned to face him, seeing for the first time the underlying anxiety in his eyes. It made her want to weep again. Why were the innocent made victims of other people's desires and pain?

"I'm sorry for upsetting you with my crying, Jamie. Your father and I had an argument. Parents sometimes do, you know."

He nodded gravely, but he wasn't satisfied. "I've never heard you cry like that. It went on for a long time."

She thought of him lying in the dark, listening, and was ashamed of letting herself go so much. It had felt as though her whole world was breaking up, ending, but it wasn't really. It was going to be a different world whether Phil came back or not. It could never be the same again. She recognised that now. But she would cope with it. Somehow.

"Things change, Jamie," she said sadly. "Sometimes it's not easy to accept the change."

His face suddenly assumed a bullish expression, and his eyes took on a fierce glitter. "Has Dad gone off to another woman?"

She was shocked. "What makes you think that?" The words tripped off her tongue, not in denial, simply in appalled wonder that he had leapt to so much. Or had he heard part of their argument?

"Half the kids in my class have divorced parents. I get to hear things." He looked too wise. "Dad's been coming home late and not here most of the weekends."

"Work. He's had a lot of work to do." That was the excuse Phil had given.

"Why isn't he home tonight?"

"Because he…wants to be somewhere else," she finished limply.

"Is he coming back?" Hard suspicion, giving no quarter.

"I don't know." She couldn't lie to him. On the other hand, the trouble with saying anything more was that it couldn't be unsaid later, and Rowena didn't want Jamie completely alienated from Phil. "If you don't mind, Jamie, I'd rather not talk about this right now. Your father and I... We need some time to work things out. Okay?"

He considered for several moments before nodding. "Okay, Mum." Then with a flash of fierce feeling, "I just want you to know that whatever Dad does, you'll always have me."

"Oh, Jamie..."

She heard her voice waver and swallowed hard. Before she could speak again, Jamie was off the stool, around the counter and flinging his arms around her waist, his head pressing against her breasts as he hugged her hard. So loyal, so protective, so intensely loving. Her hands curled around his head, fingers stroking his hair. Her son, Keir's son. If only Keir had been worthy of him.

"I don't want you to cry like that any more, Mum," came the muffled plea, revealing his deep inner distress at her breakdown.

"I won't, Jamie," she gently promised him. "I was feeling very alone. But I'm not really alone, am I?"

"No. You've got me."

"And I'll never forget that again. Thank you for reminding me."

"That's okay."

What courage he had! Courage, resolution, caring. Rowena savoured the comforting warmth of holding him, her boy holding her. For the past year or so he had shied away from "soppy stuff." He didn't seem to mind it right now, but she didn't want him to start feeling awkward about it.

"What are you reading?" she asked.

His head came up and his arms dropped. "It's a book about rabbits called *Watership Down*."

She slid her hands to his shoulders and smiled. "Why don't you take it to bed and read it there? I'm going to watch TV for a while."

"Will you be all right by yourself, Mum?"

"I'll be fine," she assured him warmly. "Light out at nine o'clock, remember."

He collected his book, said good night and went off with the jaunty confidence of having settled what needed to be settled.

Rowena wished that life could be so simple. She made herself a mug of coffee, switched on the television, sank into her usual armchair and idly flicked through the channels, stopping at what appeared to be a documentary on train travel. What was on the screen was irrelevant, its only purpose to provide a semblance of normality to the evening in case Jamie checked on her.

Her mind ran endlessly over memories of her marriage, both good and bad, sifting through what had contributed to the highs and the lows. She found her thoughts coloured by the opinions given by Adriana and Keir, especially Keir's, despite her efforts not to think of him.

You want a husband who needs to be rescued from another woman?

She didn't. She wanted a husband who would always put her first. As Adriana had pointed out, she was guilty of putting the children first at times, but they were Phil's children as well as hers. They certainly weren't another man.

The problem was, even if Phil did come back to her, Rowena didn't think she could ever feel right with him again. And that could only lead to more problems. Whichever way she looked at it, there were unhappy times ahead.

A noise caught her attention. Was that the front door opening...and closing?

CHAPTER SIX

ROWENA HURRIEDLY CLICKED off the television set and pushed herself to her feet. Phil—it had to be—come home. Yes, footsteps heading for the kitchen. What did it mean?

She glanced at her watch. Nine-forty. He'd waited until the children were asleep. Out of the way. Maybe he found it easier to face her without a watching audience, especially if he intended to admit a mistake.

She moved unsteadily towards the counter where Jamie had sat, instinctively wanting something solid separating her and the man who had betrayed his commitment to her and their family. She felt defensive, although she told herself she had no reason to be. It was he who had put their marriage under threat.

She also shied away from the thought of being touched. Phil had undoubtedly come from Adriana. If he reached out for her now... No, she couldn't bear it, not with the image of Adriana so fresh in her mind.

Phil came into the kitchen in aggressive mode. It wasn't hard to see he was not bent on reconciliation. He glared at her, his blue eyes ablaze with fury. "What the hell do you think you were doing, going to Delahunty's today?" he demanded in a voice laced with outrage.

It was like a punch in the stomach. Didn't he realise how desperate she'd been to put herself on the line against his other woman? Didn't it tell him how much their marriage meant to her? Was there no appreciation at all of what she was going through because of him?

"I wanted to see the woman you prefer to me and the children," she answered, needing to focus his mind on the real issue.

It floated over his head. "To go to my boss... God damn it, Rowena! You put me in an invidious position, dragging Keir into this."

The realisation hit her that this rage was about appearances. She had made him look bad in his boss's eyes. That was what had brought him here. Not her and the children. Phil hated looking bad.

A great distance yawned between them as she totted up the clean-cut handsome face, the perfectly groomed dark blonde hair, the buttoned-down collar of his expensive white shirt, the silk tie perfectly in place, the smartly tailored double-breasted suit that was an up-to-date fashion statement. It had always been so very important to Phil to look good. She had been proud of him looking good. She hadn't known it was more important to him than her and the children.

"Emily wanted to show you her latest painting," she said, waving to the corkboard on the wall above the kitchen counter, hoping it would jolt him out of his self-centredness.

He didn't spare it so much as a glance. "Don't drag the children into this. I want to know what went on between you and Keir Delahunty."

Jealous? Was Keir right about jealousy bringing Phil to heel? She frowned. It was so grubby, somehow.

"You were with him before and after you saw Adriana," he went on in fuming accusation.

Rowena instinctively minimised what had happened.

"We met accidentally in the car park. He knew about you and Adriana. He guessed why I'd come. He offered his office for privacy."

"Why should he do that?"

"To prevent an unpleasant scene. More gossip."

"Adriana said he was holding your hand. And he took your side. I'm one of his top executives, and he's hardly met you. Why should he care about you? Tell me that!"

Had Keir really cared, or was he an opportunist like Adriana? Rowena felt wretchedly confused about Keir's motives. Perhaps he regretted not having pursued her. And the attraction was still there. If he hadn't lied... That was the killing point.

"He knows me from a long time ago," she said quietly, trying to defuse Phil's anger and suspicion. "Our families were once friends."

A fierce resentment flared. "You never mentioned this before. I've been working with him for almost two years, and neither you nor he has ever referred to having known each other."

She shrugged. "I imagine he didn't want to remember it any more than I did. The friendship ended when my brother died in Keir's car. My parents blamed Keir."

"Was he guilty?"

Rowena hated the speculative spark in Phil's eyes. Did he want to hold something over Keir? "No, he wasn't. It was an accident. Brett was driving. My parents were too distraught to accept that it was Brett's fault. As they saw it, if Keir's parents hadn't given him a sports car and if he hadn't let Brett drive it, the accident wouldn't have happened."

"Then he should feel bitter towards you, not— Hold on a moment." He was clearly struck by another train of thought. "Weren't you seventeen when your brother died?"

"Yes. As I said, a long time ago."

"When was it exactly?"

"New Year's Day." The memory was still stark, the shock, the grief— Brett and Keir, and the guilty relief that Keir was still alive. Still alive now, and making more trouble for her. She shouldn't have gone to his office, shouldn't have stayed talking to him.

Phil's fist crashed down on the counter. "He's the father, isn't he?"

The yelled words rang in her ears. She looked at Phil's furiously pugnacious face and was too stunned to make any reply.

"Jamie's birthday is in September, nine months after the accident that killed your brother. Oh, it adds up now, doesn't it?" Phil jeered. "That's why Jamie's father didn't stand by you. Your parents blamed Keir Delahunty for your brother's death and sent you off to your aunt in Queensland."

He flung up his hands and swung away from her, marching around the kitchen, smacking his fist into his other hand. "And you let me take a job with the father of your son," he shouted at her in savage condemnation.

Rowena snapped herself out of the shock of Phil tying Keir to her pregnancy. "Jamie is your son. *Your* son," she cried in a desperate attempt to set things straight. "You're the only father he's known. Please stop this. It has nothing to do with—"

"Nothing?" he shouted. "You call it nothing for you to fob Keir Delahunty's son onto me?"

"Jamie is my son. And you adopted him as yours," she countered fiercely.

"Well, he's not any more."

She couldn't believe this. How could he turn on Jamie as though their father-and-son relationship had meant nothing? "That's very convenient, Phil. Are you going to suggest the girls have other fathers, too?" she demanded heatedly.

"Leave them out of this."

"You keep saying that, but you can't leave them out. Or is that what you really want? Not to think about them. Grasping any excuse not to think about Jamie."

"All these years, keeping it a secret from me…"

"All these years you haven't been the least bit concerned about who Jamie's biological father is. You looked after him, cared about him, played with him. You were proud to own him as your son. How do you wipe it all out, Phil? Tell me that!"

He flushed, evading her gaze for a moment, then swinging back to turn guilt into anger again. "You had no right not to tell me before I accepted the job at Delahunty's."

"You wanted the job. It was a feather in your cap. I wanted you to be happy. If I'd known it would lead to your meeting Adriana Leigh and deserting all of us for her—"

"I have every intention of remaining a father to Emily and Sarah."

At least he had that much conscience, Rowena thought, wondering where the rest of it was. "So it's only Jamie you're going to dump," she said, wanting to bludgeon every shred of his conscience into reviewing what he was doing. "Is it because Adriana doesn't want to be bothered with him? Little girls are much more malleable for a woman like her. Or maybe you haven't got the guts for answering sticky questions from Jamie."

The flush deepened. "I haven't heard you deny he's Keir Delahunty's bastard kid."

Rowena seethed over that demeaning phrase. She barely held herself back from flying at him tooth and claw. "I don't have to deny anything," she fired at him. "You adopted Jamie in good faith. You just want to muddy things up so you'll feel justified in what you're doing, and you have no justification. None at all!"

He slapped his hands on the counter and leaned towards her in belligerent challenge. "Look me straight in the eye, Rowena, and deny that you and Keir Delahunty were lovers and that Jamie is his natural son."

She stared at him, hating the feeling of being cornered, hating all the connotations he was putting on a love affair that ended long before she had met Phil and married him, and hating his evasion of responsibilities he had willingly taken on.

Even so, she couldn't bring herself to lie. In some strange way she felt a pride in Jamie's natural heritage and didn't want to deny it. After all, Keir Delahunty had certainly made his way in the world. He was also Phil's boss, hardly a comedown in the genetic pool. Yet to make a claim...

"Keir doesn't know. He doesn't know," she repeated with passionate emphasis.

"Well, maybe he ought to know." Phil straightened up, a triumphant gleam in his eyes. "Maybe he should take over the support of the boy I've been supporting all these years."

"No," she gasped, appalled that he should even think it.

He looked smug, in control. "Stay out of my business, Rowena. That's my territory. And Adriana's. And I don't want you messing with it."

"So it's all right to keep working for Keir now, is it?" she snapped bitterly.

"He doesn't know, and you don't want him told. That puts me in the driver's seat."

He was feeling good again. It was crazy. He was disowning a son who had done nothing to deserve rejection, and believing he held some kind of trump card over her and Keir. What kind of twisted thinking was that? Rowena couldn't relate to it.

He shook a finger at her. "No more putting Adriana on the spot. Keep out of our lives, Rowena. I told you last night you can keep this house. You've got a home for yourself and the children. That's more than fair."

She supposed she had to concede it was generous, though there was no telling how long the spirit of generosity would last once Adriana got to work on him.

"I'll be seeing a solicitor tomorrow," he informed her. "I don't want any hassle about reasonable access to my daughters."

Her heart bled for Jamie, but what could she do against such unfair intransigence? What more could she say? "That's it, is it, Phil? All that we had together has come to an end?"

Guilt flickered briefly in his eyes. "You were the wrong woman for me, Rowena. I'm sorry, but that's the truth."

"How was I wrong? You didn't think I was wrong when you married me. When did I change?"

"You didn't change."

"Then explain it to me, Phil. I need to know where I failed."

He heaved a discomforted sigh. "You were what I thought I wanted in a wife. It just didn't turn out how I visualised it."

"I don't understand," she pleaded.

He grimaced but went on reluctantly. "Well, you represented the ideal I had in my mind. You were happy for me to be the breadwinner, happy to have children and make a home for us, looking after everything on the domestic side."

"You saw me as the old-fashioned housewife."

"With the family. The whole bit. I hadn't had it. You know my parents were divorced," he said tersely.

And he was about to visit that upon his own children, Rowena thought grimly.

"And you're quite beautiful in your own way," he grudgingly conceded. "I was proud to have you at my side."

"Then why? Why let it all go?" she cried in anguished bewilderment.

"I told you. It was good for a while, but it's not what I want now."

"You believe Adriana is better for you?"

"It's not just Adriana," he said petulantly. "I want freedom. I want stimulation, excitement, the fun of doing things with spontaneity instead of having to live up to your ideals."

"By fun I assume you mean infidelity."

Anger bloomed again. "You expected too much of me. I'm tired of it. I want out. Is that clear enough for you?"

"Yes. Thank you."

It all made sense now. She had been Phil's fantasy. His mistake was in underestimating how much he needed to put into his role for the fantasy to become real. Looking good wasn't enough.

"So you're just walking out and leaving me to it," she said flatly, having had any last bit of caring for Phil drained out of her.

He shrugged. "You've gained a home, remember. And you'll find someone else. You're still young and attractive." He turned his back on her and walked towards the door as though she'd never been anything to him.

It struck a vengeful streak in Rowena. "Maybe I'll find Keir Delahunty. How will you like that?"

He stopped, his back rigid. Rowena knew he didn't like it one bit. He swung a glittering gaze to her. "Try it,

Rowena, and this house won't be yours. It will be sold, and I'm entitled to half the proceeds."

She bit down on her wayward tongue. She had to consider the children's welfare. Wild threats were only self-defeating. She had no intention of inviting Keir Delahunty back into her life.

Satisfied he had won his point, Phil walked out. Rowena didn't follow him to the front door. She wouldn't follow him anywhere anymore. He had severed the last sense of bonding with him.

CHAPTER SEVEN

KEIR DELAHUNTY GAVE up trying to concentrate on work. There was too much on his mind, and telling himself that none of it was his business didn't help one iota. He rolled his chair away from the drawing board, stood up and strolled around his office, ending up where Rowena had been yesterday, behind the table, looking down at the streets of Chatswood.

He'd had to tell Phil about her visit. It would have been unnatural not to when he'd come to give his report on the Pyrmont warehouse. Adriana would have had no qualms about telling him. Phil's embarrassment, the barely suppressed anger in his eyes did not bode well for Rowena.

Had she suffered a backlash from him last night?

Keir groaned inwardly. The frustration of not being able to help, not being able to go to her was eating into him. Phil didn't want her. Rowena had no reason to still feel committed to him and their marriage. How could she keep loving him in the face of such demeaning infidelity? Surely it was impossible.

His mind replayed every minute he'd spent with her yesterday, the words spoken, the tension, the eye contact. When he'd held her, he'd had such a strong sense of connecting with her again, but her rejection had been so swift, so vehement, maybe he'd been fooling himself.

Nevertheless, he didn't believe her conflict with Phil was entirely responsible for her intensely emotional responses to him. She might not want to acknowledge it, but the attraction was still there, surging between them.

Liar...

He shook his head. The word kept ringing in his ears, a death knell to any hope of recapturing what he'd once had with Rowena. But it wasn't true. If there had been a lie, it wasn't his.

He could still remember the sickening emptiness he'd felt when Rowena's mother had shown him the photograph, a totally devastating reinforcement of her father's insistence that their daughter didn't want him in her life and to stay right out of it and not bring her any more grief.

He'd stared disbelievingly at the photograph, Rowena with a baby on her lap, a man crouched adoringly beside them. Married, her parents had said, married to a good man, mother of a fine baby boy and happily settled in Queensland. There was no place for Keir Delahunty in any of their lives.

It had to have been a lie if Rowena had waited years for him. And he couldn't disbelieve her. He couldn't forget the blazing passion in her eyes as she had accused him, condemned him for having done what Phil Goodman was doing to her now, betraying her love, deserting her.

It must have been someone else's baby she'd been holding, simply a fortuitous photograph her parents had maliciously used to get rid of him. Or to give him the pain of loss they felt. As though losing his best friend and suffering through all those operations to walk again wasn't enough, Keir thought bitterly. They'd made him lose Rowena, too.

Vengeance, indeed. And for what? Brett had almost killed him, as well as himself. If that dog hadn't run onto the road… Keir shut his eyes tight, wanting to erase the memory of the last frantic moments before the car had crashed. Better to forget everything. But he couldn't.

Liar…

Would Rowena believe him about the photograph? Did she believe he'd written to her? He had no evidence to back up either claim. At least she didn't blame him for Brett's death. That was one small comfort, although it didn't balance the rest of the ledger against him. Was his word enough to get past her distrust?

The telephone on his desk rang.

He swung around in irritation. He'd told Fay to take all his calls this morning. Why wasn't she handling this? He was tempted not to answer, but there had to be a cogent reason for her to disobey his instructions, and he trusted Fay's judgment. He strode to his workstation and snatched up the receiver.

"What is it?"

"You have a visitor."

"I said no appointments."

"Keir, you remember yesterday when I brought in the coffee and sandwiches?"

"What are you getting at Fay?"

"I'm very sensitive to vibrations, you know. I think you'll want to see this visitor."

"Who is it?"

"Mrs. Goodman's son. He's come to see you. Very specifically you, Keir. He does not intend to go away until he does see you."

That knocked the wind out of any further protest and triggered a buzz of questions. Why would Rowena's son come here? To him? Where was Phil? What was happening to Rowena?

"Bring him in, Fay." The quiet command belied the turmoil in his mind.

He put down the receiver, hesitated over where best to place himself to meet the boy, then moved out of the work-station to greet him as he entered.

Fay opened the connecting door to her office and waved forward a schoolboy—eight, nine, ten? Surely too tall to be any younger. Black hair like Rowena's. He didn't have her green eyes. They were similar in shape but they were hazel. He was smartly dressed in a school uniform and carrying what was obviously his school bag.

He should be in his classroom right now, Keir thought. His parents undoubtedly believed he was. Yet there was no trace of guilt or concern in the boy's expression about having his truancy found out. He looked directly at Keir, curiously, assessingly, as though measuring him against some preconceived image.

"Jamie, this is Mr. Delahunty. Jamie Goodman, Keir." Fay introduced them, giving Keir a roll of her eyes that clearly said, Well, the fat's in the fire now, and this is what you get for involving yourself in other people's intimate problems.

Keir stepped forward, smiled encouragingly and offered his hand. "How do you do, Jamie?" Rowena's son. Another chance to reach her?

The boy put down his bag and gravely took his hand. "I'm pleased to meet you, sir."

Drilled in good manners. He didn't show any pleasure in the meeting. No responding smile. He seemed caught up in studying Keir's face, feature by feature.

"Please see that we aren't interrupted, Fay," Keir instructed and gave her a nod of approval for making an exception to orders for Rowena's son. "Thank you."

She left them together.

Jamie withdrew his hand and his scrutiny and cast his questing gaze around Keir's office. "Is this all yours?" he asked.

"All mine," Keir affirmed. "I designed it, as well. Would you like a tour?"

A flash of keen interest. "Yes, please."

Keir wondered how many tests he had to pass before Jamie Goodman revealed why he was here.

He proceeded to explain the purpose of all his architect's tools in his workstation, demonstrated how the drawing board could be adjusted, showed how he drew visualisations of his designs on the computer and answered a comprehensive range of intelligent questions. The boy was extremely bright.

"How old are you, Jamie?" Keir asked as he ushered him over to the model display.

It earned another speculative look. "How old are you?"

Keir had to smile at such a direct retort. "I'm thirty-five."

Jamie frowned, "That makes you older than—" He clamped down on whatever comparison he had been about to make and turned to examine the models.

Apparently the subject of age was not to be pursued, yet Keir was tantalised by it. Rowena had stated she had waited years for him. If that were the case, this boy could only be eight at most, yet he looked and sounded older.

"I've seen this one. It's been built at Manly," Jamie remarked, pleased at recognising the town houses Rowena had commented on yesterday.

"Yes. Your mother said she liked the design."

Jamie moved on to the next model. "Do you like my mum?"

The question sounded offhand but Keir knew intuitively it wasn't. "Yes, I do. We were close friends once. Unfortunately, your mother's brother was killed in a car accident. I was injured in the same crash. My parents flew me to the United States for special medical treatment, and I didn't see your mother again for a long time."

The boy was still, not looking at Keir, but the sense of him weighing every word Keir said was very strong. "What did you need treatment for?" he asked.

"My pelvis and both my legs were broken in many places. There was some doubt I would ever walk again."

Jamie turned and looked at Keir's legs. "How long did it take for you to mend?"

"Eighteen months."

Jamie nodded as though the answer met whatever check list he had in his mind. "You must have been badly smashed up," he remarked sympathetically.

Keir grimaced. "It wasn't much fun."

"No, I guess it wasn't." Jamie's eyes travelled up in open assessment of Keir's physical condition. "You're okay now, though," he decided.

"In top shape," Keir agreed.

Jamie pointed to the glass wall across the room. "Do you mind if I have a look at the view?"

"You're welcome."

Keir watched him walk around the table and stand where his mother had stood, looking out. It was uncanny. He wondered how close the bond was between mother and son.

"You sure can see a lot," the boy said appreciatively.

"It also gives me plenty of natural light," Keir answered, playing along with the game of not hastening to the purpose of the visit.

"Are you and Mum friends now?"

The question caught Keir unprepared, and it was loaded with pitfalls. What was behind it? Had there been an argu-

ment between Phil and Rowena last night, heated words
that Jamie had overheard and possibly misconstrued? Keir
swiftly decided that honesty was the best policy.

"I would like to be friends, Jamie," he said slowly, "but
I don't think your mother feels the same way."

"Why not?"

As an inquisitor, Jamie Goodman was excelling at putting Keir on the spot. "Well, there's your father," Keir
started tentatively.

"He's not my father."

The hard, vehement denial stunned Keir into turbulent silence. His mind leapt into overdrive. Rowena had
had an illegitimate child? When? By whom? The man in
the photograph? His back had been turned to the camera,
unidentifiable. But if he was the father, Rowena had not
waited. Unless the pregnancy had resulted from...from
an act of rape.

Keir was inwardly recoiling from this last thought when
Jamie swung around, an oddly adult look of set deter-
mination on his young face. Keir was reminded of not
Rowena but...

"I'm ten years old."

"Ten," Keir repeated, still trying to pinpoint the familiarity.

"My birthday is the twenty-eighth of September," the
boy stated with portentous emphasis.

The date sent Keir's mind reeling.

"And *you* are my father."

CHAPTER EIGHT

IT WAS BEST to keep busy, Rowena told herself, setting out all the ingredients for the Christmas pudding. Apart from which, just because Phil would not be with them for Christmas didn't mean that anything else had to change. She would proceed as though everything were normal. It would be less upsetting for the children if they saw her carrying on as usual.

"Sultanas for me, please, Mummy?"

She smiled at Sarah, wriggling excitedly on the stool behind the kitchen counter, her big green eyes agog at all the fruit that went into a pudding. "In a minute, darling. Wait until I weigh what I need, and then you can have what's left in the packet. Okay?"

"Okay." Blissful contentment.

Sarah was so easily pleased, delighted with the world and everything in it. Rowena hoped her bright little girl's happy outlook on life wouldn't be too dimmed by her father's absence.

Emily would take it the worst. She would need a lot of loving reassurance. Her disappointment when Phil wasn't here again this morning had put her in a sulky mood. She had started to whine about Daddy being away too much. Jamie had cut her off, telling her to stop acting like a baby and get ready for school.

Jamie, the man of the house, protecting her.

Rowena sighed. She couldn't let Jamie shoulder her burdens. Emily had to be told the situation. They each had to be told. Was it better done all together or separately?

Rowena pondered the problem as she poured sultanas onto the kitchen scales. Having measured the right quantity, she tipped them into the mixing bowl and handed the largely emptied packet to Sarah. The currants were another simple measuring job, but the raisins, dates and cherries needed cutting up.

After considerable thought, Rowena decided to leave the dreaded announcement for one more day. The school term finished tomorrow. She didn't want Emily upset in front of her friends and classmates. This was strictly a family problem, and it was better for Emily to have the whole Christmas vacation to come to terms with it.

As for Jamie... Rowena sighed again. How was she going to tell him his father didn't want him any more?

The door chimes sounded.

"I'll go, Mummy," Sarah cried eagerly, scrambling off the stool in her hurry to greet a visitor.

But who was visiting? Rowena wasn't expecting anyone. "Wait, Sarah. We need to wash our hands first."

A quick trip to the sink, and the stickiness of the fruit was removed from both sets of hands. The door chimes rang again. Rowena hastily threw a cloth over the mixing bowl. She glanced at the wall clock as she ushered Sarah out of the kitchen. Almost lunchtime. Who would be calling at this hour? Well, there was only one way to find out.

Sarah skipped down the hallway ahead of her but pulled up in the foyer, waiting for Rowena. The front door was always kept locked for security. There were two shapes visible through the stained-glass panels. One was considerably shorter than the other, about the same height as

Jamie, in fact. For some reason this was reassuring. With her sense of apprehension fading, Rowena opened the door.

Shock hit her like a cannon ball.

Keir Delahunty and Jamie together. Keir, eyeing her with steady resolution, holding Jamie's hand as his claim of passage. Jamie, who should be at school, looking at her with an air of triumphant satisfaction.

"He knows. I told him," her son announced as though it was a deed well done. "He's going to help you, Mum."

"May I come in, Rowena?" Keir's request was politely put, but he emanated an air of relentless purpose that clearly said no amount of wild horses would drag him away.

"Who's he?" Sarah inquired of her older brother.

"His name is Keir Delahunty and he's my real father," Jamie declared with pride.

Rowena closed her eyes. She felt the blood drain from her face as her world spun out of control. Keir's voice rang in her ears. "Jamie, look after your little sister. Your mother needs to sit down." An arm came around her waist, hugging her close to a wall of warmth and strength, supporting her as she was walked into the lounge and settled onto the closest armchair. "Head down, Rowena."

"What's wrong with Mum?" Jamie demanded in alarm.

"A little faint, I think. Nothing serious," Keir answered. "Did she eat any breakfast this morning?"

"I didn't see her have anything except coffee."

"Mummy's making a Christmas pudding," Sarah supplied helpfully.

"Jamie, could you make your mother a cup of coffee and find some biscuits or cake for her?"

"Sure I can. You'll look after Mum?"

"Yes."

"I want some biscuits, too, Jamie."

Rowena lifted her head, her eyes clearing enough to see Sarah trailing after her brother, leaving her alone with Keir.

"Take a few deep breaths, Rowena," he advised gently. "I'll just go and shut the front door so everything's secure."

Secure? Rowena felt a bubble of hysteria rising and hastily clamped down on it. Her mind whirled around the realisation that Jamie must have eavesdropped on all that had been said between her and Phil last night, and bringing Keir into their lives was his solution to the situation. But it was no solution at all. It was a massive complication!

Then Keir was back, crouching in front of her, taking her hands, rubbing them between his.

"I'm all right," she croaked.

"I'm sorry about the shock, Rowena. There was no easy way."

Concern and caring in his voice. Of course he cared! He'd just been presented with a son, hadn't he? Jamie would impress anyone as a boy a man would be proud of fathering. Any man except Phil! And now everything was going to be ten times worse.

"Jamie shouldn't have—"

"He had your interests at heart, Rowena."

She looked up wildly, her eyes filled with chaotic torment. "Then he's hopelessly mistaken, isn't he?"

Keir held her gaze steadily. "Give me the chance to show he's not."

"Phil threatened to sell this home and put us out of it if I got involved with you. Even if I wanted you, I can't afford you in our lives, Keir."

"I'll give you a home that no one else can sell. I'll put it in your name. Absolute security of tenure."

It was a mind-boggling offer, too big to be believed, tossed off as though it was the easiest thing in the world for him to do. She stared at him, the seeds of mistrust growing, multiplying. Was it another grandiose lie to impress her?

"Why on earth should you do that?" she asked suspiciously.

His gaze didn't waver, direct, intense, compelling. "If for no other reason, I owe it to you and Jamie."

Maybe he felt some indebtedness right now. Rowena could accept that he did. But things changed when it came down to the nitty-gritty. Phil had left her in no doubt of that.

"You're in the first flush of finding out you have a son, Keir. What about tomorrow and tomorrow and tomorrow? How long will the sense of responsibility last?"

"For the rest of my life," he said quietly.

She wanted to believe it. She wanted to but she couldn't. She wrenched her eyes from his and looked at her hands, still warmly enfolded. She pulled them out of his grasp and shrank into the deeply cushioned armchair, frightened of letting him get too close to her. It was too tempting to swallow the dream he was offering.

"I've heard promises before. I'm sitting in the middle of broken promises," she said, more to herself than him. "I think I'd rather manage my own life than count on support that doesn't stay true."

He stood up, very tall, very formidable, rock solid in his purpose. "There is Jamie to consider, Rowena."

"And my other children," she fiercely insisted, her maternal instinct rushing to the fore. "I won't have my children separated by fathers who only care about their own. If you think you can overlook the rest of my family in your plans for a future with Jamie—"

"I have no intention of overlooking anything. Not this time," he said grimly.

"What is that supposed to mean?"

"It means I want you in my life, Rowena. I want Jamie in my life. I don't want to lose out on any part of either of you. And that includes your daughters, Jamie's sisters."

She steeled herself against any melting towards him. "I heard the same from Phil. About Jamie. Only now it suits him to disown the son he adopted." The still raw pain of that rejection flashed out at Keir. "We're not pieces of baggage to be passed around."

"I'm not Phil."

He was right. Keir was more powerful, more self-assured, more focused on her and her needs than Phil had ever been. And probably more capable of answering them. She didn't doubt he had the wealth to buy her a house. She suspected he was harbouring the expectation of living in it with her, too. Yet he couldn't want her that much. It had to be the idea of having Jamie that was spurring him on to such sweeping declarations.

"You think you can just walk in here and take over me and my family?" she asked, trying to gauge how far he had considered what he was doing.

"No, I don't. I think I have to earn those privileges."

"It will take a lot of earning, Keir," she warned.

"I'm not acting on impulse, Rowena. I've had many years to consider what is meaningful in my life. I don't come here lightly."

He looked unshakable.

She remembered how convincing he had been about his love for her all those years ago. It hadn't proven true. Words were easy. They were also empty unless backed up by real substance.

On the other hand, maybe she was being too harsh, too sweeping in her demands. Expecting too much. Ideals were fine, but when they didn't work, compromises had to be made. Jamie was entitled to have a father in his life, and since Phil had abdicated the role, why not Keir? He could give Jamie more advantages in a material sense than she ever could alone. But if he let Jamie down, as he had let her down...

"Are you sure you want to be father to Jamie, Keir?"

"Yes."

"Are you aware of how much it costs to bring up a child, physically, financially and emotionally?"

"Whatever it takes, I'll meet it."

His confidence niggled her. He was untried, inexperienced, and words were cheap. Promises were cheap. "In that case you won't mind making provision for him," she said, driven to make him realise the consequences of commitment.

"No problem."

Put him to the test, a mutinous little voice whispered. "As an act of good faith, you could open a trust account for Jamie that will cover his keep and his education," Rowena rattled off. "When you show me how committed you are to being his father and all it entails, I'll agree to your seeing Jamie on a regular basis."

He didn't so much as blink. "And you, Rowena?"

"I come at a higher price," she said loftily, determined to test him to the limit. "You see, I've been supposedly loved and discarded once too often. You'll have to buy me a house of my own before I even begin to think of involving myself with you on any personal basis."

He observed the hard glitter in her eyes for several moments before answering her challenge. "Would you then begin to think, Rowena, or is this simply an act of vengeance for what you've suffered?"

Was it vengeance? She hesitated, not liking that image of herself. No, it was common sense, the little voice whispered. To let herself be fooled again would be too damaging, both to herself and her children.

"Call it what you will," she answered him, grimly resolved on keeping her feet on the ground. "I want protection for my children. Give me that, Keir, and I'll certainly consider you worth having in my life. You can risk it or not, as you please, but I'm not risking anything more."

"The hurt goes so deep," he murmured, his eyes softening with compassion.

It made Rowena squirm inside. But she had nothing to be ashamed of. It wasn't she who had betrayed her commitments. "I didn't ask you to come here," she said resentfully.

"No. Jamie did. He was worried for you. With good reason."

"I'm not a basket case. I can cope. I've done it before and I can do it again."

Though she was hopelessly rusty on her secretarial skills. She would have to do some computer courses to update herself before applying for a job. If that became necessary. She didn't know what the law was on maintenance payments. Phil was seeing a solicitor today. Maybe she should see one, too. At least find out what her position was.

"You don't have to cope this time," Keir said, shrewdly reading her uncertainties. "Just let me do it for you."

How could he be so confident of delivering what Phil had found too oppressive? "You're welcome to try, Keir. But let me tell you, when you really get hit in the face with the difficulties, it can be another story. I'll be more impressed with action," she informed him, her eyes broodingly sceptical.

"Did it ever occur to you to act yourself, Rowena? To let me know you were pregnant?"

The softly spoken challenge sliced through the bank of

defences she'd been feeding. It plucked at her heart. There was pain in his eyes, pain she couldn't dismiss.

"If only you'd told me," he went on, such infinite regret in his voice, the pain of loss, all the years he had been deprived of knowing Jamie, the baby years and the wonderful little-boy years, starting school, sports days where Jamie always won his races, the fun and the joy of so many things.

Rowena was suddenly gripped by guilty confusion. She had blamed Keir for not coming back to her, but was the blame all his? What did she know of his life in the years following the accident? The need to justify her own course impelled her to speak.

"I was only seventeen, Keir, and my parents… It was so bad, I was frightened of even mentioning your name, let alone…" She winced at the memory of endlessly fraught days, weeks, months. "And you didn't write to me, didn't let me know."

"I did, Rowena," he asserted quietly.

He'd said that yesterday, too. He could have written, for all she knew. She shook her head in helpless anguish. "You don't understand. Everything to do with you was destroyed. It was like living in a nightmare, and when Mum realised I was pregnant and I had to tell her you were the father, she was so unbalanced—"

"I'm sorry," Keir murmured. "You shouldn't have had to be so alone." He crouched again and gently squeezed her knees. "I'm sorry it was like that for you."

She doubted he could ever imagine what it had been like. No one could. "They wanted me to have an abortion," she stated flatly. "I refused. So they sent me to my aunt in Queensland. It seemed best. I knew you weren't in a position to help me, and I didn't want to add to whatever you were going through. It was all such a mess."

"My parents would have helped."

"I would have been disowned by my parents if I'd gone to them, Keir."

"Yes, of course."

"I thought the only thing to do was to ride it through and wait until you came home. I thought... I believed..."

He grimaced. His eyes begged more belief from her. "There were good reasons I didn't seek you out, Rowena. But I swear to you, if I'd known you'd had my child, nothing would have kept me away. Nothing."

Was it true? He seemed so sincere. Maybe she had judged him unfairly, without enough knowledge of his side. What did he consider good reasons?

"I would have given you and Jamie everything I could," he went on vehemently.

I'll never know that, Rowena thought sadly, *never know what might have happened if I'd somehow got in touch with him.* She didn't want to think about it. It was all too late. "It's pointless going over what might have been, Keir."

"Yes, it is," he agreed, withdrawing his touch and rising again. "And you want proof." He suddenly grinned, his whole face lighting up with pleasurable anticipation. "Action you will have aplenty, Rowena."

She stared at him, forcibly reminded of how attractive he was and how much she had once felt for him. But she wouldn't make the mistake of falling in love with him again. That would only be asking for more heartache. This time she would follow her head, not her heart. He hadn't said what his good reasons were for not seeking her out.

Before she could pursue the point, Jamie came in, carefully balancing a cup of coffee on its saucer. Sarah followed, bearing a plate of cookies. Impossible to continue an intimate conversation in front of the children.

"Are you feeling better, Mum?" Jamie asked anxiously

as he set his offering down on the occasional table beside her armchair.

"Yes, thank you, Jamie."

"These are my favourite cookies. You'll like them, Mummy," Sarah encouraged, handing her the plate.

"Thank you, Sarah."

They all proceeded to sit down, Keir in the armchair opposite her, the two children on the lounge. Both Jamie and Keir watched her, waiting for her to eat and drink what had been ordered and brought for her. Sarah studied Keir with keen interest.

At least her younger daughter didn't appear confused or upset by Jamie's identification of Keir as his real father, Rowena observed in some relief. Sarah was clearly consumed with curiosity.

But what about Emily? Rowena worried as she dunked a cookie into her coffee and lifted it quickly to her mouth to satisfy the onlookers. The cat was out of the bag, well and truly. Jamie would hold his tongue if she asked him to, but Sarah couldn't be trusted not to blurt out everything. She was too young to understand tact and discretion.

So much for waiting another day, Rowena thought disconsolately. Now she had to explain about two fathers going missing, and the return of one was not the one Emily would want. Keir would have his work cut out to win her older daughter over to accepting him as a replacement for Phil on any terms whatsoever.

She finished the cookie and took a sip of coffee.

"Are you and Mum friends now?" Jamie asked Keir hopefully.

Rowena almost choked.

"Your mother needs some convincing that I mean what I say, Jamie," Keir answered quietly. "That will take a little time."

"You're not going to give up?" Jamie pressed.

"No. Nothing will make me give up," Keir assured him.

"See?" Jamie said to Sarah, nudging her to take notice.

"Yes," she agreed, gravely nodding her approval at Keir. "A real prince never gives up."

"A prince!" Rowena spluttered over her coffee cup.

Sarah looked at her as though she was slow off the mark. "Jamie said it was like a fairy tale. The wicked witch took Daddy away, so the prince has come to look after us. And he's going to take us to a castle where nothing bad can happen to us."

"Oh, my God!" Rowena groaned, appalled at the licence Jamie had taken in explaining the situation to his little sister.

"I have to show your mother that the castle is hers first, Sarah. That could take a few days," Keir warned indulgently.

"Stop!" Rowena cried, crashing her cup down and standing to take command. "Jamie, take Sarah out to the family room and stay there until I join you. I want a private talk with—with your father. And no more fairy tales. That's an order."

Jamie sighed and stood up, tugging Sarah with him.

"I like fairy tales, Mummy," Sarah protested.

"No more today," Rowena amended.

"Come on, Sarah," Jamie urged. "We'll build a castle with your blocks."

"Yes," Sarah gleefully agreed and skipped along beside him as they exited from the lounge room.

"I like fairy tales, too," Keir remarked, rising from his chair. He gave Rowena a warm smile of approval. "Thank you for calling me Jamie's father. It sounded good."

Rowena found her tongue. "How dare you encourage this—this fantasy when—when...?" She floundered.

"I like your daughter very much," Keir said, still smiling as he moved closer to her.

"You're making trouble for me," she cried in anguished protest.

"Rowena." His arms enfolded her and his eyes glowed with a compelling intensity. "I want a happy ending. The only person who can stop that happening is you. All I ask is that you give it a chance."

"You're deluding yourself."

"Let's see if I am."

"Life isn't like a fairy tale. It's…"

His head was bending towards hers. There was a purposeful glitter in his eyes, a simmering glitter, a mesmerising glitter. Rowena forgot what words she had meant to say. Her mouth remained open.

His lips brushed hers and ignited a field of electric tingles. She gasped. His mouth blanketed the sensitive area, soothing it with a warm pressure that was too captivating to resist. It tugged at memories…her very first kiss on her sixteenth birthday.

She'd been waiting and waiting for it to be Keir who gave her that first kiss. How she'd longed for it, willing him to see she was grown-up enough for him, and it had been so right, so perfect, the touch like thistledown at first, and then…

He was doing it now, the slide of his tongue over the sensitive inner tissues of her lips, so tantalising, exciting… But she shouldn't be letting him do it. He shouldn't be stimulating these feelings. She wasn't sixteen any more. Nor seventeen. Yet there was a need in her to know if it would all be the same as it had been then.

Keir lifted his head, ending the kiss, leaving her mouth aquiver with anticipation. He stroked her cheek with feather-light fingertips. His eyes held a soft tenderness that curled into her heart. "A new start, Rowena," he murmured.

No, that was impossible, her mind dictated. The fantasy of reliving her youth crumbled against the stark force of the realities she had to face. "We can't go back, Keir."

"We can move forward." He smiled. "I'll go now and start the action to prove it."

He was at the doorway to the foyer before she recollected herself enough to say, "You don't appreciate how difficult this will be. There's Emily."

He paused to look back, still smiling. "I look forward to meeting her."

"She's older than Sarah."

"Jamie told me. Don't worry. I'll handle it." He grinned. "I'll fight all your dragons, Rowena. I have a quest."

And on that quixotic note he left. His devil-may-care grin stayed behind, stamped indelibly on Rowena's mind. He didn't know. He didn't understand. He didn't care what barriers he had to jump over or negotiate around. He had a quest.

CHAPTER NINE

"WHAT'S THE WICKED witch's name?" Emily demanded again.

Rowena sighed. Her careful explanation of the present situation had been completely supplanted by Jamie's fairy tale. Apparently it had more appeal. Children had a habit of judging things in black and white. Greys, Rowena reflected, were probably too difficult a concept to grasp.

"Her name is Adriana Leigh, and I told you, Emily, she's not a wicked witch," Rowena answered with somewhat frayed patience as she bent to kiss her older daughter good night.

"She is so, too, if she took Daddy away," came the petulant reply.

"Your father wanted to go, Emily."

"She put a spell on him," Sarah piped up. "That's what wicked witches do."

It was a fairly apt interpretation of what had happened, Rowena thought, although if it hadn't been Adriana, it would have been someone else sooner or later. Adriana had merely hastened what had been brewing.

"Can we undo the spell, Mummy?" Emily asked hopefully.

Rowena gently stroked her hair. "I'm afraid not, darling. But your daddy did say he'd come and see you."

"When?"

"I guess when he's ready to, Emily."

"For Christmas?"

"I don't know. Perhaps."

"He'd better. Or she is so, too, a wicked witch," Emily declared with conviction.

Rowena could only silently agree. Whatever Phil's faults, Adriana was pandering to them, not caring who got hurt. On the other hand, Adriana's influence didn't exonerate Phil of responsibility for his actions.

She gave Emily an extra good night kiss. "Go to sleep now and don't worry about it. Daddy will call us and let us know. All right?"

"All right, Mummy."

She snuggled obediently into her pillow. Rowena moved to the door, checking that Sarah was still settled. She was well burrowed down, her head barely visible. Yet as Rowena switched off the light, Sarah had the last word.

"Anyhow, we've got the prince on our side, Emily."

A more comforting thought than any she'd been able to give, Rowena conceded ruefully, but if the prince fell down on his quest, the collapse of the fairy tale would cause more trauma than Rowena cared to contemplate. Did Keir even begin to comprehend all the ramifications of what he had put in motion?

Jamie was waiting for her in the kitchen, seated on the counter stool again, his book ostensibly open. "Are you mad at me, Mum?" he asked without preamble.

What he had done was irrevocable. There was no point in recriminations. Besides, perhaps it would turn out for the best. *Give me a chance,* Keir had said. She had no other option now. She forced a smile. "No, I'm not mad at you, Jamie."

His face lit with relief, and a wide grin broke through his cautious control. "The flowers look great, don't they?"

Beyond him, on the coffee table in the family room, sat a glorious basket of flowers, Christmas bells, dark red lilies, scarlet carnations, yellow daisies, a profusion of blooms in season. It had come just after Emily had arrived home from school, and attached to it was a card that read, "To cheer you, Keir."

It had lent substance to the fairy tale.

Rowena had to concede it had also given her heart a lift. It had been years since Phil had given her flowers. "They're beautiful, Jamie. It was nice of Keir to send them," she added warmly, wanting to erase any guilt Jamie might have about going to Keir behind her back.

"He explained about you being separated by the accident and all that. He really does care about us, Mum. I could tell."

"Yes, I think he does," Rowena agreed, wishing she had heard the *all that*. She would like to know Keir's good reasons for not seeking her out when he'd returned to Australia from California. Not that it really mattered now.

A new start. Was he courting her with flowers?

"You won't have to worry about Dad getting nasty on you any more, Mum. Keir said he would fix everything," Jamie said with satisfaction.

Rowena hoped Jamie's faith in his new-found father was well-placed. She couldn't quite quell her fears over what might eventuate now that Keir had thrown his hat in the ring. She frowned over Jamie's use of his Christian name. "I don't think you should call him Keir, Jamie."

"He suggested it. He said it would be easier for Emily and Sarah if we all called him Keir. That way they won't get mixed up about fathers. I thought it was a good idea."

It amazed and impressed Rowena that Keir had been

considering the girls' reaction to him even before he met them. It showed he really did care how they felt. "What about you, Jamie? Did you want to call him Dad?"

"No. Not yet anyway. It didn't feel right."

Too soon. Too big a leap in one day. Phil had been his dad for so long, Jamie couldn't be expected to suddenly transfer that identity to a virtual stranger. "How do you feel about Keir?"

Another wide grin. "He passed all my tests, Mum. For my real father, I don't know that I could have got much better."

She had to smile. "Well, I hope he lives up to his test score."

"He's doing good so far."

"Time will tell, Jamie."

Would Keir pass her tests, as well? Rowena wondered. Even her son had been wary of giving his trust. Rejection cast a long shadow.

Caution—that was what was needed. Having been plunged into the wilderness by Phil's defection, it was very tempting for her to be swept along on what might feel like a magic carpet, but she couldn't squash the sense of dangers lurking at the edges, ready to grab them all if she wasn't vigilant.

Rowena's apprehensions, however, received one telling blow the next day. The mail was delivered at ten o'clock, and amongst an assortment of Christmas cards was an official letter from a Chatswood bank. It was not the bank Phil usually dealt with, and it was addressed to her. Mystified, Rowena opened the envelope and read the letter enclosed.

It informed her that trust accounts had been opened in the names of her three children. If she would call at the bank, at her convenience, the paperwork could be completed for her to become the signatory for each account.

Rowena was totally stunned at the speed with which Keir had moved to fulfil her demand. More than her demand. He had not only opened a trust account for Jamie, but for Emily and Sarah, as well. He must have done it straight after he left her yesterday for this letter to have come in the mail this morning.

She reread it to make absolutely sure she wasn't hallucinating. Still she could hardly bring herself to believe it. There was only one way of checking if it was bona fide—go to the bank in question and present it to whomever was in charge of such things.

Emily and Jamie would not be home from their last school day of the year until three-thirty. She had plenty of time to get herself to Chatswood and back. She dressed in her navy suit again, feeling the need to look smart. Sarah was happy to have the opportunity to wear her best dress. It was made of a pretty red and white print, with a white yoke and pockets. Sarah loved red.

The drive from their home in Killarney Heights only took fifteen minutes. Rowena entered the bank with Sarah in tow at eleven forty-five and made her way to the inquiries counter. A young woman came to attend to her needs, and Rowena handed her the letter. "My name is Rowena Goodman and I've come to settle this business," she said, hoping everything was in order.

The woman read the letter then smiled at Rowena. "Would you please take a seat, Mrs. Goodman? I'll check if the bank manager can see you now."

Rowena did as she was told, but her heart pounded with apprehension. Did bank managers oversee new accounts? Her only experience with a bank manager was over a home loan with Phil, and that had involved a lot of money. Phil had only recently finished paying off the mortgage on the house.

A few highly nervous minutes later, the door to a side office opened and a semi-bald, middle-aged man wearing gold-framed spectacles made a beeline for Rowena, his hand already stretched out in greeting. "Mrs. Goodman, delighted to meet you. I'm Harvey Ellis, the manager."

Rowena stood and shook his hand. "How do you do, Mr. Ellis." The letter had to be genuine! She wouldn't be welcomed like this if it wasn't. "This is my daughter Sarah," she offered belatedly.

"Hello, Sarah." His voice dripped with indulgence and he beamed at Sarah as though a three-year-old girl was his idea of a Christmas box.

"Hello," Sarah replied, staring at his shiny, bald pate.

"Come right this way, Mrs. Goodman. We can sit comfortably in my office while you do the necessary signatures. I trust you have identification with you."

"Yes." Her mind whirled. Driver's licence, credit cards... But she had really only come to satisfy her curiosity, to know if Keir had truly done it.

It was a very streamlined executive office. Rowena and Sarah were ushered to comfortable chairs, and Mr. Ellis settled behind his massive desk. Its clean surface made Rowena wonder if any real work was done here. However, there was one folder in front of the bank manager, and he proceeded to open it.

"Now, as you undoubtedly know, Mr. Delahunty has placed one hundred thousand dollars in each of the children's trust accounts. Jamie, Emily and of course—" he smiled benignly "—Sarah."

"One..." Rowena shook her head. Her mind was buzzing with astronomical figures. She must have misheard. "I beg your pardon, Mr. Ellis. Would you please run that past me again?"

"Mr. Delahunty..."

It was the same the second time. Rowena sat dazed, vaguely aware that the bank manager was explaining her part as signatory for the children, but none of it sank in. Then he was shoving papers at her and offering her a pen. All she could think of was the enormity of what Keir was handing over to her. It was far, far beyond any expectation she'd had of him.

"Mrs. Goodman?" It was a prompt.

"I have to speak to Mr. Delahunty first. This isn't quite what I thought it was," she said distractedly.

Harvey Ellis looked surprised. "Well, if you'd like to use my phone, Mrs. Goodman…"

"Yes, please."

He pushed it towards her.

"I need to speak to him privately," Rowena pressed, too embarrassed to reveal the true situation to the bank manager.

"I'll leave you to it," he said obligingly, standing up. "Will ten minutes be enough?"

"Yes. Thank you."

She didn't know if it was or not, but the moment he'd gone she leapt from her chair, snatched up the receiver and feverishly jabbed the numbers for Delahunty's, knowing them off by heart from calling Phil. She was put through to Keir's secretary.

"Good morning. Keir Delahunty's office. How may I help you?" Her welcoming voice instantly conjured up the homely image.

"It's Rowena Goodman. Is it possible for me to speak to Keir, please?"

"One moment, Mrs. Goodman. I'm sure he'll be happy to take your call," came the warm reply.

Rowena wildly wondered if the news of Keir's interest in her and Jamie was all over the building. If so, Phil might…

"Rowena, what can I do for you?"

"Does Phil know about Jamie's visit? And about you coming to me?"

"I haven't told him."

"Your secretary…"

"Everything held in the strictest confidence. Has something happened, Rowena?"

"No, I—I'm at the bank, Keir."

"I hope Harvey Ellis is treating you as he should."

"That's not the point. This—all this money…"

"Educating children is expensive. Over the years—"

"Keir, I can't accept it!"

"It's simply a safeguard against the future."

"But three hundred thous—" She bit down on the last word, remembering belatedly that Sarah had a mind like a sponge. "It's far too much," she said curtly.

"It's ready cash. I changed my will yesterday, making you and the children my beneficiaries. If anything should happen to me—"

"Keir, for heaven's sake!"

"It's protection for you until we're married."

"Married! Keir, I *am* married. I've only been separated from my husband for two and a half days. It'll be a year before a divorce becomes possible. And I'm not going to be rushed into anything!"

"Rowena, you wanted proof of commitment from me," he said gently. "I want to give it to you. I want to give you everything you need."

"I can't say I'll marry you, Keir. I don't know. It mightn't work. There's so much—"

"I promise I won't rush you," he soothed. "All I ask is that you give us a chance. We'll take one step at a time."

"This step is too big."

"No, it's easy, Rowena. Just attach your signature to whatever needs signing. I can afford to give your children financial security, and I choose to do it. Okay?"

"It's…it's madness."

He laughed. "The best kind of madness there is, Rowena. Are you and the children free tomorrow?"

"Yes. Unless…" It was Saturday tomorrow. Phil might want to see the girls.

"Unless what?"

Then again, he might not. He hadn't called. Why should they wait around on his and Adriana's convenience? Phil had forced separate lives upon them. *Let us lead separate lives,* Rowena thought defiantly. Besides, Keir was showing more caring than her husband—her *ex*-husband—had. A lot more!

"It doesn't matter," she declared with determination. "What do you have in mind?"

"A castle."

Rowena suddenly had a vision of ramparts and turrets. "You can't mean that."

"Well, it's really a house. But we can call it a castle. I'd like you to see it. Will ten o'clock suit for me to pick the family up?"

A smile tugged at her mouth. The magic carpet ride was zipping along at supersonic speed, and she really ought to get off and plant her feet firmly on the ground, but she couldn't help feeling fascinated about where it might lead next. "Yes. Ten will be fine," she heard herself say.

"Now do what Harvey says, Rowena. Then you can go home and bask in a sense of security."

No, she couldn't do it, no matter what argument Keir used. She would feel as though he was buying her. Such a huge commitment from him automatically placed a commitment on her, one she wasn't prepared to give at this juncture in her life.

"The gesture is enough, Keir. I really can't take the money from you, but thank you for placing so much value on my children," she said warmly.

"I want you to feel safe."

"It's good of you. I appreciate it very much. And thank you for the flowers. They're lovely."

"My pleasure. Tomorrow at ten."

She smiled. "We'll be ready." She dropped the receiver in its cradle, feeling distinctly light-headed.

"Was that the prince you were talking to, Mummy?" Sarah asked.

"Yes, it was the prince." In a giddy moment of delight that Keir had proved as good as his word, Rowena scooped Sarah from her chair and hoisted her up against her shoulder. "He's going to sweep us off to a castle tomorrow," she told her darling little daughter.

"A real castle?"

Rowena laughed. She hadn't laughed so light-heartedly for a long, long time. It felt good. "Not quite, Sarah. A home. If the home is right, it feels like a castle."

Sarah grinned. "I like the prince."

He was certainly scoring well at the moment, Rowena thought happily.

"If you marry him, you could be a princess, Mummy."

That brought Rowena down to earth with a thump. The talk about marriage had clearly filtered into Sarah's active little brain, and she might blurt it out at the worst possible moment, creating trouble Rowena could well do without.

"We mustn't think about that yet, Sarah. The prince has to do a lot of brave deeds first."

"He said he wouldn't give up," Sarah reminded her.

"Let's wait and see. He might not mean to give up but

it's better to wait and see. It might be bad luck to talk about marrying him. We wouldn't want to give him bad luck, would we?"

Sarah gravely shook her head.

Rowena was relieved to have that settled. She hoped. There was always an unpredictable element with Sarah.

The bank manager entered the office. She turned to him with beaming confidence. "Mr. Ellis, thank you so much for your time, but I can't continue with this business right now. Mr. Delahunty will be making further arrangements with you."

"Oh! Well, thank you for coming in, Mrs. Goodman."

He escorted her and Sarah to the bank door, showing them every courtesy. Rowena felt the pleasurable glow of being worth three hundred thousand dollars even though she didn't have it. She also felt good about showing Keir she wasn't out for vengeance.

A new start.

Magic words.

She wasn't going to do anything she didn't want to do, but she saw no harm in giving Keir a chance.

He had earned it.

CHAPTER TEN

KEIR DELAHUNTY FINISHED signing the letters his secretary had brought him and handed her the sheaf of papers.

"Is everything all right?"

He glanced at Fay, surprised by her question. "Are you concerned about any of the letters?"

"No. Horses for courses. You looked so grim. I wondered…" She gave him a rueful smile. "Well, Mrs. Goodman sounded anxious when she called you."

He sighed and leaned back in his chair, brooding over the note of fear in Rowena's voice when she'd asked if Phil knew what had developed over Jamie. Was it fear of losing her home or fear that the door would be shut on any chance of Phil coming back to her? Did she still want him?

"It's not an easy time for her," he said.

Fay gave him her owl look. "It's messy, Keir, with Phil working for you."

"Don't I know it," he agreed, flicking her a derisive look for stating the obvious. "I've been considering what to say to him."

"It'll be blood on the floor," Fay warned.

"Maybe. Maybe not. Either way, I will not have Rowena frightened," he said decisively. "I'm going to straighten Phil out on that point."

"Good for you," Fay approved.

He gave her a wry smile. "Not much gets past you, does it, Fay?"

"Old eagle eye strikes again. If it's not too much of an impertinence…" She paused, eyeing him warily.

"Go on."

"Is Mrs. Goodman the reason you haven't married?"

He nodded. He didn't mind Fay knowing. She could be trusted, and in a way, it made his situation less lonely. "I've loved Rowena all my life," he revealed. "But she's been hurt, Fay. Badly hurt. Through no fault of her own."

"It's a hard road when someone's been damaged, Keir," Fay advised softly.

He frowned as he remembered the anguish in Rowena's eyes yesterday, the tests of commitment she had thrown down as a challenge to his caring, her fear of him making more trouble for her and her children.

"Somehow I've got to fix it," he said resolutely.

"I wish you luck." She smiled. "I was impressed with Jamie. Your son?"

"Yes," he acknowledged with pride. "How did you know?"

"Well, he's not exactly a dead ringer in looks, but he gets a set expression on his face that is pure you. When he declared he would wait all day if he had to…" She rolled her eyes.

He grinned, his heart lightening momentarily at the strength of character his son had displayed. "Persistence often pays off."

"I hope it does for you this time," Fay said sympathetically.

His grin turned lopsided. "It won't be for want of trying."

"You do have the boy on your side, Keir. That's a big plus."

"I've got to win Emily."

"Who's Emily?"

"Rowena's older daughter. I haven't met her yet. All going well, I shall tomorrow."

Rowena had agreed to his plan for tomorrow, but Keir didn't feel he could take it for granted. *Unless,* she had said. Unless what? Was she hoping, wanting Phil to call? Would she still accept a reconciliation at this point?

Over my dead body, Keir thought grimly. To his mind, Phil had burnt his boats with his rejection of Jamie. Keir was not about to stand by and watch Rowena hurt any further, either.

He looked at his secretary, who was still hovering, and made his decision. "Call Phil up, Fay. I'll talk to him now. It's best done before the weekend."

"Right!" She nodded agreement then waved a salute as she turned to go. "Battle stations at the ready."

He stood and wandered down his office to the table at the far end. Rowena filled his mind. The way she had accepted his kiss yesterday, the bemused, almost hopeful look on her face as he had left her to start proving himself in her eyes. The attraction *was* still there. He was certain of it. The task was to build on it.

His instincts told him speed was critical to success. He had to block Phil out of her mind, fill it with thoughts of a different, happier, easier future. With him. Fay was right about Jamie being on his side. Keir foresaw no problem with Sarah. She was delightfully open. Emily, at five, could be a stumbling block. He would have to be very alert to Emily's sensitivities.

He was pleased Rowena had refused the money for the children, though he wouldn't have begrudged a cent of it. It showed a softening of her stance against him, a return of some faith in his word. He wanted to tell her about the photograph and how it had been used to crush his hopes and dreams, but he wasn't sure she was ready to believe him yet. What if her parents denied showing him any such thing?

No, it was better to concentrate on a new start. Forget the past. It was gone. Rowena had different needs now, urgent needs, and he had to answer them. First and foremost was protection.

A knock on the door alerted Keir to Phil's arrival. He swung around to face one of the most important diplomatic meetings he'd ever had to deal with. He needed a win-win result to set the ground for the future he wanted.

"Keir, you just caught me. I was on my way out to lunch. Something urgent?" Phil asked, a tense edge to the bluff heartiness he was trying to project.

"Urgent and important. I'm sorry if I've inconvenienced you."

"Not at all. Fire away."

"Take a seat, Phil."

Keir gestured to the chairs on the other side of the table and sat down himself, careful to avoid any suggestion of a superior position. Phil Goodman's pride was very much at stake here. Keir knew he had to set the scene for a man-to-man talk, removing any threat his employer status carried.

This had nothing to do with work. Phil had to be assured of that. He had to be left feeling comfortable, not ill-affected in any way by what Keir planned. In fact, the optimum result would be for Phil to feel advantaged by Keir's stepping into the breach. It would prevent any negative fallout on Rowena.

Highly aware of the thin line he had to tread, Keir waited until Phil relaxed in his chair, then looked him straight in the eye and said, "I had a visit from your son, Jamie, yesterday. He informed me that I was his natural father. He gave me facts to substantiate his claim, and I have no doubt whatsoever that he is my child."

Phil looked stunned. "Jamie came to you?"

"Yes." Keir carefully kept his voice level and matter-of-fact. "I subsequently visited Rowena, who confirmed what Jamie told me. She was, however, extremely shocked and upset by his revelation. She had not intended me to know."

Phil ruminated over that for several moments before asking, "How did Jamie find out?"

"He didn't say. It came as a shock to me."

Phil gave a nervous, derisive laugh. "And to me. I only found out myself the other night."

Time for some judicious ego stroking, Keir thought. As much as he disliked any form of manipulation, he was prepared to use every tactical move he could think of to free Rowena from this man's destructive capabilities.

"Jamie is a fine boy, Phil," he said admiringly. "You've done a great job of bringing him up."

"That's mostly Rowena's doing," he conceded without thought. Then wryly, "She's a good mother."

"You were there for him. And you supported him. I can't thank you enough for that. Rowena and I...we were separated by circumstances that I'd rather not go into."

"I understand," Phil put in hastily.

"But things change. As with your marriage. Sometimes a relationship doesn't work out and it's better to part and move on. People grow and want to take different directions. Is that how it is with you, Phil?"

He flushed but manfully replied, "Yes, it is."

"These things happen. No one's fault. But I find myself presented with a situation where a responsibility that should have been mine can very properly and appropriately be taken up by me."

Keir paused. Phil's expression had turned wary, uncer-

tain, as though he sensed he was being pushed into a corner from where there was no exit. Keir pushed.

"*You* have shouldered that responsibility long enough,
Phil. Do you mind if I take over Jamie's care and support?"

He looked surprised, relieved. "No, that's fine by me,
Keir. He is, after all, your boy."

"Thank you. I feel I've missed out on a good deal of
Jamie's life. I want to make up for it."

"Yes. It's a shame you were…well, left out. As I said before, I wasn't aware you were Jamie's father until a couple
of nights ago, and I felt I had to respect Rowena's decision
not to tell you."

Abrogation of responsibility complete. Keir hid his
inner contempt. Although it suited him and it was what
he wanted, Phil Goodman's dumping of Jamie stirred an
urge to smash his face in. Keir controlled the primitive
reaction with some difficulty.

"Yes, after all, Rowena was left holding the baby," he
couldn't resist saying, hating the fact that it was true of
himself, but it was even more true of the man across the
table from him. "I appreciate now that I let her down," he
continued, concentrating on the next step. "I want to make
up for that, too."

A gleam of speculative interest. "What do you have
in mind?" Phil was clearly fishing for what might be in
it for him.

"Marriage, if she'll have me." Keir plunged straight in.

Phil's mouth tightened. Anger flared in his eyes. He
didn't like it one bit that Rowena might end up winning
more than he did.

Keir shifted it to a matter of principle. "It's what I would
have done had I known about her pregnancy with Jamie.
Even though he's ten years old now, I feel the same way
about it."

A nasty little smile tilted one corner of Phil's mouth. "Very noble of you, Keir. I admire you for taking your responsibility so seriously. But man to man, you should get to know Rowena again first before proposing. She expects one hell of a lot from a man."

And how many times did you let her down? Keir thought caustically. "I did know Rowena for a long time," he said, keeping his tone level and matter-of-fact.

"Knowing her and living with her are two different things," Phil said, scoffing.

"I'm prepared to take my chances on that."

"Your problem," was the mocking concession.

Keir's fingers began to clench into a fist. It took an act of will to relax them. For Rowena's sake, he had to remain civilised. It was better that Phil vented his sour grapes on him, where it couldn't hurt. One day, Keir vowed, when he'd won the right to stand by Rowena's side, Phil Goodman would get what was coming to him if he insulted Rowena again.

"Thank you for your advice, Phil," he said, keeping the savage streak at bay. "I take it you don't actually object to my marrying Rowena."

He brooded over the proposition for several moments, not caring for it but having no reasonable grounds for objection. "The girls are mine," he said possessively.

"No question. I respect that, Phil," Keir soothed. "Do you intend to contest custody of them?"

"No." He flushed again. "They're better off with Rowena," he added quickly. "I can't recommend her as an understanding wife—" another spiteful stab "—but she is a good mother."

"I thought she would be."

"Of course, I'll be paying maintenance for Emily and Sarah and I expect reasonable access."

Putting a good face on it, Keir thought cynically. He was tempted to test the depth of Phil's devotion to his daughters. "Should Rowena consent to marry me, Phil, I wouldn't mind supporting them. You've supported Jamie all these years."

"No, no, they're my daughters," he protested. "You didn't know about Jamie."

"I just feel I owe you so much."

"I appreciate that, Keir." He liked it, too. "As you remarked, these things happen."

"They do indeed."

And Keir wouldn't be at all surprised if the maintenance payments and the paternal feeling wilted away as time went on. Especially if Adriana Leigh had her way. That calculating lady didn't have a maternal bone in her body, and she wouldn't take kindly to the money going out instead of coming in.

Rowena was right not to trust her ex-husband. Phil Goodman was looking for ways out. Keir instinctively increased the carrot.

"You're a generous man, Phil. I understand you're leaving Rowena the family home."

"It's for the family," he agreed, then had quick second thoughts. "Though should Rowena remarry and the house is sold, the proceeds of the sale would be divided between us."

"That would certainly happen if I can persuade Rowena to marry me," Keir assured him. "As far as I'm concerned, you could have all the proceeds, but Rowena might feel entitled to half."

Phil's mouth curved into a self-satisfied little smile. "I wish you, luck, Keir. Rowena couldn't do better than you."

"That's big of you." It was worth the pay-off to get him off Rowena's back. "I hope you'll be happy with your decisions. I thought it better to have all this out in the open so everyone knows where they stand."

"Good idea." Warmly approved.

"Well, I won't hold you up from your lunch any longer."

Keir stood and offered his hand. Phil Goodman rose and gripped it.

Deal done.

Keir watched him leave, savagely wishing it was the last he ever had to see of Phil Goodman, but he knew he had to live with his presence for a while. Alienating the man would inevitably rebound on Rowena and her children.

He wondered how Rowena could have been so deceived about the character of the man she had married.

The need to feel loved, he decided. The words she had hurled at him echoed painfully through his mind. *He gave me what you didn't give.*

It ill behove him to forget that. Besides, Phil could look good and sound good, and he *was* good at his job. Keir had chosen to employ him. Rowena had chosen to marry him. But for Phil Goodman, they might never have met again, might never have had a second chance to come together. That was a sobering truth.

Could love rise out of hurt?

Tomorrow, Keir thought. Tomorrow he had to get everything right for Rowena. And give her all that she needed to be given. He must not fail her this time. His second chance was, in all probability, his last chance.

CHAPTER ELEVEN

"HE'S HERE, MUM!" Jamie's excited voice rang through the house.

Rowena's heart skittered. It was not quite ten o'clock. Keir was five minutes early. Not that it mattered. She was ready. They were all ready. But she couldn't help worrying how Phil was going to react to her involvement with Keir Delahunty. Her ebullient mood of yesterday had wilted overnight.

She heard the front door open, Jamie running out to greet his father. His real father. Whom he had a right to know. Impossible to stop that now.

"Come on, Emily," Sarah urged, her voice high with excitement, too. "The prince is here to take us to the castle."

Rowena winced. She shouldn't have embellished the fairy tale in Sarah's mind. Maybe she was doing everything wrong.

"I'll wait for Mummy."

Sarah dashed through the kitchen to follow Jamie.

Emily hung back, unsure of her place in this new situation.

Rowena picked up her handbag from the counter. Her gaze fell briefly on the large crystal bowl of big black cherries. It had been delivered by taxi yesterday afternoon. From Keir. He had remembered her favourite fruit.

Flowers, cherries, the trust accounts, a house... She took a deep, calming breath. It was good to feel valued again, she told herself, even if it was a risky business.

She turned to Emily with an encouraging smile and held out her hand. "Keir is a nice man," she assured her. "You'll like him."

"Will he like me?" Emily asked, trustingly slipping her hand into Rowena's.

Rowena squeezed it lightly. "Of course. He has to or he's not a prince."

That was the truth of it, though Rowena instantly wished she hadn't said it. This fairy tale business had to stop. It was too facile, too fertile a ground for future disillusionment. She didn't want her children subjected to another, possibly worse, disappointment in their young lives. If Keir didn't live up to the expectations he'd raised, how was she going to explain it all away, compensate?

As she and Emily stepped onto the front porch, he was coming up the path with Jamie and Sarah dancing around him. He was wearing blue jeans and a red T-shirt, and Rowena was instantly struck by a sense of déjà vu, Keir as a university student in happier times, coming to collect Brett for a football game or a cricket match, her at her parents' front door, waiting to ask if she could tag along, too.

He smiled as he saw her, just as he always had, and her heart turned over. Keir... Then Jamie's and Sarah's voices reminded her that time hadn't slipped back, and the years of separation from that age of innocence made their former relationship irrecoverable. Emily's little hand gripped hers more tightly. It rammed home that the past was gone.

"Good morning," Keir greeted them warmly, his gaze sweeping from her to the little girl hugging her side.

"Hello, Keir," Rowena returned as naturally as she could. "This is my daughter Emily."

"I'm happy to meet you, Emily." He crouched to be more her height. "What lovely blue eyes you have!"

"They're like my daddy's."

"So they are."

"Do you know my daddy?"

Rowena tensed. Emily was clearly fixated on her father and holding Keir at a distance.

Keir gave her a reassuring smile. "Yes, I know him. He works with me." The open establishment of a link made him less of a stranger.

"I've got green eyes like Mummy," Sarah piped up.

"I noticed that, Sarah. They're lovely, too," Keir assured her.

"Your hair is the same as Jamie's," Emily said, stepping forward to touch the cowlick at his left temple.

Keir laughed. "Well, I guess we've all got a bit of everyone. That's what families are like."

"Yes, they are," Emily agreed, pleased at having found a familiarity that made Keir properly acceptable.

Rowena's inner tension eased. The initial awkwardness with Emily had been smoothed, and Keir had managed to end it on a positive note.

He straightened to include Jamie in the group. "Now what I need to know is can you all swim?"

"Mum and I can but the girls can't," Jamie informed him.

"Aren't we going to the castle?" Sarah demanded.

"We most certainly are, but the castle has a moat."

"Keir," Rowena reproved.

"I mean the house has a swimming pool," he swiftly corrected, but the whimsy was still there as he added, "It doesn't matter if you can't swim because we can float across it on a raft, but you will need swimming costumes. Have you got some?"

"Yes," they all shouted and dived into the house, Emily as eager as the other two.

"You look breathtakingly beautiful in green," Keir said softly.

It caught Rowena off guard. She flushed. The emerald-green linen skirt with gingham trim on its pockets, teamed with a white T-shirt and a matching green overblouse, was the kind of smart-casual outfit she had thought suitable for today's outing. She hadn't expected a compliment, hadn't anticipated the warm male appreciation in Keir's eyes. It made her feel nervous, unprepared.

"I thought we were looking at a house," she said.

"We are. I own it, so we can do as we please. If you and the children like it, it's yours."

Just like that! Speechless, Rowena searched his eyes and found nothing but steady conviction. "I didn't mean it," she said in helpless agitation. "Not really."

"I do."

He was serious. Deadly serious. Rowena flailed around for an adequate explanation for the way she had behaved, the wild demands she had made. "It felt like everything was crashing around me, Keir. And Phil..."

"I've spoken to Phil. You have nothing to worry about, Rowena. He accepts that I'm seeing you and the children. He sees quite a lot of advantages to him if you marry me."

"You told Phil you were going to marry me?" Rowena squeaked. Keir was moving too far, too fast.

"I informed him it was what I wanted."

"What about what *I* want?" Her mind whirled chaotically around the image of Phil happily shifting all his responsibilities over to Keir, not only Jamie but... "Our home. He'll sell it up."

"I'll provide you with another home, Rowena."

The affirmation of his seriousness threw her into total

panic. "But that ties me to you, Keir, and I'm not ready to make such a huge decision. You can't expect it of me. We…it's been so long and…and there's the children…"

"Rowena, you're tied to me anyway. Through Jamie," he stated quietly.

That was true. She steadied for a moment. That was unavoidably true. And she could no longer count on Phil for anything. He had undoubtedly passed the buck to Keir. But *she* was not going to be passed to him. Keir had better believe that.

Her eyes flashed a fierce autonomy. "Don't take me for granted, Keir."

"I don't. I never will," he replied gently.

The soft, caring expression in his eyes reduced her insides to mush. A deep yearning welled up, making her chest ache. A passionate cry filled her mind. *Please let it be true. Please…*

"What about towels?" Jamie called out.

"No need," Keir called back, not missing a beat.

The immediate practicalities of the present snapped Rowena out of the thrall of emotional need. She had to be wary of a rebound effect from Phil's desertion. She had to take stock, be sensible, not surrender to the weakness of leaning on Keir just because he was here and offering her all his strength. How could she know it wouldn't be a mistake that she'd rue as time went on?

"Rowena, why not relax and simply enjoy the day?" Keir suggested quietly. "There'll be no pressure from me. Not for anything."

"Promise?" It sounded hopelessly childish, the kind of thing she'd said to him in their teens when she'd desperately wanted him to grant her a favour.

He grinned. "Promise."

Did he remember, too? His grin was like a burst of

sunshine, warming her with the happy beams of the past, making her feel like a teenager again. And this was their first date, just Keir and her, without Brett...without Phil.

The children broke the dreamy bubble, rushing out of the house, urging her to get her swimming costume so they could go. As she went to collect it, she told herself very sternly to keep her feet firmly planted on the ground. Keir had always been attractive to her. He still was. But that didn't mean everything in the garden was rosy.

She automatically stuffed her costume, a comb and sun-block cream in a beach bag while she tried to calculate the dangerous pitfalls in Keir's plan. She would lose her independence if she accepted Keir's house.

It was different with this home. She felt she had earned half of it over her years of marriage to Phil, and he owed the rest of it to their daughters. It was his choice as much as hers to have a family, and he shouldn't be able to slide out of it now.

It offended Rowena's sense of justice.

No doubt Adriana would profit by it, too, and that scraped raw wounds. What had the wicked witch ever done to deserve to pick up the fruits of Rowena's hard work? *Love Phil as he wanted to be loved,* came the sobering answer.

Rowena sighed away the pain of it. She had to stop thinking of Adriana as the wicked witch. If Phil hadn't wanted Adriana, nothing would have happened. The plain truth was Phil regarded her as the wrong woman for him, and he had certainly proved the wrong man for her.

Better to concentrate on Keir.

He was definitely going too fast for her. She didn't want to reject him, but she did want to slow him down as far as big commitments were concerned. It was important for her to have time to sort herself out and figure out her best future course.

It was an easy matter not to like his house, she decided. There was sure to be something wrong with it, unsuitable for the children, too small a kitchen, a shower stall instead of a proper bath. That was enough to stop Keir from putting the property in her name, which he might be mad enough to do. The experience with the trust accounts demonstrated he was not fooling around.

Satisfied she had wrested back some control of her life, Rowena emerged from the house to find the children already packed into the back seat of Keir's BMW. Keir was standing by the open front passenger door, waiting for her. Rowena's heart skittered again as she locked the door of the house that represented her marriage to Phil Goodman. Somehow it seemed fateful.

CHAPTER TWELVE

ROWENA *LOVED* KEIR'S house.

Set on a battleaxe block of land and overlooking a nature reserve leading down to Lane Cove River, it was constructed in a widened U shape to take full advantage of the view. The high central section made an impressive entrance, with tall columns flanking the front doors. Rowena was fascinated by the graduation of roof levels that ran down the two wings of the house. The entire roofline was suggestive of a phalanx of birds rising up to the sky. She knew intuitively that Keir had designed it.

"It's big," Jamie commented.

"Castles are always big," Sarah said authoritatively.

"Will we get lost in it?" Emily asked, her insecurity showing.

"No," Keir assured her with a warm smile. "Once you see how it's planned inside, you'll know how easy it is to get where you want to go, Emily."

They entered a spacious foyer backed by a wall of panelled Western red cedar. Dominating it was a breathtaking Pro Hart landscape, spotlighted for immediate impact. Keir ushered them to the right, where a gallery overlooked a wonderful, homey living area, leather lounges, television set, a log fireplace, thick fluffy mats on the slate floor, a breakfast setting in front of glass doors that opened onto an extensive sundeck, and behind the foyer wall a state-of-the-art kitchen and pantry, which left absolutely nothing to be desired.

"This is the heart of the house, Emily," Keir explained. "You start here and always come back to here. Now if we go farther along the gallery we come to the bedroom wing."

There were four bedrooms, two with private ensuites and two sharing a bathroom that had both bath and shower facilities. The master bedroom featured a walk-in wardrobe, and the cupboard space in the other rooms was more than ample. The wing also contained a laundry with every convenience, a boxroom for extra storage and a private study with a computer, photocopier and fax machine.

Jamie's eyes lit up at seeing the computer. "Do you play games on it, Keir?" he asked eagerly.

"No. But we can soon buy some, Jamie," came the obliging reply.

"Great!"

A father-and-son activity was cemented. It was just what Jamie needed, Rowena thought, and becoming familiar with computers also had to help with his education for today's world. Whatever else happened, it was good, for Jamie's sake, that he had gone to Keir.

Rowena could find nothing to criticise. It would be very easy to be seduced by Keir's castle, she reflected, as he led them to its heart and then down the left wing. A powder room off the foyer was followed by the formal dining room and lounge. Both had a casual elegance that pleased the eye without being intimidating.

The pièce de résistance was the completely enclosed pool and spa room, which also had a bar, a change room with piles of towels and an adjoining shower and toilet. Comfortable cane furniture was spread around for easy entertaining. The entire area was roofed with fibreglass shingles to let in the sunlight. The walls were mainly of glass bricks, and a profusion of ferns and exotic plants gave it a wonderful, tropical atmosphere.

Keir had every conceivable safety aid ready for the children, floaties to go on the girls' arms to make them unsinkable, inflated tyres and rafts. Simply for fun he also supplied a water polo ball and plastic ducks and boats. The children were wild to instantly try out "the moat," clamouring to get changed as fast as possible. Which, of course, meant Rowena and Keir getting changed, too.

Rowena suffered some initial disquiet at seeing Keir nearly naked in his brief, black swimming costume. The sheer male beauty of his body had always had the power to set her hormones racing, and it was disconcerting to find it was no different now. It made her acutely aware of her own body, clad only in a sleek yellow maillot, but the self-consciousness gradually eased under Keir's relaxed and friendly manner.

The water was heated to a lukewarm temperature. It invited swimming. With no initial chill factor to overcome, it made slipping into the water a real pleasure. Keir helped with the girls, laughing and playing with them, teaching them how to move their arms and legs to propel themselves around the pool. They were soon confident of manoeuvring themselves to wherever they wanted to go. Jamie teased them into being braver.

"This is marvellous, Keir," Rowena happily enthused as she watched the girls frolic like born waterbabies with Jamie pretending to be a submarine. "What made you think of an indoor pool?"

They were sitting on the steps that led into the water, ready to go to the rescue if needed.

She turned to him quite naturally, appealing for the

answer that hadn't come. "I don't remember swimming being a passion for you."

His smile held a touch of irony. "I guess it became a habit. The kind of injuries I had led to a lot of hydrotherapy. And swimming was the best exercise for strengthening my leg muscles again."

She had noticed the faded but still discernible scars on his legs and wondered how many operations it had taken to put everything right. It had been a long time since she had considered how much pain he had suffered, not only physical but emotional, as well.

"What was in the letter you wrote me, Keir?" she asked, suddenly impelled to know, to understand what he had felt in those sad, broken months following Brett's death.

He grimaced.

"You don't have to tell me if you don't want," she said quickly, realising she had contravened the new-start agreement and not really wanting to dredge through the past again. It wasn't fair, after all this time. People did change. She had changed. Probably for the worse, she thought ruefully.

"I wanted to know how you were," he answered slowly, as though feeling for the words. He scooped up a handful of water and watched it trickle through his fingers. "I knew Brett's death would have hit you hard," he continued. "The shock and the grief, the sudden empty hole in your life. It worried me...how you were coping. With everything."

With him gone, as well? Had he any idea how much she had missed him? He lifted his gaze to meet hers, and the deep, dark regret in his eyes made her heart miss a beat. It also convinced her he spoke the truth as he went on.

"It worried me that I hadn't used any protection on New Year's Eve. I hadn't planned what happened between us that night, Rowena. You were simply irresistible to me.

Afterwards… Well, I asked you in the letter if you'd fallen pregnant. And to contact me immediately if you were."

"What would you have done if I had?" she asked, glad he had thought of the risk they'd taken and the possible consequences.

"Got my parents to fly you to the States so we could plan what was best for you."

"No marriage?" she mocked lightly, disappointed with the answer.

"I didn't think it would be right to tie you to me in the circumstances, Rowena," he said softly. "It was more likely than not that I'd be crippled for life."

"Oh!" She turned away as she felt the hot burn of a flush race up her neck. He had been thinking of marriage, but caring more about *her* future.

"I also wrote, if you weren't pregnant to get on with your life, go to university as you'd planned and do your arts course. Since it might be a very long wait before I could come back to you, I said to feel free about going out with other guys and having fun. I wanted you to enjoy all there was to enjoy because that was what being young was for, exploring life and finding out what you really wanted."

"Didn't you believe I wanted you?" she asked in a very small voice, wishing she had never started this conversation.

"Rowena, I didn't want you to waste the years if I could never walk again."

"And that's why there was only one letter," she said sadly. "You set me free."

"I thought I'd done that, yes."

She had to know it all now, had to know the truth. "How long did it take for you to walk again?"

"Eighteen months. I worked very hard at it so I could come back to you."

"Then why didn't you?" She turned to him with anguished eyes. "What were the good reasons, Keir?"

"Rowena…" He didn't want to tell her. She could see the reluctance, the uncertainty over her reaction. Then he took a deep breath and said, "Your parents…"

"Go on," she urged.

His eyes focused intensely on hers, willing her to listen and accept what he said. "They showed me a photograph of you with a baby in your lap. There was a man crouched beside you. They said you were married, Rowena."

Her heart stopped. She had the numb sense of totally suspended animation. Her mind floated back, and she could see it—the terrible turning point in her life, Keir's life, that her parents had forced upon them in their bitter vendetta against Keir, the photograph she had sent them in the hope of healing the rift with the gift of their grandchild. And it was her cousin, Aunty Bet's son, who had been squatting beside her, playing with Jamie's toes to make him smile. She could see it all. And then her mind shattered under the dreadful enormity of what had been done to them.

The lie—not Keir's, her parents'. And she had accused him, blamed him, rejected him out of hand for dismissing her from his life. The awful injustice of her behaviour towards him rushed in on her. And still she hadn't killed his feeling for her. She couldn't bear the shame of it, the guilt. Tears spurted into her eyes.

"I'm sorry. I'm sorry," she gulped, then turned and fled into the pool, swimming hard, thrashing the water with her arms and legs, her chest hurting with so much pent-up feeling, her heart bleeding from all the might-have-beens.

She reached the other end of the pool. There was nowhere to go, nowhere to hide. She clutched the ledge just below the water level and tried to catch her breath. The water erupted around her as Keir's head and shoulders emerged from it.

"Mummy won!" she heard Sarah crow.

"Keir gave her a good start," Jamie pointed out.

"But Mummy won," Emily said with pride.

Rowena felt proud of nothing. She hadn't won. Too much had been lost.

"It's not your fault," Keir said in a low, intense voice.

She looked at him with agonised eyes. "But I said... I thought..."

"It's not your fault, Rowena. It was your parents' doing. And they're probably not going to like any reconciliation between us, either."

"They're dead."

"How? When?" He looked concerned.

"My father said my mother died of a broken heart. That was when Emily was one. My father then proceeded to drown his sorrows and his liver. He died last year."

"I'm sorry."

"I'm not. I'm glad they're dead," she said savagely. "I'd never forgive them if they were alive. They had no right to interfere so...so—"

"They were hurting," Keir cut in quietly. "Some people can't ever put the hurt behind them, Rowena. If you can't forgive them, you'll never be able to put it aside and move on, either."

How could he be so understanding when...?

"They're beyond hurting now," he softly pointed out. "Let it go, Rowena. Let it all go. We can make a new start."

"Can we? Can we really, Keir?" She felt as though her life was a total mess.

"Just give us time, Rowena. You'll see."

He was so sure, so confident, it eased some of the sick

churning inside her. If he could forgive and forget, maybe she could, too.

But the sense of having been cheated of the life she should have had remained with her, and it was difficult to maintain a facade of good humour for the children, who were unaware of what had transpired between Keir and herself.

The excitement and exercise in the pool soon made them hungry. They changed into their dry clothes and Keir led them out to the sundeck in front of the kitchen where he barbecued sausages, which he served with an array of tempting salads and crispy bread rolls. This was followed by ice cream, scooped into cones for easy licking. It was a relaxed and happy family luncheon, thoroughly enjoyed by the children. Even Emily's blue eyes sparkled at Keir.

He should have been their father, not just Jamie's, Rowena couldn't help thinking. She was haunted by the words Keir had thrown at her. *Is it my fault that the woman I loved married someone else? That the children I wanted with her are Phil Goodman's?* Would he ever be able to forget the girls were Phil's and treat them as his own?

He was good with them. Would he always be?

She felt a fierce love for her daughters. Even though Phil was their father, they were very much part of her. Keir had said that, too. Maybe he could put aside the fact they'd been fathered by another man. On the other hand, Phil had seemed to do so with Jamie, but when it had come to the crunch...

But Keir was different to Phil. It wasn't fair to judge him by another man's failings. Despite the passage of all these years, Keir remained steady in his love for her. Or was he clinging to a dream that had been lost a long time ago?

Time. Time would tell. She had told Jamie that.

"I wish I could swim like Jamie," Emily said with a wistful sigh.

"Would you like me to teach you?" Keir offered.

"Can you?" Her eyes lit with hope.

"Well, I taught your mother when she was a little girl."

"Did he, Mummy?"

"Yes, he did, Emily." How she had adored him, even as a little girl. He had been kinder and far more patient with her than her brother, Brett.

"Can you teach me now? This afternoon?" Emily pressed.

"We could have your first lesson. It might take a few before you take off like a mermaid," Keir warned.

Emily giggled. "Mermaids have tails, Keir."

"Legs are probably better," he returned with a grin.

He hadn't lost his giving nature, Rowena thought warmly.

They cleaned away the luncheon dishes and returned to the pool. Sarah was flagging, ready for her afternoon nap. She was happy to curl up on one of the cane lounges and watch Emily's swimming lesson. Rowena sat with her. Jamie elected to help Keir by showing Emily how to follow his instructions. Learning how to float was the first step, and Keir quickly earned her trust.

"Is teaching Emily how to swim a brave deed, Mummy?" Sarah whispered.

Rowena had to smile. "Yes, it is, Sarah."

"The prince will do it," came the vote of confidence. Demonstrating her complete trust in him, Sarah closed her eyes, gave a contented little sigh and went to sleep.

By the end of the day, Rowena had to acknowledge that Keir had done a great deal towards gaining both acceptance and real liking from her three children. After Emily's swimming lesson and Sarah's nap, he put on a video of Walt Disney's *Aladdin*, which was greatly enjoyed. For their evening meal he took them to a McDonald's, always considered a treat.

When they arrived home, the girls clamoured for him to stay and tell them a bedside story about when Mummy was a little girl. Then Jamie wanted to discuss the merits of the computer games in the catalogue Keir had found and given him. As a new-family-togetherness day, it had to be counted as highly successful.

But it was only one day, Rowena told herself, not wanting to build too many hopes on it. Nevertheless, she deeply appreciated all the effort Keir had put into giving joy and pleasure. The children had been wonderfully distracted from the misery Phil's desertion could have brought.

Rowena tried to examine her own feelings. She could not deny the underlying yearning for the fulfilment of her youthful dreams, yet the break-up with Phil had eroded her confidence in being able to live up to Keir's expectations. What if she fell short? What if the rightness she felt with him was simply a desire to feel it because she was frightened of standing alone? It was a scary world for someone who had been out of the work force as long as she had.

"Jamie said to tell you good night." Keir's voice broke into her private reverie. "I've put his light out."

She swung around from the laundry tub where she had been rinsing swimming costumes. "Thank you, Keir. For everything," she added in a rush of gratitude for his being the man he was.

"Would you like me to go now?" he asked quietly.

"No, I..." Was it wise to be alone with him when she was feeling so...needful? He stood in the doorway, almost filling it—big, solid, strong—and the urge to step forward and lean on him, to feel his arms enfold her with the promise of holding her safe forever, coursed through

Rowena with close to irresistible force. "Would you like a cup of coffee?" she blurted.

He smiled. "Very much."

His smile curled around her heart, squeezing it tight. It was the smile of the Keir she had loved, who had loved her. There was a dull ache in her stomach, a faint quiver in her thighs. It shocked her into action.

I'm playing with fire, she thought, as she hurried ahead of him to the kitchen. It was wrong to want another man when she was still married to Phil. But Phil had Adriana. Why should she care what he thought, what anyone thought? Who cared about her? Only Keir.

And the children, she sternly corrected herself. She had to remember the children.

She was reaching for the electric jug when the wall phone above it rang. She grabbed the receiver as though it was a lifeline out of her internal churning. "Hello. Rowena Goodman speaking," she said, turning to wave Keir to one of the armchairs in the family room. It was sensible to establish space between them.

"Well, it's about time you were home," a voice drawled in her ear.

The tempting excitement of a moment ago drained into a sick hollowness.

It was Phil.

CHAPTER THIRTEEN

GUILT AT HAVING been out all day was swiftly dissipated by a strong surge of self-determination. Why should she be at Phil's beck and call? He had chosen to be with Adriana. He couldn't expect the wife he had scorned to dance attendance on him, as well. Any meeting they had should be by mutual consent, with consideration given to both sides.

"I'm home now, Phil," she stated, her tone deliberately neutral.

Keir froze midway from the kitchen to the family room. His gaze swung sharply to her, assessing her reaction to the call. She had the sense of something fiercely primitive emanating from him, as though he were a warrior of old, poised to do battle to protect his territory.

"I suppose you've been with Keir Delahunty," Phil said snidely.

Rowena felt her face tighten. No doubt Phil would like to justify his actions by putting her involvement with Keir on the same level as his with Adriana. She would not give him that exoneration.

"What do you want to talk to me about?"

He laughed. "No need to get your knickers in a twist, Rowena. I know what's going on."

He made it sound dirty, and it wasn't. She had nothing

to be ashamed of. "Is there some purpose to this call?" she demanded coldly.

"I came to visit the girls this afternoon."

Guilt struck again. Rowena stubbornly repelled it. Phil could have given her fair warning. "I'm sorry your trip was wasted. If you'd—"

"Oh, it wasn't wasted. I picked up all my things. Our bedroom is now completely yours."

A chill ran down her spine at the thought of Phil coming in and removing all his personal possessions from their home. It was such a final act. Seven years...gone. And she hadn't even been here to witness it. Maybe it was easier that way, but it seemed underhand, like a thief in the night.

"I see," she said tightly. "Thank you for letting me know it wasn't burglary."

"Don't tell me you were about to ring the cops."

"No. I haven't been in our—my—bedroom since coming home."

"Busy with the kids, I take it," he said sardonically.

Conscious of Emily's need to see her daddy, Rowena smothered her resentment at his mockery of proper parenting and said, "We'll be home tomorrow if you want to visit the children."

"I have other plans for tomorrow."

Not so much as a pause to reconsider, Rowena thought. It was typical of his self-centred attitude. "Then could we make an arrangement so they don't miss you next time?" she pressed, wanting something definite so she could organise herself accordingly.

"Well, as you pointed out, Christmas is coming up next week. I'll take the girls out for a while on Christmas morning, get them out of your hair while you're cooking the turkey."

No mention of Jamie. Rowena instantly resolved to in-

vite Keir for Christmas Day. She would not have Jamie
left out of having a father. "I presume you won't be staying for the turkey."

"No. Adriana and I are booked in at a hotel for their
festive spread."

No work for Adriana. Not that Rowena cared about that.
She would much prefer to have a family Christmas in her
home than go to a hotel where the children wouldn't feel
at ease. "What time should we expect you?" she asked.

"Oh, ten-thirty, eleven o'clock, whatever," he answered
carelessly.

She wanted to say, *Don't bother,* but she held her tongue,
mindful that it wasn't only her feelings to be considered.
"You will come, won't you, Phil? I don't want to tell the
girls if they might be disappointed."

"I said I'll be there. You can have the girls waiting for
me."

Rowena burned. Had they always danced at Phil's convenience? Looking back, she could see they had, for the
most part. As the breadwinner, Phil expected it, and she
had thought he deserved the extra consideration. She had
tried so hard to be a good wife to him.

"By the way, I've taken the stereo from the lounge, and
my favourite CDs."

She frowned, wishing he hadn't done it while she was
away, but she didn't begrudge him his precious sound system. It did surprise her he'd been able to fit so much equipment into his Mazda convertible.

"And Adriana took a few bits and pieces she liked."

Adriana? She'd been with him, picking over the corpse
of their marriage for what she could get out of it? Snooping
through personal possessions, ransacking the house while
no one was here to watch over anything? No doubt she had
brought her car, too, to carry off the spoils.

Outrage billowed through Rowena, making her heart thump hard and her head pound with the hurtful injury of having her privacy wantonly invaded by a woman who had already taken her husband.

"You invited Adriana into my home?" She barely found voice enough to ask the question.

Phil snorted. "Don't tell me Keir Delahunty hasn't been there."

It wasn't the same. Not the same at all. "What bits and pieces did she take?"

"Nothing I didn't buy, Rowena. You're not entitled to everything, you know."

"I am entitled to be consulted, Phil. Please keep that in mind, or I shall call the police if anything more is taken without my knowledge or consent."

She was shaking. She fumbled the receiver onto its wall bracket, unsure what her rights were but too upset to argue the point. She would have to see a solicitor. She would have to...

"Rowena," Keir called softly, "if there's anything I can do..."

She stared blankly at him, too caught up in the tatters of her marriage to consider what he was saying. The need to know the worst impelled her feet forward, faster, faster, down the hall to the lounge. Open the door. Light on. The far end of the room bare without the stereo equipment. The china cabinet emptied of the crystal wineglasses, the Capo Di Monte figurine of the card players gone from its pride of place on top of the cabinet. Her gaze swung to the-no, no, not the lamp, too. Not the beautiful wisteria lamp he had bought her for their first wedding anniversary.

Tears welled into her eyes. An arm curled around her shoulders and turned her to a broad chest. She sagged against it, needing comfort, needing a solidity that wouldn't be stolen away from her. "Why?" she cried brokenly. "It was good once. Couldn't he leave it like that, Keir? Does it all have to be destroyed?"

"No. It shouldn't be," he murmured.

"He brought her here," she sobbed. "He let her take my lamp. I was pregnant with Emily when he gave me that. How could he? How could he?"

"I don't know."

"It's like my parents, getting rid of everything to do with you. It was so awful. Like murdering the memories."

"But I'm not gone, Rowena. I'm here with you now," he soothed. "And we'll never be parted again."

"Oh, Keir!" She burst into uncontrollable weeping.

He held her tight and stroked her hair. "I'm sorry I can't wipe all the hurt away. I wish I could."

"Not your fault," she sobbed.

"It's not your fault either, Rowena. You always did your best at everything you undertook. Don't think you're any less of the beautiful person you are because of this. Phil is the lesser person, not you."

"Why is Mum crying?"

Jamie! She'd promised him not to cry. She struggled to control the tears.

"There was a lamp. It's gone," Keir answered.

"So's the stereo. And the—" A hiss of breath. "Did Dad take them?"

"He was here with his friend while we were out. It could have been his friend who took some of the things," Keir added in mitigation. "Jamie, could you bring your mother a box of tissues, please?"

"Sure."

He was back in a trice, and Keir gave Rowena a handful of tissues to mop up her face.

"I'm sorry, Jamie," she choked out. "You can go back to bed now. I'm all right."

"I don't think so," Keir said gravely. "Jamie, can you get the girls up? Your mother is too upset to stay here. I think we should go back to my house tonight."

"No...no, I can't," Rowena protested, afraid of where that might lead and too wrought up to handle any decisions properly.

"It's okay, Mum. Keir will look after you," Jamie assured her. "I'll get Emily and Sarah."

He raced off again.

"Keir," Rowena appealed desperately.

"I can't leave you here, Rowena. Everywhere you turn you'll feel a sense of violation. It's better that you all come with me."

"But..."

"Don't worry. You'll have a bedroom to yourself. One that Phil and Adriana haven't been in."

She shuddered. Would they have? In the light of what had happened, anything was possible.

"You left your bag and keys in the kitchen, didn't you?"

"Yes."

"Come on. We'll collect them and get on our way."

He kept her hugged warmly to his side as they walked to the kitchen. Rowena couldn't think in any coherent fashion. There were too many mixed-up emotions running rampant. With all the upheaval and revelations of the past week, she felt her life had been turned upside down and inside out, and nothing made any sense any more.

When they returned to the hall, her three children were standing in the open doorway to the lounge, staring at the empty spaces.

"See?" said Jamie.

"I bet the wicked witch did it," Emily declared, trying to be loyal to her father.

Sarah turned to Keir. "Can the wicked witch get into the castle?"

"No. I guard the gate, Sarah. You'll be absolutely safe there," he promised.

"It's good to have a brave prince, isn't it, Mummy?"

"Yes," Rowena said weakly, too drained to take anyone to task over the fairy tale.

"Let's go," Jamie urged, leading the way.

Keir took charge of everything. He switched off lights, locked the house, settled Rowena in the front passenger seat of his car and made sure the children had their safety belts fastened in the back seat before taking his place on the driver's side.

Rowena stared at the darkened house as he started the car. It looked abandoned, empty, empty of love and commitment, dead to any happy future. The car moved onto the street and accelerated away. Keir's hand reached across and grasped hers, enveloping it in warmth, linking her to him.

"Trust me, Rowena," he said softly.

A brave prince, she thought. *Brave to take me on, and all the baggage I bring with me.*

She looked at their hands, feeling the strength of his seep into her veins. A helping hand, a loving hand, a hand she could hold onto. It wouldn't slip away from her, would it?

Trust me.

But could she trust herself to do right by him? She was no longer sure what *right* was. Only that Keir's hand felt right in hers. Was that enough on which to let the past go and forge a future together?

CHAPTER FOURTEEN

THE CHILDREN HAD fallen asleep without any problem. Keir wasn't worried about them. He was confident of answering their needs and concerns as they arose. There was a wonderful simplicity about children.

He could see Rowena in all three of them, even Emily, trying her best to learn how to swim. It was easy to love them, to give them the attention that made them feel happy within themselves, knowing they had their special place in the affections of the people who counted most in their lives.

Rowena's parents had robbed her of that precious feeling. They had let Brett's death overshadow everything. She hadn't counted any more. Phil had just done the same thing to her. It was like crushing out of her all the value she had as a person, and it was so wrong, so hurtful. It was fortunate that Phil Goodman wasn't within striking distance, because the violence Keir felt towards him was close to murderous.

At least Rowena now knew he hadn't dismissed her, too. He hoped she was beginning to realise how meaningful she was to him. He desperately wanted to heal her hurts, to give her the love and life she deserved. He had to pull her through this, win her trust, give her back the bubbling joy that had once been naturally hers.

He paused by her door to listen again, worrying about

her state of mind. The shower in the ensuite had been running for the past half hour. It was a relief not to hear it. He hadn't known whether it was a lethargy of mind and spirit that had kept her standing under the beat of the spray, or some sense of wanting to wash away the rotten distaste of what Phil and Adriana had done.

Whatever…it had stopped now. He had given her one of his soft, cotton T-shirts to wear to bed. Maybe she was already settled for the night, but he doubted that sleep would come easily. He remembered a habitual nightly routine from her childhood, and headed for the kitchen.

A mug of hot Milo. It didn't matter if it was no longer a habit with her. It would recall happier times. He tipped two heaped spoonfuls of the sweet chocolate grains into a mug, poured in milk, stirred the mixture vigorously and slid it into the microwave for two minutes.

Happier times…

There had been several little occurrences today when he had felt they had been recaptured, if only fleetingly. This morning… Rowena waiting for him on the front porch as he walked up the path to her. When she had appeared in her swimming costume and looked at him in his, barriers had slipped away momentarily, he was sure of it. Then tonight, in the laundry, that vibrant moment when he sensed her wanting to reach out to him, wanting to try what he offered.

If Phil hadn't phoned…

But Phil's crass insensitivity had resulted in Rowena coming here, under his protection. That was a plus. If he could persuade her to stay, it would give him his best chance to show her how it could be for them. They had so many years to make up. He didn't want a second of this new start wasted, didn't want a second of the rest of their future wasted. If only she could see it as he did.

The microwave clicked off. He took out the steaming hot mug, stirred the Milo through the milk again, then, hoping Rowena would welcome it, returned to her bedroom door and knocked.

"Yes?" Definitely awake.

"It's Keir. I've got some hot Milo for you. It might help you sleep."

"Hang on till I put the bedside light on," she called.

He waited, wondering if this was such a good idea after all. It might help Rowena sleep, but seeing her in bed was bound to arouse thoughts and feelings that would make sleep difficult for him. He wanted her so much it was almost a constant ache inside him.

"It's okay. You can come in now."

Think of her as the child she had once been, he sternly advised himself. He had waited years for her to grow into a young woman. He could wait…please, God, not years again.

He left the door ajar to assure her he had no desirous intent. It was important she feel safe with him. Absolutely safe. She was sitting up, propped against the pillows. She looked like a lost waif, the sleeves of his T-shirt dangling shapelessly around her elbows, her black hair in damp wisps around her wan face.

"Are you okay?" he asked.

"More or less." She managed an ironic little smile. "Thanks, Keir. It was kind of you to think of the Milo."

"I hope it helps." He set the mug on the bedside table. "Is there anything else I can do for you, Rowena?"

"Are the children all right?" she asked anxiously.

"Yes. Fast asleep."

"You were good with them today. And tonight." Her big green eyes were darkly soulful. "I appreciate it. Very much."

"It's a pleasure."

"You really mean that, don't you?"

"Yes."

"Keir..." She flashed him a look of vulnerable appeal. "Sit with me?" She shifted somewhat gracelessly, nervously, to make room for him beside her on the bed.

It left him no option but to oblige her request. She would interpret any retreat as rejection. Unfortunately, her movement had pulled the soft fabric of the T-shirt so that her breasts were delineated too clearly for Keir's comfort. He tore his gaze away from them as he lowered himself gingerly on the bed, determined to be the friend she needed.

"Will you hold my hand?" she asked huskily, offering it for him to take.

He shot her a swift, searching look, wondering if she felt frightened and lonely. Her lashes were lowered, her gaze fixed on the inviting hand. Her face had a soft, pearlescent glow in the lamplight. Her lips were slightly apart as though waiting to shape more words. Or perhaps anticipating, wanting the kind of kiss he had given her before starting on his quest.

Keir grimly leashed in that thought. He couldn't afford to give in to temptation when Rowena already had too much to deal with. He turned more towards her so he could enfold her hand in both of his, feeling both tender and possessive as his fingers stroked softly over her inner wrist.

Her pulse leapt under his touch. Again he glanced at her, sharply questioning. Her gaze remained fixed on their hands, and she was absolutely still, as though even her breathing was suspended.

What was she thinking? What did his touch mean to her?

"I want you to..." She hesitated, drew in a deep breath. "I want us..." She spoke more strongly, but with a slight quaver that suggested she was screwing up her courage. "To make love."

His heart stopped, then seemed to catapult around his chest with chaotic abandonment of any control whatsoever. Her gaze flew to his, her eyes dark, swirling pools of tortured uncertainties, yet overlaid with a desperate pleading for him to sort them out for her.

No, no, his mind screamed. He wanted it free and clear of anyone else, proving nothing, a joyous celebration of finding each other again, loving because it was beautiful to love. Yet he felt his body stir, urging him to appease the need that had raged in him for so long. She would respond. She had to. Or there was no sense in any of the feelings he'd nursed all these years.

"Tell me it's not because of what Phil Goodman did to you," he heard himself say, his voice uncharacteristically harsh, riven with deep and violent emotions. "If this is some hit back at him, Rowena..."

"No! It's not, Keir."

He saw the recoil in her eyes and both gloried in it and regretted it. Was he spoiling everything? He couldn't help himself. The need to have her all to himself, cleaving only to him, was so powerfully imbedded it reeked of the primitive, but he didn't care. He couldn't be civilised about this. She was his woman, and he didn't want the slightest taint of another man coming between them when they made love.

"I need to know...about us, Keir," she pleaded. Her fingernails scraped the palm of his hand in her agitation at his reaction. Her eyes begged him to understand.

Not another test, he thought in violent rejection. She couldn't turn making love with him into a test. He wouldn't let her. It was too demeaning, too repugnant to him.

He set her hand on the bedclothes and stood up. He couldn't bear her look of hurt. "I have needs, too, Rowena," he stated baldly. He hurt, as well. He hurt all over. He turned aside lest he break and give in to her, even knowing it was wrong and possibly destructive to both of them. He walked away from her because he had to, or nothing would turn out right. Even his bones ached.

"Keir..." Anguish.

He felt it, too. "I hear you, Rowena. I hear your grief and your pain, your doubts and your fears. I understand them all. But I can only give so much." He reached the door he had left ajar and held it to reinforce his resolve to go when he'd said what needed saying.

"Don't you want me?"

The lost little-girl voice pierced his heart and shattered his defences. The passions he had tried so hard to contain exploded through his mind and ripped through his body. "Want you!" The breath hissed from his lungs. He slammed the door shut and wheeled to face her.

"Want you!" he repeated, words jamming in their tumult to be expressed, then spilling into a torrent. "Have you any idea how it felt to be suddenly confronted with you last year, you at Phil Goodman's side, his wife? I didn't even dare ask you to dance with me. It made me sick to watch you with him, wanting...wanting what I couldn't have."

She stared at him, dumbstruck by his vehemence. At least he had her full attention, Keir thought with fierce satisfaction.

"And I had to work with your husband, knowing he went home to you every night," he said, hammering the emotional dilemma *he* had faced. "I couldn't make myself get rid of him. I'd given him a well-paid executive job. Maybe you needed the money, I reasoned. But the truth, the deep-down basic truth was I didn't want to give up the link to you, Rowena."

She shook her head, as though dazed by his revelations.

It spurred him to lay it all out for her, so she would understand and realise the length and depth and breadth of what she was asking of him.

"I could hardly believe it when Phil started flirting with Adriana. At first I was angry on your behalf. How could he play around when he had you as his wife? Then as the affair ripened into full-blown infidelity, I took a different attitude."

He paused, warning signals flashing in his brain. Was he flagellating her with too much honesty?

"What?" she asked.

It was enough to goad him on. "I wanted your marriage to break up. I wanted him out of your life so I could step into it. And if that shocks you, I'm sorry, but it's a measure of my wanting."

She said nothing. She simply stared at him.

Too late to retract anything now. He felt too raw himself to do any healing. "Then you came to fight for him." He flung the words at her. "To fight for a man who cared so little about hurting you. While I... I'd die for you, Rowena."

Utter stillness from her. Silence.

His hands lifted and fell in a gesture of despair. "Want you..." The words were a whip to tortured passion. "I've wanted you most of my life. But when we made love all those years ago, Rowena, you came to me as a woman who wanted me equally as much, and I will not accept less. To ask me to make love on the chance that it might make you feel better about yourself—"

"No, Keir. It wasn't that," she swiftly denied.

"Then what? A test of what you feel with me?"

She didn't answer. Her eyes lost focus as though she was looking inside herself.

"You want a test?" he demanded hoarsely. "I'll give you

a test, Rowena." He hauled off his T-shirt and tossed it on the floor. "I've already stripped myself naked for you in every other way. Let's get down to the absolute basics."

She made no protest as he savagely removed his other clothes. Then he stood before her, ostensibly at ease, arms akimbo, deliberately challenging her with his nudity, his eyes blazing forth his need. "You want us to make love?" His voice shook with the force of it. "Then come to me, Rowena. Show me you want me. Not as some panacea for other ills, but wanting me for the man I am."

Her focus was certainly on him now.

The air between them was charged with tension.

Decision time.

She moved. Keir could hardly believe it. Hope tingled through him, electrifying every nerve end. Bedclothes tossed aside, long bare legs reaching for the floor. His heart pounded in his ears. She stood. Her arms crossed, hands bunching folds of the T-shirt. Without hesitation she yanked it over her head and hurled it aside.

Keir's stomach contracted as the full flood of her nakedness hit him, more womanly than he remembered, softer, lushly feminine. His loins tightened, desire shooting through him, vessels expanding, wanting. This was Rowena now, Rowena who had borne him a son in her rounded belly, suckled his baby at her breasts, such glorious breasts, their nipples tightly pointed at him.

There was a magnificent air of pride and confidence in the way she held herself as she walked towards him, shoulders back, hips swaying, her gaze fixed unwaveringly on his, her eyes fiercely aglow. No defeat in her, no grief. Keir exulted in the breaking of those deadly chains, exulted in the freedom with which she came to him.

"I want you, Keir." Her husky voice caressed the last dregs of torment from his mind. "I've always wanted you."

Her words burned the scars from his heart. "And that's the naked truth," she said, touching him.

The dark, empty places in his soul exploded in a cascade of light, like brilliant fireworks erupting in showers of stars, wondrous patterns imprinting themselves in renewed bursts, the ecstatic revival of all he had feared lost.

As her hands slid up his chest and linked around his neck, he crushed her body to his, craving the oneness he knew was theirs, unlocked from seemingly impassable doors that had been shut so devastatingly between them. His mouth found hers with a hunger she returned, her passion matching his, her need as wild and as insatiable. The kisses were long and infinitely sweet in their total lack of inhibition.

But they weren't enough. Not nearly enough. His hands swept down the sensual curve of her back, curled around her bottom, cradling the intimate heat of her closer, wanting the ultimate joining, his flesh sheathed in hers, together as they had been, would be.

She stretched on tiptoe, as eager as he for the exquisite sensation of desire fulfilled. "Lift me, Keir," she urged, parting her legs for him, winding them around his hips as he hoisted her higher, ready for the seeking, the finding, the thrust that took him inside her, deep as she settled around him, her muscles convulsing with the pleasure of containing him.

The ecstasy of it, Rowena wanting him as he wanted her. He swung her around in sheer elation, carrying her with him to the bed, smoothly accommodating her position on top of him, inciting the rhythm with hands and thighs, moving to match her, to excite, to thrill to the beat, the slide and the plunge. And her lovely full breasts dangling above him, inviting capture, suction.

The fantastic freedom of drawing her flesh into his

mouth, lashing the taut nipple with his tongue, pulling, tugging, the seductive music of her gasps and moans of pleasure as he moved from one breast to the other, taking them in tandem, greedy for the taste of her, for the feel of her response to him, the silky heat of her bathing his pulsing shaft until her shattered cry and the milky flood of her climax spurred him to take the control that had melted for her.

Gently he rolled her onto the pillows where she sank into languid abandonment of any further action. Her thighs were still aquiver. He cradled her hips and pushed to the place that he knew would increase her pleasure. She arched as he reached it, caressed it. An inarticulate cry broke from her throat. Her eyes flew open, and their wonderment filled him with joy as they mirrored the intense inner world he built for them, the soft undulations and the high peaks.

He sustained it as long as he could, but when she lifted her hands and ran her fingertips over his shoulders and chest, his entire body was ignited with excitement and the dance he had orchestrated fell apart to the drumbeat of uncontrollable need. He drove hard and fast, and she lifted herself to give him the fullness of his pleasure, welcoming the ultimate release of his love for her, her arms waiting to receive him as the final melding came.

It was good simply to hold her close in the blissful contentment of knowing all the barriers had been crossed. *Mine at last,* he thought, intensely happy, uncaring of any problems that might arise from what might be viewed as a premature coupling. It wasn't to him. It wasn't to Rowena, either. The wanting had been deep and mutual.

CHAPTER FIFTEEN

ROWENA LAY IN his arms, incredulity, awe, bliss, drifting across her mind, like shining clouds, pierced by a sun that dispelled all gloom.

Keir.

His name alone embodied a wealth of feeling for Rowena. She had forgotten or suppressed the magic of loving and being loved by him. And to think she had spent eleven years without this brilliant sense of being utterly, poignantly, beautifully alive.

She nestled closer to him, tucking her head under his chin, giving herself more reach to play her hand over Keir's magnificently male body. He hadn't changed at all, not in nature, not in heart, not in any way that counted. He was Keir, her first love, the love that would always endure. She knew that now.

How bravely and passionately he had ripped the scales from her eyes, torn aside the shadows in her mind and smashed the shackles of the eleven long years that had parted them. *My prince, slaying all my dragons,* she thought in smiling whimsy.

"Thank you for being you, Keir," she said with a happy sigh.

"And you…you're a miracle, Rowena," he answered softly. "More than I dared dream of."

"I lost faith in dreams," she confessed. "I'm sorry, Keir. I should have trusted you. I should have known. Will you forgive me my blindness?"

He stroked her back, sending delicious little shivers over her skin. "There's nothing to forgive. You had a lot of baggage to carry, Rowena," he said, generously excusing her of any fault.

"I still have," she said, thinking of the children. "You really don't mind about getting a ready-made family?"

"What's yours is mine," he stated simply. "They're great kids. All three of them."

The warmth in his voice left her in no doubt that he accepted them without reservation. And he wouldn't disown any of them. Not like Phil. It wasn't in Keir to renege on commitment.

"Are you worried about them accepting us?" he asked.

Rowena considered the question seriously, then consciously dismissed every niggle of concern. Perhaps she had made the mistake of putting the children's needs first in her marriage to Phil, although certainly not all the time, as Adriana had suggested. What she knew now, with utter conviction, was the love she and Keir shared would always come first. What they had was so special it would rub off on the children, anyway. They could only benefit by it, even if it took some time for it to permeate their lives.

"No, I'm not worried," she replied with firm confidence.

"Good! Then how do you feel about moving in here with me tomorrow?"

She laughed and hitched herself up to see the expression in his eyes. The need and want so clearly emblazoned in their shining depths sobered her. So much time wasted. And who knew how long their lives would be?

"We'll do it," she said decisively.

"You don't mind returning to the house to pack your things?"

She shook her head. Nothing in that house could touch her now. What had been there was gone, irrevocably. Keir was the future, every minute of it.

He grinned. "I'd better give Sarah swimming lessons, too. The sooner they learn, the better. Then you won't have any cause to worry."

He was so generous with everything. "What can I give you, Keir?"

His eyes sparkled with mischief and desire as he rolled her onto her back and leaned over her. "I could suggest many things— " he kissed her, and his voice dropped to a husky throb of contentment " —but the gift of yourself is enough for me, Rowena." He kissed her again, more passionately, thrillingly.

She would think of something to give him, Rowena silently vowed. Something he wasn't expecting. A gift of love that he would know was especially for him, for being the man he was.

CHAPTER SIXTEEN

THE WEEK LEADING up to Christmas sped by.

There was no protest from the children about moving in to the castle. To Sarah it was a natural progression of the fairy tale. Emily reasoned that Daddy had packed up and left what had been the family home, so it was only right to do the same. Jamie's energy level hit a new high. He could barely contain his excitement at beginning a new life with his real father. Plus a computer to play with.

Keir was marvellous. Both Sarah and Emily learnt to swim very quickly under his patient tuition. He bought video games for the computer, some of which were simple enough for the girls to play, too, although Jamie was put in charge of them and had the responsibility of showing and helping.

The highlight of the week was the Christmas pantomime of *Cinderella,* which was showing in the city. Keir provided them with tickets to a matinee, and the performance was an absolute delight, much talked about afterwards, with the children giving Keir renditions of the parts they loved best. His enjoyment of their mimicking added enormously to their pleasure in the outing.

None of them questioned her sharing a bedroom with Keir. Maybe they accepted it as natural, Rowena thought, given the fact of living together as a family. Maybe they wanted everything to feel natural. She hoped that when Phil came to see the girls on Christmas morning, he wouldn't stir up any uneasy feelings about it.

Keir had informed Phil they had left the house at Killarney Heights and were living with him at Lane Cove. Only personal belongings had been taken with them, so if Phil wished to dispose of the furniture he could do what he liked with it. Rowena and the children would not be returning to the house, which could be put on the market immediately if Phil and Adriana had no use for it.

Phil was also informed that the move in no way affected his right to see his daughters, and both Emily and Sarah had been told of his intention to visit them on Christmas morning. Keir assured Rowena that the conversation had been conducted in a civilised manner, but she could not help having some trepidation about Phil's manner with the girls when he had them to himself.

Keir opened a bank account for her and urged her to spend freely. He wanted this Christmas to be the best ever for all of them. They decorated a marvellous tree in the living room. Rowena had already bought most of her gifts for the children, but she added a few more for extra surprises, and indulged herself in finding some special gifts for Keir.

She laid the festively wrapped parcels out under the tree once she was sure the children were asleep on Christmas Eve. To her astonishment, Keir added a heap of his own, which he'd kept hidden in the boot of his car.

"It's great having kids for Christmas," he told her with a happy grin. "I can't remember when I've had so much fun shopping."

It slid into Rowena's mind that Phil had always left gift shopping for the children to her. Too much hassle with the crowds and too little time to think about it, he had excused himself. She should have known Keir would be different.

Thinking about what would give them pleasure was second nature to him. Doing it *was* his pleasure.

As expected, they were woken early on Christmas morning with cries of feverish excitement. Every gift was unwrapped with gleeful anticipation and greeted with delight. Keir had made some inspired choices. Best of all to the children was a three-dimensional jigsaw puzzle of a fantasy castle. The picture of the completed construction showed it had turrets, balconies, open arches, drawbridges and a moat, as well as cobblestoned courtyard gardens with realistic grass, water and rocks. It was, in fact, a detailed model of a classic medieval castle.

One of Keir's gifts to Rowena was the title deed of his house, transferred into her name, making her the legal owner. On its accompanying Christmas card he had written, "The security I want you to have, with all my love, Keir."

Impossible to protest. Rowena wished again there was something special she could give him, something of similar value in so far as it would answer a need he had. She was busy in the kitchen, preparing the traditional roast turkey, when Jamie, in response to some question from Keir, fetched the photograph album devoted to him. The answer Rowena had been looking for struck her forcefully as Keir leafed through the album.

Photos of Jamie as a baby, as a toddler, his first day at kindergarten. There was a sad, regretful look on Keir's face—years forever lost to him, joys he hadn't shared. She remembered his words—*the children I wanted with her.*

A baby, Rowena thought.

She was only twenty-eight. She wouldn't mind having another baby with Keir, and he would love it so, sharing intimately the experience of birth and a new life unfolding. She was privately revelling in the pleasure it would give him when the door chimes rang.

Phil!

She had been half hoping he wouldn't come at all, not wanting the day to be soured in any way. But he was the girls' father, and rights had to be observed. Emily and Sarah looked up from their new toys.

"Is that Daddy?" Emily asked.

It had just gone ten-thirty. "I think so," Rowena answered, giving them an encouraging smile to put them at ease. "Shall we go and see?"

"Well, I'm going to play my new computer game," Jamie announced, proudly independent of Phil. "Want to have a look with me, Keir?"

"Yes. It should be quite a challenge for you, Jamie," he obliged, moving to give his son the reassurance he needed.

It felt wrong to have the family separated like this, but there was nothing that could be done about it. Rowena gathered up the girls, who had gone oddly quiet, looking after Jamie and Keir as they walked along the gallery to the study and not expressing any excitement whatsoever over the visit by their father. Nevertheless, they compliantly followed Rowena to the front door and didn't hang back when she opened it.

One step onto the porch and all three of them came to a dead halt.

Phil was accompanied by Adriana Leigh.

Neither of them looked as though they had come to entertain two little girls. Phil was in a smart navy blue suit and Adriana was semi-clothed in a red and gold sundress that showed plenty of cleavage and leg. Rowena and the girls were wearing jeans and T-shirts printed with bright Christmas motifs. The contrast in dress instantly created a distance between the two parties.

"Well, how are my girls?" Phil began with forced heartiness, not bothering with Christmas greetings to Rowena.

"Who is *she*?" Sarah demanded, eyeing Adriana up and down with hostile suspicion.

"Don't be rude, Sarah," Rowena softly reproved. "Your father will introduce you."

"This is my friend Adriana. We're going to take you and Emily to a big park where you can play on the swings and the slippery dip," Phil said unctuously.

While they sat and twiddled their thumbs until time was up, Rowena thought. Adriana's high heels were definitely not park shoes. Which raised the question of how much supervision the children would get.

Sarah gave Adriana a baleful stare and bluntly stated her decision. "I'm not going anywhere with the wicked witch!"

"What?" Phil snapped.

Rowena barely stopped herself from rolling her eyes.

"She'll put a spell on me," Sarah explained. "I'm going back inside the castle. She can't get me there because the prince won't let her."

Before anyone could stop her she turned tail and ran into the foyer, heading full pelt towards the gallery.

"What the hell is this, Rowena?" Phil demanded testily. "Have you been bad-mouthing Adriana to my daughters?"

"No, I haven't. Sarah has her own way of working things out, Phil. You know she does," she pleaded in mitigation.

"You could have corrected her," he accused.

"I tried." Though not very hard, she had to admit to herself. After all, she couldn't see why she should defend Adriana in the circumstances. The woman was not interested in children, and that was as obvious as the dress she wore.

"I didn't think you'd be spiteful," Phil said, sniping.

Rowena held her tongue, wondering how he described his actions to himself.

He gave up badgering her and dropped to his haunches to court Emily. "How's Daddy's girl? Have you missed me?"

Emily shrank back against Rowena. "Why did you leave us, Daddy?" she bravely asked.

Phil sighed. "Well, it's hard to explain. I wasn't really happy with your mother, Emily."

"Don't you love Mummy any more?"

"I'm much happier with Adriana," he stated firmly. "That's why I'm with her. And you'll like her very much once you get to know her."

Emily looked at Adriana, who obliged with an indulgent smile, which was enough to turn Rowena's stomach. Emily wasn't much taken with it, either. She returned her gaze to her father and continued her childish inquisition.

"What about me, Daddy? Weren't you happy with me?"

"Emily…" Phil flushed uncomfortably. "When you're grown up, you need to be with another grown-up. That doesn't mean I don't love my little girl. I've got lots of Christmas presents in the car for you."

"Have you got Mummy's lamp for her? The one with the blue beads hanging down?"

"No, I haven't," he growled. "Now let's get going. We haven't got all day." He straightened up and offered his hand to her.

Emily looked doubtfully at Adriana, then shook her head, her hand seeking Rowena's, not Phil's. "I want to stay with Mummy."

"Emily, I've come out of my way to see you," Phil said tersely. "Your mother said you wanted me to."

"Yes." She nodded gravely. "Thank you for seeing me,

Daddy, but I don't want to go with you," she said in a very little voice.

"All right," Phil snapped. "If that's the way you want it, I'll give all your presents to the Smith family."

"Phil," Rowena reproved quickly. "You can't force things. It would have been wiser to come without Adriana this time."

"You can say that when you're living openly with Keir Delahunty?" he scoffed.

Keir appeared in the doorway, Sarah's hand firmly clasped in his, Jamie on his other side. "Is there a problem?" he asked, politely nodding to Phil and Adriana.

"No. No problem," Phil mocked. "I only came to do my duty, and that's done. Have yourself a happy family Christmas." He stepped smartly back to Adriana and took her arm. "Come on, darling. We've spent enough time here."

"Happy Christmas!" Adriana trilled, delighted to have the duty disposed of.

Keir stepped out to stand at Rowena's side. Jamie came forward to put his arm around Emily's shoulders in big-brotherly support. They all watched Phil and Adriana get into what had to be Adriana's car, since it wasn't the red Mazda convertible.

"He said he'd give our presents away, Sarah," Emily said mournfully.

"I don't want them anyway," Sarah declared unequivocally. "I bet the wicked witch touched them."

She was undoubtedly right, Rowena thought. Phil would have got Adriana to buy them for him. She had the feeling it would be a long time before Phil came visiting again.

"He didn't bring Mummy her lamp, either," Emily added, clearly affected by the injustice of it all.

The car zoomed away from the kerb and disappeared down the street.

"We've got the prince, Emily," Sarah said, her satisfaction in the choice abundantly clear.

"Yes. We've got the prince," Emily agreed with fervour.

Jamie gave Keir a smug look. "And we've got lots of presents inside," he reminded the girls.

"Yes!" they shouted in unison.

"Let's play!" It was like a bugle call.

"Yes!"

Jamie led the charge into the house, the girls on his heels, the encounter with Phil shrugged off and left behind them with what seemed like extraordinary ease. Emily, at Jamie's urging, ran with him to the study to see what was on the computer screen, and Sarah skipped down the gallery, as carefree as an impish little fairy.

Keir closed the front door and drew Rowena into a gentle embrace, his dark velvet eyes scanning hers for stress. "Are you all right?" he asked. "Phil didn't upset you?"

"No." She released her inner tension with a sigh, then smiled her relief at the unexpected outcome of Phil's visit. "Children can be so amazing."

"Their logic is very direct," he said dryly.

"Keir…" She wound her arms around his neck and pressed closer. Her eyes projected all the desire in her heart, desire for him, desire to please, to give, to share all life had to offer. "Let's have another baby. Together."

Surprise and delight lit his eyes. "You mean it, Rowena? You really want another child?"

She laughed, her heart lifting exultantly at his response. "Well, we needn't stop at one if you want more," she teased. "I'm pretty good at being a mother, you know."

"The best." He grinned. "I'd love a big family, Rowena. Having been an only child…"

Of course! That was why he and Brett had been inseparable—the only child in each family until she had come along, the much-loved little sister.

"But what about you?" He quickly changed tack. "I thought you might like to pick up the arts course you'd wanted to do."

"I can do that in my thirties. Or my forties. I'm planning on a long life."

He laughed, his eyes shining with unadulterated happiness. "A very long and a very full life."

"How could it be anything else with you?"

"And with you."

Their lips met in a kiss that sealed so many things— the love and the giving and the open trust and the sense of completely bonded togetherness.

A new start.

CHAPTER SEVENTEEN

FAY PENDLETON, KEIR'S wonderful all-purpose secretary, bustled around them in the nave of the church, making sure the bridal procession was arranged to proceed perfectly.

Jamie was in the lead, dressed in a formal black page-boy suit, carrying a white satin cushion on which lay the two gold wedding rings.

Emily came next, then Sarah, both looking absolutely exquisite in flower-girl gowns of ivory raw silk. Seed pearls enhanced the lace on their bodices and outlined the waistline. Frills and bows ornamented softly puffed sleeves, and the full skirts were caught at the back with a feature bow. Around their hair were circlets of little pink florabunda roses and baby's breath, and they carried beautifully decorated baskets of rose petals to sprinkle down the aisle.

"There! Now don't twitch or anything," Fay advised Rowena. "I've got the train just right. You're ready to go. I'll signal the organist before taking my seat."

Rowena smiled. "Thank you for organising everything for me, Fay. You've been marvellous."

"It's been a real pleasure, Rowena. Like having a daughter."

She moved to the head of the aisle and gave them one last look-over, nodded approval, then set off for her seat

at the front of the church. It would be easy for the organist
to spot her, Rowena thought. Fay had her hair dyed a fiery
copper and was wearing a vibrant violet outfit.

Sarah disobeyed the eyes-forward edict and turned her
head to catch one more admiring eyeful of her transformed
mother. "You look just like a princess, Mummy," she whispered, a note of awe in her voice.

"Thank you, Sarah," Rowena whispered back, her heart
swelling with happiness.

She *felt* like a princess. Keir had insisted they be married in a traditional fairy-tale wedding, and she was to
buy the dress of her dreams, no expense spared. When
she had seen this wedding gown she had just stared and
stared at it, spellbound, finding it utterly magical and perfect in every detail.

It was made of ivory silk duchess satin and had an air of
elegant majesty about it. The empire sleeves, cinched waist
and deep neckline evoked a bygone era. The wide flare of
the skirt created a wonderful balance to the tightly fitted
bodice. It featured a centre gore encrusted with lace and
pearls, repeating the pattern sewn onto the flared lower
half of the sleeves.

In keeping with the style of the dress, the veil was attached to a tiara of fine gold and tiny ivory flowers. Rowena's hair had been swept up into a high topknot, which the
tiara encircled. Around her neck she wore a fine gold chain
supporting a beautiful gold and pearl-encrusted cross.

Keir hadn't seen any of it. She hoped—no, she knew—
she was everything he wanted in a bride. To him, she
would look beautiful whatever she wore, and part of feeling like a princess was knowing her prince was at the
altar, waiting for her.

The soft organ playing stopped. There was a hushed
expectancy in the church. The "Wedding March" started.

Jamie set off down the aisle, keeping in perfect time with the music. Emily correctly paced her entrance, gently scattering rose petals from her basket. Sarah followed on cue, apparently deciding a shower of rose petals was more appropriate. Or more fun.

Rowena couldn't help smiling. She smiled all the way down the aisle—to the friends she had met and made over the past sixteen months while living with Keir, to Aunty Bet and her son and his family, who had flown down from Queensland for the wedding, to Keir's parents, who were so delighted to be getting Rowena as their daughter-in-law, and finally to the man she loved and always would love.

Keir.

He looked stunningly handsome in black, peak-lapel tails and white wing-collar shirt, so elegant and debonair. The classic style gave him such a distinguished air. But it was the expression in his eyes that mattered most to Rowena, the shining of a love that had spanned so many years without ever faltering.

She wished her parents could have been here, not as they were after Brett's death, but before, when they had been happy to have Keir as almost a second son, happy for her to go out with him. She hoped they had found peace and perhaps were even looking down at her and Keir right now, knowing it was right for them to have come together again.

The marriage service began.

She thought fleetingly of her marriage to Phil, wondering if he was as happy as he wanted to be with Adriana. He had resigned from Delahunty's over a year ago, investing the money from the sale of the house in a real estate business on the Gold Coast of Queensland. The fast-paced life there suited them better, he had said, and the girls could come and have a vacation with him when they were old enough to travel alone.

Their parting was reasonably amicable. So was their divorce. There was no question over the custody of the children, and formal visiting rights were waived. The girls could contact him if they wanted to, but basically he had simply dropped out of their lives, and Rowena didn't believe he was missed.

Keir more than filled the gap.

Keir.

Their commitment to each other was at last being formalised in this marriage service, husband and wife in the eyes of the world, yet the inner bonding went back a long, long way and would go on forever. Rowena was certain of that. No doubts. No fears. The rapture in her heart was completely unshadowed.

Keir slid the gold ring on her finger. She slid the matching ring on his. They said the words that sealed the promise of togetherness. They kissed. They signed the marriage certificate. They were one.

Then Keir's parents came forward, his mother lovingly laying Keir's and Rowena's new baby son in Rowena's arms. He was clothed in the same beautiful ivory christening robes Keir had worn thirty-six years ago. They moved over to the christening font. Fay Pendleton proudly joined them as designated godmother. Aunty Bet's son, Darren, who was godfather to Jamie, stepped up to take on the same responsibility for Jamie's new brother. The children clustered around to complete the family grouping.

Brett Keir Delahunty.

To Rowena the name symbolised so much that was good—friendship, trust, sharing and caring.

Once the christening ceremony was over, Jamie declared he had something to say, and he and Emily and

Sarah had agreed that this was the time to say it. The girls nodded vigorously. Keir smiled at his older son, his eyes shining with love and pride.

"Say what's on your mind, Jamie," he invited, happily confident it would not be amiss.

"It's like this," Jamie started, then turned to address Rowena. "When Brett gets a bit older and begins learning words, he'll be saying Dada when he sees Keir, won't he, Mum?"

Rowena hadn't thought that far. "It would be the natural thing, Jamie," she answered, feeling strongly that Keir shouldn't be deprived of the joy of hearing Dada for the first time.

"And he's our brother," Jamie went on, "so he might get confused if we don't call Keir Dad. We're all in the same family."

His reasoning was wonderfully clear, beautifully clear. A brilliant smile burst from Rowena's heart. "That's true, Jamie," she encouraged.

He looked at Keir. "So if it's okay with you, Emily and Sarah and I would like to call you Dad from now on."

Emily and Sarah lifted brightly expectant faces to him.

"I'd like that very much," Keir assured them all, his voice deepening with emotion, a sheen of tears making his eyes even shinier.

"I'd rather call you Daddy," Emily appealed.

"Daddy is fine, Emily. Whatever you're comfortable with," Keir said warmly.

She beamed.

Rowena's heart turned over. Such full acceptance from Emily meant she really felt she belonged to Keir.

"I like Dada," Sarah declared. "Dada, Dada, Dada," she trilled with uninhibited glee. "Brett will learn real fast from me, Dada."

Keir laughed. "I'm sure he will, Sarah."

And he'll live in a fairy-tale wonderland with Sarah as his guide, Rowena thought. Her younger daughter was utterly entranced with the baby, and her attachment to Keir had never been in question. He had entered her life as the prince, and Rowena suspected that when Sarah grew up, there would be many a man who'd find himself being measured against the prince, and woe betide them if they didn't reach the mark.

"That's it, Dad," Jamie said with a huge grin. "We can move out now."

Keir returned the grin, father to son. "Lead the way, Jamie."

Rowena passed baby Brett to Keir and curled her arm around his for the long walk down the aisle and out of the church. Their eyes caught in a magic moment of love, utterly fulfilled.

His wife, Keir thought, his heart so full it was fit to burst. He looked down at the baby cradled in his other arm. His son. He watched Emily and Sarah take their places in the procession behind Jamie. His family.

To be so blessed…the wonder and glory of it.

Their wedding day.

* * * * *

HIS BOARDROOM
MISTRESS

Emma
DARCY

Many thanks for Phil Asker and his wonderful team for providing me with so many amazing experiences on The Captain's Choice Tour of Southeast Asia—all in such a safe and friendly atmosphere. Great memories!

CHAPTER ONE

'THE kind of man you want, Liz, is the marrying kind.'

The quiet authority of her mother's voice cut through the buzz of suggestions being tossed around by her three sisters, all of whom had succeeded in marrying the men of their choice. This achievement made them feel qualified to hand out advice which Liz should take, now that she had been forced to confess her failure to get a commitment from the man who'd been her choice.

Brendan had told her he felt their relationship was stifling him. He needed space. So much space he was now in Nepal, half a world away from Sydney, planning to find himself or lose himself in the Himalayas, meditate in a Buddhist monastery, anything but make a life with a too managing woman.

It was shaming, humiliating to have to admit his defection to her family, but there was no excuse for not attending her father's sixtieth birthday luncheon today and no avoiding having to explain Brendan's absence.

The five of them—her mother, her sisters and herself—were in the kitchen, cleaning up after the long barbecue lunch which had been cooked by the male members of the family, now relaxing out on the patio

5

of her parents' home, minding the children playing in the backyard.

Liz knew she had to face up to her situation and try to move on from it, but right now she felt engulfed by a sense of emptiness—three years of togetherness all drained away—and her mother's statement hit a very raw place.

'How can you know if they're the marrying kind or not?' she tossed back derisively.

Mistake!

Naturally, her wonderfully successful siblings had the answers and leapt in to hit Liz over the head with them.

'First, you look for a man with a good steady job,' her oldest sister, Jayne, declared, pausing in her task of storing leftovers in the refrigerator to deliver her opinion. 'You want someone to support you when the kids come along.'

Jayne was thirty-four, the mother of two daughters, and married to an accountant who'd never deviated from forging a successful career in accountancy.

'Someone with a functional family background,' Sue contributed with a wise look. 'They value what they've had and want it for themselves.'

Sue was thirty-two, married to a solicitor from a big family, now the besotted father of twin sons, loving his wife all the more for having produced them.

Liz silently and bitterly conceded two black marks against Brendan who'd never held a steady job—preferring to pick up casual work in the tourist indus-try—and had no personal experience of a functional family background since he'd been brought up by a series of foster parents.

There was no longer any point in arguing that she earned enough money to support them both. A small family, as well, if Brendan would have been content to be a house husband, as quite a few men were these days. The traditional way was not necessarily the *only* way, but Jayne and Sue weren't about to appreciate any other view but theirs, especially with the current inescapable proof that Liz's way hadn't worked.

'What about your boss?'

The speculative remark from her younger sister, Diana, jolted Liz out of maundering over her failures. 'What about him?' she retorted tersely, reminded that Diana, at only twenty-eight, was rather smug at having scooped the marriage pool by snagging her own boss, the owner of a chain of fashion boutiques for which she was still a buyer since they had no immediate plans to start a family.

'Everyone knows Cole Pierson is rolling in money, probably a billionaire by now. Isn't his divorce due to go through? He's been separated from his wife for ages and she's been gallivanting around, always in the social pages, linked to one guy or another. I'd certainly count Cole Pierson available and very eligible,' Diana declared, looking at Liz as though she'd been lax at not figuring that out for herself.

'Get real! That doesn't mean *available* to me,' Liz threw back at her, knowing full well she didn't have the female equipment to attract a man of his top-line attributes.

'Of course it does,' Diana persisted. 'He's only

thirty-six to your thirty, Liz, and right on the spot for you to snaffle. You could get him if you tried. After all, being his P.A. is halfway there. He depends on you...'

'Cole Pierson is not the least bit interested in me as a woman,' Liz snapped, recoiling absolutely from the idea of man-hunting where no love or desire was likely to be kindled.

Besides, she'd long ago killed any thought of her boss *that way* and she didn't want to do anything that might unsettle what had become a comfortable and satisfying business relationship. At least she could depend on *its* continuing into the foreseeable future.

'Why would he be interested?' Diana countered, apparently deciding she'd done her share of the cleaning up, propping herself on a stool at the island bench and examining her fingernails for any chipped varnish. 'You've been stuck with Brendan all the time you've been working for Cole Pierson, not giving out any availability signals,' she ran on.

'He is quite a hunk in the tall, dark and handsome mould,' Jayne chimed in, her interest sparked by the possibility of Liz linking up with the financial wizard who managed the money of several of her accountant husband's very wealthy clients. As she brought emptied salad bowls to the sink where their mother was washing up and Liz drying, she made a more direct remark. 'You must feel attracted to him, Liz.'

'No, I don't,' she swiftly denied, though she certainly had been initially, when he'd still been human and happily married. He'd been very distractingly attractive *then*, but being the remarkable man he was and having a beautiful wife in the background, Liz had listed him in the no hope category.

Besides, she'd just found Brendan—a far more realistic and reachable choice for her—so she'd quelled any wayward feelings towards her boss.

'How couldn't you be?' Sue queried critically, frowning over what she assumed was totally unnatural. 'The few times I've dropped in on you at your office and he's appeared…the guy is not only a stunner but very charming. Fantastic blue eyes.'

Cold blue eyes, Liz corrected.

Cold and detached.

Ever since he'd lost his baby son eighteen months ago—a tragic cot death—Cole had retreated inside himself. The separation from his wife six months later had not come as a surprise to Liz. The marriage had to be in trouble. Her boss had moved beyond *connecting* to anyone.

He switched on a superficial charm for clients and visitors but there was no real warmth in it. He had a brilliant brain that never lost track of the money markets, that leapt on any profitable deal for his clients' investments, that paid meticulous attention to every critical detail of his business. But it was also a brain that blocked any intrusion to whatever he thought and felt on a personal level. Around him was an impenetrable wall, silently but strongly emitting the message—*keep out.*

'There's just no spark between us,' she told Sue, wanting to dampen this futile line of conversation. 'Cole is totally focused on business.'

Which made *him* appreciate her management skills,

she thought with black irony. He certainly didn't feel *stifled* by her being efficient at keeping track of everything. He expected it of her and it always gave her a kick when she surprised him by covering even more than he expected. He was a hard taskmaster.

'You need to shake him out of that one-track mind-set,' Diana advised, persisting with her get-the-boss idea.

'You can't change what drives a person's life,' Liz flashed back at her, realising she'd been foolish to think she could change any of Brendan's ingrained attitudes.

Diana ignored this truism. 'I bet he takes you for granted,' she rattled on, eyeing Liz assessingly. 'Treats you as part of the office furniture because you don't do anything to stand out from it. Look at you! When was the last time you spent money on yourself?'

Liz gritted her teeth at the criticism. It was all very well for Diana, who had a rich husband to pay for everything she wanted. *She* didn't need to siphon off most of her income to make the payments on a city apartment. Liz had figured the only way she'd ever have a home to call her own was to buy it herself. Besides which, real estate was a good solid investment.

'I keep up a classic wardrobe for work,' she argued, not bothering to add she had no use for fancy clothes anyway. She and Brendan had never gone anywhere fancy, preferring a much more casual lifestyle, using whatever spare money they had to travel where they could. Jeans, T-shirts and jackets took them to most places.

'Dullsville,' Diana said witheringly. 'All black suits and sensible shoes. In fact, you've let yourself get positively drab. What you need is a complete makeover.'

Having finished putting everything away, her two older sisters joined Diana on stools around the island bench and jumped on this bandwagon. 'I've never thought long hair suits you,' Jayne remarked critically. 'It swamps your small face. And when you wear it pulled back like that, it does nothing for you at all. Makes your facial bones appear sharper. No softening effect. You really should get it cut and styled, Liz.'

'And coloured,' Sue said, nodding agreement. 'If you must wear black suits, mouse brown hair doesn't exactly give you a lift.'

'There's no *must* about it,' Diana declared, glaring a knowing challenge as she added, 'I bet you simply took the cheap route of having a minimal work wardrobe. Am I right or not, Liz?'

She couldn't deny it. Not making regular visits to a hairdresser saved her time and money and it was easy enough to slick back her long hair into a tidy clip at the back of her neck for work. Besides, Brendan had said he liked long hair. And the all-purpose suits she wore meant she didn't have to think about putting something smarter together—a sensible investment that actually cost less than a more varied range of clothes.

'What does it matter?' she countered with a vexed

sigh at being put under the microscope like this. 'I get by on it,' she added defiantly. 'Nobody criticises me at work.'

'The invisible handmaiden,' Diana scoffed. 'That's what you've let yourself become, and you could be a knockout if you made the effort.'

'Oh, come off it!' she protested, losing patience with the argument. 'I've always been the plain one in this family. And the shortest.'

She glared at tall, willowy Jayne with her gorgeous mane of dark wavy hair framing a perfectly oval face and a long graceful neck. Her eldest sister had thickly fringed chocolate brown eyes, a classical straight nose, a wide sensuous mouth, and a model-like figure that made everything she wore look right.

Her gaze moved mockingly to Sue who was almost as tall but more lushly feminine, round curves everywhere topped by a pretty face, sparkling amber eyes and soft, honey-coloured curls that rippled down to her shoulders.

Lastly she looked derisively at Diana, a beautiful blue-eyed blonde who turned heads everywhere she went, her long hair straight and smooth like a curtain of silk, her lovely face always perfectly made up, her tall slim figure invariably enhanced by fabulous designer clothes. Easy for her to catch the eye of *her* boss. He'd have to be blind not to appreciate what an asset she was to him.

Next to her sisters Liz felt small, and not just because she was only average height and had what could be called a petite figure. She felt small in every sense. Her hair was a mousy colour and far too thick to manage easily. It did swamp her. Not only that, her eyes were a murky hazel, no clear colour at all, there was a slight bump in her nose, and her cheekbones and chinline *were* sharply angular. In fact, her only saving grace was good straight teeth.

At least, people said she had a nice smile. But she didn't feel like smiling right now. She felt utterly miserable. 'It's ridiculous to pretend I could be a knockout,' she stated bitingly. 'The only thing I've got going for me is a smart brain that keeps me in a good job, and it's been my experience that most men don't like too much smart in their women when it comes to personal relationships.'

'A smart man does, Liz,' her mother said quietly.

'And Cole Pierson is incredibly smart,' Diana quickly tagged on. 'He'd definitely value you on that score.'

'Would you please leave my boss out of this?' Liz almost stamped her foot in frustration at her younger sister's one-track mind. Any intimate connection with Cole was an impossible dream, for dozens of reasons.

'Regardless of your boss, Liz,' Jayne said in a serious vein. 'I truly think a makeover is a good idea. You're not plain. You've just never made the most of yourself. With some jazzy clothes and a new hairdo...'

'A lovely rich shade of red would do wonders for your hair,' Sue came in decisively. 'If you had it cut and layered to shape in just below your ears, it could look fantastic. Your skin is pale enough for red to look great with it and such a positive contrast would bring out the green in your eyes.'

'They're not green!' Liz cried in exasperation. 'They're...'

'More green than amber,' Sue judged. 'Red would definitely do the trick. Let me make an appointment with my hairdresser for you and I'll come along to advise.'

'And I can take you shopping. Outfit you in some smashing clothes,' Diana eagerly tagged on.

'At a discount price,' Jayne leapt in. 'Right, Diana? Not making it too frightfully expensive?'

'Right!'

'Hair first, clothes second,' Sue ordered.

'A visit to a beautician, too. Get the make-up right to match the new hair.'

'And accentuate the green in her eyes.'

'Don't forget shoes. Liz has got to get out of those matronly shoes.'

'Absolutely. Shapely legs should be shown off.'

'Not to mention a finely turned ankle.'

They all laughed, happy at the thought of getting their hands on their little sister and waving some magic wand that would turn her into one of them. Except it couldn't really happen, and as her sisters continued to rave on with their makeover plan, bouncing off each other, meaning well...she knew they *meant well*...Liz found herself on the verge of tears.

'Stop! Please stop!' she burst out, slamming her hands onto the island bench to gain their undivided attention. 'I'm me, okay? Not a doll for you to dress up. I'm okay as me. And I'll live my life my own way.'

The shaking vehemence in her voice shocked them

into silence. They stared at her, hurt showing on their faces at the blanket rejection of their ideas. They didn't understand where she was coming from, had never understood what it was like to be *her,* the odd one out amongst them. The tears pricked her eyes, threatening to start spilling.

'I'd like some time alone with Liz.'

Her mother's quiet demand floated over Liz's shoulder. She was still at the sink, wiping it back to its usual pristine state. Without a word of protest, her other three daughters got to their feet and trooped out to the patio. Liz turned to her mother, who slowly set the dishcloth aside, waiting for the absolute privacy she'd asked for, not turning until the others were gone.

Having screwed herself up for more talking, Liz was totally undone when her mother looked at her with sad, sympathetic understanding. Impossible to blink back the tears. Then her mother's arms were around her in a comforting hug and her head was being gently pressed onto a shoulder that had always been there for her to lean on in times of strife and grief.

'Let it out, Liz,' her mother softly advised. 'You've held in too much for too long.'

Control collapsed. She wept, releasing the bank of bad feelings that had been building up ever since Brendan had rejected all she'd offered him, preferring to be somewhere else.

'He wasn't right for you,' her mother murmured when the storm of tears eased. 'I know you tried to make him right for you, but he was never going to be, Liz. He's footloose and rootless and you like to be grounded.'

'But I did enjoy the travelling with him, Mum,' she protested.

'I'm sure you did, but it was also a way of going off independently, not competing with your sisters. You may not think of it like that, but being different for the sake of being different is not the answer. By attaching yourself to Brendan, you virtually shut them out of your life. They want back in, Liz. They want to help you. They're your sisters and they love you.'

She lifted her head, looking her mother in the eye. 'But I'm not like them.'

'No, you have your own unique individuality.' Her mouth curved into a tender, loving smile. 'My one brilliant daughter.'

Liz grimaced. 'Not so brilliant. Though I am good at my job.'

Her mother nodded. 'That's not the problem, is it? You're not feeling good about yourself as a woman. I don't think you have for a long time, Liz. It's easy to sweep away your sisters' makeover plan as some kind of false facade, but you could treat it as fun. A new look. A new style. It might very well give you a lift. Don't see it as competing with them. See it as something new for you.'

'You're urging me to be their guinea pig?'

This drew a chiding shake of the head. 'They're proud of your career in high finance, Liz. They admire your success there. How about conceding that they have expertise in fields you've ignored?'

She winced at the pointed reminder that in the feminine stakes, her sisters certainly shone and undoubt-edly had an eye for things she hadn't bothered with. 'I guess they do know what they're talking about.'

'And then some,' her mother said dryly.

Liz sighed, giving in more because she was bereft of any plans for herself than in any belief that her life could be instantly brightened, along with her hair. 'Well, I don't suppose it will hurt.'

'You could be very pleasantly surprised. Jayne is right. You're not plain, Liz. You're just different.' Her mother patted her cheek encouragingly. 'Now go and make peace with them. Letting them have their way could be a very positive experience for all of you.'

'Okay. But if Diana thinks a new me will make any difference to Cole Pierson, she's dreaming.'

Her boss occupied a different planet.

A chilly one.

Even fiery red hair wasn't about to melt the ice in that man's veins. Or make him suddenly see her as a desirable woman. Why would he anyway, when he'd had Tara Summerville—a top-line international model—as his wife? Even Diana wasn't in that class.

A totally impossible dream.

CHAPTER TWO

His mother was upset.

Cole didn't like his mother being upset. It had taken her quite a while to get over his father's death and establish a life on her own. For the past few years she'd been happy, planning overseas trips and going on them with her bridge partner, Joyce Hancock, a retired school principal who was a natural organiser, a person he could trust to look after his mother on their travels. As misfortune would have it, Joyce had fallen and broken her hip so the tour they'd booked to South-East Asia had to be cancelled.

He'd spent the whole weekend trying to distract his mother with his company, cheer her up, but she'd remained down in the dumps, heaving miserable sighs, looking forlorn. Now, driving her back to her Palm Beach home after visiting Joyce in Mona Vale Hospital, Cole saw she was fighting tears. He reached across and squeezed her hand, trying to give sympathetic comfort.

'Don't worry about Joyce. Hip replacement is not a dangerous procedure,' he assured her. 'She'll be up and about soon enough.'

'She's annoyed with me for not going ahead with the trip by myself. But I don't want to go on my own.'

Unthinkable to Cole's mind. His mother would undoubtedly get flustered over the tour schedule, leave things in the hotel rooms, be at the wrong place at the wrong time. She'd become quite fluffy-headed in her widowhood, not having to account to anyone anymore, just floating along while Cole took care of any problems that were troublesome. He saw to the maintenance of her far too large but beloved home and looked after her finances. It was easier than trying to train her into being more responsible for herself.

'It's your choice, Mum. Joyce probably feels guilty about disappointing you,' he soothed.

She shook her head dejectedly. 'I'm disappointing her. She's right about *The Captain's Choice Tour Company*. Their people do look after everything for you. They even take a doctor along in case anyone gets sick or injured. Joyce wants me to go so I can tell her all about it. She says I'll meet people I can talk to. Make new friends...'

'That's easy for her to say,' Cole said dryly, knowing Joyce was the kind of person who'd bulldose her way into any company and feel right at home with it. His mother was made of more fragile stuff.

Her hands twisted fretfully. 'Maybe I should go. Nothing's been cancelled yet. I was going to do it tomorrow.'

Clearly she was torn and would feel miserable either way. 'You need a companion, Mum,' Cole stated categorically. 'You'll feel lost on your own.'

'But there's no one in our social circle who's free to take up Joyce's booking.'

He frowned at this evidence of her actively trying to find someone congenial to travel with. 'You really want to go?'

'I've been looking forward to it for so long. Though without Joyce...' Her voice wavered uncertainly.

Cole made a decision. It meant a sacrifice on his part. Liz Hart had been on vacation for the past two weeks and her fill-in had tested his tolerance level to the limit. He hated doing without his efficient personal assistant. Nevertheless, when it came to entrusting the management of his mother to someone else, he couldn't think of anyone better. No hitches with Liz Hart.

'I'll arrange for my P.A. to take up Joyce's booking and accompany you on the tour,' he said, satisfied that he'd come up with the perfect solution, both for his mother's pleasure and his peace of mind.

It jolted her out of her gloom. 'You can't do that, Cole.'

'Yes, I can,' he asserted. 'I'll put it to Liz first thing in the morning. I'm sure she'll agree.'

'I don't even know the girl!' his mother cried in shocked protest.

'You can come into the city tomorrow and I'll set up a lunch meeting. If you approve of her...fine. If you don't, I'm afraid the trip will be off.'

The lure of the tour clearly held a lot of weight. After a few moments, his mother gave in to curiosity. 'What's she like...this personal assistant of yours?'

'She's the kind of person who can handle anything I throw at her,' he replied, smiling confidently.

'Well, she'd have to be, wouldn't she, to keep up with you, Cole,' came the dryly knowing comment. 'I meant...what is she like as a person?'

He frowned, not quite sure how to answer. 'She fits in,' was the most appropriate description he could come up with.

This earned an exasperated roll of the eyes. 'What does she look like?'

'Always neat and tidy. Professional.'

'How old is she?'

'Not sure. Late twenties, I guess. Maybe early thirties.'

'What colour are her eyes?'

He didn't know, couldn't recall ever noticing. 'What does eye colour have to do with anything?'

His mother sighed. 'You just don't look, do you? Not interested. You've closed off all involvement with anyone. You've got to get past this, Cole. You're still a young man.'

He gritted his teeth, hating any reference to all he'd put behind him. 'Her eyes are bright.' he answered tersely. 'They shine with intelligence. That's more important to me than colour.'

The blank look her temporary fill-in had given him too many times over the past fortnight had filled him with frustration. He'd have to second someone else to take Liz Hart's place while she was off with his mother.

'Is she attractive...pretty...big...slight...tall... short...?'

Cole sighed over his mother's persistence on irrelevant detail. 'She's ordinary average,' he said impatiently. 'And always obliging, which is the main point here. Liz will ensure you have a trouble-free tour, Mum. No worries.'

His mother sighed. 'Do try to tell me more about her, Cole.'

She should be satisfied with what he'd already told her but he stretched his mind to find some pertinent point. 'She likes travel. Spends most of her time off travelling somewhere or other. I expect she'll jump at the chance of accompanying you to South-East Asia.'

'Then it won't be a completely burdensome chore for her, escorting me around?'

'Of course not. I wouldn't load you with a sourpuss. I'm sure you'll find Liz Hart a delight to be with.'

'Do you?'

'Do I what?'

'Find her a delight to be with.'

'Well, I'll certainly miss her,' he said with feeling.

'Ah!'

He glanced sharply at his mother. Her 'Ah!' had carried a surprising depth of satisfaction, making him wonder what she was thinking.

She smiled at him. 'Thank you, Cole. You're quite wonderful at fixing things for me. I'll look forward to meeting your Liz tomorrow.'

'Good!'

Problem solved.

His mother wasn't upset anymore.

Monday morning...

Cole heard Liz Hart arrive in the office which adjoined his—promptly at eight-thirty as she did every workday. Totally reliable, he thought with satisfaction.

He had not qualms whatsoever about entrusting his mother's well-being and pleasure in this upcoming South-East Asia tour to his punctual and efficient personal assistant.

It didn't occur to him that the request he was about to make was tantamount to inviting Liz Hart into his personal and private life. To his mind it was simply a matter of moving people into position to achieve what had to be achieved. He could manage another two weeks more or less by himself, asking the absolute minimum of another temporary P.A., while his mother enjoyed a stress-free trip. Once the fortnight was over, everything would shift back to normal.

He rose from his desk and strode to the connecting door, intent on handing the tour folder to Liz so she could get straight to work on doing what had to be done to become Joyce Hancock's replacement. In his business, time was money and his time was too valuable to waste on extraneous matters. Liz would undoubtedly see to everything required of her—passport, visas, whatever.

He opened the door to find some stranger hanging her bag and coat on Liz's hatstand, taking up personal space that didn't belong to her. Cole frowned at the unexpected vision of a startling redhead, dressed in a clingy green sweater and a figure-hugging navy skirt with a split up the back—quite a distracting split, leading his gaze down a pair of finely shaped legs encased in sheer navy stockings, to pointedly female high-heeled shoes.

Who was this woman? And what did she think she was doing, taking up Liz's office? He hadn't been informed that his P.A. had called in, delaying her scheduled return to work. Unexplained change was not acceptable, especially when it entailed having someone foisted on him without his prior approval.

His gaze had travelled back up the curve of thigh and hip to the indentation of a very small waist before the unwelcome intruder turned around. Then he found himself fixated on very nicely rounded breasts, emphatically outlined by the soft, sexy sweater, with more attention being drawn to them by a V-neckline ending in a looped tie that hung down the valley of her cleavage.

'Good morning, Cole.'

The brisk, cool greeting stunned him with its familiarity. His gaze jerked up to an unfamiliar mouth, painted as brightly red as the thick cropped hair that flared out in waves and curls on either side of her face. The eyes hit a chord with him—very bright eyes—but even they looked different, bigger than they normally were and more sparkly. This wasn't the Liz Hart he was used to. Only her voice was instantly recognisable.

'What the devil have you done to yourself?' The words shot out, driven by a sense of aggrievement at the shock she'd given him.

A firmly chiseled chin which he'd previously thought of as strong, steady and determined, now tilted up in provocative challenge. 'I beg your pardon?'

He was distracted by the gold gypsy hoops dangling from her earlobes. 'This is not you, dammit!' he grated, his normal equilibrium thrown completely out of kilter by these changes in the person who worked most closely with him, a person he counted on not to rock his boats in any sense whatsoever.

Her eyes flashed a glittery warning. 'Are you objecting to my appearance?'

Red alert signals went off in his brain...sexual discrimination...harrassment...Liz was calling him on something dangerous here and he'd better watch his step. However disturbingly different she looked today, he knew she had a core of steel and would stand up for herself against anything she considered unreasonable or unjust.

'No,' he said decisively, taking firm control over the runaway reactions to an image he didn't associate with her. 'Your appearance is fine. It's good to have you back, Liz.'

'Thank you.' Her chin levelled off again, fighting mode discarded. She smiled. 'It's good to be back.'

This should have put them on the correct footing but Cole couldn't help staring at her face, which somehow lit up quite strikingly with the smile. Maybe it was the short fluffy red hair that made her smile look even whiter and her eyes brighter. Or the bright red lipstick. Whatever it was, she sure didn't look average ordinary anymore.

He wanted to ask...why the change? What had happened to her? But that was personal stuff he knew he shouldn't get into. He liked the parameters of their business relationship the way they were. Right now they felt threatened, without inviting further infringements on them.

He had to stop staring. Her cheeks were glowing pink, highlighting bones that now seemed to have an exotic, angular tilt. They must have always been like that. It made him feel stupid not to have noticed before. Had she been deliberately playing herself down during business hours, hiding her surprisingly feminine figure in unisex suits, keeping her hair plain and quiet, wearing only insignificant make-up?

'Is that something for me to deal with?' she asked, gesturing to the folder he was holding.

Conscious that his awkward silence had driven her to take some initiative, he didn't stop to reconsider the proposition he'd prepared. 'Yes,' he said, gratefully seizing on the business in hand. 'I need you to go to South-East Asia with my mother,' he blurted out.

She stared at him, shocked disbelief in her eyes.

Good to serve it right back to her, Cole thought, stepping forward and slapping the folder down on her desk, a buzz of adrenalin shooting through him at regaining control of the situation.

'It's all in here. The Captain's Choice Tour. Borneo, Burma, Nepal, Laos, Vietnam, Cambodia— all in fifteen days by chartered Qantas jet, leaving on Saturday week. You'll require extra passport photos for visas and innoculation shots for typhoid, hepatitis, and other diseases. You'll see the medical check list. I take it you have a usable passport?'

'Yes,' she answered weakly.

'Good! No problem then.'

She seemed frozen on the spot, still staring at him, not moving to open the folder. He tapped it to draw her attention to it.

'All the tickets are in here. Everything's been paid

for. You'll find them issued in the name of Joyce Hancock and first thing to do is notify the tour company that you'll be travelling in her place.'

'Joyce Hancock,' she repeated dazedly.

'My mother's usual travelling companion. Broke her hip. Can't go. None of her other friends can take the trip at such short notice,' he explained.

Liz Hart shook her head, the red hair rippling with the movement like a live thing that wasn't under any control. Very distracting. Cole frowned, realising she was indicating a negative response. Which was unacceptable. He was about to argue the position when she drew in a deep breath and spoke.

'Your mother...Mrs. Pierson...she doesn't even know me.'

'*I* know you. I've told her she'll be safe with you.'

'But...' She gestured uncertainly.

'Primarily my mother needs a manager on this trip. I have absolute faith in your management skills, not to mention your acute sense of diplomacy, tact, understanding, and generally sharp intelligence. Plus you're an experienced traveller.' He raised a challenging eyebrow. 'Correct?'

Another deep breath, causing a definite swell in the mounds under the clingy sweater which was a striking jewel green, somewhere between jade and emerald, a rich kind of medieval colour. The fanciful thought jolted Cole. He had to get his mind off her changed appearance.

'Thank you. It's nice to have my...attributes... appreciated,' she said in a somewhat ironic tone that sounded unsure of his end purpose. 'However, I do think I should meet with your mother...'

'Lunch today. Book a table for the three of us at Level 21. Twelve-thirty. My mother will join us there. She is looking forward to meeting you.'

'Is Mrs. Pierson…unwell?'

'Not at all. A bit woolly-headed about directions in strange places and not apt at dealing with time changes and demanding schedules, but perfectly sane and sound. She'll lean on you to get things right for her. That's your brief. Okay?'

'She's…happy…about this arrangement?'

'Impossible for her to go otherwise and she wants to go.'

'I see. You want me to be her minder.'

'Yes. I have every confidence in your ability to provide the support she needs to fully enjoy this trip.'

'What if she doesn't like me?'

'What's *not* to like?' he threw back at her more snappishly than he'd meant to, irritatingly aware that his mother would think this new version of Liz Hart was just lovely. And she would undoubtedly mock his judgment at having called his P.A. ordinary average.

No answer from Liz. Of course, it would be against her steely grain to verbally put herself down. Which increased the mystery of why she had *played* herself down physically these past three years. Had it been a feminist thing, a negation of her sexuality because she wanted her intellect valued?

Why had she suddenly decided to flaunt femininity now?

Dammit! He didn't have time to waste on such vagaries.

He tapped the folder again. 'I can leave this with you? No problems about dealing with it?' His eyes locked onto hers with the sharp demand of getting what he expected.

'No problems I can see,' she returned with flinty pride.

Her eyes were green.

With gold speckles around the rim.

'Fine! Let me know if you run into any.'

He stalked off into his own office, annoyed at how he was suddenly noticing every detail about a woman who'd been little more than a mind complementing his up until this morning. It was upsetting his comfort zone.

Why did she have to change?

It didn't feel right.

Just as well she was going off with his mother for two weeks. It would give him time to adjust to the idea of having his P.A. looking like a fiery sexpot. Meanwhile, he had work to do and he was not about to be distracted from it. Bad enough that he had to take time off for the lunch with his mother, which was bound to be another irritation because of Liz Hart's dramatic transformation.

Bad start to the morning.

Bad, bad, bad.

At least the food at Level 21 was good.

Though he'd probably choke on it, watching his mother being dazzled by her new travelling companion. No way was *she* going to be upset by a *colourful* Liz Hart, which was some consolation, but since he was decidedly upset himself, Cole wasn't sure that balanced the scales.

CHAPTER THREE

LIZ took a deep, deep breath, let it out slowly, then forced her feet to walk steadily to her desk, no teetering in the high-heels, shoulders back, correct carriage, just as Diana had drilled her. It was good to sit down. She was still quaking inside from the reaction her new image had drawn from Cole Pierson.

Diana had confidently predicted it would knock his socks off but Liz had believed he would probably look at her blankly for a few seconds, dismiss the whole thing as frivolous female foibles, then get straight down to business. Never, in a million years, would she have anticipated being *attacked* on it. Nor looked at so…so *intensely*.

It had been awful, turning around from the hatstand and finding those piercing blue eyes riveted on her breasts. Her heart had started galloping. Even worse, she'd felt her nipples hardening into prominent nubs, possibly becoming visible underneath the snug fit of the cashmere sweater.

She'd clipped out a quick greeting to get his focus off her body, only to have him stare at her mouth as though alien words had come out of it. Even when he had finally lifted his gaze to hers, she'd been totally rattled by the force of his concentration on how she looked. Which, she readily conceded, was vastly different to what he was used to, but certainly not

31

warranting the outburst that came. Nor the criticism it implied.

Her own fierce response to it echoed through her mind now—*I will not let him make me feel wrong. Not on any grounds.*

There was no workplace law to say a woman couldn't change the colour of her hair, couldn't change the style of her clothes, couldn't touch up her make-up. It wasn't as if she'd turned up with hair tortured into red or blue or purple spikes or dreadlocks. Red was a natural hair colour and the short layered style was what she'd call conservative modern, not the least bit outlandish. Her clothes were perfectly respectable and her make-up appropriate—certainly not overdone—to match the new colouring.

In fact, no impartial judge would say her appearance did not fit the position she held. All her sisters had declared she was now perfectly put together and Liz herself had ended up approving the result of their combined efforts. Her mother was right. It did make her feel good to look brighter and more stylish. She'd even started smiling at herself in the mirror.

And she wasn't about to let Cole Pierson wipe *that* smile off her face, just because he'd feel more comfortable if she merged into the office furniture again so he could regard her as another one of his computers. Though he had attributed her with management skills, diplomacy, tact, understanding, and sharp intelligence, which did put her a few points above a computer. And amazingly, he trusted her enough to put his mother into her keeping!

Having burned off her resentment at her boss's totally intemperate remarks on what was none of his business, Liz focused on the folder he'd put on her desk. Surprises had come thick and fast this morning. Apart from Cole's taking far too much *physical* notice of her, she had been summarily appointed guardian to a woman she'd never met, and handed a free trip to South-East Asia, no doubt travelling first-class all the way on The Captain's Choice Tour.

Right in the middle of this, Cole had listed Nepal amongst the various destinations.

Brendan was in Nepal.

Not that there was any likelihood of meeting up with him, and she didn't really want to...did she? What was finished was finished. But there was a somewhat black irony in her going there, too. Especially in not doing everything on the cheap, as Brendan would have to.

You can do better than Brendan Wheeler, her mother had said with a conviction that had made Liz feel she had settled for less than she should in considering a life partner.

Maybe her mother was right.

In any event, this trip promised many better things than bunking down in backpacker hostels.

On the front of The Captain's Choice folder was printed 'The leader in luxury travel to remote and exotic destinations.' Excitement was instantly ignited. She opened the folder and read all about the itinerary, delighted anticipation zooming at the places she would be visiting, and all in a deluxe fashion.

The accommodation was fantastic—The Hyatt Regency Hotel in Kathmandu, The Opera Hilton in

Hanoi, a 'Raffles' hotel in Phnom Penh. No expense spared anywhere…a chartered flight over Mount Everest, and a chartered helicopter to Halong Bay in Vietnam, another chartered flight to the ancient architectural wonder of Angkor Wat in Cambodia, even a specially chartered steam train to show them some of the countryside in Burma.

She could definitely take a lot of this kind of travel. No juggling finances, no concern over how to get where, no worry about making connections, no trying to find a decent meal…it was all laid out and paid for.

Even if Cole's mother was a grumpy battleaxe, Liz figured it couldn't be too hard to win her over by being determinedly cheerful. After all, Mrs. Pierson had to want this trip very much to agree to her son's plan, so mutual enjoyment should be reached without too much trouble.

Tact, diplomacy, understanding…Liz grinned to herself as she reached for the telephone, ready now to get moving on sealing her place for this wonderful new adventure. Her changed appearance had probably knocked Cole's socks off this morning, though in a more negative way than Diana had plotted, but he had still paid her a huge compliment by giving her this extra job with his mother. Better than a bonus.

It made her feel good.

Really good.

She zinged through the morning, booking the table at Level 21—no problem to fit Cole Pierson's party in at short notice since he regularly used the restaurant for business lunches—then lining up everything nec-

essary for her to take Joyce Hancock's place on
the tour.

Cole did not reappear. He did not call her, either.
He remained secluded in his own office, no doubt
tending meticulously to his own business. At twelve-
fifteen, Liz went to the Ladies' Room to freshen up,
smiled at herself in the mirror, determined that nothing her boss said or did would unsettle her again, then
proceeded to beard the lion in his den, hoping he
wouldn't bite this time.

She gave a warning knock on the door, entered his
office, waited for him to look up from the paperwork
on his desk, ignored the frown, and matter-of-factly
stated, 'It's time to leave if we're to meet your mother
at twelve-thirty.'

Since Cole's financial services company occupied
a floor of the Chifley Tower, one of the most prestigious buildings in the city centre, all they had to do
was catch an elevator up to Level 21, which, of
course, was also one of Sydney's most prestigious
restaurants. This arrangement naturally suited Cole's
convenience, as well as establishing in his clients'
minds that big money was made here and this location
amply displayed that fact.

Cold blue eyes bored into hers for several nerve-
jangling moments. He certainly knew how to put a
chill in a room. Liz wondered if she should have put
her suitcoat on, but they weren't going outside where
there was a wintery bite in the air. This was just her
boss, being his usual self, and it was good that he had
returned to being his usual self.

Though as he rolled his big executive chair back

from his work station and rose to his full impressive height, Liz did objectively note that Sue was not wrong in calling him tall, dark and handsome, what with his thick black hair, black eyebrows, darkly toned skin, a strong male face, squarish jaw, firm mouth, straight nose, neat ears. And those piercing eyes gave him a commanding authority that accentuated his *presence*.

The Armani suits he invariably wore added to his presence, too. Cole Pierson had dominant class written all over him. Sometimes, it really piqued Liz. It didn't seem fair that anyone should have so much going for him. But then she told herself he wasn't totally human.

Although the robotic facade *had* cracked this morning.

Scary stuff.

Better not to think about it.

Move on, move on, move on, she recited, holding her breath as Cole moved towards her, mouth grim, eyes raking over her again, clearly not yet having come to terms with her brighter presence.

'Did you call up to see if my mother had arrived?' he rapped out.

'No. I considered it a courtesy that we be there on time.'

'My mother is not the greatest time-keeper in the world.' He paused beside Liz near the door. 'Which is why she needs you,' he rammed home with quite unnecessary force.

'All the more reason to show her I'm reliable on that point,' she retorted, and could have sworn he breathed steam through his nostrils as he abruptly waved her to precede him out of both of their offices.

It made Liz extremely conscious of walking with straight-backed dignity. It was ridiculous, given his icy eyes, that she felt the bare nape of her neck burning. He had to be watching her, which was highly disconcerting because usually his whole attention was claimed by whatever was working through his mind. She didn't want his kind of intense focus trained on her. It was like being under a microscope, making her insides squirmish.

She breathed a sigh of relief when they finally entered the elevator and stood side by side in the compartment as it zoomed up to Level 21. Cole held his hands loosely linked in front of them and watched the numbers flashing over the door. It looked like a relaxed pose, but he emanated a tension that erased Liz's initial relief.

Maybe he was human, after all.

Was it *her* causing this rift in his iron-like composure, or the prospect of this meeting with his mother?

This thought reminded Liz that *she* should be thinking about his mother, preparing herself to answer any questions put to her in a positive and reassuring manner. Of course, her response depended largely on the kind of person Cole's mother was. Liz hoped she wasn't frosty. Cole had said fluffy, but that might only mean her mind wasn't as razor-sharp as his.

Liz was fast sharpening her own mind as they were met at the entrance to the restaurant by the maitre d' and informed that Mrs. Pierson had arrived and was enjoying a drink in the bar lounge.

'Must be anxious,' Cole muttered as they were led to where a woman sat on a grey leather sofa, her attention drawn to the fantastic view over the city of Sydney, dramatically displayed by the wall of windows.

Her hair was pure white, waving softly around a slightly chubby face which was relatively unlined and still showing how pretty she must have been in her youth. About seventy, Liz judged, taking heart at the gentle, ladylike look of the woman. Definitely not a battleaxe. Not frosty, either. She wore a pink Chanel style suit with an ivory silk blouse, pearl brooch, pearl studs in her ears, and many rings on her fingers.

'Mum!'

Her son's curt tone whipped her head around, her whole body jerking slightly at being startled. Bright blue eyes looked up at him, then made an instant curious leap to Liz. Her mouth dropped open in sheer surprise.

'Mum!' Cole said again, the curt tone edged with vexation now.

Her mouth shut into a line of total exasperation and she gave him a look that seemed to accuse him of being absolutely impossible and in urgent need of having his head examined.

Liz thought she heard Cole grind his teeth. However, he managed to unclench them long enough to say, 'This is my P.A., Liz Hart...my mother, Nancy Pierson.'

Nancy rose to her feet, her blue eyes glittering with

a frustration that spilled into speech as she held out her hand to Liz. 'My dear, how *do* you put up with him?'

Tact and diplomacy were right on the line here!

'Cole is the best boss I've ever had,' Liz declared with loyal fervour. 'I very much enjoy working with him.'

'Work!' Nancy repeated in a tone of disgust. 'Tunnel vision...that's what he's got. Sees nothing but work.'

'Mum!' Thunder rolled through Cole's warning protest.

Liz leapt in to avert the storm. 'Cole did cover your trip to South-East Asia this morning, Mrs. Pierson.' She beamed her best smile and poured warmth into her voice as she added, 'Which I think is wonderful.'

It did the trick, drawing Nancy out of her grumps and earning a smile back. She squeezed Liz's hand in a rush of pleasure. 'Oh, I think so, too. Far too wonderful to miss.'

Liz squeezed back. 'I'm simply over the moon that Cole thought of me as a companion for you. Such marvellous places to see...'

'Well...' She gave her son an arch look that still had a chastening gleam. 'Occasionally he gets some things right.'

'A drink,' Cole bit out. 'Liz, something for you? Mum, a refill?'

'Just water, thank you,' Liz quickly answered.

'Champagne,' Nancy commanded, and suddenly there was a wickedly mocking twinkle in her eyes.

'I'm beginning to feel quite bubbly again, now that I've met your Liz, Cole.'

His Liz? Exactly what terms had Cole used to describe her to his mother? Nothing with a possessive sense, surely.

'I'm glad you're happy,' he said on an acid note and headed for the bar.

Nancy squeezed Liz's hand again before letting go and gesturing to the lounge. 'Come and sit down with me and let us get better acquainted.'

'What would you like to know about me?' Liz openly invited as she sank onto the soft leather sofa.

'Not about work,' came the decisive dismissal. 'Tell me about your family.'

'Well, my parents live at Neutral bay…'

'Nice suburb.'

'Dad's a doctor. Mum was a nurse but…'

'She gave it up when the family came along.'

'Yes. Four daughters. I'm the third.'

'My goodness! That must have been a very female household.'

Liz laughed. 'Yes. Dad always grumbled about being outvoted. But he now has three sons-in-law to stand shoulder to shoulder with him.'

'So your three sisters are married. How lovely! Nice husbands?'

Under Nancy's eager encouragement, Liz went on to describe her sisters' lives and had just finished a general rundown on them when Cole returned, setting the drinks down on the low table in front of them and dropping onto the opposite sofa. Into the lull follow-

ing their 'thankyous,' Nancy dropped the one question Liz didn't want to answer.

'So what about your social life, Liz? Or are you
like Cole...' a derisive glance at her son. '...not having one.'

It instantly conjured up the hole left by Brendan's
defection. She delayed a reply, picking up the glass
of water, fiercely wishing the question hadn't been
asked, especially put as it had been, linking her to her
boss who was listening.

Unexpectedly he came to her rescue. 'You're getting too personal, Mum,' he said brusquely. 'Leave it
alone.'

Nancy aimed a sigh at him. 'Has it occurred to you,
Cole, that such a bright, striking young woman could
have a boyfriend who might not take kindly to her
leaving him behind while she travels with me?'

He beetled an accusing frown at Liz as though this
was all her fault, then sliced an impatient look at his
mother. 'What objection could a boyfriend have? It's
only for two weeks and you can hardly be seen as a
rival.'

'It's short notice. The trip takes up three weekends.
They might have prior engagements,' came the ready
arguments. 'Did you even ask this morning, or did
you simply go into command mode, expecting Liz to
carry through your plan, regardless?'

A long breath hissed through his teeth.

Liz felt driven to break in. 'Mrs. Pierson...'

'Call me Nancy, dear.'

'Nancy...' She tried an appeasing smile to cover
the angst of her current single state. '...I don't have

a boyfriend at the moment. I'm completely free to take up the amazingly generous opportunity Cole handed me this morning. I would have told him so if I wasn't.'

Tact, diplomacy…never mind that the hole was humiliatingly bared.

'Satisfied?' Cole shot at his mother.

She smiled back at him. 'Completely.' It was a surprisingly smug pronouncement, as though she had won the point.

Liz was lost in whatever byplay was going on between mother and son, but she was beginning to feel very much like the meat in the sandwich. Anxious to get the conversation focused back on the trip, she offered more relevant information about herself.

'I haven't been to Kuching but I have travelled to Malaysia before.'

Thankfully, Nancy seized on that prior experience and Liz managed to keep feeding their mutual interest in travel over lunch, skilfully smoothing over the earlier tension in their small party. Cole ate his food, contributing little to the table talk, though he did flash Liz a look of wry appreciation now and then, well aware she was working hard at winning over his mother.

Not that it was really hard. Nancy seemed disposed to like her, the blue eyes twinkling pleasure and approval in practically everything Liz said. Oddly enough, Liz was more conscious of her boss watching and listening, and whenever their eyes met, the understanding that flashed between them gave her heart a little jolt.

This had never happened before and she tried to analyse why now? Because his mother made this more personal than business? Because he was looking at her from a different angle, seeing the woman behind the P.A.? Because she was doing the same thing, seeing him as Nancy's son instead of the boss?

It was confusing and unsettling.

She didn't want to feel...*touched*...by this man, or close to him in any emotional sense. No doubt he'd freeze her out again the moment this meeting with his mother was over.

'Now, are you free this Saturday, my dear?' Nancy inquired once coffee was served.

'Yes?' Liz half queried, wondering what else was required of her.

'Good! You must come over to my home at Palm Beach and check my packing. Joyce always does that for me. It eliminates doubling up on things, taking too much. Do you have a car? It's difficult to get to by public transport. If you don't have a car...'

Liz quickly cut in. 'Truly, it won't be a problem. I'll manage.'

She'd never owned a car. No need when public transport was not only faster into the city, but much, much cheaper than running a car. Palm Beach was, however, a fair distance out, right at the end of the northern peninsula, but she'd get there somehow.

'I was going to say Cole could bring you.' She smiled at her son. 'You could, dear, couldn't you? Don't forget you're meeting with the tradesman who's going to quote for the new paving around the pool on Saturday.' She frowned. 'I think he said eleven o'clock. Or was it one o'clock?'

Cole sighed. 'I'll be there, Mum. And I'll collect and deliver Liz to you,' he said in a tone of sorely tried patience.

Oh, great! Liz thought, preferring the cost of a taxi to being a forced burden loaded onto her boss's shoulders. But clearly she wasn't going to get any say in this so she might as well grin and bear it. Though she doubted Cole would find a grin appropriate. He was indulging his mother but the indulgence was wearing very, very thin.

'You'd better come early. Before eleven,' Nancy instructed, then smiled at Liz. 'We'll have a nice lunch together. I've so enjoyed this one. And, of course, we have to be sure we've got all the right clothes for our trip.'

Liz had been thinking cargo pants and T-shirts for daywear and a few more stylish though still casual outfits for dinner at night, but she held her tongue, not knowing what Nancy expected of her. She would see on Saturday.

A great pity Cole had to be there.

He was probably thinking the same thing about her.

In fact, Liz wondered if Nancy Pierson was deliberately putting the two of them together to somehow score more points off her son. She might be fluffy-headed about time, but Liz suspected she was as sharp as a tack when it came to people. And she was looking smug again.

'Everything settled to your satisfaction, Mum?' Cole dryly inquired.

'Yes.' She smiled sweetly at him. 'Thank you, dear. I'm sure I'll have a lovely time with your Liz. So good of you to give her to me. I imagine you'll be quite lost without her.'

'No one is indispensable.'

A chill ran down Liz's spine. She threw an alarmed look at Cole, frightened that she'd somehow put her job on the line by courting his mother. The last thing she wanted at this uncertain point in her life was to lose the position that gave her the means to move on.

Cole caught the look and frowned at the flash of vulnerability. 'Though I must admit it's very difficult to find anyone who can remotely fill Liz's shoes as my P.A.,' he stated, glowering at her as though she should know that. 'In fact, I may very well take some time off work while she's away to save myself the aggravation.'

Both Liz and Nancy stared at him in stunned disbelief.

Cole taking time off work was unheard of. He ate, drank, and slept work.

Surprises were definitely coming thick and fast today!

The best one, Liz decided with a surge of tingling pleasure, was the accumulating evidence that Cole Pierson really valued her. That made her feel better than good. It made her feel...*extra special*.

CHAPTER FOUR

COLE had expected Liz Hart to manage his mother brilliantly. That had never been in doubt. However, while the meeting had achieved his purpose—his mother happily accepting his P.A. as her companion for the trip—there were other outcomes that continued to niggle at his mind, making the rest of Monday afternoon a dead loss as far as any productive work was concerned.

Firstly, his mother considered him a blind idiot.

That was Liz's fault.

Secondly, his mother had neatly trapped him into some ridiculous matchmaking scheme, forcibly coupling him with Liz on Saturday.

While he couldn't entirely lay the blame for that at his P.A.'s door, if she hadn't completely changed how she looked, his mother wouldn't have been inspired to plot this extraneous togetherness.

Thirdly, what had happened to the boyfriend? While Cole had never met the man in Liz Hart's life and not given him a thought this morning, he had been under the impression there was a long-running relationship. The name, Brendan, came to mind. Certainly on the few occasions Liz had spoken of personal travel plans, she'd used the plural pronoun. 'We…'

Had she lied to put a swift end to the fuss his

mother had made? Surely insisting her boyfriend wouldn't object could have achieved the same end.

Cole wanted that point cleared up.

Maybe the departure of the boyfriend had triggered the distracting metamorphosis from brown moth to bright butterfly.

Lastly, why would Liz feel insecure about her job? She had every reason to feel confident about holding her position. He'd never criticised her work. She had to know how competent she was. It was absurd of her to look afraid when he'd said no one was indispensable.

The whole situation with her today had been exasperating and continued to exasperate even after she left to go home. Cole resolved to shut it all out of his mind tomorrow. And for the rest of the working week. Perhaps on the drive to his mother's house on Saturday he'd get these questions answered, clear up what was going on in Liz's head. Then he'd feel comfortable around her again.

On Tuesday morning she turned up in a slinky leopard print outfit that totally wrecked his comfort zone, giving him the sense of a jungle cat prowling around him with quiet, purposeful manoeuvres. She also wore sexy bronze sandals with straps that crisscrossed up over her ankles, making him notice how fine-boned they were.

Wednesday she gave the tight navy skirt with the slit up the back a second wearing, but this time topped with a snug cropped jacket in vibrant violet, an unbelievably stunning combination with the red hair. Cole found his gaze drawn to it far too many times.

Thursday came the leopard print skirt with a black sweater, and the gold hoop earrings that dangled so distractingly. *Striking,* his mother had said, and it was a disturbingly apt description. Cole was struck by thoughts he hadn't entertained for a long time. If Liz Hart was free of any attachment…but mixing business with pleasure was always a mistake. Stupid to even be tempted.

Friday fueled the temptation. She wore a bronze button-through dress which wasn't completely buttoned through, showing provocative flashes of leg. A wide belt accentuated her tiny waist, the stand-up collar framed her vivid hair and face, and the strappy bronze sandals got to him again. The overall effect was very sexy. In fact, the more he thought about Liz Hart, the more he thought she comprised a very desirable package.

But best to leave well enough alone.

He wasn't ready for a serious relationship and an office affair would inevitably undermine the smooth teamwork they'd established at work. Besides which, he reflected with considerable irony, Liz had not given any sign of seeing *him* in a sexual light. No ripple of disturbance in her usual efficiency.

She did seem to be smiling at him more often but he couldn't be sure that wasn't simply a case of the smile being more noticeable, along with her mouth, her eyes, and everything else about her. Nevertheless, the smile was getting to be insidious. More times than not he found himself smiling back, feeling a lingering pleasure in the little passage of warmth between them.

No harm in being friendly, he told himself, as long

as it didn't diminish his authority. After all, Liz had worked in relative harmony with him for three years. Though getting too friendly wouldn't do, either. A line had to be drawn. Business was business. A certain distance had to be kept.

That distance was clearly on Liz's mind when she entered his office at the end of their working week, and with an air of nervous tension, broached the subject—'About tomorrow...going to your mother's home at Palm Beach...'

'Ah, yes! Where and when to pick you up.'

Her hands picked fretfully at each other. 'You really don't have to.'

'Easier if I do.' Cole leaned back in his chair to show that he was relaxed about it.

'I've worked out the most efficient route by public transport. It's not a problem,' she assured him.

'It will be a problem for me if I arrive without you,' he drawled pointedly.

'Oh!' She grimaced, recalling the acrimony between mother and son. Her eyes flashed an anxious plea. 'I don't want to put you out, Cole.'

'It's my mother putting me out, not you. I don't mind obliging her tomorrow, Liz.' He reached for a notepad. 'Give me your address.'

More hand-picking. 'I could meet you somewhere on the way...'

'Your address,' he repeated, impatient with quibbling.

'It will be less hassle if...'

'Do you have a problem with giving me your address, Liz?' he cut in.

She winced. 'I live at Bondi Junction. It would mean your backtracking to pick me up...'

'Ten minutes at most from where I live at Benelong Point.'

'Then ten minutes back again before heading off in the right direction,' she reminded him.

'I think I can spare you twenty minutes.'

She sighed. 'I'd feel better about accepting a lift from you if we could meet on the way. I can catch a train to...'

'Are you worried that your boyfriend might object if I pick you up from your home?' The thought had slid into his mind and spilled into words before Cole realised it was openly probing her private life and casting himself in the role of a rival.

She stared at him, shocked at the implications of the question.

Cole was somewhat shocked at the indiscretion himself, but some belligerent instinct inside him refused to back down from it. The urge to know the truth of her situation had been building all week. He stared back, waiting for her answer, mentally commanding it.

A tide of heat flowed up her neck and burned across her cheekbones, making their slant more prominent and her eyes intensely bright. Cole was conscious of a fine tension running between them, a silent challenge emanating from her, striking an edge of excitement in him...the excitement of contest he always felt with a clash of wills, spurring on his need to win.

'I told you on Monday I don't have a boyfriend,' she bit out.

'No. You told my mother that, neatly ending her blast at me.'

'It's the truth.'

'Since when? The last I heard, just before you left on vacation, you had plans to travel with...is it Brendan?'

Her mouth compressed into a thin line of resistance.

'Who's been floating around in your background for as long as you've been working with me,' Cole pushed relentlessly. 'Probably before that, as well.'

'He's gone. I'm by myself now,' she said in defiant pride.

'Send him packing, did you?'

'He packed himself off,' she flashed back derisively.

'You're telling me he left you?'

'He didn't like my style of management.'

'Man's a fool.'

Her mouth tilted into a wry little smile. 'Thank you.'

No smile in her eyes, Cole noted. They looked bleak. She'd been hurt by the rejection of what she was, possibly hurt enough to worry about how rightly or wrongly she managed her job, hence the concern about losing it, too.

Satisfied that he now understood her position, Cole restated his. 'I shall pick you up at your home. Your address?'

She gave it without further argument, though her tone had a flat, beaten quality he didn't like. 'I was only trying to save you trouble,' she muttered, excusing her attempt to manage him.

'I appreciate the value you place on my time, Liz.' He finished writing down her address and looked up, wanting to make her feel valued. 'You're obliging my mother. The least I can do is save *you* some of your leisure time. Does ten o'clock suit?'

'Yes. Thank you.' Her cheeks were still burning but her hands had forgotten their agitation.

He smiled to ease the last of her tension. 'You're welcome. Just don't feel you have to indulge all my mother's whims tomorrow. Do only what's reasonable to you. Okay?'

She nodded.

He glanced at his watch. 'Time for you to leave to get those injections for the trip.' He smiled again. 'Off you go. I'll see you in the morning.'

'Thank you,' she repeated, looking confused by his good humour.

Cole questioned it himself once she left. He decided it had nothing to do with the fact she was free of any attachment. That was irrelevant to him. No, it was purely the satisfaction of having the mysteries surrounding her this week resolved. Even the change of image made sense. Given that Brendan was stupidly critical, no doubt she'd been suppressing her true colours for the sake of falling in with what he wanted.

Liz was well rid of that guy.

He'd obviously been dragging her down.

Cole ruefully reflected that was what his ex-wife had accused him of doing, though he'd come to recognise it had been easier to blame him than take any responsibility herself for the breakdown of their marriage. At the time he hadn't cared. All that had been good in their relationship had died...with their baby son.

For several moments the grief and guilt he'd locked away swelled out of the sealed compartment in his mind. He pushed them back. Futile feelings, achieving nothing. The past was past. It couldn't be changed. And there was work to be done.

He brought his concentration to bear on the figures listed on his computer monitor screen. He liked their logical patterns, always a reason for everything. Figures didn't lie or deceive or distort things. There were statiticians who used them to do precisely that, but figures by themselves had a pure truth. Cole was comfortable with figures.

He told himself he'd now be comfortable again with Liz Hart. It was all a matter of fitting everything into place—a straightforward pattern built on truth and logic. It wouldn't matter what she wore or how she looked tomorrow, he wouldn't find it distracting. It was all perfectly understandable.

As for the sexual attraction...a brief aberration.

No doubt it would wear off very quickly.

His desk telephone rang, evoking a frown of annoyance. No Liz to intercept and monitor his calls. He didn't talk to clients off the cuff, but it could be an in-house matter being referred to him. Hard to ignore the buzzing. He snatched up the receiver.

'Pierson.'

'Cole…finally,' came the distinctive voice of his almost ex-wife.

'Tara…' It was the barest of acknowledgments. He had nothing to say to her. An aggressive tension seized his entire body, an instinctive reaction to anything she might say to him.

'I tried to get hold of you all last weekend. You weren't at the penthouse…'

'I was with my mother at Palm Beach,' he cut in, resenting the tone that suggested he should still be at Tara's beck and call. She'd been *enjoying* the company of several other men since their separation, clearing him of any lingering sense of obligation to answer any of her needs.

'Your mother…' A hint of mockery in her voice.

It had been one bone of contention in their marriage that Cole spent too much time looking after his mother instead of devoting his entire attention to what Tara wanted, which was continual social activity in the limelight. Not even her pregnancy and the birth of their baby son had slowed her merry-go-round of engagements. If they hadn't been out at a party, leaving David in the care of his nanny…

'Get to the point, Tara,' he demanded, mentally blocking the well-worn and totally futile *if only* track in his mind.

She heaved a sigh at his bluntness, then in a sweetly cajoling tone, said, 'You do remember that our divorce becomes final next week…'

'The date is in my diary.'

'I thought we should get together and…'

'I believe our respective solicitors have covered

every piece of that ground,' he broke in tersely, angry at the thought that Tara was thinking of demanding even more than he had conceded to her in the divorce settlement.

'Darling, you've been more than generous, but…do we really want this?'

The hair on the back of his neck bristled. 'What do you mean?' he snapped.

She took a deep breath. 'You know I've been out and about with a few men since our separation, but the truth is…none of them match up to you, Cole. And I know you haven't formed a relationship with anyone else. I keep thinking if David hadn't died…'

His jaw clenched.

'It just affected everything between us. We both felt so bad…' Another deep breath. 'But time helps us get over these things. We had such a good life going for us, Cole. I was thinking we should give it another shot, at least try it for a while…'

'No!' The word exploded from him, driven by a huge force of negative feelings that were impossible to contain.

'Cole…we could try for another child,' she rolled on, ignoring his response, dropping her voice to a soft throaty purr that promised more than a child. 'Let's get together tomorrow and talk about it. We could have lunch at…'

'Forget it!' he bit out, hating what could only be a self-serving offer. Tara had never *really* wanted a child, hadn't cared enough about David to spend loving time with him. The nanny had done everything

Cole hadn't done himself for his son—the nanny who'd been more distraught than Tara when...

'I'll be lunching with Mum tomorrow,' he stated coldly, emphasising the fact he was not about to change any plans at this point. 'I won't be doing anything to stop the divorce going through. We reached the end of our relationship a long time ago, Tara, and I have no inclination whatsoever to revive it.'

'Surely a little reunion wouldn't hurt. If we could just talk...'

'I said forget it. I mean precisely that.'

He put the receiver down, switched off his computer, got up and strode out of the office, the urge for some intense, mind-numbing activity driving him to head for the private gymnasium where he worked out a couple of times a week.

He didn't want sex with his almost ex-wife.

It was sex that had drawn him into marrying Tara Summerville in the first place. Sex on legs. That was Tara. It had blinded him to everything else about her until well after the wedding. And there he'd been, trapped by a passionate obsession which had gradually waned under one disillusionment after another.

He might have held the marriage together for David's sake, but he certainly didn't want back in. No way. Never. If he ever married again it would be to someone like...he smiled ironically as Liz Hart popped into his mind.

Liz, who was valiantly trying to rise above being dumped by her long-term lover, revamping herself so effectively she'd stirred up feelings that Cole now recognised as totally inappropriate to both time and circumstance.

No doubt Liz was currently very vulnerable to being desired. It was probably the best antidote for the poison of rejection. But he was the wrong man in the wrong place to take advantage of the situation. She needed to count on him as her boss, not suddenly be presented with a side of him that had nothing to do with work.

Still the thought persisted that Liz Hart could be the perfect antidote to the long poisonous hangover from Tara.

Crazy idea.

Better work that out of his mind, too.

CHAPTER FIVE

FORTUNATELY, Liz wasn't kept waiting long at the medical centre. The doctor checked off the innoculations on the yellow card which went straight into the passport folder, along with the reissued tickets and all the other paperwork now acquired for the trip to South-East Asia. *Done,* Liz thought, and wished she was flying off tomorrow instead of having to accompany Cole Pierson to his mother's home.

It was quite scary how conscious she'd become of him as a man. All this time she'd kept him slotted under the heading of her boss—an undeniably male boss but the male part had only been a gender thing, not a sexual thing. This past week she'd found herself looking at him differently, reacting to him differently, even letting her mind dwell on how very attractive he was, especially when he smiled.

As she pushed through the evening peak hour commuter horde and boarded the train for Bondi Junction, she decided it had to be her sisters' fault, prompting her into reassessing Cole through their eyes. Though it was still a huge reach to consider him a possible marriage prospect. First would have to come...no, don't think about steps towards intimacy.

If her mind started wandering along those lines while she was riding with him in his car tomorrow, it could lead her into some dubious response or glance that Cole might interpret as trouble where he didn't want trouble. As it was, he was probably putting two and two together and coming up with a readily predictable answer—boyfriend gone plus new image equals man-hunting.

She would die if he thought for one moment she was hunting him. Because she wasn't. No way would she put her job at risk, which would certainly be the case if anything personal between them didn't work out. Bad enough that this trip with his mother had bared private matters that were changing the parameters of how they dealt with each other.

It didn't feel *safe* anymore.

It felt even less safe to have Cole Pierson coming to her home tomorrow, picking her up and bringing her back. Liz brooded over how he'd torpedoed her alternative plan, making the whole thing terribly personal by questioning her about Brendan and commenting on the aborted relationship.

She must have alighted from the train at Bondi Junction and walked to her apartment on automatic pilot, because nothing impinged on her occupied mind until she heard her telephone ringing in the kitchen.

It was Diana on the line. 'How did it go today?' Eager to hear some exciting result that would make all her efforts worthwhile.

'My arm is sore from the injections,' Liz replied, instinctively shying from revealing anything else.

'Oh, come on, Liz. That bronze dress was the pièce de résistance. It had to get a rise from him.'

'Well, he did notice it...' making her feel very self-conscious a number of times '...but he didn't *say* anything.'

Diana laughed. 'It's working. It's definitely working.'

'It might be angry notice, you know,' Liz argued. 'I told you how he reacted on Monday.'

'Pure shock. Which was what he needed to start seeing you in a different light. And don't worry about anger. Anger's good. Shows you've got to him.'

'But I'm not sure I want to get to him, Diana. It's been a very...uneasy...week.'

'No pain, no gain.'

Liz rolled her eyes at this flippant dictum. 'Look!' she cried in exasperation. 'It was different for you. A fashion buyer operates largely on her own, not under her boss's nose on a daily basis. There was room for you to pursue the attraction without causing any threat to your work situation.'

'You're getting yourself into a totally unnecessary twist, Liz. Cole Pierson is the kind of man who'll do the running. All you have to do is look great, say *yes,* and let things happen.'

'But what if...'

'Give that managing mind of yours a rest for once,' Diana broke in with a huff of impatience. 'Spontaneity is the key. Go with the flow and see where it takes you.'

To not being able to pay the mortgage if I lose my job, Liz thought. Yet there was something insidiously tempting about Diana's advice. She'd been *managing* everything for so long—*stifling* Brendan—and where had it got her?

On the discard shelf.

And Diana was right about Cole. He'd rolled right over the arrangements she'd tried to manage for tomorrow. If there was any running to be done, he'd certainly do it his way. Of course the choice to say yes or no was hers, but where either answer might lead was still very tricky.

'Maybe nothing will happen,' she said in her confusion over whether she wanted it to or not.

'He's taking you to a meeting with his mother tomorrow, isn't he?'

Liz wished she hadn't blabbed quite so much to Diana on Monday night. 'It's just about the trip,' she muttered.

'Wear the camel pants-suit with the funky tan hip belt and leave the top two buttons of the safari jacket undone,' came the marching orders.

'That's too obvious.' The three buttons left undone on her skirt today had played havoc with her nerves every time Cole had glanced down.

'No, it's not. It simply telegraphs the fact you're not buttoned up anymore. And use that *Red* perfume by Giorgio. It smells great on you.'

'I'm not good at this, Diana.'

'Just do as I say. Got to go now. Ward's arrived home. Good luck tomorrow and don't forget to smile a lot.'

Liz released a long, heavy sigh as she put the receiver down. This linking her up with Cole Pierson was turning into a personal crusade for her younger sister. Liz had tried to dampen it down, to no avail. She had the helter-skelter feeling that wheels had been set in motion on Monday and she had no control over where they were going.

At least she'd had little time to feel depressed over her single state. This weekend could have looked bleak and empty without Brendan. Instead of fretting over how to act with Cole, she should be grateful that the Piersons—mother and son—had filled up tomorrow for her.

Besides, she had Diana's instructions to follow and she carried them out to the letter the next morning, telling herself the outfit would undoubtedly please Nancy Pierson's sense of rightness. Classy casual. Perfect for a visit to a Palm Beach residence, which was definitely in millionaire territory. After all, she did want to assure Cole's mother she was a suitable companion for her in every way.

Her doorbell rang at five minutes to ten. Cole had either given himself more time than he needed to get here, or was keen to get going. Liz grabbed her handbag on the way to the door, intent on presenting herself as ready to leave immediately. She wasn't expecting to have her breathing momentarily paralysed at sight of him, but then she'd never seen him dressed in anything other than an impeccably tailored suit.

Blatant macho virility hit her right in the face. He wore a black polo sweater, black leather jacket, black leather gloves, black jeans, his thick black hair was slightly mussed, adding an air of wild vitality, and his eyes were an electric blue, shooting a bolt of shock straight through Liz's heart.

'Hi!' he said, actually grinning at her. 'You might

need a scarf for your hair. It's a glorious morning so I've put the hood of my car down.'

Scarf…the tiger print scarf for this outfit, she could hear Diana saying. 'Won't be a moment,' she managed to get out and wheeled away, heading for her bedroom to the beat of a suddenly drumming heart, leaving him standing outside her apartment, not even thinking to invite him in. Her mind was stuck on the word, scarf, probably because it served to block out everything else.

Despite the speedy collection of this accessory, Cole had stepped into her living room and was glancing around when she emerged from the bedroom. 'Good space. Nice high ceilings,' he commented appreciatively.

'Built in the nineteen thirties,' she explained on her way to the door, feeling his intrusion too keenly to let him linger in her home.

'Do you own or rent?' he asked curiously.

'It's partly mine. I'm paying off the bank.'

'Fine investment,' he approved.

'I think so. Though primarily I wanted a place of my own.'

'Most women acquire a home through marriage,' he said with a slightly cynical edge.

Or through divorce, Liz thought, wondering how much his almost ex-wife had taken him for and whether that experience had contributed to his detachment from the human race.

'Well, I wasn't counting on that happening,' she said dryly, holding the door and waving him out—a pointed gesture which was ignored.

'You like your independence?' he asked, cocking a quizzical eyebrow at her.

She shrugged. 'Not particularly. I've just found it's better to only count on what I know I can count on.'

'Hard lesson to learn,' he remarked sympathetically.

Had he learnt it, too?

Liz held her tongue. He was finally moving out, waiting for her to lock the door behind them. She didn't know what to think of the probing nature of his conversation. Or was it just casual chat? Maybe she was too used to Cole's habit of never saying anything without purpose.

Still, the sense of being targeted on a personal level persisted and it was some relief that he didn't speak at all as they descended the flight of stairs to street level. Perversely the silence made her more physically aware of him as he walked beside her. She was glad when they emerged into the open air.

It was, indeed, a glorious morning. There was something marvellous about winter sunshine—the warmth and brightness it delivered, the crisp blue of a cloudless sky banishing all thought of cold grey. It lifted one's spirits with its promise of a great day.

'Lucky we don't have to be shut up in the office,' Liz said impulsively, the words accompanied by a smile she couldn't repress.

'An unexpected pleasure,' Cole replied, his smile raising tingles of warmth the sun hadn't yet bestowed.

Liz was piqued into remarking, 'I thought work was the be-all and end-all for you.'

His laser-like eyes actually twinkled at her. 'My life does extend a little further than that.'

Her heart started fluttering. Was he *flirting?* 'Well, obviously, you do care about your mother.'

'Mmmh...a few other things rate my attention, too.'

His slanted look at her caused a skip in her pulse beat and provoked Liz into open confrontation. 'Like what?'

He laughed. He actually laughed. Liz was shocked into staring at him, never having seen or heard Cole Pierson laugh before. It was earth-shaking stuff. He suddenly appeared much younger, happily carefree, and terribly, terribly attractive. The blue eyes danced at her with wicked amusement, causing her to flush in confusion.

'What's so funny?' she demanded.

'Me...you...and here we are.' Still grinning, he gestured to the kerb, redirecting her gaze to the car parked beside it.

Hood down, he'd said, alerting her to the fact that he had to be driving some kind of convertible. If anything, Liz would have assumed a BMW roadster or a Mercedes sports, maybe even a Rolls-Royce Corniche—very expensive, of course, but in a classy conventional style, like his Armani suits.

It was simply impossible to relate the car she was seeing to the boss she knew. She stared at the low-slung, glamorous, silver speed machine in shocked disbelief, her feet rooted on the sidewalk as Cole moved forward and opened the passenger door for her.

'You drive…a Maserati?' Her voice emerged like a half-strangled squawk.

'Uh-huh. The Spyder Cambio Corsa,' he elaborated, naming the model for her.

'A Maserati,' she repeated, looking her astonishment at him.

'Something wrong with it?'

She shook her head, belatedly connecting his current sexy clothes to the sexy car and blurting out, 'This is such a change of image…'

'Welcome to the club,' he said sardonically.

'I beg your pardon?'

She was totally lost with this Cole Pierson, as though he'd changed all the dimensions of his previous persona, emerging as a completely different force to be reckoned with. To top off her sense of everything shifting dangerously between them, he gave her a sizzling head-to-toe appraisal that had her entire skin surface prickling with heat.

'You can hardly deny you've subjected me to a change of image this week, Liz,' he drawled, 'And that was at work, not at play.'

Was he admitting the same kind of disturbance she was feeling now? Whatever…the old boat was being severely rocked on many levels.

'So this is you…at play,' she said in a weak attempt to set things right again.

'One part of me.' There was a challenging glint in his eyes as he waved an invitation to the slinky low black leather passenger seat. 'Shall we go?'

Diana's voice echoed through her head… *Go with the flow*.

Liz forced her feet forward and dropped herself onto the seat as gracefully as she could, swinging her legs in afterwards. 'Thanks,' she murmured as the door was closed for her, then trying for a light note, she smiled and added, 'Nothing like a new experience.'

'You've never ridden in a high-performance car?' he queried as he swung around to the driver's side.

'First time,' she admitted.

'Seems like we're clocking up a few first times between us.'

How many more, Liz thought wildly, acutely aware of him settling in the seat next to her, strong thigh muscles stretching the fabric of his jeans.

'Seat belt,' he reminded her as he fastened his own.

'Right!'

He watched her pull it across her body and click it into place. It made Liz extremely conscious of the belt bisecting her breasts, emphasising their curves.

'Scarf.' Another reminder.

She flushed, quickly spreading the long filmy tiger-print fabric over her hair, winding it around her neck and tying the floating ends at the back.

'Sunglasses.'

It was like a countdown to take-off.

Luckily she always carried sunglasses in her hand-bag. Having whipped them out and slipped them on, she dared a look at him through the tinted lenses.

He gave her a devil-may-care grin as he slid his own onto his nose. 'You want to watch those jungle prints, Liz. Makes me wonder if you're yearning for a ride on the wild side.'

Without waiting for a reply—which was just as well because she was too flummoxed to think of one—he switched on the engine, put the car into gear, and they were off, the sun in their faces, a wind whipping past, and all sorts of wild things zipping through Liz's mind.

CHAPTER SIX

LIZ couldn't help feeling it was fantastic, riding around in a Maserati. The powerful acceleration of the car meant they could zip into spaces in the traffic that would have closed for less manoeuvrable vehicles. Pedestrians stared enviously at it when they were stopped at traffic lights. They looked at her and Cole, too, probably speculating about who they were, mentally matching them up to the luxurious lifestyle that had to go with such a dream car. After one such stop, Liz was so amused by this she burst out laughing.

'What's tickling your sense of humour?' Cole inquired.

'I feel like the Queen of Sheba and a fraud at the same time,' she answered, grinning at the madness of her being seen as belonging to a Maserati, which couldn't be further than the truth.

'Explain.'

The typical economical command put her on familiar ground again with Cole. 'It's the car,' she answered happily. 'Because I'm your passenger, people are seeing me as someone who has to be special.'

'And you think that's funny?'

'Well, it is, isn't it? I mean you are who you are...but I'm just your employee.'

'Oh, I don't know.' His mouth quirked as he

glanced at her. 'You do have a touch of the Queen of Sheba about you today.'

This comment wasn't boss-like at all. Liz tried to laugh it off but wasn't sure the laughter sounded natural. She was glad he was wearing sunglasses, dimming the expression in the piercing blue eyes. As it was, the soft drawl of his voice had curled around her stomach, making it flutter.

'And why shouldn't they think you're special?' he continued with a longer glance at her. 'I do.'

Liz took a deep breath, desperate to regather her scattered wits. 'That's not the point, Cole. I mean...this car...your wealth...I'm sure you take it all for granted, but it's not me.'

'Do you categorise anyone born to wealth as *special?*' he demanded critically.

'Well...they're at least privileged.'

'Privileged, yes. Which, more times than not, means spoiled, not special.' He shook his head. 'I bought a Maserati because I like high performance. You've remained my P.A. because you give me high performance, too. In my view, you match this car more than any other woman who has ridden in that passenger seat.'

More than the fabulous Tara Summerville?

Liz couldn't believe it.

Unless Cole had acquired the Maserati *after* the separation with his wife.

On second thoughts, he'd been talking performance, not appearance, which reduced the compliment to a work-related thing, puncturing Liz's bubble of pleasure.

'You know, being compared favourably to how well an engine runs doesn't exactly make a woman feel special, Cole,' she dryly informed him.

He laughed. 'So how do I answer you? Hmm...' His brow furrowed in concentration. 'I think you were being a fraud to yourself all the time you were with Brendan, but now you're free of him, the real you has emerged in a blaze of glory and everyone is seeing the shine and recognising how special you are, so you're not a fraud today.' He grinned at her. 'How's that?'

She had to laugh. It was over the top stuff but it did make her feel good, as though she really had shed the miserable cloak of feeling less—deserving less—than her beautiful sisters. 'It wasn't so much Brendan's influence,' she felt obliged to confess. 'I guess I've had a problem with self-esteem for a long time.'

'What on earth for?' he demanded, obviously seeing no cause for it.

She shook her head, not wanting to get into analysing her life. 'Let me relish *blaze of glory*. I can smile over that for the rest of the trip.' Suiting action to words, she gave him her best smile.

He shook his head, still puzzled. 'Would it help for you to know I hold you in the highest esteem?'

'Thank you. It's very kind of you to say so.'

'I can hear a *but* in there.'

Her smile turned rueful. 'I guess what you're giving me is respect for what I can carry out for you. And I'm glad to have your respect. Please don't think I'm not. But I've never felt...incompetent...in that area, Cole. Though I have wondered if being too damned smart is more a curse than a blessing.'

'It's a gift. And it's stupid not to use it. You won't be happy within yourself if you try denying it. You know perfectly well it pleases you to get things right, Liz.'

'Mmmh...but I'm not happy living in a world of my own. I want...' She stopped, realising just how personal this conversation had become, and how embarrassing it might be in retrospect, especially on Monday when she had to face Cole at work again.

'Go on,' he pressed.

She tried shrugging it off. 'Oh, all the usual things a woman wants.'

'Fair enough.'

To Liz's immense relief, he let it go at that. She'd been running off at the mouth, drawn into speaking from her heart instead of her head, all because Cole had somehow invaded her private life and was involving himself in it.

Her gaze drifted to the leather gloved hands on the steering wheel. Power controlling power. A convulsive little shiver of excitement warned her she should get her mind right off tempting fantasies. But it was very difficult with Cole looking as he did, driving this car, and dabbling in highly personal conversation.

She did her best to focus on the passing scenery, a relatively easy task once they hit the road along the northern beaches, passing through Dee Why, Collaroy, Narrabeen, then further on, Bilgola, Avalon, Whale Beach. Apart from the attraction of sand and sea, there were some fabulous homes along the way, making the most of million dollar views. Liz had never actually visited this part of Sydney, knew it only by repute, so it was quite fascinating to see it firsthand.

Finally they came to Palm Beach, right at the end of the peninsula, where large mansions overlooked the ocean on one side and Pittwater the other. Cole turned the Maserati into a semicircular driveway for what looked like a palatial Mediterranean villa with many colonnaded verandahs. It was painted a creamy pink and positively glowed in the sunshine. A fountain of dolphins was centred on the front lawn and a hedge of glorious pink and cream Hawaiian hibiscus lined the driveway.

'Wow!' Liz breathed.

'It is far too large for my mother, requires mountainous maintenance, but she won't leave it,' Cole said in a tone of weary resignation.

'Neither would I,' Liz replied feelingly, turned chiding eyes to Nancy's son. 'She must love it. Leaving would be a terrible wrench.'

Cole sighed. 'She's alone. She's getting old. And she's a long way out from the city.'

Liz understood his point. 'You worry about her.'

He brought the Maserati to a halt, switched off the engine. 'She is my mother,' he stated in the sudden quiet.

And he loved her, thereby passing the functional family background test, unlike Brendan. Liz clamped down on the wayward thought and pushed her mind back onto track.

'I *will* look after her on this trip, Cole.'

He smiled. 'I know I can count on you. And while your ex-boyfriend may not have appreciated your responsible streak, I do. And I don't count on many people for anything.'

Over the past year she had considered him totally self-sufficient. Coldly self-sufficient. It gave Liz a rush of warm pleasure to hear him express some dependence on her, even if it was only peripheral.

No man is an island, she thought.

No woman is, either.

Liz was very conscious of needs that remained unanswered. They'd just been highlighted by Cole's comparing himself to Brendan.

Deliberately highlighted?

For what purpose?

He took off his sunglasses and tucked them into the top pocket of his leather jacket. Liz was prompted into taking hers off, too. She was about to meet his mother again and she didn't need any defensive barrier with Nancy Pierson.

'Want to remove your scarf before we go inside?'

She'd forgotten the scarf, forgotten her hair. Cole sat watching as she quickly unwound the protective cover and tucked it under the collar of her jacket, letting the ends fall loose down the front. Having whipped out a brush from her handbag, she fluffed up her flattened hair and trusted that she hadn't eaten off her lipstick because painting her mouth under Cole's gaze was not on. As it was, she was super conscious of him observing her actions and their effect.

'Okay?' she asked, turning to show herself for his approval.

His eyes weren't their usual ice blue. They seemed to simmer over her face and hair, evoking a flush as he drawled, 'All things bright and beautiful.'

Then he was out of the car and at the passenger door before Liz found the presence of mind to release her seat belt. As she freed herself and swung her feet to the ground, he offered his hand for the long haul upright. It was an automatic response to take it, yet his grip shot an electric charge up her arm and when she rose to her full height, they were standing so close and he seemed so big, she stared at the centre of his throat rather than risk looking up and sparking any realisation of her acute physical awareness of him.

She could even smell the leather, and a hint of male cologne. His broad shoulders dwarfed hers, stirring a sense of sexual vulnerability that quite stunned her because she'd never felt overwhelmed by the close presence of any other man. And this was her boss, who should have been familiar, not striking these weird chords that threatened to change everything between them.

'I didn't realise you were so small,' he murmured in a bemused tone.

Her head jerked up as a sense of belittlement shot through her. The gold sparks in her green eyes blazed at him. 'I hate being *small*.'

His brows drew together in mock concern. 'Correction. Dainty and delicate.'

'Oh, great! Now I sound breakable.'

'Woman of steel?'

His eyes were twinkling.

She took a deep breath and summoned up a wry smile. 'Sorry. You hit a sore point. Unlike you, I was behind the door when God gave out height.'

He openly grinned. 'But you weren't behind the door when God gave out quick wit. Which you'll undoubtedly have to use to keep my mother in line.'

With that comment he led off towards the front door of the pink mansion and Liz fell into step beside him, still fiercely wishing she was as tall as her sisters, which would make her a much better physical match for him. Somehow that 'small' comment felt as though she'd been marked down in the attraction stakes.

On the other hand, she was probably suffering from an overactive imagination to think Cole was attracted at all, and she'd do well to concentrate her mind on exercising the quick wit he credited her with, because the real purpose of this trip was about to get under way.

The front door was opened just as they were stepping up onto the ground floor verandah. 'At last!' Nancy Pierson cried in a tone of pained relief.

Cole checked his watch. 'It's only just eleven, Mum.'

'I know, dear, but I've been counting the minutes since Tara arrived. You could have warned me...'

'Tara?' Cole's face instantly tightened. 'What the devil is she doing here?'

Nancy looked confused. 'She said...'

'You shouldn't have let her in.'

The confusion deepened, hands fluttering a helpless appeal. 'She *is* still your wife.'

'A technicality. One that will end next week.'

This evoked a huff of exasperation from his mother. 'Tara gave me the impression it was arranged for her to meet you here.'

'There's no such arrangement. You've been manipulated, Mum.'

'Well, I'm glad you recognise Tara's skill at doing that, Cole,' came the swift and telling retort. Clearly Nancy held no warm feelings for the woman her son had married. 'I set out morning tea in the conservatory. She's there waiting for you, making herself at home as though she had every right to.'

'Makes for one hell of a scene,' Cole ground out.

'Well, it's not my place to shut her out of your life. It's you who has to make that good. If you have a mind to.'

'Tara's made you doubt it?'

Another huff of exasperation. 'How am I supposed to know what you feel, Cole? You never talk about it. For all I know, you've been pining over that woman...'

'No way!'

'Then you'd better go and convince her of that because she's acting as though she only has to crook her little finger at you and...'

'An act is what it is, Mum.' He flashed a steely glance at Liz. 'As you've just heard, we have some unexpected company for morning tea.'

'I'll take Liz upstairs with me,' Nancy rushed out,

shooting an anguished look at her. 'I'm sorry, dear. This isn't what I planned.'

'Which is precisely why you won't scurry off with Liz,' Cole broke in tersely. 'I will not have her treated like some backroom nonentity because my almost ex-wife decides to barge in on us.'

Nancy looked shocked. 'I didn't mean...'

'It's an issue of discretion, Cole,' Liz quickly supplied. 'I don't mind giving you privacy.'

'Which plays right into Tara's scheme. We're not changing *anything* for her.' Angry pride shifted into icy command. 'Mum, you will lead back to the conservatory. Liz, you will accompany my mother as you normally would. We are going to have the morning tea which has been prepared for *us*.'

He gestured her forward, unshakable determination etched on his face. Liz glanced hesitantly at his mother whom she was supposed to be pleasing today. The anguish was gone from Nancy's expression. In fact, there seemed to be a look of smug delight in her eyes as she, too, waved Liz into the house.

'Please forgive me for not greeting you properly, dear,' she said with an apologetic smile. 'These problems in communication do throw one out.'

'Perfectly understandable,' Liz assured her. Then taking her cue from Cole's command to act normally, she smiled and said, 'I love the look of your home, Nancy. It's very welcoming.'

'How nice of you to say so!' Nancy beamed her pleasure as she hooked her arm around Liz's and drew her into a very spacious foyer, its tiled floor laid out in a fascinating mosaic pattern depicting coral and seashells. 'I picked everything myself for this house. Even these tiles on the floor.'

'They're beautiful,' Liz said in sincere admiration, trying not to be too conscious of Cole closing the door behind them, locking them into a scene that was bound to be fraught with tension and considerable unpleasantness, since Tara Summerville had obviously come expecting to gain something and Cole was intent on denying her.

Nancy continued to point out features of the house as she showed Liz through it, feeding off the interest expressed and enjoying telling little stories about various acquisitions, quite happy not to hurry back to her uninvited guest. Liz suspected Nancy was taking satisfaction in keeping Tara waiting.

Cole didn't push his mother to hurry, either, seemingly content to move at her pace, yet Liz sensed his seething impatience with the situation that had been inflicted on all of them by the woman he'd married.

He must have loved her once, Liz reasoned.

Had the love died, or had husband and wife been pulled apart by grief over the loss of their child?

She had never speculated over her boss's marriage—none of her business—but the exchange between mother and son at the door had ignited a curiosity Liz couldn't deny now. She wanted to see how Cole and Tara Summerville reacted to each other, wanted to know the cause of the ruction between them, wanted to feel Cole was now truly free of his wife...*which may not be the case.*

Surely a private meeting would have served his purpose for ending it more effectively.

Was his angry pride hiding a vulnerability to his wife's power to manipulate his feelings?

Was he using Liz and his mother as a shield, not trusting himself in a one-on-one situation?

As they approached the conservatory, Nancy's prattling began to sound nervous and the tension emanating from Cole seemed to thicken the air, causing Liz to hold her breath. She sensed something bad was about to happen.

Very bad.

And she found herself suddenly wishing she wasn't in the middle of it.

CHAPTER SEVEN

LIZ caught a quick impression of abundant ferns, exotic plants, many pots of gorgeous cyclamens in bloom, all forming a glorious backdrop to settings of cane furniture cushioned in tropical prints. However, even as she entered the conservatory her gaze was drawn to the woman seated at the far end of a long rectangular table.

'Cole, darling…' she drawled, perfect red lips pursing to blow a kiss at him as she rose from her chair, giving them all the full benefit of what the media still termed 'the body' whenever referring to Tara Summerville.

She wore a black leather jacket that moulded every curve underneath it, with enough buttons undone to promise a spillage of lush feminine flesh if one more button was popped. This was teamed with a tight little miniskirt, also in black leather, and with a front split that pointed up the apex of possibly the most photographed legs in history—long, long legs that led down to sexy little ankle high boots. A belt in black and white cowhide was slung jauntily around her hips and a black and white handkerchief scarf was tied at the base of her very long throat.

Her thick mane of tawny hair tumbled down to her shoulder-blades in highly touchable disarray and her artfully made-up amber eyes gleamed a provocative

challenge at the man she was intent on targeting. Not
so much as a glance at Liz. Nor at Nancy Pierson.
This was full power tunnel vision at Cole and Liz
suspected the whole beam of it was sizzling with sexual invitation.

'I'm glad you're on your feet, Tara,' Cole said in
icy disdain of this approach. 'Just pick up your bag
and keep on walking, right out of this house.'

'Very uncivil of you, darling, especially when *your
mother* invited me in,' she returned with a cat-like
smile, halting by a side chair and gripping the back
of it, making a stand against being evicted.

'You lied to her,' came the blunt rebuttal.

'Only to get past your pride, Cole. Now that I'm
here for you, why not admit that pride is…' She rolled
her hips and moved her mouth into a sensual pout.
'…a very cold bedfellow.'

'Waste of time and effort, Tara. Might as well
move on. I have,' he stated emphatically.

'Then why haven't I heard a whisper of it?' she
mocked, still exuding confidence in her ability to get
to him.

'I no longer care to mix in your social circle.'

'You're *news,* Cole. There would have been tattle
somewhere if you'd…*moved on.*'

'I prefer to guard my privacy these days.'

He was stonewalling, Liz thought. If there'd been
any woman in his life since Tara, some evidence of
the relationship would have shown up, at least to her
as his personal assistant—telephone calls, bookings to
be made, various arrangements. Was it pride, resisting

the offer Tara was blatantly making? Or did he truly not want her anymore?

'Don't tell me you've taken to slumming it,' Tara tossed at him derisively.

'Not every woman has your need for the limelight,' Cole returned, icy disdain back in his voice. 'And since I'll never be a party to it again, I strongly recommend you go and find yourself a fellow game player to shine with. You're not about to win anything here.'

Her eyes narrowed, not caring to look defeat in the face. For the first time, her gaze slid to Liz. A quick up and down appraisal left her feeling she'd been raked to the bone. The fact that Nancy was still hugging her arm didn't go unnoticed, either. Without any warning, Tara flashed a bolt of venom at Cole's mother.

'You never did like me, did you, Nancy?'

Liz felt the older woman stiffen under the direct attack, but she was not lacking in firepower herself. 'It's difficult to like such a totally self-centred person as yourself, Tara,' she said with crisp dignity.

A savagely mocking smile was aimed right back at her. 'No doubt you've been producing sweet little protégées for Cole ever since I left.' Her glittering gaze moved to Liz. 'So who and what is this one?'

'*I* brought Liz with me,' Cole stated tersely. 'Her presence here has nothing to do with you and your exit is long overdue.'

'*Your* choice, Cole?' One finely arched eyebrow rose in amused query. 'In place of *me?*'

The comparison was meant to humiliate, but on

seeing his wife in the flesh again, Liz had already conceded she'd never be able to compete in the looks department. She just didn't have the female equipment Tara Summerville had. Not even close to it. But since it could be argued there was something positive to be said for an admirable character and an appealing personality—neither of which was overly evident in Cole's wife—the nasty barb didn't hit too deeply. What actually hurt more was Cole's response to it.

'Oh, for God's sake! Liz has been my personal assistant for the past three years. You used to waltz past her on your way to my office in times gone by, though typically, you probably didn't bother noticing her.'

It was a curt dismissal of the *his choice* tag, implying there was no chance of her ever being anything more than his personal assistant. It shouldn't have felt like a stab to her heart, but it did.

'The little brown mouse!' Tara cried incredulously, then tossed her head back as laughter trilled from her throat.

Liz's stomach knotted. She knew intuitively that Tara Summerville hadn't finished with her. The nerve-jangling laughter was bound to have a nasty point to it. The amber eyes glinted maliciously at her as the remarks rolled.

'How handy, being Cole's P.A.! Saw your chance and took it, jazzing yourself up, making yourself *available,* and here you are, getting your hooks into Mummy, as well, playing Miss All-Round-Perfect.'

The rush of blood to Liz's head was so severe she didn't hear what Cole said, only the angry bark of his voice. She saw the response to it though, Tara swinging back to pick up her bag, slinging the strap of it over her shoulder, strutting towards Cole, pausing to deliver one last broadside.

'You've been *had,* Cole. No doubt she's hitting all the right chords for you...but I bet she can't match me in bed. Think about it, darling. It's not too late to change your mind.'

Both of them left the conservatory, Tara leading off like a victor who'd done maximum damage, Cole squeezing Liz's shoulder first in a silent gesture of appreciation for her forebearance, then following Tara out to enforce her departure and possibly have the last word before she left.

Liz was so sick with embarrassment, she didn't know what to do or say. The worst of it was, Tara had literally been echoing Diana's calculated plan to *get the boss.* While that had not been part of Liz's motivation for going along with her sisters' makeover plan, Tara's accusations had her squirming with guilt over the feelings that had emerged this past week, the growing desire for Cole to find her attractive.

Fortunately, Nancy moved straight into hostess mode, drawing Liz over to the table and filling the awkward silence with a torrent of words. 'Tara always did make an ugly scene when she wasn't getting her own way. You mustn't take anything she said to heart, dear. Pure spite. You just sit yourself down and relax and I'll make us a fresh pot of tea. Help yourself to a pastry or a scone with strawberry jam and cream. That's Cole's favourite. I always make him Devonshire tea.'

Liz sat. Her gaze skated distractedly over a selection of small Danish pastries with fillings of glazed fruit—apricot, apple, peach—the plate of scones beside dishes of cream and strawberry jam. Nothing prompted an appetite. She thought she would choke on food.

Nancy moved to what was obviously a drinks bar, easily accessible to the swimming pool beyond the conservatory. She busied herself behind it, apparently unaffected by the suggestion that Liz and Cole were having an affair, though she must be suspecting it now, adding in the fact that Cole had arranged for his P.A. to accompany her on a pleasure trip. It was, after all, an extraordinary thing to do, given there was no closer connection between them than boss and employee.

Liz couldn't bear Nancy thinking she was Cole's mistress on the side. It made her seem underhand, sleazy, hiding the intimacy from his mother, pretending everything was straight and aboveboard.

'I'm not having a secret affair with Cole. I've never slept with him...or...or anything like that,' she blurted out, compelled to clear any murkiness from their relationship.

Nancy looked up from her tea-making, startled by the emphatic claim. Her blue eyes were very direct, projecting absolute certainty as she replied, 'I have no doubt whatsoever about that, dear. I questioned Cole about you before we met on Monday. His answers revealed...' She heaved a deep sigh. '...he only thought of you as very capable.'

The flush in Liz's cheeks still burned. Although she'd known Cole had not been aware of her as a woman, certainly not before this past week, that truth was not quite so absolute now. He *was* seeing her differently, and even though it might not *mean* what Diana wanted it to mean, Liz couldn't let Tara's interpretation of her changed appearance go unanswered.

'I'm not out to *get* him, either.'

Nancy heaved another deep sigh, then gave her a sad little smile. 'I almost wish you were, dear, but I don't think it's in your nature.'

It startled Liz out of her wretched angst. 'You wish…?'

'I probably shouldn't say this…' Nancy's grimace revealed her own inner angst. '…but I'm very afraid Cole is still stuck on Tara. What she said is all too true. And I'm sure you must know it, as well. There hasn't been any other woman in his life since she left him. It's like he's sealed himself off from every normal social connection.'

Liz nodded. She was well acquainted with *the untouchable ice man.*

Nancy rattled on, voicing her main concern. 'But if Tara is now determined on getting her hooks into him again…' A shake of the head. 'I can only hope Cole has the good sense to go through with the divorce and have done with her.'

Liz kept her mouth shut. It wasn't appropriate for her to comment on Cole's personal life when it had nothing to do with her. The stress of Tara's visit had wrung this confidence from Nancy, just as it had driven Liz to defend herself. Where the truth lay about Cole's feelings for his wife, she had no idea.

Though now that Nancy had spelled out her viewpoint, it did seem he had to be carrying a lot of emotional baggage from his marriage—baggage he'd systematically buried under intensive work.

Was the physical confrontation with his wife stirring it all up? He hadn't come back from seeing her out of the house. Maybe they were still talking, arguing as couples do when neither of them really wanted to let go. Any foothold—even a bitter one—was better than none. And Cole was unhampered by witnesses now. What if Tara had thrown her arms around him, physically pressing for a resumption of intimacy? Was it possible for him to be totally immune to what 'the body' was offering?

A sick depression rolled through Liz. Cole had only noticed her this past week because *the little brown mouse* didn't fit that label anymore. Which was probably still an annoyance to him. Or a curiosity, given his questioning about Brendan. Nothing to do with a sudden attraction which she'd probably fabricated out of her own secret wanting it to be so.

A foolish fantasy.

Why on earth would a man like him—a handsome billionaire—be attracted to her when he could snap his fingers and have the Tara Summervilles of this world? She must have been mad to let Diana influence her thinking. Or desperate to feel something excitingly positive after being dumped by Brendan.

'Oh! There's Cole with the tradesman!' Nancy cried in relief.

The remark halted Liz's miserable reverie and directed her gaze out to the pool area where Nancy was looking. Cole was, indeed, with another man, pointing out a section of paving and leading him towards it.

'He must have arrived while Cole was seeing Tara out. They've come down the side path,' Nancy prattled on, her spirits perking up at this evidence that her son's delayed return did not mean he was being vamped by his almost ex-wife. 'The appointment was at eleven o'clock, after all. So fortuitous.'

It didn't guarantee that Cole had maintained his rejection of any reunion, but it certainly minimised the opportunity for persuasion on his wife's part. Liz found herself hoping that Tara had not *won* anything from him, and not just because of being interrupted by the arrival of the tradesman. Nancy didn't like the woman and Liz certainly had no reason to. But no doubt the power of sex could turn some men blind to everything else.

'Now we can enjoy our morning tea,' Nancy declared, carrying an elegant china teapot to the table and setting it down with an air of happy satisfaction. Clearly danger had been averted in her mind. She settled on the chair opposite to Liz's and eyed her with bright curiosity.

'Pardon me for asking, dear, but was it just this week that you…uh…jazzed yourself up?'

'During my vacation,' Liz answered, not minding the question from Nancy, knowing she could find out from Cole anyway. 'My sisters ganged up on me, saying I'd let myself become drab, and hauled me off to do their Cinderella trick.'

'Well, whatever they did, you do look lovely.'

'Thank you.'

'Tea?'

'Yes, please.'

Nancy poured. 'So you came back to work on Monday with a new image,' she said, smiling encouragement.

'Yes.'

'Did Cole notice any difference?'

Liz grimaced. 'He didn't like it.'

'Didn't like how you looked?'

'Didn't like me looking different, I think.' Liz shrugged. 'No doubt he'll get used to it.'

'Milk and sugar?'

Liz shook her head. 'Just as it is, thank you.'

'Do have a scone, dear.'

Liz took one out of politeness, though she did feel calmer now and thought there'd be no problem with swallowing. It was a relief to have Nancy understanding her situation. It would have been extremely uncomfortable accompanying Cole's mother on the trip, with her still thinking all sorts of horribly false things.

Having cut the scone in half, Liz was conscientiously spooning strawberry jam and cream onto her plate when her ragged nerves received another jolt.

'Oh, good! Cole is coming in for his tea,' Nancy announced, causing Liz to jerk around in her chair to see her boss skirting the pool and heading for the conservatory, having left the tradesman to measure the paving area and calculate the cost of the work to be done.

Totally mortified by the tide of heat that rushed up her neck again, Liz focused hard on transferring the jam and cream to the halved scone. If she shoved the food into her mouth and appeared to be eating, she reasoned that Cole might only speak to his mother. It might be a cowardly tactic but she didn't feel up to coping with his penetrating gaze and probing questions. She didn't even want to look at him. He might have lipstick smudged on his mouth.

Which was none of her business!

Why she felt so violent about that she didn't know and didn't want to know. She just wanted to be left out of anything to do with Tara Summerville.

She heard a glass door slide open behind her and it felt as though a whoosh of electric energy suddenly permeated the air. Her hands started trembling. It stopped her from lifting the scone to her mouth. She glared at her plate, hating being affected like this. It wasn't fair. She'd done nothing wrong.

'Liz…'

She gritted her teeth.

He had no right to put her on the spot, commanding her attention when they weren't even at work. She was here in her spare time, as a favour to his mother, not as *his* personal assistant.

'Are you okay?' he asked, amazingly in a tone of concern.

Pride whipped her head around to face him. There was no trace of red lipstick on his mouth. His expression was one of taut determination, the piercing blue eyes intensely concentrated, aimed at searching her mind for any trouble.

Her chin tilted in direct challenge as she stated, 'I have no reason not to be okay.'

He gave a slow nod. 'I didn't anticipate a collateral hit from Tara. I regret you were subjected to it.'

'A hit only works if there's damage done. I've assured your mother there's no truth in what was assumed about me...and you.' *And don't you dare think otherwise,* she fiercely telegraphed to him.

His gaze flicked sharply to Nancy. 'You didn't believe that rank bitchiness, did you, Mum?'

'No, dear. And I told Liz so.'

'Right! No harm done then,' he said, apparently satisfied. 'Got to get back to check that this guy knows what's he's quoting on.'

'What about your tea?' Nancy asked.

'I'll have it later.'

He stepped outside, closed the door, and to all intents and purposes, the nasty incident with Tara Summerville was also closed. Liz certainly wasn't about to bring the subject up again. She realised her hands were clenched in her lap and consciously relaxed them. The scone was waiting to be eaten. She'd eat it if it killed her. It proved she was okay.

'Well, isn't that nice?' Nancy remarked, beaming pleasure at her as Liz lifted one half of the scone from her plate.

She looked blankly at Cole's mother, completely lost on whatever had struck her as *nice.*

'He cares about you, dear.' This said with a benevolent smile that thoroughly approved of the supposed caring.

Liz felt too frazzled to argue the point.

She only hoped that Cole had completely dismissed the idea—planted by Tara—that his personal assistant was focused far more on climbing into bed with him than doing the work she was employed to do.

CHAPTER EIGHT

MAKE another baby...

Cole seethed over Tara's last toss at him and all the memories it aroused. He ended up accepting the quotation for the paving work around the pool without even questioning it. He didn't care if the guy was overcharging. As long as the job was done by a reputable tradesman, the cost was irrelevant. All the money in the world could not buy back the life of the baby son he'd lost. Though it could obviously buy back a wife who was prepared to pay lip-service to being a mother again.

A mother...

What a black joke that was!

And the gross insensitivity of Tara's even thinking he'd consider her proposition was typical of her total lack of empathy to how he felt. God! He wouldn't want her in the same house as any child of his, let alone being the biological mother to it, having the power to affect its upbringing in so many negative ways.

David had only ever been a show-off baby to her—trotting him out in designer clothes when it suited her, ignoring him when he needed her. *Their son* hadn't even left a hole in her life when he died, and she'd resented the huge hole he'd left in Cole's—impatient with his grief, ranting about how cold he was to her,

93

seeking more cheerful company because he was such *a drag*.

Did Tara imagine he could forget all that just because they'd started out having great sex and she still had 'the body' to excite him again if she put her mind to it?

He hadn't even felt a tingle in his groin when she'd tried her come-on this morning.

Not a tingle.

Though he had felt a blaze of fury when she'd painted Liz in her own manipulative colours, casting her as a calculating seductress, mocking her efforts to look more attractive. Which she certainly did, though Cole had no doubt the change had been motivated by a need to lift herself out of the doldrums caused by Brendan's defection. Nothing to do with him.

If Liz withered back into a little brown mouse now...because of Tara's bitchiness...Cole seethed over that, too, as he made his way back to the conservatory after seeing the tradesman off. Liz had insisted she was okay, but she hadn't wanted to look at him when he'd asked. When she had turned to answer, her eyes had been all glittery, her cheeks red hot. She'd denied any damage done but Cole suspected her newly grown confidence in herself as a woman had been badly undermined. He wanted to fix that but how...?

Liz and his mother were gone from the conservatory by the time he returned to it, Just as well, since he had no ready antidote for Tara's poison. At least he could trust his mother to be kind to Liz, involve her in the business of packing for their trip. Probably overkind, trying to make up for the nasty taste left behind by her uninvited guest.

He'd made one hell of a mistake marrying that woman. Five more days and the divorce would become final. Thursday. It couldn't come fast enough for Cole.

He made himself a fresh pot of tea, wolfed down a couple of scones, found the morning newspaper and concentrated on shutting Tara out of his mind. She didn't deserve space in it and he wouldn't give it to her.

Having read everything he deemed worth reading, he was attacking the cryptic crossword when his mother returned to the conservatory, wheeling a tray-mobile loaded with lunch things. Liz trailed behind her, looking anywhere but at him.

'Well, we've worked everything out for the trip,' his mother declared with satisfaction. 'Do clear the table of that newspaper, Cole. And if you'd open a good bottle of red—Cabernet Sauvignon?'

'What are we eating?' he asked, hoping some mundane conversation would make Liz feel more relaxed in his company.

'Lasagne and salad and crispy bread, followed by caramelised pears. And we must hurry because Liz needs to do some shopping and it's after one o'clock already.'

'How much shopping?' he asked as he moved to the bar. 'Mum, have you been pressing Liz to buy a whole lot of stuff to fit what *you* think is needed?'

'Only a few things,' she answered airily. 'Liz didn't understand about the colonial night at The

Strand Hotel in Rangoon where the ladies are invited to wear white, and...'

'Surely it's not obligatory.'

'That's not the point, dear. It's the spirit of the thing.'

He frowned, wondering how much expense his mother was notching up for her companion—costs he simply hadn't envisaged. 'I didn't mean for Liz to be out of pocket over this trip.'

His mother gave him one of those limpidly innocent smiles that spelled trouble. 'Then you could take her shopping so she'll feel right...everywhere we go together.'

'No!' Liz looked horrified by the suggestion, stopping in her setting of cutlery on the table to make a firm stand on the issue. 'You're giving me the trip free, Cole,' she reminded him with vigour. 'And Nancy, I'll get plenty of use out of what I buy anyway. It's no problem.'

The line was drawn and her eyes fiercely defied either of them to cross it.

Cole felt the line all through lunch.

He was her boss.

She was here on assignment.

She would oblige his mother in every way in regard to the trip, but the block on any personal rapport with the man who employed her was rigidly adhered to. She barely looked at him and avoided acknowledging his presence as much as she could without being openly rude. It was very clear to him that what Tara had said about her—and him—was preying on Liz's mind.

It was even worse in the car travelling back into the city. She sat almost scrunched up in the passenger seat, making herself as small as possible, her hands tightly interlinked in her lap. No joy in riding in the Maserati this time, though Cole sensed she was willing the car to go as fast as it could, wanting the trip over and done with so she could get away from him.

It made him angry.

He hated Tara's power to do this to her.

Just because Liz wasn't built like Tara didn't make her less attractive in her own individual way. He liked the new hairstyle on her. It was perky. Drew more attention to her face, too, which had a bright vitality that was very appealing. Very watchable. Particularly her eyes. A lot of power in those sparkly green eyes. As for her figure, certainly on the petite side, but definitely feminine. Sexy, too, in the clothes she'd been wearing. Not in your face sexy. More subtle. Though strong enough to get to him this past week.

Cole was tempted to say so, but he wasn't sure she'd want to hear such things from him, coming on top of Tara's coupling them as she had. It might make Liz shrink even more inside herself, thinking he *was* about to make a move on her. It was damned difficult, given their work situation and her current fragile state.

'I'd appreciate it if you'll drop me off along Military Road at the Mosman shopping centre,' she said abruptly.

He glanced at his watch. Almost three o'clock. Most shops closed at five o'clock on Saturday, except in tourist areas, and Mosman was more a classy suburb. 'I'll park and wait for you. Take you home when you're through shopping.'

'No, please.' Almost a panicky note in her voice. 'I don't want to hold you up.'

'*You'll* be held up, getting public transport home. Apart from which, you wouldn't be shopping but for my mother making you feel you have to,' he argued. 'I'll sit over coffee somewhere and wait for you.'

'I truly don't want you to do that, Cole.' Very tense. 'It will make me feel I have to hurry.'

'Take all the time you want,' he tossed back at her, assuming a totally relaxed air. 'I have nothing in particular to go home to.'

And he didn't like the sense of her running away from him.

A compelling urge to smash the line she had drawn prompted him into adding, 'Actually, I think I'll tag along with you. Give an opinion on what looks good.'

That shocked her out of her defensive shell. Her head jerked towards him. The sunglasses hid the expression in her eyes but if it was horror, he didn't care.

'I will not let you buy anything for me,' she threw at him, a feisty pride rising out of the assault on her grimly held sense of propriety. 'You are not responsible for...for...'

'My mother's love of dressing up for an occasion?' he finished for her, grinning at the steam he'd stoked. 'I couldn't agree more. The responsibility is all yours for indulging her. And you probably don't need me along. Have to admit the clothes you've been wearing this past week demonstrate you have a great eye for what looks good on you.'

Got in that little boost to her confidence, Cole thought, and continued on his roll with a sense of triumphant satisfaction. 'But most women like a man's opinion and since I'm here on the spot, why not? More interesting for me than sitting over coffee by myself.'

'Cole, I'm your P.A., not your...your...'

Lover? Mistress? Wife?

Clearly she couldn't bring herself to voice such provocative positions. Cole relieved her agitation by putting their relationship back on terms she was comfortable with.

'As your boss, who instigated this whole situation, it's clearly within my authority to see that you don't spend too much on pleasing my mother.'

'I'm not stupid!' she cried in exasperation. 'I said I'd only buy what I'll make use of again.'

'Then you can't have any objection to my feeling right about this. Besides, I'll be handy. I'll carry your shopping bags.'

She shook her head in a helpless fashion and slumped back into silence. Cole sensed that resistance was still simmering but he was now determined on this course of action and he was not about to budge from it. Tara was not going to win over Liz Hart. One way or another, he was going to make Liz feel great about herself.

As she should.

She was great at everything she did for him.

Probably make a great mother, too.

Cole grimaced over this last thought.

Time he got Tara out of his head, once and for all. She'd left one hell of a lot of scar tissue but that was no reason for him not to move on. In fact, he'd told her he had, which had spurred the attack on Liz.

Well, at least he was moving on neutralising that— one step in the right direction.

CHAPTER NINE

LIZ's heart was galloping. Why, why, why was Cole being so perverse, insisting on going shopping with her, foiling her bid to escape the awkwardness she now felt with him? Didn't he realise how personal it was, giving his opinion on what clothes she chose, carrying her shopping bags, acting as though they were *a couple?*

She took several deep breaths in an attempt to calm herself down. Her mind frantically re-examined everything he'd said, searching for clues that might help her understand his motivation. It came as some relief to realise he couldn't think she'd been making a play for him this past week. His comment on the clothes she'd worn to work had been a compliment on her taste, no hint of suspicion that they could have been especially aimed to attract *his* notice.

He'd said he had nothing in particular to go home to and tagging along with her would be more interesting than drinking coffee alone. But weren't men bored by clothes shopping? Brendan had always been impatient with any time spent on it. *That'll do,* had been his usual comment, never a considered opinion on how good anything looked on her.

Maybe with having a famous model as his wife, Cole had learnt some of the tricks of the trade, but thinking of Tara made Liz even more self-conscious about parading clothes in front of him. She couldn't compete. She didn't want to compete. She just wanted to be left alone to lick her wounds in private.

But Cole was already parking the car, pressing the mechanism that installed the hood, getting ready to leave the Maserati in the street while he accompanied her. She knew there'd be no stopping him. Once Cole Pierson made up his mind to do something, no force on earth would deter him from pursuing his goal. But what was his goal here?

Was it just filling in time with her?

She could minimise the shopping as much as seemed reasonable to him.

Reasonable might be the key. He'd said he wanted to *feel right* about what she bought. Which linked this whole thing back to indulging his mother. Nothing really personal at all.

The frenzy in her mind abated. She could cope with this. She had to. Cole was now out of the car and striding around it to the passenger door. Liz hastily released her safety belt and grabbed her handbag from the floor. The door was opened and once again he offered his hand to help her out. Ignoring it was impossible. Liz took it and was instantly swamped by a wave of dynamic energy that fuzzed the coping sector in her mind.

Thankfully he didn't hold on to her hand, releasing it to wave up and down the street, good-naturedly asking, 'Which way do you want to go?'

Liz paused a moment to orient herself. They were in the middle of the shopping centre. Mosman had quite a number of classy boutiques, but her current budget wasn't up to paying their prices, not after the big splurge she'd just had on clothes. She hadn't wanted to ask Diana for help with these extras for the trip. Her sister would inevitably pepper her with questions about her boss, and Liz didn't want to hear them, let alone answer them. There was, however, one inexpensive shop here that might provide all she needed.

'Across the road and to our left,' she directed.

Cole automatically took her arm to steer her safely through the cruising traffic to the opposite sidewalk. She knew it was a courtesy but it felt like a physical claim on her. She was becoming far, far too conscious of her boss as a man. It wasn't even a relief when he resumed simply walking side by side.

'Do you have a particular place in mind?' he asked, glancing at display windows they passed.

'Yes. It's just along here.' She kept her gaze for ward, refusing to be tempted by what she couldn't afford. It was the middle of winter but the new spring fashions were already on show everywhere.

'Hold it!' Cole grabbed her arm to halt her progress and pointed to a mannequin dressed in a gorgeous green pantsuit. 'That would be fantastic on you, Liz.'

'Not what I'm looking for,' she swiftly stated, knowing the classy outfit would cost mega-dollars.

He frowned at her as she tugged herself loose and kept walking. 'What are you looking for?'

'A couple of evening tops to go with black slacks and something in white,' she rattled out.

'Black,' he repeated in a tone of disapproval.

'You're going into the tropics, you know. Hot and humid. You should be wearing something light.'

'Black goes anywhere,' she argued.

'I like green on you,' he argued back.

'What you like isn't really relevant, Cole. You won't be there,' she reminded him, glad to make the point that she wasn't out to please *him*.

'My mother would like what I like,' he declared authoritatively. 'I think we should go back and...'

'No. I'm going to look in here,' she insisted, heading into the shop she had targeted.

It was somewhat overcrowded with racks of clothes, but promising a large range of choice which was bound to yield something suitable. However, Liz had barely reached the first rack when Cole grabbed her hand and hauled her outside.

'A second-hand shop?' he hissed, his black brows beetling down at her.

'Quite a lot of second-hand designer wear,' she tersely informed him. 'Classy clothes that have only been worn a few times, if that. They're great bargains and perfectly good.'

'I will not have you wearing some other woman's cast-offs,' he said so vehemently Liz was stunned into silence, not understanding why he found it offensive. His hand lifted and cupped her cheek, his thumb tilting her chin up so the piercing blue eyes bored into hers with commanding intensity. 'I will not have you thinking you only rate seconds. You're a class act, Liz Hart. Top of the top. And you are going to be dressed accordingly.'

He dropped his hand, hooked her arm around his

and marched her back down the street before Liz could find her voice. Her cheek was still burning from his touch and her heartbeat was thundering in her ears. It was difficult to think coherently with his body brushing hers, his long stride forcing her to pick up pace to keep level with him. Nevertheless, something had to be said.

'Cole, I've…I've spent most of my spare money on…on…'

'I'll do the buying,' he cut in decisively. 'Consider it a bonus for being the best P.A. I've ever had.'

Bonus…best P.A.…top of the top…the heady words buzzed around her brain. The compliments were so extraordinary, exhilarating. And suddenly she recalled what his mother had said—*He cares about you.*

Her feet were almost dancing as he swept her into the boutique she had bypassed before. 'We'll try that green,' he told the saleswoman, pointing to the pant-suit on the display mannequin.

There was such a strong flow of power emanating from Cole, the woman virtually jumped to obey. Liz was ushered into a dressing-room and handed the garments in her size in double-quick time.

'I want to see that on,' Cole continued in commanding vein. 'And while Liz is changing, you can show me anything else you have that might do her justice.'

Wearing second-hand clothes had never bothered her, but Cole's determination to *do her justice* was too intoxicating to resist. She fell in love with the apple green pantsuit and his raking look of male appreciation and resounding, 'Yes,' set her heart fluttering with wild excitement. He really did see her as special…and attractive.

Next came a lime green cotton knit top, sleeveless but with a deep cowl neckline that could be positioned many clever ways. It was teamed with white pants printed with lime green pears, strawberries and mangos—the kind of fun item she'd never indulged in. But it did look brilliant on her and she was tempted into striking a jaunty pose when showing the outfit to Cole. He grinned at her, giving a thumbs up sign, and she grinned back, enjoying the madness of the moment. Both green tops would dress up her black slacks, she decided, trying to be a bit sensible.

'That's it for here,' he declared. 'We'll try somewhere else for the white.'

Somewhere else turned out to be a Carla Zampatti boutique, all stocked up with the new spring range from one of the top designers in Australia. With the help of the saleswoman Cole selected a white broderie anglaise skirt with a ruffle hem and a matching peasant blouse. The correct accessories included a dark auburn raffia hip belt featuring a large red, brown and camel stone clip fastening, long Indian earrings dangling with beads and feathers in the same colours, high wedge heeled sandals in white, with straps that crisscrossed halfway up Liz's calves.

The whole effect was absolutely stunning.

Liz couldn't believe how good she looked.

Fine feathers certainly did make fine birds, she thought giddily, waltzing out of the dressing-room on cloud nine. Cole's gaze fastened on her ankles and slowly travelled up, lingering on her bare shoulder where the saleswoman had pulled down the peasant neckline for *the right effect*. A sensual little smile was directed at the exotic earrings and when he finally met her eyes, she saw the simmer of sexual interest in his—unmistakable—and felt her toes curling in response.

'This strappy bandeau top in camel jersey also goes with that skirt,' the saleswoman informed, showing the garment.

'Yes,' Cole said eagerly. 'Let's see it on.'

It fit very snugly, moulding her small firm breasts, which didn't go unnoticed by Cole whose interest in dressing her as *he* liked seemed to gather more momentum. 'I like that filmy leopard print top, too,' he said, pointing to a rack of clothes.

'The silk georgette with the hanky hemmed sleeve?' It was held up for his approval.

'Mmmh...very sexy.'

'It teams well with the bronze satin pants, and the bronze tassel belt,' the saleswoman encouraged, seizing advantage of the obvious fact that Cole was in a buying mood.

Liz felt driven to protest. 'I don't need any more. Truly.'

'Just this one extra lot then,' came the blithe reply. He grinned at her. 'I know you've got bronze shoes. Saw you wearing them last week. And the jungle motif is definitely your style.'

He would not be deterred. Liz couldn't help feeling both elated and guilty as they left the boutique, both of them now laden with shopping bags.

'Happy?' he asked, triumph sparkling in his eyes.

'Yes. But I shouldn't have let you do that.'

He arched a cocky eyebrow at her. 'The choice was all mine.'

She heaved a sigh in the hope of relieving the wild drumming in her chest. 'You've been very generous. Thank you.'

He laughed. 'It was fun, Liz. Maybe that's what both of us need right now. Some fun.'

His eyes flirted with hers.

It was happening. It really was happening. Just as Diana had predicted. But could a classy appearance achieve so much difference in how one was viewed? It didn't seem right. Surely attraction shouldn't depend entirely on surface image. Yet Cole had *married* Tara Summerville, which pointed to his being heavily swayed by how a woman looked.

But he knows me, the person, too, Liz quickly argued to herself. We've worked together for three years. *Best P.A. I've ever had.* And he did like her. Trust and respect were also mixed in with the liking. So this suddenly strong feeling of attraction was acceptable, wasn't it? Not just a fleeting thing of the moment?

They reached the Maserati and Cole unlocked the boot to stow away the host of shopping bags. 'What we should do now...' he said as they unloaded themselves. '...is drop this stuff off at your apartment, then go out to dinner to celebrate.'

'Celebrate what? Your outrageous extravagance?'

'Worth every cent.' He shut the lid of the boot with an air of satisfaction, then smiled at her. 'Pleasure can't always be so easily bought, Liz, and here we are, both of us riding a high.'

She couldn't deny it, but she knew her high was fired by feelings that hadn't been stirred for a very long time, feelings that had nothing to do with new clothes. Not even fabulous clothes. 'So we're celebrating pleasure?'

'Why not?' He took her arm to steer her to the passenger side, opening the door for her as he added, 'Let's put the blight of our ex-partners aside for one night and focus on having fun.'

One night...

The limitation was sobering. So was the reference to ex-partners. As Liz stepped into the car and settled on the passenger seat, she forced herself to take stock of what these remarks could mean. She herself had completely forgotten the blight left by Brendan in the excitement of feeling the sizzle of mutual attraction with Cole. However, she did have three weeks' distance since last being with Brendan. Cole had been very freshly reminded of his relationship with Tara this morning.

Earlier, before the shopping spree, he'd said he had nothing to go home to. Tara had clearly left a huge hole in his life. Had he just been buying a filler for that hole? As well as some sweet private revenge on the woman who'd taken him for much more than Liz would ever cost him?

She glanced sharply at him as he took the driver's seat beside her. One night of fun could mess with their business relationship. Had Cole thought of that or was he in the mood not to care?

He switched on the engine and threw her a smile that quickened her pulse-beat again. 'How about Doyle's at Rose Bay? Feel like feasting on oysters and lobster?'

Oh, why not? she thought recklessly. There was nothing for her to go home to, either. 'Sounds good. But it's Saturday night. Will we get a table?' The famous seafood restaurant on Sydney Harbour was very popular.

'No problem,' he confidently assured her. 'I'll call and book from your apartment.'

No doubt he wouldn't care what it cost for the restaurant to *find* an extra table for two. Cole was on a roll, intent on sweeping her along with him, and Liz decided not to worry about it. Fun was the order of the night and there was nothing wrong with taking pleasure in each other's company.

Diana's advice slid into her mind.

Go with the flow.

For too much of her life Liz had been managing situations, balancing pros and cons, thinking through all the possible factors, choosing what seemed the most beneficial course. She wanted to be free of all that...if only for one night...to simply *go with the flow* and let Cole take care of whatever happened between them.

After all, he was the boss.

The man in command.

CHAPTER TEN

COLE had never thought of his P.A. as delightful, but she was. Maybe it was the influence of the champagne, loosening inhibitions, bringing out bubbles in her personality. It was the first time she'd ever drunk alcohol in his presence. First time they'd ever been away from their work situation, dining together as a social twosome. She was enjoying the fine dinner at Doyle's and he was thoroughly enjoying her company.

Aware that she liked travelling, he'd prompted her into relating what trips she'd like to take in future—the old silk route from Beijing to Moscow, the northwest passage to Alaska, the Inca trail in South America—places he'd never thought of going himself. He'd hit all the high spots—New York, London, Paris, Milan, Hong Kong—but they hadn't been adventures in the sense Liz was talking about—reliving history and relating culture to geography.

Watching her face light up with enthusiasm, her eyes sparkle in anticipation of all there was yet to see and know, Cole mentally kicked himself for allowing his world to become so narrow, so concentrated on the challenge of accumulating more and more money. He should take more time out, make a few journeys into other areas. Though he'd probably need Liz to guide him into seeing what she saw.

Future plans…he had none. Not really. Just keep on doing what he'd been doing. He looked at Liz, taking pleasure in her vitality, in her quest for new experiences, and a question popped into his mind—a question he asked without any forethought of what its impact might be on her.

'Does marriage and having a family fit anywhere in your future, Liz?'

A shadow instantly descended, wiping the sparkle from her eyes, robbing her face of all expression. Her lashes lowered to half mast, as though marking the death of her hopes in that area, and Cole mentally kicked himself for bringing up what must be a raw subject for her with Brendan having walked away from their long-term relationship.

Her shoulders squared. An ironic little smile tilted one corner of her mouth. Her eyes flashed bleakly at him. 'I guess I'm a failure at being desirable wife material. I haven't met anyone who wants to marry me,' she said in a tone of flat defeat.

Cole barely bit down on the urge to tell her she was intensely desirable in every way. Words were useless if they didn't match her experience. But they were true nonetheless. It had been growing on him all day…how different she was to Tara, how much he liked her, how sexy she looked in the right clothes.

His gaze fastened on her mouth. He wanted to kiss away the hurt that had just been spoken, make her smile with joy again, as she had this afternoon, twirling around in that very fetching white skirt. She'd felt all woman then, failing in nothing, and certainly stirring a few pressing male fantasies in Cole.

'What about you?' she asked. 'Would you come at marriage again?'

It jolted him into a harsh little laugh. 'Not in a hurry.'

'Bad experience?'

'Bad judgment on my part.' He shrugged, not wanting to talk about it. 'Though I would like to be a father again,' he added, admitting that joy and sorrow from his marriage.

She nodded, her eyes flashing heartfelt sympathy. 'I would hate to lose a child of mine.'

It had barely caused a ripple in Tara's life, which made her proposition today all the more obscene. He had no doubt Liz would manage motherhood better, probably dote on a child of her own. He recalled her speaking of a number of sisters to his mother and asked about her family, moving the conversation on.

She was an aunt to two nieces and nephews, had a big extended family, lots of affection in her voice. Good people, Cole thought, and wondered how much he'd missed by being an only child. His father hadn't wanted more, even one being an intrusion on the orderly life he'd liked. Though he had been proud of Cole's achievements.

His mother would have liked a daughter. Someone like Liz with whom she could really share things. Not like Tara.

Liz Hart...

Why hadn't he thought of her like this before?

Blind to what was under his nose.

Tara getting in the way, skewing his view, killing

any desire to even look at a woman, let alone involve himself with one.

Besides which, Liz had been attached—might still be emotionally attached—to the guy who'd used her for years, then dumped her. Though clearly she'd been trying to rise out of those ashes, firing herself up to make something else of her life. Still, she'd definitely been burned, thinking of herself as a failure in the female stakes.

It wasn't right.

And on top of that, Tara putting her down this morning.

So wrong.

The rank injustice that had been done to Liz lingered in Cole's mind, even as he drove her home from Doyle's. She was quiet, the bubbles of the night having fizzed out. Facing the prospect of a lonely apartment, he thought, and memories that would bring misery. He didn't like this thought. He didn't like it one bit.

It was just a one off night, Liz told herself, trying to drum it into her foolish head. And she'd probably talked far too much about herself, her tongue let loose by the free flow of beautiful French champagne, delicious food, and Cole showing so much personal interest in her.

But it hadn't been a two way street. Very little had come back to her about him, and on the question of marriage, Cole's instant and derisive reply—*Not in a hurry*—had burst Liz's fantasy bubble. In fact, reflecting on his manner to her over dinner, Liz decided he undoubtedly dealt with clients in the same fashion, drawing them out, listening intently, lots of eye contact, projecting interest. *Charm,* Jayne had called it.

It didn't *mean* anything.

He'd spelled it out beforehand—one night of fun. And now he was driving her home. Nothing more was going to happen. She just wished her nerves would stop leaping around and she'd be able to make the parting smooth and graceful, showing she didn't expect any more from him.

But in her heart she wanted more.

And trying to argue it away wasn't working. The wanting had been building all day. It was now a heaviness in her chest that was impossible to dislodge. A tight heaviness that was loaded down with sadness, as well. Crying for the moon, she thought. Which had shone on her for a little while this evening but would inevitably keep moving and leave her in the dark again.

Cole parked the car outside her apartment, switched off the headlights. Liz felt enveloped in darkness—a lonely darkness, bereft of the vital power of his presence as he left her to stride around to the passenger side. *Get used to it, girl,* she told herself savagely. *He's not for you.*

The door opened and she stepped out, not taking the offered hand this time, forcing herself upright on her own two legs because if she took that hand it would heat hers, sending the tingling message of a warm togetherness that wasn't true. Cole was her boss. He would do her the courtesy of accompanying her to her door and then he would leave her. Back to business on Monday.

She put her head down and walked, acutely conscious of the sound of their footsteps—the quick clacking of her heels, the slower thump of his. They seemed to echo through the emptiness of her personal life, mocking dreams that had never been fulfilled, recalling her mother's words—*The kind of man you want, Liz, is the marrying kind.*

Why couldn't she meet someone who was?

Want someone who was.

Someone who was at least…reachable!

Tears blurred her eyes as they started up the stairs to her apartment. She shouldn't have drunk those glasses of champagne, giving her a false high, making the down worse. It was paramount now that she pull herself together, get out her door key, formulate a polite goodbye to her boss who had done her many kindnesses today. Kind…generous…making her feel special…

A huge lump rose in her throat. She blinked, swallowed, blinked, swallowed, managed somehow to get the key in the lock, turned it, pushed the door open enough for a fast getaway, retrieved the key, dropped it in her bag, dragged a deep breath into her aching chest, and turned to the man beside her.

'Thank you for everything, Cole,' she recited stiltedly and tried to arrange her mouth into a smile as she lifted her gaze, knowing she had to briefly meet his eyes and desperately hoping no evidence of any excess moisture was left for him to see. 'Goodnight,' she added as brightly as she could. 'It was fun.'

Cole's whole body clenched, resisting the dismissal. He stared at her shiny eyes. Wet eyes. Green pools, reflecting deep misery. The smile she'd forced was quivering, falling apart, no fun left to keep it in a natural curve.

He should let her go.

They were on very private ground now.

If he crossed it, there'd be no going back.

She was his employee...

Yet he stepped forward, his body responding to a primal tug that flouted the reasonable workings of his mind. Raising a hand, he gently stroked the tremulous corner of her mouth, wanting to soothe, to comfort, to make her feel safe with him. A slight gasp whispered from her lips. Her eyes swam with a terrible vulnerability, fearful questions begging to be answered.

It laid a responsibility on him, instantly striking a host of male instincts that rose in a strangely exultant wave, urging him to fight, to hold, to take, to protect—the age-old role of man before current day society had watered it down into something much less.

A sense of dominant power surged through his veins. She would submit to it. He would draw a positive response from her. He sensed it waiting behind the fear and confusion, waiting to be ignited, to flare into hot fusion with the desire pounding through him.

He slid his hand over her cheek, felt the leap of warmth under her skin, the firm yet fragile line of her jaw, the delicate curl of her small ear. Even as his thumb tilted her chin, his fingers were reaching to the nape of her neck, ready to caress, to persuade, to possess.

He lowered his head...slowly, savouring the moment of impact before it came. She had time to break away. His hold on her was light. She stood still, as though her entire being was poised for this first intimate contact with him, caught up in a breathless anticipation that couldn't be turned aside.

His lips touched hers, settling over their softness, drawing on them with light sips, feeling their hesitant response, teasing them into a more open kiss, wanting an exchange of sensation, reining in the urge to plunder and devour. She was willing to experiment, her tongue tentatively touching his as though she wasn't sure this was right. It fired a fierce desire in Cole to convince her it was. He turned the kiss into a slow, sensual dance, intent on melting every inhibition. She followed his lead, seduced into playing his game, savouring it herself, beginning to like it, want it, initiating as well as responding.

Excitement kicked through Cole. This was so different to Tara's all-too-knowing sexual aggression. He had to win this woman, drive the memory of her lost partner out of her mind and supplant it with what *he* could make her feel. The challenge spurred him into sweeping her into his embrace.

Her spine stiffened, whether in shock or resistance he didn't know. Shock was probably good. Resistance was bad. Before he could blast it with a passionate onslaught of kisses, her palms pressed hard against his chest and her head pulled back from his—a warning against force that he struggled to check, sensing her need for choice here, even while gathering himself to sway it his way.

He felt the agitated heave of her breasts as she sucked in a quick breath. Her lids fluttered, lashes half veiling the eloquent confusion in her eyes. Satisfaction welled in him, despite the frustration of being halted. It wasn't rejection on her mind. She didn't understand what was going on in his.

'Why are you doing this?' The words spilled out, anxious, frightened of consequences that he should know as well as she.

The lack of any calculation in her question, the sheer exquisite innocence of it evoked a streak of tenderness that Cole would have sworn had died with his son. His own chest heaved with the sudden surge of emotion. He dropped a soft kiss on her forehead.

'Because it feels right,' he murmured, feeling the sense of a new beginning so strongly, his heart started racing at the possibility it was really true. He could move past Tara. Even past David. Perhaps it was only hope but he wasn't about to step away from this opportunity of taking a future track which might bring him all he'd craved in his darkest nights.

'But I'm not really a...a date, am I?' she argued, trying to get a handle on what he meant by kissing her.

'No. You're much more.'

She shook her head, not comprehending. 'Cole, please...' Anguished uncertainty in her eyes. '...we have to work together.'

'We do work together. That's precisely the point. We work very well together.' He stroked the worry line between her brows. 'I'm just taking it to another level.'

'Another level?' she repeated dazedly.

He smiled into her eyes, wanting to dispel the cloudiness, to make her see what he saw. 'This feels right to me, Liz. Don't let it feel wrong to you because it's not,' he insisted, recklessly intent on carrying her with him. On a wild burst of adrenalin he added, 'I'm damned sure I can give you more than Brendan ever could or would.'

'Bren...dan.'

The name seemed to confuse her further. Cole silently cursed himself for bringing it up. He didn't want to compete. He wanted to conquer—wipe the guy out, take the woman, make her his. He didn't care how primitive that course was. It burned in his gut and he acted on it, sweeping Liz with him into her apartment, closing the door, staking his claim on her territory.

Before she could even think of protesting, he threw off his leather jacket, needing no armour against the cold in here, nor any barrier to the enticing heat of her body, and he captured her within the lock of his arms, intent on her surrender to his will. She felt small against him, and all the more intensely feminine because of it, but he knew she had a backbone of steel that could defy the might of his physique. Triumph zinged through his brain as her spine softened, arched into him, and her hands slid up over his shoulders, around his neck, and she lifted herself on tiptoe, face tilted to his, ready to be kissed again.

The darkness of the room seemed to sharpen his

senses. He could smell her perfume, enticingly erotic. His fingers wove through the silky curls of her hair, revelling in the tactile pleasure of it. His body hardened to the yielding softness of hers. He was conscious of their breaths mingling as his mouth touched hers, touched and clung with a voracious need that demanded her compliance.

She kissed him back with a passionate defiance that challenged any sense of dominance over her. No submission. It was as though a fire had erupted in her and Cole caught the flame. It flared through him, firing his desire for her to furnace heat. The power of it raced out of control, taking them both, drawing them in, sucking them towards the intense thrill of merging so completely there could be no turning back.

He removed her jacket.

She lifted his sweater, fearless now in matching him step for step.

Discarding clothes...like walls coming down, crashing to the floor, opening up the way...the ravenous excitement of flesh meeting flesh, sliding, caressing, hot and hungry for more and more intimacy.

Kissing...like nothing he knew, sliding deep, a sensual mating of tongues, a fierce response generated in every cell of his body, the sense of immense strength, power humming.

He scooped her off her feet, cradled her against his chest, carried her, intuitively picking the route to the room where she had gone to get her scarf this morning. Her head rested on his shoulder, her face pressed to his neck, the whole feel of her soft and warm and womanly, giving, wanting what he wanted.

She made him feel as a man should feel.

Essentially male.

And all that entailed.

CHAPTER ELEVEN

LIZ was glad of the darkness. It wasn't oppressive now. It was her friend and ally, heightening the vibrant reality of Cole making love to her while it hid the same reality in comforting shadows. It allowed her to stifle the fear of facing the sheer nakedness of what they were doing and revel in the incredible pleasure of it. She could even believe she was as desirable as Cole made her feel. In the darkness.

He laid her on the bed—a bed she had shared only with Brendan—and she felt a sharp inner recoil at the memory, not wanting it. Why had Cole referred to him? Brendan was gone. Long gone from her bed. And he'd made mincemeat of her heart—the heart that was now pounding with wild excitement as Cole loomed over her, so big and strong and dynamically male, as different as any man could be to Brendan.

Purpose...action...energy focused on carrying through decisions...and unbelievably that focus was now on her...a totally irresistible force that kept swamping the reservations that should be in her brain, but he'd blown them away as though they didn't count. And maybe they didn't at this level, wherever this level was taking them.

She could barely think. Couldn't reason anymore. His arms slid out from under her and the solid mass of him straightened up, substance not fantasy, Cole taking charge, wanting her with him like this. She saw his arm reach for the bedside lamp and reacted with violent rejection of the action he had in mind.

'No!'

The arm was momentarily checked. 'No what?' he demanded.

'No light. I don't want light.'

'Why not?'

'You'll see...'

'I want to see you.'

'It won't be right,' she argued desperately. Her mind was screaming, *I'm not built like Tara. My breasts are small. My legs aren't long. I don't have voluptuous curves.*

'I promise you it will be,' he said, his voice furred with a deep sensuality that did promise, yet she couldn't believe he wouldn't compare her body to that of the woman he'd married and find her wanting.

'I don't have red hair down there,' she cried frantically, clutching at anything to stop him from turning on the light. 'You'll see it and think of me as a little brown mouse again.'

'I never thought of you like that,' he growled. 'Never!'

It got him onto the bed, lying beside her, the lamp forgotten, his hand sliding down over her stomach, fingers thrusting into the tight curls below it. 'I always saw you as bright, Liz Hart. Bright eyes. Bright intelligence. And behind it a fire which occasionally leapt out at me. There's not an ounce of mouse in you.'

This emphatic string of statements was very reassuring as to her status in his eyes, but Liz was highly distracted from it by the further glide of his fingers, delving lower, probing soft sensitive folds, exciting nerve ends that melted into slick heat.

'I thought this past week…she's showing her true colours. Reflecting the real Liz instead of covering her up,' he went on, still wreaking exquisite havoc with his hand, caressing, tracing, teasing. 'You don't need a cloak of darkness. You can't hide from me anymore. I know the fire inside you. I can feel it…'

A finger slid inside the entrance to her body and tantalisingly circled the sensitive inner wall, raising convulsive quivers of anticipation for the ultimate act of intimacy. He leaned over, his face hovering above hers. She saw the flash of a smile.

'…and taste it.'

He kissed her, long and deeply, and the tantalising fingertip plunged inward, stroking in the same rhythmic action as his tongue, a dual invasion that drove her wild with passionate need, a need that swelled inside her, arching her body in an instinctive lift towards his, wanting, yearning. He didn't instantly respond so she reached for him with her hands, turned towards him, threw a leg over his, and her heart leapt at the hard muscular strength it met. Huge thighs. She'd forgotten how big he was, had a moment's trepidation…how would it be when he took her?

I promise you it will be right…

It had to be.

She didn't want to stop.

Not now.

Not when she was awash with a tumultuous

need to have him...if only this once. It was madness...dangerous madness...risking what should have been kept safe. But it was his choice. *She* was his choice. And feeling him wanting her—Cole Pierson wanting her—it was like being elevated above any other woman he could have had, above Tara, making her feel...marvellous!

He broke the kiss and moved, but not as she expected, craved. His mouth fastened over the pulse at the base of her throat, radiating a heat that suffused her entire skin. She heard herself panting, barely able to breathe. Her arms had locked around his neck, but his head slipped below their circle, his lips tracing the upper swell of one breast, shifting to its tip...

Her stomach contracted as the feeling of inadequacy attacked her again. Her breasts weren't lush. He'd be disappointed in them. Oh, why, why couldn't he just...

Sensation exploded through her as he drew the tense peak into the hot wetness of his mouth and sucked on it. Swept it with his tongue. Another rhythmic assault that moved in tandem with the caressing hand between her thighs, driving her to the edge of shattering. Her fingers scrabbled blindly in his hair, pressing, tugging, protesting, inciting.

He moved to her other breast, increasing her ache for him, and her flesh seemed to swell around his mouth, throbbing with a tight fullness that totally erased any concern about levels of femininity. He made her feel she was all the woman he wanted and he wouldn't be denied any part of her.

Again he shifted and her body jerked as his tongue

swirled around her navel, a hot sweep of kisses trailing lower, lower. Her hands grabbed ineffectually at the bunched muscles of his shoulders as fear and desire warred through her mind.

No hesitation in his. Ruthless purpose. Lips pressed to her curls, fingers parting the way, his tongue touching, licking. The intensity of feeling rocked her, drenched her with desire, rendered her utterly helpless to stop anything even if she'd wanted to. And she didn't. She was on fire and he was tasting her because he wanted to.

He wedged his shoulders between her thighs, lifted her legs, clamped his hands on her hips and held her fast as he replaced the caress of his hand with the incredibly intimate caress of his mouth, his lips encircling her, his tongue probing with such artful sensual skill, she couldn't breathe at all as the intensity of feeling grew, ripping through her. She tried to ride the tide of it, her hands gripping the bedcover, holding on, holding on, but a rush of heat broke through her inner walls, overwhelming her with a wave of excruciating delight. A cry broke from her throat as she lost all sense of self, falling into a deep well of pleasure that engulfed her in sweet, molten heat.

Then Cole was surging over her. She could see him, feel him, but her muscles were so limp, she was unable to react. Her mind was filled with awe that he had taken her this far before satisfying himself. Yet she sensed he was not unsatisfied with what he had done, but pleased, even triumphant, as though he'd found his feasting very much to his liking.

I promise you it will be right...

Impossible to deny it, feeling as she did.

Having set himself to enter her, he pressed forward, pushing into her slowly, letting her adjust to the thick fullness of him, a completely different sensation and one that re-electrified all her senses. He eased back, lifting her hips, stuffing a pillow under her.

'Put your legs around me,' he murmured.

Somehow she managed to do it, locking her ankles so that they wouldn't slip apart. This time his thrust was firm, pushing deep, deeper, filling her to a breath-taking depth, then bracing himself on his arms as he bent his head to join his mouth to hers, and the kiss was different, too, like an absolute affirmation of him being inside her, having him there, an intensely felt sensation of possessing and being possessed, exulting in it, absorbed by it.

'Now rock with me,' he instructed, flashing a smile as he lifted his head.

Joy rippled through her. He was happy with where they were. She was, too. It re-energised her body, making it easy now to move as he did, matching the repetitive undulation, even touching him, stroking him, encouraging him, running her hands over the warm skin of his back, inciting the rise of heat with each delicious rhythmic plunge.

It was a wild, primitive dance that she gloried in, flesh sliding against—into—flesh, fusing, yet still gliding with a strong, relentless purpose, friction building to ecstatic peaks, wave after wave of intense sensation rolling through her...so much to feel...flaring, swirling, pooling deep inside her, touching her heart, stirring indefinable emotions...too much to pin down...far beyond all her previous experience.

Rapture as he groaned and spilled himself inside her. She sighed his name as his hard body collapsed on her, spent, and she wrapped her arms around him, holding him close, loving him, owning him if only for these few precious moments in time. He'd given himself to her, all that he was, and she silently revelled in the gift, unable to see ahead to what came next, not caring, listening to his heart thundering, elated that he had reached a pinnacle of pleasure with her.

He raised himself to kiss her again, her name whispering from his lips as they covered hers, soft, lingering sips that demanded nothing, merely sealing a tender togetherness that tasted of true and total contentment. Then his arms burrowed under her and he rolled onto his back, carrying her with him so that she lay with her head under his chin, her body sprawled over his.

Done, she thought, and wondered where it would lead. But with no sense of anxiety. She felt too amazingly replete to worry about tomorrow. Only luxuriating in this blissful sense of peace mattered. As long as it lasted. It awed her that she had lived so many years without realising how fantastic intimacy could be with a man. With the right man. Cole...Cole Pierson. Was it asking too much to want him thinking the same about her?

Probably it was.

This could be just a timing thing with him—a backlash against Tara's assumption that she could rope him in again, making the alleged intimacy between him and his personal assistant real because it had been planted in his mind, and it was an act of defiance against any desire he might have left for his almost ex-wife.

People did do reckless things on the rebound.

Was he thinking of Tara now...mentally thumbing his nose at her?

Liz felt herself growing cold at these thoughts and fiercely set them aside. Cole was with her. He'd chosen her. She moved her hand, suddenly wanting to stoke his desire again, feel it burning through her, obliterating everything else with the intense sense of possession.

A long sensual caress from his armpit, down his rib-cage, over the hollows underneath his hipbones, his firm flesh quivering to her touch, pleasured by it. She levered herself to a lower position so she could close her mouth over his nipple, kissing it, lashing it with her tongue. His chest heaved, dragging in a sharp breath, reacting swiftly to the sexual energy that had roared around them and was sparking again, gathering momentum.

She reached further, her hand closing around him, fondling, stroking. He groaned, his whole body tensing as her thumb brushed delicately over the sensitive head of his shaft. Elated at his response, she seized him more firmly, felt the surge of rampant strength grow hard, harder...

Hands gripped her waist, lifting her. 'Straddle me,' came the gravelled command. 'Put me inside you.'

It was an even more incredible sensation, lowering

herself onto him, engineering the penetration herself, feeling her inner muscles convulse and adjust to the pressing fullness of him, loving the sense of taking him, owning him. His hands moved to her hips, helping her sink further as he raised his thighs behind her, forming a cradle for her bottom, a cradle he rocked to breathtaking effect.

'Lean forward.'

She wanted to anyway, wanted to kiss him as he'd kissed her when he was deep inside her. She placed her hands on his shoulders and merged her mouth with his, plunging into a cavern of wild passion, drawn into a whirlpool of need that he answered with ravishing speed, his hands on her everywhere, stroking, shaping, kneading, strong fingers clutching, gentle fingers loving, sensitising every inch of her flesh to his touch.

She lifted herself back and he rubbed his palms over her nipples, rotating the hardened buds, exciting them almost beyond bearing, then latching onto them one by one with his mouth, his hands back on her hips, moving her from side to side, up and down, stirring a frenzy of sensation that rocketed through her, shattering every last vestige of control.

Even as she started to collapse on him he caught her face, drew it down to his, and devoured her mouth again, a sweet devastating plunder that she could only surrender to, helplessly yet willingly because the intoxication of his desire for more and more of her was too strong an exhilaration to deny.

Then amazingly, he was surging upright, swinging his legs off the bed, holding her pinned to him across his lap, hugging her tightly, her breasts crushed so intimately against his chest, the beat of his heart seemed to pound through them, echoing the throb of her own. And he remained inside her, a glorious sensual fullness, as his fingers wound through her hair and his lips grazed over her ear.

'I have never felt anything as good as this,' he murmured, his voice furred with a wonderment that squeezed her heart and sent elation soaring through her bloodstream. He tilted her head back, rained kisses over her face, her forehead, her eyelids, her cheeks, his lips hovering over hers as he added with compelling urgency, 'Tell me it's so for you. Tell me.'

'Yes.' The word spilled out automatically, impossible not to concede the truth, and he captured it in his mouth and carried it into hers, exploding the force of it with a fierce enthralling passion, holding her caged in his arms, swaying to reinforce the sense of his other insertion, pressing the heated walls of the passage he filled, making her feel him with commanding intensity.

'So, good, it has to be right,' he said rawly as he broke the kiss and cupped her chin, his eyes burning into hers. 'So don't you doubt it tomorrow. Or on Monday. Or anytime in the future.'

Emphatic words, punching into her dazed mind. She wasn't sure what he was saying. Her brain formed its own message. 'Right...for one night,' she sighed, knowing she would never forget the feelings he'd aroused in her, was still arousing. She didn't care if it was only one experience. It was the experience of a lifetime.

'No.' His hands raked through her hair, pressing for concentration. 'This isn't an end. It's a beginning. You and me, Liz. Moving forward, moving together. Feel it. Know it. Come with me.'

He moved his thighs, driving an acute awareness of their sexual connection. He was still strongly erect, probing her inmost self, demanding she yield to him, and what else could she do? She wanted this deeper bonding, wanted it to last far beyond now.

'Liz...' An urgent demand poured through her name.

She lifted her limp, heavy arms and locked them around his neck...for better or worse, she thought, her mind aswim, drowning in the need for Cole to keep wanting her, making her feel loved as a woman.

'Yes.' It was the only word humming through her mind. Yes to anything, everything with him.

'Yes-s-s...' he echoed, but with a ring of triumphant satisfaction, powerfully realised.

One hand skated down the curve of her spine, curled under the soft globes of her bottom, clasping her to him as he rose to his feet and turned to lower her onto the bed again, her head and shoulders resting on the coverlet as he dragged pillows under her hips, then knelt between the spread of her legs, leaning over her, hands intertwining with hers, a wild grin of joy on his face.

'We'll both come,' he promised wickedly, then began to thrust in a fast driving beat, rocking deeply into her, and she felt her body receive him with an exultant welcome, opening to him over and over again. And he claimed all she gave, imprinting himself so completely on her consciousness, her entire body was focused on the erotic friction he built and built...only pausing, becoming still when he felt the powerful ripples of her release, savouring them before he picked up the rhythm again, all restraint whipping away as he pursued his own climax, broken breaths, moans of mounting tension, climbing, climbing, bursting into a long, intense rapture, waves of heat spilling, swirling, fusing them, lifting them into a space where they floated together in ecstatic harmony.

And Liz no longer questioned anything.

A sense of perfect contentment reigned.

Sliding slowly and languorously into a feast of sensuality that lasted long into the night...the night that he said was a beginning, not an end.

CHAPTER TWELVE

COLE was gone when Liz awoke. She vaguely remembered him kissing her, murmuring he had to keep an appointment. He'd been fully clothed, ready to leave. She was almost sure she'd mumbled, 'Okay,' before dropping back into a heavy sleep.

It came as a shock that her bedside radio now showed 11:47, almost midday. There was only one afternoon of the weekend left and she had washing to do, food shopping. She bolted out of bed and headed straight into the bathroom, cold wintry air hitting her nakedness, making her shiver.

A hot shower dispelled the chill and soaping her body brought back all the memories of last night's intimacies with Cole...delicious, indelible memories. If she wasn't in love with the man, she was certainly in lust with him. He was an incredible lover. And he'd made her feel sexier than she'd ever felt in her life. Sexy, beautiful, special...

Her mind flitted to how it had been with Brendan. Why had she accepted *so little* from him? Compared to Cole...but she hadn't known any better at the time. In fact, Brendan had been mean about a lot of things—a taker, not a giver. Whereas Cole...the beautiful clothes yesterday, the sumptuous dinner last night, the loving...she felt wonderfully spoilt, as though all her Christmases had come at once.

She desperately hoped it *was* right to have plunged into this intimate relationship with him. Her job was very definitely at risk if it turned wrong. Oddly enough, work security didn't weigh so heavily on her mind now. Losing him would be far more devastating. Which was the problem with being raised to giddy heights. The fall...

But she wasn't going to think about that.

Nor was she going to worry about Cole being her boss. As Diana had predicted, *he* had done the running, and Liz was now determined on *going with the flow,* wherever it took her. There really was no other choice, except dropping entirely out of his life. And why would she do that when he made her feel...so good?

The somewhat sobering recollection slid into her mind—he was in no hurry to marry again.

So what? she quickly argued. Did she have any prospects leaping out at her? Not a one. Besides, there was no guarantee of permanence with any relationship. It went that way or it didn't. Though everything within her craved for this new relationship with Cole to last, to become truly solid, to have it fulfil...all her impossible dreams.

As she stepped out of the shower, dried herself and dressed, a wry little smile lingered on her lips. Perhaps hope *was* eternal. In any event, it was a happy boost to her spirits. So was emptying yesterday's shopping bags, remembering the zing of parading the clothes in front of Cole as she hung them up in her wardrobe, knowing now that he did see her as a desirable woman—a woman he wanted.

She rushed through the afternoon, doing all the necessary chores, planning what she'd pack for the trip with Cole's mother, making sure everything was clean, ready to wear. She wondered what Nancy would think of her son becoming attached to his personal assistant. Better me than Tara, Liz cheerfully decided. Nancy hadn't liked Tara at all.

She was still riding a high when her telephone rang just past seven o'clock. She hesitated over answering it, thinking it might be Diana with another stream of advice. She didn't want to share what had happened with Cole. Not yet. It suddenly felt too precious, too fragile. And she didn't know how it might be tomorrow.

On the other hand, it might be her mother who wasn't pushing anything, only for her daughter to be happy about herself, and Liz was happy about herself right now, so she snatched up the receiver and spoke with a smile. 'Hi! Liz here.'

'Cole here,' came the lilted reply, warm pleasure threading his voice.

'Oh!' A dumb response but he'd taken her by surprise.

'Oh good, I trust?'

The light teasing note brought the smile back. 'Yes. Definitely good.'

He laughed. 'I've been thinking of you all day. Highly distracting.'

'Should I say I'm sorry?' It was fun to flirt with him, though it amazed her that she could.

'No. The distraction was very pleasurable.' He drawled the last words, sending pinpricks of excitement all over her skin. 'I'm currently having to restrain myself from dashing to your door, telling myself I do need some sleep in order to function well tomorrow.'

'You have a string of meetings in the morning,' she said primly, playing the perfect P.A. while inwardly delighted that his restraint was being tested. It spoke volumes about the strength of attraction he felt. Towards *her*.

'Mmmh…I was wondering how to alleviate the problem of people getting in the way of us.'

Us…such an exhilarating word. 'We do have work to get through, Cole,' she reminded him, though if he didn't care, she wasn't about to care, either.

'True. But you could wear that bronze dress with the buttons down the front. Very provocative those buttons. One could say…promising.'

Liz felt her thighs pressing together, recapturing the sensations of last night when he'd…

'And wear stockings,' he continued. 'Not those coverall pantihose. Stockings that end mid-thigh, under the skirt with the buttons. And no one will know but you and me, Liz. I like that idea. I like it very much.'

His voice had dropped to a seductive purr, and her entire body was reacting to it, an exquisite squirming that actually curled her toes.

'If you'll do that I think I'm sure to perform at a high peak tomorrow,' he went on, conjuring up breathtaking images that dizzied her brain. 'Won't feel deprived at all during those meetings. There's nothing quite like waiting on a promise.'

A shiver ran down her spine. Did he mean…after the meetings…at the office? He wanted sex with her there?

'Liz?'

'Yes?' It was like punching air out her lungs.

'Have I shocked you?'

'Yes…no,' she gabbled. 'I mean…I wasn't sure what you'd want of me tomorrow.'

'You. I want you. In every way there is,' he answered with a strength of purpose that thudded straight into Liz's heart, making her feeling intensely vulnerable about how he would deal with her in the end if she trod this path with him. Was it only sex on his mind? How much did she count as a person?

She couldn't find anything to say, her mind riddled by doubts and fears, yet physically, sexually, she was aware of an overwhelming yearning to follow his lead, to be the woman he wanted in every way.

'Remember how right it felt?' he dropped into her silence.

'Yes,' she answered huskily, her voice barely rising over a huge emotional lump in her throat.

'It will be tomorrow, too. That's my promise, Liz.' Warm reassurance.

'I'll come as you say,' she decided recklessly.

'Good! I'll sleep on that. Sweet dreams.'

The connection clicked off.

Goal achieved, she thought, then shook her head dazedly over the power Cole Pierson could and did exert. Being the focus of it was like nothing she had ever known before. In the past, she had always done the running, not very effectually where men were concerned. No truly satisfying success at all. In actual fact, a string of failures, probably because she'd tried to manage things to turn out right instead of them just being right.

She had no control with Cole.

He'd seized it.

Was still wielding it.

And maybe that was how it should be.

So let it be.

Cole sat at his desk in his office, his computer switched on, the screen flashing figures he should be checking, but he was too much on tenterhooks, waiting for Liz to arrive. He couldn't remember ever being this tense about seeing a woman again. Would he win or lose on last night's gamble?

He wasn't sure of her.

The sex on Saturday night had been fantastic. No doubting her response to everything they'd done together—a more than willing partner in pleasure, once he'd moved her past the initial inhibitions—storming barriers before she could raise them. Barriers that had undoubtedly been built during the Brendan era—damage done by a selfish lover who didn't have the sense to appreciate the woman he had.

Cole knew he could definitely reach her on the sexual level. It was what he was counting on to bind her to him. He'd moved too fast to take a slower route now, and be damned if he was going to let her slip away from him. He'd sensed her second thoughts during the telephone call. Perhaps the better move would have been to stay with her all yesterday. But her

apartment was her ground and she would have had
the right to ask him to go.

Best to keep the initiative.

She'd come to work this morning—his ground.
And after their conversation over the phone, she
would have gone to bed last night thinking of him,
tempted by the promise of more pleasure, remembering what they'd already shared, wanting more...

Cole dragged in a deep breath, trying to dampen
the wild surge of desire rising at the thought of what
she would wear today. Compliance or defiance? At
least the signal would be clear, the moment she
walked into his office. Yes...no. He fiercely willed it
to be yes. And why not? She had the fire in her to
pursue pleasure. He'd lit the flame. She wouldn't let
it go out...would she?

A knock on his door.

'Come in!' he called, his voice too terse, on edge.

She stepped into his office, wearing the bronze
dress with the buttons down the front.

His heart thundered as a lightning burst of triumph
flashed through his mind.

'Good morning,' she said brightly.

He saw courage in the red flags on her cheeks, in
the high tilt of her head, the squared shoulders, the
smile that wavered slightly at its corners. Courage
defying fear and uncertainty. It touched him to a surprising depth.

'I think it's a great morning,' he rolled out, his
smile ablaze with admiration and approval.

She visibly relaxed, walking forward, holding out

a Manila folder. 'I brought in the file for your first meeting.'

Straight into business.

Not quite yet, Cole thought. 'I seem to remember that the last time I saw you in that dress, there were several buttons towards the hem undone.'

It was a challenging reminder and she halted, looking down at her skirt in hot confusion.

'Three,' he said. 'I recall counting three undone.'

Her gaze lifted, eyes astonished. 'You counted them?'

He grinned. 'I'm good at counting.'

A little laugh gurgled from her throat. 'So you are.'

'And here you are all buttoned up today, which doesn't look right at all. I much preferred it the other way. I think you should oblige me and undo at least one button before we get down to serious business.'

'One button,' she repeated, her eyes sparkling at the mischievous nonsense.

Fun was the key here. There was never enough fun in anyone's life. She'd had fun trying clothes on during the buying spree on Saturday. What could be more relaxing and seductive than having fun with some knowingly provocative undressing?

'Okay. One button for now,' he agreed. 'Though I think it would relieve the pressure of these meetings if an extra button got undone after each session.'

'That makes four buttons.'

'I knew you were good at counting, too.'

She gave him an arch look, joining in the game he was playing. 'You might find that distracting.'

'No. I'll think of it as my reward for outstanding concentration.'

She placed the folder on the desk. Then with an air of whimsical indulgence, she flicked open the bottom button, straightened up, took a deep breath and boldly asked, 'Happy now?'

'We progress. Let's say I'm...briefly...satisfied.' He ran his gaze up the row of buttons from hem to neckline, then smiled, meeting her eyes with deliberately wicked intent.

She flushed, realising he had no intention of stopping anywhere. *And may she burn with anticipation all morning,* Cole thought as he drew the folder over to his side of the desk and opened it, ostensibly ready to familiarise himself with the financial details of the client who would soon be arriving.

He'd thrown his net, caught Liz with it, and he'd draw her closer and closer to him as the morning wore on. The whole encounter had sharpened his mind brilliantly. He felt right on top of the game.

An hour later, the first client had been dealt with. Without saying a word, Cole stared at Liz's skirt. Without a word from her, she undid a button, then handed him the next file.

Exhilarated by the silent complicity, Cole ploughed through the next meeting, sparking on all cylinders.

Another button hit the dust.

He could see above her knee now when she walked, the skirt peeping open far enough to tease him with flashes of leg. Was she wearing stockings as he'd requested?

Excitement buzzed through his brain. Restraint was

like a refined torture. He forced it over the desire simmering through him and satisfied the third client with a fast and comprehensive exposition on the state of the money markets. Even as he ushered the man out of his office, his gaze targeted the next button, wanting it opened, commanding it done…now…this instant.

He saw her hands move to do it as he walked his client through Liz's office. Anticipation roared through him. It was an act of will to keep accompanying the man to the elevator, farewelling him into the compartment before turning back to the woman who had to be wanting an acceleration of action as much as he did.

He'd planned the sexual tease. He'd meant it to go on all day, but here he was, too caught up with the need it had evoked in him to wait for tonight. To hell with work. It was lunch time anyway. Though his appetite for Liz Hart wiped out any thought of food. The energy driving him now did not require more fuel.

He strode into her office, locked the door against any possible interruption. She stood at one of the filing cabinets, putting the last folder away. The click of the lock caused her to throw a startled glance over her shoulder. Their eyes met, the sizzling intent in his causing hers to widen.

'It's all right,' he said, soothing any shock. 'We're alone. Private. And I want you very urgently, Liz Hart.'

She didn't move, seemingly entranced by the force of need emanating from him. Then he was behind her, his arms caging her, pulling her back against him, finding some solace for his fierce erection in pressing it against the soft cleft of her sexy bottom.

He heard, felt her gasp, kissed the delicate nape of her neck, needing to give vent to the storm of desire engulfing him. He was so hungry for her. His hands covered her stomach, pushing in, making her feel how much he wanted her. Then he remembered the buttons, stockings, bare thighs, and his desire for her took another turn. He dropped his hands, fingers moving swiftly, opening the skirt.

And yes, yes...it was how he'd envisaged, stockings ending, naked flesh above them, quivering to his touch, the crotch of her panties hot, moist, telling evidence of her excitement, boosting his.

He whirled her over to her desk, sat her on it, took her chair, spread her legs, lifting them over his shoulders as he bent to taste the soft, bare, tremulous inner walls of her thighs, kissing, licking, smelling her need for him, exulting in it, knowing she was his to take as he wanted.

Liz could hardly believe what was happening. He was spreading the silk of her panties tight, kissing her through the thin screen, finding the throbbing centre between her folds, sucking on it. Pleasure rushed from the heat of his mouth, sweeping through her like a tidal wave. She had to lie back on the desk to cope with it, though there was no coping, more a melting surrender to the flow of sensation.

And she had once thought him an ice man!

He let her legs slide from his shoulders as he rose,

seemingly intent on following her, bending over her, his eyes dark, ringed with burning blue—no ice!—and she felt the silk being drawn aside as the hot hard length of him pushed to possess the space waiting for him, aching for him.

The intense focus of his eyes captured hers, held it as he drove the penetration home. 'This is how it is…in the light,' he said raggedly. 'You don't need the dark, Liz. It's better this way, seeing, knowing…'

He withdrew enough to plunge again, and it *was* thrilling to see the tension on his face, the concentrated flare of desire in his eyes, to watch him moving in the driving rhythm that pleasured them both in ever increasing pulse beats of intense excitement. The final release was incredibly mutual, and instinctively she wrapped her arms around his head and drew his mouth to hers, kissing him with the sweet knowledge that his desire for her was very real, not some accident of fate because she was simply on hand at a time of need.

This was proven to her over and over again as the days—and nights—rolled on towards the date of departure for the trip to South-East Asia. For the most part, restraint ruled in the office, but then they would go to her apartment, his apartment, make wild needy love, proceed to a nearby restaurant for dinner, enjoy fine food and wine while they whetted their appetite for more lovemaking.

It was exhilarating, addictive, a whirlwind of un-inhibited passion, and Liz was so completely caught up in it, she heartily wished she wasn't going off travelling with his mother…until Cole made an announcement over dinner on Thursday night that gave her pause for thought.

'My divorce was settled this afternoon. I'm finally a free man again.'

It was the relief in his voice that unsettled her, as though his freedom had remained threatened until the law had brought his marriage to Tara Summerville to an end. It instantly brought to mind the confrontation between them last Saturday, with Tara firing all her guns to win a reconciliation, and Cole savagely denying her any chance of it.

Since then—apart from Sunday when he had been occupied elsewhere—he had virtually immersed himself in a white-hot affair with the very woman Tara had accused of a sexual connection to Cole. Had it become so concentrated in order to keep Tara completely shut out? No space for her, not in his mind, not in his life, ensuring the final line was drawn on a marriage he'd written off as a case of bad judgment.

One could settle things in one's head that didn't necessarily get translated into physical and emotional responses. In a kind of reverse situation, Liz knew she'd reasoned out a million things about Brendan, trying to keep positive about their relationship, even when her body and heart were reacting negatively. The old saying, mind over matter, didn't really work. It only covered over stuff that kept bubbling underneath.

Liz couldn't help wondering if Cole had chosen her as the best possible distraction to take him through to the finishing line with Tara. Yet the sexual chemistry they shared had to be real. He couldn't perform as he

did unless he felt it. And he'd noticed how many buttons had been undone on the bronze dress last week,
before that meeting with Tara. Which surely meant
Liz could trust the attraction between them.

It was just that Cole had such a formidable mind.
Once he decided something, he went at it full bore
until the goal was achieved. And Liz didn't know
what his goal was with her, except to satisfy a very
strong sexual urge—made right because she wanted
the same satisfaction. Although secretly she wanted
more from him. Much more.

But nothing was said about any future with her.
Too soon, Liz told herself. After dinner, Cole drove
her home. This was their last night together for more
than two weeks while she toured through South-East
Asia with his mother. She had Friday off to pack and
generally get ready for the trip so she wouldn't be
seeing him at work tomorrow. It had been arranged
for her to meet Nancy Pierson at the airport Holiday
Inn at six o'clock for a tour group dinner and they
would fly off early Saturday morning.

Cole stayed late, seemingly reluctant to part from
her even when he finally chose to leave. 'I wish you
weren't going on this trip,' he said with a rueful
smile, then kissed her long and hard, passionately reminding her of all the intimacy they'd shared. 'I'll
miss you,' he murmured against her lips.

In every sense, Liz hoped, silently deciding the trip
was a timely break, giving them both the distance to
reflect on what they'd done, where they were going
with it and why.

She felt she'd been caught up in a fever-pitch compulsion that completely blotted out everything else beyond Cole Pierson. Distance might give her enough perspective to see if it truly was good...or the result of influences that had pulled them somewhere they shouldn't be.

Which wouldn't be good at all.

CHAPTER THIRTEEN

BY MIDAFTERNOON Friday, Cole found himself totally irritated by the temporary assistant taking Liz's place. He wasn't asking much of her. Why did she have to look so damned intimidated all the time? He hoped his mother appreciated the sacrifice he was making, giving her Liz as a companion for this trip.

Which reminded him to call his mother before the limousine arrived to transport her to the airport Holiday Inn, make sure she wasn't in a tizz about having everything ready to go. He picked up the telephone and dialled the number for the Palm Beach house.

'Yes?' his mother answered breathlessly.

'Just calm down, Mum. The limousine can wait until you're sure you haven't left anything behind.'

'Oh, Cole! I was just going around the house to check everything was locked.'

'I'll drive out tomorrow and double-check the security alarm so don't worry about it. Okay?'

A big sigh. 'Thank you, dear. There's always so much to think about before I leave. I did call your Liz and she assured me she's all organised.'

His Liz. A pity she wasn't his right now. In more ways than one. 'She would be,' he said dryly.

'Such a nice girl!' came the voice of warm approval. 'I rather hope we do run into her boyfriend at

Kathmandu. I can't imagine he's not having second thoughts about leaving her.'

'What?' The word squawked out of the shock that momentarily paralysed Cole's brain.

'You must know about him,' his mother said reasonably. 'Brendan Wheeler. He and Liz have been together for the past three years.'

'Yes, I know about him,' Cole snapped. 'But not that he was in Kathmandu. When did Liz tell you this?'

'Last Saturday when we were working out what clothes to take. It seemed wrong that she didn't have a boyfriend, so I asked her...'

'Right!' *Before he'd made his move. She couldn't want the guy back now...could she?* 'Brendan dumped her, Mum, so don't be getting any romantic ideas about their getting together again,' he said tersely.

'But it might have been only a case of him getting cold feet over commitment, Cole. If he comes face to face with Liz over there...'

'I am not paying for my personal assistant to run off with a guy in Kathmandu!' Cole thundered into the receiver. 'If you assist this in any way whatsoever...'

'Oh, dear! I didn't think of that. Well, I don't think she would actually run off, Cole. As you said, Liz is very responsible. I'm sure she'd insist on Brendan following her back home to prove good faith.'

'Better that the situation be avoided altogether,' he grated through a clenched jaw.

'You can't block Fate, dear,' his mother said blithely.

Fate was a fickle fool, Cole thought viciously, recalling how quickly Liz had agreed to the trip. He'd listed off Nepal as one of the destinations when he put the proposition to her. She must have instantly thought...Kathmandu...Brendan. And she'd played his mother brilliantly at lunch that day, clinching the deal.

No reluctance at the possibility of meeting him over there.

She'd even told his mother where the guy was.

'Mum, you keep your nose right out of this,' Cole commanded. 'No aiding and abetting. I'm telling you straight. Brendan was no good for Liz.'

'No good?' came the critical reply. 'Then why did she stay with him so long? She didn't have a child to consider...like you did with Tara. And Liz didn't do the leaving,' his mother reminded him with pertinent emphasis.

He wanted to shout, *Liz is with me, now,* but knew it would be tantamount to ringing wedding bells in his mother's ears and Cole was not prepared to deal with that.

'He repressed her. He put her down. He made her feel like a failure,' he punched out. 'I know this, Mum, so just let it be. Liz is better off without him. Okay?'

A long pause, then...'You really do care about her, don't you?'

Care? Of course, he cared. And he certainly didn't want to lose her to an idiot who hadn't cared enough to keep her. However, what he needed here was to seal his mother's sympathy to the cause of holding Liz away from Brendan.

'She's had a rough time, Mum,' he said in a gentler tone. 'I want you to ensure she enjoys this trip. No pain.'

'I'll do my best,' came the warm and ready promise.

Mother hen to the rescue of wounded bird.

Cole breathed more easily.

'Right! Well, I hope you have a wonderful time together.'

'Thank you. I'm sure we will. Oh, there's the limousine now. Must go, dear. Goodbye! Thanks for all your help.'

Gone!

He put the receiver down and stared at the telephone for several seconds, strongly tempted to call Liz, but what more could he say? He'd told her last night he would miss her, shown her how very desirable she was to him. There could be no possible doubt in her mind that he wanted her back, wanted her with him.

Surely to God she wouldn't throw what they'd shared aside and take Brendan back!

She couldn't be that much of a fool!

Or did he have it all wrong?

Cole rose from his chair and paced around the office, unsettled by the sudden realisation that much of what he'd told his mother comprised assumptions on his part. Maybe Liz had felt secure enough in her relationship with Brendan not to bother about feminine frippery, saving money towards a marriage and having a family...which had slipped away from her because... *He didn't like my style of management.*

That was all she had actually told him about the relationship.

He'd interpreted the rest.

What if he was wrong?

He'd steamrolled Liz into a hot and heavy affair, to which she'd been a willing party, but he didn't really know what was going on in her mind. Was it rebound stuff for her? An overwhelming need to *feel* desired?

What if she did meet Brendan in Kathmandu and they clicked again, as they must have done in the beginning? Would she count the sex with her boss as meaning anything in any long-term sense? Had he made it *mean* anything to her?

All he'd said was it felt right.

And it did.

She'd agreed.

But was it enough to hold her to him?

Cole didn't know.

But there was nothing more he could do or say now to shift the scales his way.

Besides, Kathmandu was a big city. The tour schedule was jam-packed. The likelihood of her running into Brendan was very low. She had a full-time job to do—looking after his mother—and he'd just ensured, as best he could, that his mother wouldn't let Liz skip out on her responsibility.

Cole took a deep breath and returned to his desk.

Liz would come back.

He was wasting time, worrying over things he had no control over, but that very lack of absolute control where Liz Hart was concerned made him...uneasy.

CHAPTER FOURTEEN

LIZ quickly found she had no difficulty in travelling with Nancy Pierson. All the older woman needed was a bit of prompting on where they had to be at what time, and when their luggage was to be put outside their hotel room to be collected by the Captain's Choice staff, all of whom were brilliantly and cheerfully efficient. Nancy accepted the prompting good-naturedly, grateful that Liz took the responsibility of ensuring they did everything right.

It was quite marvellous flying off on a chartered Qantas jet with almost two hundred other tourists, everyone excited about the adventure ahead of them. The party atmosphere on the plane was infectious, helped along by the champagne which flowed from the moment they were seated.

'Oh, I'm so glad you were able to come with me,' Nancy enthused, her eyes twinkling with the anticipation of much pleasure as she started on a second glass of champagne.

'So am I. This is great. But you want to go easy on the champers, Nancy. Don't drink it too quickly,' Liz warned, concerned about her getting tipsy.

Nancy laughed. 'I'm not a lush, dear. Just celebrating.' She leaned over confidentially. 'Cole's divorce was settled on Thursday. He's completely free of that woman now.'

'Well, I guess that's a good thing,' Liz said non-committally, unsure how she should respond.

'He'd make a wonderful husband to the right woman, you know,' Nancy went on, eyeing her with a spark of hopeful eagerness.

Liz could feel a tide of heat creeping up her neck and quickly brushed the subject aside. 'A failed marriage often puts people off the idea of marrying again.'

'But Cole absolutely adored his son. It was such a terrible tragedy losing David, and it's taken a long time for him to get over it, but I'm sure he'll want to have more children and he's not getting any younger,' Nancy argued.

'Men can have children any time they like,' Liz dryly pointed out. 'It's only women who have a biological clock ticking.'

'He doesn't want to get too old and set in his ways.' A sad sigh. 'His father—my husband—was like that, unfortunately. Didn't want more than one child. But I'm sure Cole is different. He loved being a father.'

'Then perhaps he'll be one again someday.'

This drew a sharp look. 'Do you want children, Liz?'

The flush swept into her cheeks. 'Someday.'

Another sigh. 'Someday I'd love to have a grandchild in my life again. Your mother must be delighted with hers.'

'Yes, she is. Particularly the twins, being boys, after having only daughters herself.'

Luckily, this turn of the conversation diverted

Nancy from pushing Cole as an eligible husband—a
highly sensitive issue—and Liz was able to relax
again. She didn't want to speculate on her new relationship with Nancy's son. It had happened so fast.
She was banking on time away to bring some sort of
perspective to it…on both sides.

When they arrived in Kuching, it was great to im-
merse herself in a completely different part of the
world. Their hotel overlooked the Sarawak River with
its fascinating traffic of fishing boats and sampans—
smells and sights of the East. Kuching actually meant
the city of cats and it even had a cat museum featuring an amazing collection of historical memorabilia
on the feline species.

On their second morning, a bus took them to the
Semengoh Orangutan Reserve where they were able
to observe the animals closest to humans on the pri-
mate ladder, extinct now except here in Borneo. The
orangutans' agility, swinging through the trees, was
amazing but it was their eyes that Liz would always
remember—so like people's eyes in their expression.

They also visited a long house where over a thousand men, women and children lived together in the
old traditional way, with each family having their
own quarters but sharing a large verandah as a com-
munal area. No isolation here, as there was in modern
apartment buildings, Liz thought. Ready company
seemed to make for happy harmony, and sharing was
obviously a way of life, clearly giving a sense of security and contentment in continuity.

It made her wonder how much had been lost in
striving for singular achievement in western society.

She didn't want to live alone for the rest of her life, yet going back to her parents' home didn't seem right, either. She was thirty years old, had a mortgage on an apartment she was living in, but no one to share it with on any permanent basis. Her neighbours in the apartment block were like ships passing in the night. Where was she going with her life?

Would Cole ever think of marrying her?

Having a family with her?

Or was all this sexual intensity nothing more than a floodgate opening after a long period of celibacy?

It hurt to think about it. She knew the attraction had always been there on her side—suppressed because it had to be. Her boss was off limits for a variety of good reasons. Besides which, he'd shown no interest in her as a woman until...what exactly had triggered his interest? The new image? The fact that Brendan was no longer an item in her life, making her unattached and available? Simple proximity when he felt tempted by Tara's blatantly offered sexuality?

To Liz's mind, it wasn't something solid, something she could trust in any long-term sense. As much as she would like to explore a serious relationship with Cole, she wasn't sure it was going to develop that way, which made her feel very vulnerable about the eventual outcome.

She could end up in a far worse situation than when Brendan had decided enough was enough. Holding on to her job would be unthinkable, unbearable. Did Cole realise that? Had he even paused to think about it? What did *right* mean to him?

She wasn't at all sure that Diana's advice about

going with the flow was good—not if it led to a waterfall that would dash her to pieces. But there was no need to make any decision about it yet. Indeed, she didn't know enough to make a sensible decision.

The next day the tour group had a wonderful boat trip on the river to Bako National Park where they walked through a rainforest and swam in the South China Sea from a beautiful little beach. It felt like a million miles away from the more sophisticated life in Australia—primitive, sensual on a very basic level, simple but very real pleasures. Time slipped by without any worries.

They left Kuching and flew to Rangoon in Burma—or rather Yangon in Myanmar as it was now known. This had been one of the richest countries of South-East Asia and its past glories were abundantly evident. The Shwedagon Pagoda with its giant dome covered with sixty tonnes of gold and the top of the stupa encrusted with thousands of diamonds, rubies and sapphires, was absolutely awesome.

And the comfort of a past era was amply displayed in the old steam train chartered to take the tourists into the nearby countryside, through the green rice fields and the small villages where nothing had changed for centuries. Pot plants decorated the carriages, legroom was spacious, seats were far more comfortable than in modern trains, and provided with drink holders and ashtrays. The windows, of course, could be opened and it was fun waving to the people they passed, all of whom waved back.

'I feel like the queen of England,' Nancy commented laughingly. 'Such fun!'

Indeed, much of England lingered here, especially in the architecture of the city. The City Hall, Supreme and High Court Buildings, GPO, Colonial Offices—all of them would have looked at home in London, yet the city centre revolved around the Sule Pagoda which was stunningly from a very different culture, as were the temples.

On their last night in Rangoon a 'grand colonial evening' had been arranged for them at The Strand Hotel which had been built by an English entrepreneur and opened in 1901. It had once been considered 'the finest hostelry east of Suez, patronised by royalty, nobility and distinguished personages'—according to the 1911 edition of Murray's Handbook for Travelers in India, Burma and Ceylon.

The men were given a pith helmet to put them in the correct British India period, the women an eastern umbrella made of wood and paper printed with flowers. Everyone was asked to wear white as far as possible and as Liz dressed for the evening in the broderie anglaise peasant blouse and frilled skirt that Cole had bought for her, memories of their shopping spree came flooding back.

You're a class act, Liz Hart. Top of the top. And you are going to be dressed accordingly.

Cole hadn't been talking sex then.

If she really was the *top of the top* to him…but maybe that just referred to her efficiency as his P.A.

As much as she wanted to believe he could fall in love with her—was in love with her—Liz felt he only wanted sex, no emotional ties. And she'd been tempted into tasting the realisation of a fantasy which probably should have remained a fantasy. Except she couldn't regret the experience of having actually known what it was like to be his woman, if only for a little while.

'I just love that outfit on you!' Nancy remarked, eyeing her admiringly as they set off from their hotel room.

Liz bit her lips to stop the words, 'Your son's choice.' She forced a smile. 'Well I must say you look spectacular in yours, Nancy.'

She did. Her glittery white tunic was beaded with pearls at the neckline and hem, falling gracefully over a narrow skirt which was very elegant. In fact, Nancy had been right about the dressing on this tour. Casual clothes ruled during the day, but there was very classy dressing at the evening dinners which were invariably a special event.

The compliment was received with obvious pleasure. 'Thank you, dear. We must make the most of this last night here. It's off to Kathmandu tomorrow.'

Liz didn't reply. Kathmandu conjured up thoughts of Brendan. Was he happy with *the space* he'd put between them? If by some weird coincidence they should meet, would he think she had pursued him? What would his reaction be?

Didn't matter, Liz decided with a touch of bitterness. She'd wasted three years on him and wasn't going to waste another minute even thinking about their past relationship. But was she doing any better for herself with Cole? Would she look back in a few months' time and wonder at her own madness for getting so intimately involved with him?

A bus transported them to the Strand Hotel, the men laughing in their helmet hats—a pukka reminder of the British Raj—the women twirling their umbrellas with very feminine pizazz, embracing the sense of slipping back into a past era. They walked into a spacious, very old-world reception lobby, two storeys high with marvellous ceiling fans and chandeliers, wonderful arrangements of flowers, someone playing eastern music on a xylophone. Many waiters circulated with trays of cocktails and hors d'oeuvres, the refreshments adding to the convivial mood.

Overlooking the lobby was an upstairs balcony, a richly polished wood balustrade running around the four sides. Nancy was taking it all in, revelling in the ambience of the superbly kept period hotel. Liz heard her gasp, and automatically looked to where she was looking, her whole body jolting in shock as she saw what Nancy saw.

'Good heavens! There's Cole!'

He was on the balcony scanning the crowd below. Even as his mother spoke, his gaze zeroed in on them. His mouth twitched into a smile. He raised his hand in a brief salute then turned away, heading for the staircase which would bring him down to where they were.

Every nerve in Liz's body was suddenly wired with hyper-tension. Her mind pulsed with wild speculation over why Cole was here? He hadn't once suggested he might catch up with them on this trip. Had he felt compelled to check on her for some reason? Didn't he trust her with his mother?

'Well, well, well,' Nancy drawled, her voice rich

with satisfaction. 'Cole has actually taken time off
work to be with us. Isn't that wonderful!'

It jerked Liz out of her turbulent thoughts. 'Did
you…invite him to join us?' she choked out, her
throat almost too tight to force words out.

Nancy shook her head in a bemused fashion. 'I
didn't even think of it.' A lively interest sparkled in
her eyes. 'Though I do find it very encouraging that
he's done so just before we leave for Kathmandu.'

'Encouraging?' Liz echoed, not comprehending
Nancy's point.

'Oh yes, dear. It's a very good sign,' she said with
a complacent smile.

Of what?

Liz didn't have time to ask. Cole was already
downstairs and heading towards them. He cut such an
imposing figure and emanated such powerful purpose,
people automatically moved aside to give him a clear
path through the milling crowd, heads turning to stare
after him, women eyeing him up and down. He
looked absolutely stunning dressed in a white linen
suit, made classy casual by the black T-shirt he'd
teamed it with. A man in a million, Liz thought, her
heart pounding erratically at his fast approach.

He grinned, his hands lifting into a gesture that
encompassed them both as he reached them. 'Definitely the two best looking women here!' he declared.

His mother laughed. 'What a surprise to see you!'

'A happy one, I hope.' His gaze slid to Liz, the
piercing blue eyes suddenly like laser beams burning
into hers. The grin softened to a quirky smile. 'One
day in the office with your replacement was enough

to spur me into taking a vacation. You are...quite irreplaceable, Liz.'

In the office or in his bed? Did this mean he'd decided he couldn't do without her? Excitement fevered her brain. 'Have you arranged to join the tour?'

'Only for this evening. I'm actually booked into this hotel for a couple of days. I thought I'd have this one night with you...'

One night...in this hotel...

'...share what appears to be a very special occasion and escort you both to dinner.' He turned back to his mother. 'Are you enjoying yourself, Mum?'

'Immensely, dear. What are your plans for the rest of your vacation?'

'I thought I'd take a look at Mandalay while I'm in this country. It's always had a fascinating ring to it...Mandalay...'

'You're not coming to Kathmandu?'

'No.' He flicked a quick probing look at Liz. Trying to assess her reaction to this decision? Was she okay with only one night here? 'But I am flying on to Vietnam,' he added. 'I might meet up with you there.'

'We're very busy in Vietnam,' his mother warned.

He laughed. 'Perhaps I'll catch up with you for another dinner together. Hear all your news.'

Another night.

Liz's heart squeezed tight.

Was Cole expecting to whisk her away from his mother for a while...fit in a hot bit of sex?

If so, she wouldn't be a party to it, Liz fiercely decided, her backbone stiffening. She would not have

his mother thinking there was some hanky-panky going on between her son and his personal assistant, just
as his ex-wife had suggested. Nancy might even leap
to a rosy conclusion that was not currently on the
cards—marriage and grandchildren!—and her happy
allusions to it would be horribly embarrassing.

Best that she didn't so much as guess at any intimate connection. There were another eleven days of
the trip to get through and every hour of it in Nancy's
company. As it was, she was happily raving on to
Cole about what they'd seen so far, accepting his
presence here at face value. *Let it stay that way,* Liz
grimly willed.

'What about you, Liz? Having fun?' he inquired
charmingly.

'Yes, thank you.'

'No problems?' His eyes scoured hers, trying to
penetrate the guard she'd just raised.

'None,' she answered sharply.

He frowned slightly. 'I haven't come to check up
on you, if that's what you're wondering.'

She managed an ironic smile. 'That would com-
prise bad judgment and a waste of time and money,
Cole.'

He returned her smile. 'As always, your logic is
spot on.'

'Thank you. I hope you enjoy your vacation.'

The distance she was putting between them was so
obvious in her impersonal replies, he couldn't possibly mistake it. His eyes glittered at her, as though
she'd thrown out a challenge he was bent on taking
up with every bit of ammunition at his disposal. Liz

burned with aggressive determination. Not in front of your mother, she wanted to scream at him.

'Time to move on to the ballroom,' Nancy announced, observing the people around moving forward, being ushered towards the next stage of the evening—dinner, entertainment and dancing in the Strand Hotel ballroom.

'Ladies...'

With mock colonial gallantry, Cole held out both of his arms for them to hook on to, ready to parade them in to dinner. His mother happily complied. Realising it would be rude to try avoiding the close contact, Liz followed suit, fixing a smile on her face and focusing on the people moving ahead of them, doing her level best to ignore the heat emanating from him and jangling every nerve in her body.

As they walked along, Nancy hailed various new acquaintances amongst the tour group, introducing her son, distracting Cole from any concentration on Liz, for which she was intensely grateful. It left her free to glance around the ballroom which was very elegant, panelled walls painted in different shades of pinky beige, huge chandeliers hanging from very high ceilings, a highly polished wooden floor, tables set for ten with white starched tablecloths and all the chairs had skirted white slip covers, adding to the air of pristine luxury.

Nancy insisted they sit at a table on the edge of the circle left free for dancing, saying she wanted to be close to whatever entertainment had been arranged for them. Cole obliged her by steering them to seats which had a direct view of the stage. Other people quickly joined them, making up the table of ten.

Liz was glad of the numbers. Although Cole had seated himself between her and Nancy, at least she had people to talk to on her other side, a good excuse to break any private tete-a-tete he might have in mind.

Even so, he shattered her hastily thought out defences by leaning close and murmuring, 'I look forward to dancing with you tonight.'

Dancing!

Being held in his arms, pressed into whatever contact he manoeuvred, moved right out of his mother's hearing for whatever he wanted to say to her...

Panic churned through Liz's stomach.

How was she going to handle this?

How?

CHAPTER FIFTEEN

Liz barely heard the choir of street children who had been rescued by the World Vision organization. They sang a number of songs. Another troup of children performed a dance. People made speeches she didn't hear at all. Food was placed in front of her and she ate automatically, not really tasting any of it. The man sitting beside her dominated her mind and played havoc with every nerve in her body.

A band of musicians took over the stage. They played a style of old time jazz that was perfect for ballroom dancing. A few couples rose from their tables, happily intent on moving to the music. Any moment now...

She could politely decline Cole's invitation to dance with him. He couldn't force her to accept. But given the level of intimacy there had been between them, he had every right to expect her compliance. A rejection would create an awkwardness that Nancy would inevitably rush into, urging Liz to *enjoy herself.*

She could say her feet were killing her.

Except she hadn't once complained about sore feet on this tour and Nancy might make a fuss about that, too.

Cole set his serviette on the table, pushed back his chair and rose to his feet. The band was playing

'Moon River', a jazz waltz which could only be executed well with very close body contact. Liz's stomach lurched as Cole turned to her, offering his hand.

'Dance, Liz?'

She stared at the hand, riven by a warring tumult of needs.

'Go on, dear,' Nancy urged. 'I'm perfectly happy watching the two of you waltz around.'

There really was no choice. Cole's other hand was already on the back of her chair ready to move it out of her way. Liz stood on jelly-like legs, fiercely resolving not to spend the night with him, no matter how deep the desire he stirred. It was an issue of... of...

She forgot what the issue was as his fingers closed around hers in a firm possessive clasp. An electric charge ran up her arm and short-circuited her brain. It seemed no time at all before his arm had scooped her against the powerful length of his body and his thighs were pushing hers into the seductive glide of the slow waltz.

He lowered his head and murmured in her ear. 'Why aren't I welcome, Liz?'

Her lobe tingled with the warmth of his breath. It was difficult to gather her scattered wits under the physical onslaught of his strong sexuality. The very direct question felt like an attack too, forcing her to explain her guarded behaviour with him.

'I'm with your mother,' she shot out, hoping he would see the need for some sense of discretion.

'So?' he queried, totally unruffled by any embarrassment she might feel about being pressed into some obvious closeness with him.

'It's not right to...' She struggled with the sensitivity of the situation, finally blurting out, '...to give her ideas...about us.'

'What's not right about it?' he countered. 'We're both free to pursue what we want.' His hand slid down the curve of her spine, splaying across the pit of her back, pressing firmly as his legs tangled with hers in an intricate set of steps and turns. 'I want you,' he said, again breathing into her ear. 'I thought you wanted me.'

She jerked her head back, her gaze wildly defying the simmering desire in his eyes. 'That's been private between us.'

'True. But I have no problem with making our private relationship public. And I can't imagine my mother would have any objection to it, either. She likes you.'

Resentment at his lack of understanding flared. 'That's not the point.'

He raised an eyebrow, mocking her contentious attitude. 'What is the point?'

Liz sucked in a quick breath and laid out what he apparently preferred to ignore. 'Nancy will want to think it's serious. She's already expressed her hope to me that you'll marry again and...and provide her with grandchildren.'

'And you don't see marriage on the cards for us?'

It sounded like a challenge to her. As though she had made a decision without telling him. And his eyes were now burning into hers with the determined purpose of finding out precisely what was on her mind.

Liz was flooded with confusion. 'You said...you said you had no intention of marrying again in a hurry.'

'Marry in haste, repent at leisure,' he quoted sardonically. 'Not a mistake I care to repeat. But I can assure you it won't take me three years to make up my mind.'

'Three...years?'

'That's what you spent on Brendan, Liz.'

She shook her head, amazed that he was linking himself in any way to her experience with Brendan. It was all so completely different. Why even compare a blitzkrieg affair to a long siege for commitment? In any event, it reminded her of a failure she preferred to forget. Surely Cole should realise that.

The music stopped.

The dancing stopped.

Cole still held her close, not making any move to disengage or take her back to the table. She dropped her hand from his shoulder, preparing to push out of his embrace. All the other couples were leaving the dance floor.

'Why didn't you tell me Brendan was in Nepal?'

'What?' Startled, her gaze flew up to meet his and was caught in the blaze of fierce purpose glittering at her.

'You heard me,' he stated grimly.

Her mind was whirling over knowledge he couldn't have...unless... 'Did Brendan try to contact me at the office?'

'Is that what you want to hear? Did you contact him with the news you were coming?'

'No…I…' She didn't understand what this was all about.

'Have you left a message for him to meet you in Kathmandu?' Cole bored in.

'It's over!' she cried, trying to cut through to the heart of the situation.

'Not for me, it isn't!' came the harsh retort.

She glanced wildly around the emptied dance floor. 'You're making a spectacle of us, standing here.'

'Then let's take the show on the road. You want private? We'll have private.'

Before Liz could begin to protest, he had her waist firmly grasped and was leading her straight to Nancy who was keenly watching them.

'I don't want private,' Liz muttered fiercely.

'I'm not going to let you take up ignoring me again, nor pretending there's been nothing deeply personal between us. Public or private, Liz. You choose.'

Aggression was pouring from him. He'd blow discretion sky-high if she insisted on staying at the table with the tour group. Liz frantically sought a way out of the dilemma Cole was forcing. Nancy was smiling at them, pleased to see them linked together. Liz inwardly recoiled from the interpretation she would put on their *togetherness* if Cole made it clear he was involved with his P.A. on more than a professional level.

Best to seize the initiative before he said something. Liz managed a rueful smile as they closed on his mother and quickly spoke up. 'Nancy, Cole and I have some business to sort out. Will you excuse us for a few minutes?'

'Might take quite a while,' Cole instantly inserted. 'Are you okay to get back to your hotel with the tour group, Mum?'

'Of course, dear.' She beamed triumphantly. 'I even have my room key with me. Liz always checks me on that.'

Trapped by her own efficiency.

'I'm sure we won't be so long, Cole,' she said, trying to minimise this *private* meeting.

'Best to cover all eventualities,' he smoothly returned. 'Given we run late sorting out this business, Mum, I'll escort Liz to your hotel and see her safely to your room, so no need to stay up and worry about her.'

Heat whooshed up Liz's neck and scorched her cheeks. Cole had to be planning more than just talk...

'Fine, dear,' came the ready acceptance to her son's plan. Nancy smiled benevolently at Liz. 'And don't you worry about disturbing me. It's been such a very busy day I'm sure I'll sleep like a log.'

Another excuse wiped out.

Cole picked up Liz's small evening bag from the table, taking possession of her money and her room key. 'Thanks, Mum,' he said by way of taking leave, then forcefully shepherded Liz towards the exit from the ballroom.

'Give me my bag,' she seethed through clenched teeth, determined not to have control taken completely out of her hands. If driven to it, she could arrange a taxi for herself.

'Going to do a runner on me, Liz?' he mocked.

'I don't like being boxed into a corner.'

'Right!' He passed it to her. 'So now you're a lady of independent means. Before you trot off in high dudgeon at my interference with your plans, I would appreciate your telling me what use I've been to you, apart from giving you a free ticket to Kathmandu.'

'What *use?*' She halted, stunned by what felt like totally unfair accusations. 'I didn't ask you for a free ticket!'

'This is not a private place.' To prove his point, he waved at the groups of smokers who had gathered out in the foyer to the ballroom. 'Since you don't want to cause gossip that might reach my mother's ears...'

He scooped her along with him, down the steps and through the passage to the hotel lobby, moving so fast Liz had barely caught her breath when he pressed the wall button beside an elevator.

'I am not going to your room,' she declared, furious at his arrogant presumption that she would just fall in with what he wanted.

His eyes seared hers in a savage assault. 'You had no problem with doing so last week.'

Liz's heart galloped at the sheer ferocity of feeling emanating from him. 'That...that was different.'

'How was it different? I'm making this as private as you had it then. Or was I just a stepping stone to boost your confidence enough to win with Brendan tomorrow?'

Brendan again!

The elevator doors opened while Liz was still shell-shocked by Cole's incredible reading of her actions.

He bundled her into the compartment and they were on their way up before her mind could even begin to encompass what he was implying. She stared at him in dazed disbelief. 'You think I went to bed with you to boost my confidence?'

'A frequent rebound effect,' he shot at her.

She was so incensed by the realisation he actually did think she had *used* him, the reverse side of that coin flooded into her mind. 'What about you, Cole?' she shot back at him. 'Quite a coincidence that on the very day Tara suggested I was obliging you in bed, you decided to make that true.'

He looked appalled. 'Tara had nothing to do with what I felt that night. Absolutely nothing!'

'So why do you imagine Brendan had anything to do with what I felt?'

'You didn't want the light on.'

'I didn't want you comparing me to your hot-shot wife. Finding me much less sexy.'

'You think I'd even look at a Tara clone after what I've been through with her?' he thundered.

Liz was stung into retorting, 'I don't know. She was the woman you married.'

'And divorced. As soon as it could be decently achieved after the death of our child.' A hard pride settled on his face. 'Tara is a user. She doesn't give a damn for anyone but herself. And believe me, that becomes sickeningly *unsexy* after you've lived with it for a while.' His eyes flashed venomously at her as he added, 'And I don't take kindly to being used by a woman I thought better of.'

'I didn't use you,' Liz cried vehemently.

'No? Then why the freeze-off tonight?'

'I told you. Your mother…'

'Not good enough!' he snapped, just as the elevator doors opened. He hustled her out into a corridor, jammed a key in a door, and pulled her into a private suite that ensured they'd be absolutely alone together.

Liz didn't fight the flow of action. The realisation had finally struck that this was not about having sex with her tonight. It was about sorting out their relationship and what it meant to them. And Cole was in a towering rage because he believed she meant to meet Brendan tomorrow, with the possible purpose of reigniting interest in a future together.

He released his hold on her as he closed the door behind them, apparently satisfied he had shut off all avenues of escape. 'Now…now I'll have the truth from you,' he said, exuding a ruthless relentlessness that perversely sent a thrill through Liz.

He cared.

He really cared.

Hugging this sweet knowledge to herself she walked on into the massive suite, past the opened door to a huge bathroom, past two queen size beds, through an archway to an elegant sitting room. She turned to face him in front of the large curtained window at the far end. He'd followed her to the archway where he stood with an air of fierce patience—a big, powerful man who was barely reining in violent feelings.

'I didn't tell you Brendan was in Nepal because it was irrelevant to us, Cole,' she stated quietly.

'Hardly irrelevant,' he gravelled back at her. 'Because of him you stopped hiding your light under a bushel and showed me a Liz Hart I'd never seen before.'

She shook her head. 'That was my sisters' idea. To brighten me up so that other men might see me as attractive. My mother insisted it would make me feel better about myself. Brendan was gone, Cole. I never thought for one moment of trying to get him back. It was over.'

'But then…having made me see you differently, which led to my proving how very desirable you were…you had a ticket to Nepal in your hand—the chance to show Brendan what he was missing.'

'We're going to Kathmandu. I have no idea where in Nepal Brendan is or if, indeed, he's still there. I don't care. If by some freakish chance I should run into him, it won't make any difference. I don't ever want him in my life again.'

He frowned. 'Is that how you feel about me, too? I've served your purpose of…feeling better about yourself?'

She lifted her chin in a kind of defiant challenge, telling herself she had nothing to lose now. 'You want the truth, Cole?'

'Yes.' Piercing blue eyes demanded it of her.

'I've always been attracted to you. But you were married. And I was no Tara Summerville anyway so it was absurd of me to even dream of ever having you. I guess you could say Brendan was a pragmatic choice for me and I tried quite desperately to make it work. Maybe that was what drove him away in the end…me trying too hard to make something that was never quite right into something I could live with.'

Another frown. 'You never indicated an attraction…'

'That would have been futile. And I liked working with you.'

He grimaced and muttered, 'My oasis in a desert.'

'Pardon?'

He managed an ironic smile. 'You helped make my life livable during its darkest days, just by being there, Liz.'

Her smile was wry. 'The handmaiden.'

'Oh, I wouldn't put you in that category. A handmaiden wouldn't talk back, put me in my place. More a helpmate.'

Liz took a deep breath and spilled out the critical question for her. 'Was I helping you to shut Tara out of your mind in those days—and nights—before your divorce was settled?'

He shook his head, clearly vexed by such a concept. 'She was gone. A lot longer gone than Brendan was for you, Liz. Part of me was angry because he'd made you feel a failure, made you feel less than you are. And Tara had put you down, as well. I wanted to lift you up…'

'You took…*pity*…on me?' Everything within her recoiled from that idea.

'Good God, no!' He looked totally exasperated, frustrated by her interpretation, scowling as he gathered his thoughts to dispel it. 'I was angry that you felt so low, especially since you were worth so much more than the people who did that to you. I tried to tell you…show you….' He lifted his hands in an oddly helpless gesture. 'In the end, I couldn't stop myself from making love to you even though I knew I shouldn't risk our business relationship.'

'Making love…' She struggled to swallow the huge lump that had risen in her throat. 'It did feel like that, but then it seemed you only had sex on your mind. All the sex you could get.'

'With you, Liz. Only with you.' His eyes softened, warmed, simmered over her. 'You truly were like an oasis in the desert and when I finally got there, I wanted to revel in everything you gave me. It felt so good.'

So good… She couldn't deny it, didn't want to shade that truth by other things, but she needed to have all her doubts cleared away.

'To me, too,' she admitted. 'But I thought…maybe I was just handy and you were using me to…'

'No. Simply because you're you, Liz.'

'Tonight…when I saw you here…I decided I didn't want to be used like that. Not even by you, Cole.' She held tightly on to all her courage as she added, 'Though I want you more than any man I've known.'

His face broke into a smile that mixed relief with intense pleasure. 'Believe me. The feeling is entirely mutual.'

She let out the breath that had been caught in her lungs and an answering smile burst across her face. 'Really?'

'What do you think I've been fighting for?' He swiftly crossed the short distance between them and wrapped her in a tight hug, his eyes burning into hers with very serious intent. 'No pulling away from me now. We're going to see how well this relationship can work for us. Give it time. Okay?'

Not an impossible dream.

It was almost too much to believe. Her heart swelled with glorious hope. Her mind danced with future possibilities. She was being held very possessively by the man she wanted more than any other in the world. He'd left his work and flown to South-East Asia to fight anything that might part them, and now he was saying...

'Answer me, Liz.'

Commanding...

She loved this man...everything about him. Her arms flew up around his neck. 'Yes, Cole. Yes.' Joy in her voice, desire churning through her body. Mutual, she thought exultantly.

He kissed her, making *mutual* absolutely awesome.

They made love...wonderful, passionate, blissful love...long into the night. No inhibitions. Cole didn't have to sweep them away. Liz felt none. She believed she was the woman he wanted in every sense. He made her feel it. There was nothing she couldn't do with him, nothing she couldn't say to him. And she no longer worried about what his mother might think. Nancy would be happy for them.

It was almost dawn when Cole arranged for a car to transport them to the tour hotel. They'd both decided his mother might panic if Liz wasn't in their room when she woke up. Liz felt too exhilarated to sleep at all. She told herself she would have the op-

portunity later this morning, on the flight to
Kathmandu.

Which reminded her...

'How did you know Brendan was in Nepal, Cole?'

'My mother told me, just before leaving on the
trip.'

'Your mother?' Liz frowned over this unexpected
source until she recollected having answered Nancy's
questions on her ex-boyfriend. 'But why would she
do that?'

Cole smiled. 'Maybe she guessed I cared about you
and the suggestion that I might lose you was a prompt
to action if I wanted to keep you.'

Liz sighed with happy contentment. 'Well, I'm
glad you came.'

Cole squeezed her hand. 'So am I.'

She glanced down at their interlocked hands, suddenly recalling the horribly tense scene just after Tara
had left the Palm Beach house and Cole had come to
the conservatory to eliminate any distress she'd
caused.

'Well, isn't that nice?' his mother had remarked.
'He cares about you, dear.'

Liz could now smile over the memory.

Maybe mothers knew best.

Cole did care about her.

And Liz certainly felt very, very good about herself.

CHAPTER SIXTEEN

Six months later...

LIZ and her sisters were in the kitchen, cleaning up after the Sunday lunch barbecue—an informal family celebration of her engagement to Cole who was happily chatting to her father and brothers-in-law out on the patio. Her mother and Nancy Pierson had their heads together in the lounge room, conferring about the wedding which Cole had insisted be held as soon as it could be arranged.

'That man of yours truly is charming. And mouth-wateringly attractive,' Sue declared, rolling her eyes teasingly at Liz. 'You have to admit it now.'

She laughed. 'He's improved a lot since we've been together.'

'Oh, you!' Sue flicked a tea-towel at her. 'You never give anything away. Still all buttoned up within yourself.'

'No, she's not!' Diana instantly disagreed. 'She's positively blossomed since we made her over. Best idea I ever had. And look what's come out of it.' She grabbed Liz's left hand out of the sink of washing up water and suds. 'Got to see your gorgeous ring again!'

It was a magnificent ruby, surrounded by diamonds. Liz smiled at the red gleams as Diana turned it to the light.

'That's the fire in you,' Cole had said when he'd slid it on her finger. 'Every time I think of you I feel warm.' Then a wicked grin. 'If not hot.'

'This is a very serious ring,' Diana decided. 'Definitely a *to have and to hold from this day forth* ring. High-powered stuff. I hope you realise what you're getting into with this guy, Liz.'

'I have known Cole for quite some time,' she answered dryly.

It evoked a gurgle of gleeful amusement. 'Nothing like marrying the boss.'

'What impresses me…' Jayne chimed in. '…is how good he is with the children. He's like a magnet to them. They're all over him and he obviously doesn't mind a bit.'

'He doesn't. Cole loved being a father.'

Jayne heaved a rueful sigh. 'So sad about the son he lost. Is he mad keen to have a family with you, Liz?'

'Definitely keen.'

'Liz…' her mother called from the doorway. 'Would you go and fetch Cole inside to us. Nancy and I need to talk to both of you.'

'Okay, Mum.'

Liz dried her hands on Jayne's tea-towel and headed for the patio. Behind her, her three sisters broke into a raucous chorus of, 'Here comes the bride…'

Liz was laughing at their high-spirited good humour as she stepped outside. It was so good to feel at one with them instead of shut out of their charmed circle, looking in. Not that they had ever shut her out.

Liz realised now she'd done that to herself, not feeling she could ever compete with them.

It was only with Cole that she'd come to understand that love had nothing to do with competition. Love simply accepted who you were. You didn't have to be like someone else…just who you were.

And she saw his love for her in his eyes as she walked towards him. It warmed her all through, made her feel special and brilliantly alive. She smiled, loving him right back.

'Our mothers want us in the lounge room with them. I think you've thrown them a bit, insisting on a quick wedding.'

'No way are we going to put it off,' he warned, and promptly excused himself from the company of the other men. He reached her in a couple of strides and wrapped an arm around her shoulders. 'We're standing firm on this, Liz. I want us married. I'm not waiting a day longer than I have to.'

'They won't be happy if they can't organise a proper wedding. And just remember, I only intend to be a bride once.'

He slanted a look at her that crackled with powerful purpose. 'I promise you, you'll have a proper wedding.'

Cole really was unstoppable when he had a goal in his sights.

Once they were in the lounge room, their mothers regaled them with the plans they'd made. A Saturday would be best for the wedding. Impossible to book a decent reception place at such short notice. Nancy had offered her home at Palm Beach, a marquee to be put up over the grounds surrounding the pool. Catering could be arranged.

'But, Liz,' her mother addressed her seriously. 'We really should have six weeks for the invitations to go out. People need that much time to…'

'No,' Cole broke in decisively. 'A month is it. If some invited guests can't make it, I'm sorry but we're not waiting on them.'

'What is the hurry, dear?' Nancy cried in exasperation.

His piercing blue eyes speared the question at Liz.

She nodded, feeling sure enough now to share their secret.

'Liz wouldn't agree to marry me until she was three months pregnant and feeling secure that everything was okay and she'd carry our baby full term.'

'Pregnant?' Her mother gaped at Liz.

'A baby!' Nancy clapped her hands in delight.

'If I'd had my way, we would have been married before she got pregnant,' Cole informed them. 'But Liz got this fixation about having a child…'

'*Our* child,' Liz gently corrected him.

He gave her a look that melted her bones. '*Our* child,' he repeated in a thrilling tone of possessive pride and joy.

'A grandchild,' Nancy said on a sigh of pleasure.

'And Liz doesn't want to look lumpy in her wedding dress,' Cole went on.

'Of course not!' Nancy happily agreed.

'Liz…' Having recovered from her initial shock, her mother rose from her armchair, shaking her head at her daughter as she came over to enfold her in a motherly hug. '…always bent on doing it your way. Congratulations, darling.'

'I'm so happy, Mum,' Liz assured her.

'As you should be.'

'And I'm so happy for both of you,' Nancy declared, leaving her chair to do some hugging herself. 'Liz is the right woman for you, Cole. I knew it the moment I met her.'

'Amazing how anyone can be blessed with such certainty at a moment's notice,' Cole drawled, his eyes twinkling at Liz.

'Mother's intuition,' she archly informed him. 'Maybe I'll get some of that myself in six months' time.'

'Mmmh…removing logical argument from our relationship?'

'More like shortcutting it.'

'This might be stretching my love for you.'

'You swore it would stretch on forever.'

He turned to his mother. 'You see, Mum? She's too smart for me.'

'Go on with you, Cole,' Nancy laughingly chided. 'You love it.'

He grinned. 'Yes, I do. And since we now have the wedding back on track, I'm going to whisk Liz off to show her how very much I love everything about her.'

And he did.

Six months later, Liz and Cole were the besotted parents of a baby daughter, Jessica Anne, whose tiny fingers curled around one of her father's and instantly enslaved him for life.

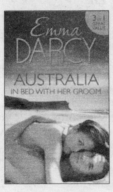
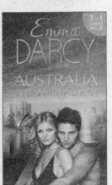

The World of
Mills & Boon®

There's a Mills & Boon® series that's perfect for you. We publish ten series and, with new titles every month, you never have to wait long for your favourite to come along.

By Request

Relive the romance with the best of the best
12 stories every month

Cherish™

Experience the ultimate rush of falling in love
12 new stories every month

Desire™

Passionate and dramatic love stories
6 new stories every month

nocturne™

An exhilarating underworld of dark desires
Up to 3 new stories every month

M&B/WORLD4a